The Dancing Kangaroos

Roy H Sach

First published in 2020 by Barrallier Books Pty Ltd,
trading as Echo Books

Registered Office: 35—37 Gordon Avenue, West Geelong, Victoria 3220, Australia.

www.echobooks.com.au

Copyright ©Roy H Sach

Creator: Sach, Roy H, Author.

Title: The Dancing Kangaroos

ISBN: 978-0-6488545-0-0 Paperback

A catalogue record for this
book is available from the
National Library of Australia

Book layout and design by Peter Gamble, Canberra.
Set in Garamond Premier Pro Display, 12/17 and MinervaSmallCaps regular.

www.echobooks.com.au

Dedication

To potentates, princes, presidents, premiers and prime ministers.

Everyone must obey state authorities, because no authority exists without God's permission, and the existing authorities have been put there by God.

Whoever opposes the existing authority opposes what God has ordered; and anyone who does so will bring judgement on himself.

For rulers are not to be feared by those who do good, but by those who do evil. Would you like to be unafraid of those in authority? Then do what is good, and they will praise you, because they are God's servants working for your own good. But if you do evil, then be afraid of them, because their power to punish is real. They are God's servants and carry out God's punishment on those who do evil.

Good News Bible. Romans 13. 1–4.

FOREWORD

This is fiction. My story is set in the future and I don't own a crystal ball. But *perhaps* some events described will happen. If rising tensions over trade persist, together with enhanced national ambitions, *perhaps* might escalate to *probably*.

I invented characters described, although there is statistical potential for names or personalities to reflect those of real people. If that occurred, it was a coincidence. As for attributions to senior officials or to their policies or to public or corporate institutions identified, I emphasise such attributions and policies were fictitious, apart from the few situations where they had been openly and widely reported. Even in those cases, I would advocate the Royal Society's advice, *nullius in verba*.

Australian aboriginal people appear in several contexts. Having once lived in Australia's Northern Territory, visited remote settlements and read the works of several historians and anthropologists, I did not write from total ignorance. Nevertheless, almost any reference to Australia's original inhabitants can become controversial. Despite the best of intentions to portray innate nobility, culture and capacity, I might have caused some dismay. If so, I apologise unreservedly.

I suppressed a longstanding addiction to nouns and verbs in favour of allowing adjectives and adverbs to reign, notwithstanding the claim that *the road to hell is paved with adverbs*. Readers will judge how successful I was, although the final paragraph of this foreword suggests I should not be too confident. Those of editorial disposition will note I sometimes used American spelling to emphasise an American dialogue.

All literary themes of which I am aware have been used innumerable times. You will find hints of *Iliad, Macbeth, Don Quixote* and *The Great Gatsby*, among others. Anyone seeking originality in this regard should stop now.

For readers inclined to reject this work for other reasons, you are in good company. My wife provided the most direct response I received to an early draft. Her comments included '*hopeless*' and '*boring*'. I persisted, perhaps unwisely, fantasising that even Nikolayevich Tolstoy's writings might have been criticised by Sophia telling him, for example, *War and Peace* was much too long.

RHS

Australia

2020

Contents

E-MAIL

That boy's same as his father, a genuine carbon-copy. All facts, no feelings. Seldom writes. Never tells me what he's eating or whether he's sleeping well. Still, I guess anything's better than nothing.

Clad in a floral-patterned housecoat, Martha Ivory tucked her slippered feet back beneath the chrome framed kitchen chair. Surrounded by pink, gloss-painted cupboards with matching benchtops and built-in white-fronted appliances, she leaned forward, bare elbows on her Formica-topped kitchen table, cradling her plump face in the palms of both hands. For a full ten-seconds she sat, motionless, staring at her iPad.

Anticipating disappointment, she reluctantly opened her son's latest e-mail. It was titled, *Australia Again.*

> Hi Mom,
>
> I'm back in Canberra, Australia's capital city. Sorry I didn't get a chance to say goodbye before leaving.
>
> My temporary office is in our Embassy. I'll probably be here for a few months. As previously, I'm fitting-in quite well. Nobody seems to notice or care I'm African American.
>
> Canberra is a pleasant place to live. Water is pure, trash collected regularly and the electricity supply reliable. A

network of recreational paths extends across the city, following an undulating landscape. Walkers, joggers, cyclists and mothers pushing strollers all use this facility.

Most Canberrans either live in freestanding houses or aspire to. Homeowners' gardens, which commonly attract native parrots, line both sides of many neat streets.

A lake, Burley Griffin, meanders across the city center, passing by public gardens, walkways and bushland. Two well-designed bridges span the lake, helping set the tone for a thoughtfully planned municipality.

Burley Griffin also divides the population into people who live north or south of 'the lake'. Canberrans, regardless of address, believe they live on the best side.

This is the fall season, so we're now approaching what they call winter. Despite a lot of grumbling, and a few threats to relocate, winter will be a wimpy event. They'll possibly get a dusting of snow once or twice. There'll be hardly any ice and they won't need to use salt on the roads.

One delightful thing about this time of year is the fabulous sunsets. The vibrant hues can be spectacular. They range from intense reds and oranges to the most delicate of pastel shades, all changing minute by minute as the sun disappears.

But despite all its good points, many Australians hold a negative opinion of this city. They regard it as artificial and divorced from 'real' Australia, whatever that might be.

Most of them have never been here so their views have been influenced by the writings of journalists who gain kudos when they deride Canberra, which is often. Also, politicians try to avoid responsibility for their own unpopular decisions or failing policies by attributing them to *Caanberra*, much like they do with Washington DC at home.

In fact, Canberra has significantly less political influence than any of the Australian States. Over 65% of its workforce is in the private sector. Canberra has absorbed a higher proportion of migrants from various nations than any other Australian city.

That's all for the moment, Mom. Please say 'hi' to Dad for me. God bless you both and may God bless and keep safe our beautiful United States of America.

Love, Allen

Hmmm, the bit about fabulous sunsets is new and different. Didn't sound like my boy at all. What the heck are they putting into that pure Canberra water?

N-Day

I t happened while a pleasant morning was introducing a mild autumn day to Canberra's central business and shopping district, known as *Civic.*

Beneath a dome of washed-blue sky a gentle breeze from the south was elevating ribbons of fog up from valleys through which they'd been drifting. Gum trees offered delicate hints of eucalypt aroma. Their deciduous cousins in public parks flaunted traces of a rich and varied regalia yet to appear.

Business-attired women and men strode purposefully to and from modern offices, the surrounding cloak of familiarity allowing them to contemplate their immediate objectives or, perhaps, to imagine other distractions. Cars, buses and assorted commercial vans were advancing in orderly procession.

Within this reassurance of normality, a mid-sized silver sedan abruptly forced its way into the passing traffic and began tail-gating any car unfortunate enough to slow its progress. As soon as a driver surrendered by pulling over, the sedan squeezed past and began harassing its next victim.

Occasionally the diplomatic-plated aggressor overtook several vehicles at a time, driving on the wrong side of the road. Some approaching cars crashed while manoeuvring to avoid head-on collisions. Wing-mirrors snapped off. Body panels of both moving and adjacent parked vehicles were scoured. Aggrieved motorists tooted loudly or shook clenched fists.

Oblivious to their rage, the rogue driver sped past the pleasant gardens of Glebe Park before turning abruptly into Torrens Street. There, he almost lost control, skidding and fishtailing slightly as his vehicle struck a frail-elderly man tottering over a pedestrian crossing.

The thump was unmistakable but the driver neither stopped nor slowed, instead muttering 'Sorry pal! Wrong place, wrong time.'

He was accelerating hard, yet again, his rear tyres squirting twin jets of rubbery fumes, when a pure-white flash filled the immediate and surrounding environments. Brighter than daylight, it illuminated all of Canberra and was clearly visible from townships in the region.

The following shockwave, travelling at 1000 kilometres per hour, converted the man and his vehicle into a mist of particles. Hyper-heat evaporated what remained of his blood and other bodily fluids. He became an inconsequential puff within the mushroom-shaped cloud now rising over a vast expanse of newly created detritus.

Allen Ivory died, frantically trying to reach and rescue the woman he loved, a tsunami of disgust and loathing replacing the patriotic faith evident in yesterday's e-mail to his mother. He'd been 523 metres from the front door of her apartment.

———

An inner-city observer, had one survived, couldn't have decided which was worse, the depressing sight or the disgusting smell.

A formerly vibrant cityscape had become an almost uniform sea of flattened brown, grey and black artefacts, punctuated by flames and embers. The eye-searing and vomit-making stench of scorched flesh, melted rubber, burning building materials and dissolved produce of every description was persistent and inescapable.

As smoke and dust settled a few structures emerged through the pall, each pointing defiantly but futilely skywards. Sections of the Australian War Memorial's facade and part of its side walls could be identified. A concrete tower on the grounds of the Australian National University still stood.

The distant silhouette of a gabled wall might have belonged to St John's church in the suburb of Reid.

Across Lake Burley Griffin some concrete-clad public buildings appeared almost unscathed, although smoke rising from various orifices pointed to interior fires consuming irreplaceable works of art and other records held in the National Gallery of Australia and the High Court.

Avant-garde architecture comprising the National Museum of Australia had disintegrated. The National Library of Australia was a pile of rubble.

Occasionally a visible patch of paved roadway would ignite into blue luminosity, then subside. Yellow flames of remembrance for the former city burned continuously from ruptured gas pipelines.

Theoretically, people and objects shielded from the initial holocaust by hills, valleys or other barriers should have survived. But in many cases that didn't happen.

Cars and trucks on a sunken section of nearby Parkes Way were crushed by steel girders swathed in molten glass when buildings from New Acton toppled and collapsed onto them. Concrete blocks and debris fell onto other sheltered roads, fatally striking vehicles or falling directly into their paths with the same result.

In and around the city's centre, humanity was annihilated. Across the immediately adjoining suburbs severely burned victims, the elderly and children alike, most with strips of skin hanging from their faces and near-naked bodies, survived for a few disoriented and horror-filled minutes. Yet further distant, people clung to life for several indescribable hours or, in a few unfortunate cases, days.

Most roadside trees in the intermediate region were species known to have volatile botanical oils, which they demonstrated by smouldering continuously.

Minimally damaged, multi-storey hospitals in the suburbs of Bruce and Woden switched to diesel-powered generators as they prepared, at first, to deal with an uncategorised emergency. But their crisis response plans had assumed continuity of water supply. As they soon discovered, the supply system had collapsed.

The hospitals had no capacity to manage sewage, cook food, launder clothing, wash bed linen or attend to the persistent needs of existing patients. Their capacity to accept casualties, most with severe burns and fractured bones, was negligible.

In any case, nobody within the medical hierarchy had contemplated treating the thousands of wretched, ragged scarecrows who came staggering toward them across a decimated landscape, beneath a malevolent dome of orange-brown sky.

The flash of light had blinded some. They were clinging to sighted victims. Parts of faces and upper bodies were glowing red from burns or bleeding. Elsewhere they'd been blackened by radioactive soot.

The more severely injured formed parallel but slower processions. Bellies downwards, using their least-injured limbs, they heaved themselves jerkily along the ground, every courageous push releasing another wave of agony.

Occasionally the ranks detoured to avoid crashed motor vehicles, human corpses or uprooted trees.

Some casualties were too shocked or injured to vocalise. Most were groaning softly in a chorus resembling the deep, mournful moan of a pipe-organ.

Had the best treatment been available, 90 per cent of them would have died within weeks. But nothing could be done. A putrid landscape of dead and dying bodies lying in pools of blood, vomit and excrement surrounded both hospitals.

Mercifully, most victims died within hours, before crows, augmented by dogs from the outer suburbs, arrived to begin feasting on this macabre cornucopia of human flesh.

And while the Grim Reaper applied his ghastly scythe, other events, some good, some bad, many impossible to categorise, were unfolding.

GENESIS

While he was a pre-schooler, Allen Ivory's family had moved from New Orleans to Oakton, in North Virginia.

From Mr and Mrs Ivory's perspective, *highs* of New Orleans had included unemployment, poverty, humid days and the threat of cyclones. Relocation to Oakton seemed like winning a lottery, despite freezing and occasionally snow-bound northern winters.

Their almost-new colonial style home blended compatibly into a street of similar but not identical houses. Paralleling the road on both sides were rows of ornamental plumtrees, planted to give a spectacular display of pink and white blossoms every springtime. New Orleans had offered a fascinating window into American history. Oakton combined middle-class comfort blended with natural beauty, showcasing the nation in its more modern livery.

Tall, taciturn and dignified, Jefferson Ivory, when at home, assisted his wife Martha if possible. However, Jefferson, now promoted by the United States Postal Service to the level of Senior Storeman, was also wedded to his job.

His attitude, strongly supported by Martha, was that life's top priority was ensuring the US mail would be delivered, undamaged and on time.

Consequently, Jefferson spent many early mornings, late nights and occasional weekends in a warehouse he liked to call *the office*.

Despite Jefferson's distractions Allen's home-life was happily consistent. The Ivory abode felt stable and secure. Drugs and even swearing were foreign. Parental disagreements, if they happened at all, were invisible.

Theirs was a faith-filled family. From Allen's early childhood, they'd worshipped together at a United Methodist Church. They now attended Sunday Services in nearby Fairfax.

Evening meals, centred on their mahogany dining table, always began with a prayer of thanks, the ceremony conveying an unmistakable sense of gratitude for blessings surrounding them.

At bedtime, Martha would kneel beside her young son, their knees comfortably cushioned by a thick, floral-patterned carpet, while Allen prayed to a Lord who watched over them and knew everything. This presence of God, through his Son the Lord Jesus Christ, provided yet another strong foundation to support the developing edifice of this boy's life.

Some of his friends came from Roman Catholic families. The walls of their homes displayed crucifixes and religious statues, unmistakable evidence of faith in God as well as the Lord Jesus and His Sacred Mother, Mary.

In Allen's home, faith and patriotism were entwined. It was beyond question that America's manifest destiny provided a channel for God the Father to shower this exceptionalist nation with His blessings. These indisputable truths left an indelible mark on the young and impressionable Allen.

Regardless of who was President of the United States of America, a framed photograph of that person would alone grace one of the deep-green ornamental-papered living-room walls.

Beside their front door, a carved rosewood-timber stand supported a staff holding the Stars-and-Stripes. On special national occasions Jefferson would reverently carry the staff and flag outside. There, he'd carefully insert the staff into a bracket bolted to the front wall and allow the flag to hang proudly.

A slim, thoughtful and often shy young Allen Ivory was first enrolled at the Mosby Woods Elementary School. Its geometric structures and modern-colonial buildings, compatible with the local architecture, housed a multiracial student population.

In time and with dawning awareness, Allen came to sense an almost indefinable wall separating the racial categories. No group considered itself superior or inferior to any of the others. Porous membranes nevertheless existed in ways he vaguely suspected would accompany him throughout his life.

One evening, Allen raised the issue of race with his father.

'Dad, why do the various races at school seem to prefer being with their own kind? We're forever being told colour is only a pigment in the skin and we are all equal.'

His father replied 'Yes Allen, it's true, the races are all equal, but they are not all identical. Each group has its own history and culture and these differences emerge in different social customs, preferred foods and attitudes.'

'Most of the time we feel more comfortable with situations that are familiar to us, so it's only natural for members of racial groups to enjoy similar company, hopefully without excluding others.'

He added 'The most important thing to remember is this; we are all citizens of the United States of America and it is to America we owe our first loyalty, not to any racial category. To be American is a privilege the citizens of other nations cannot imitate, although many would like to.'

With those last sentences, Jefferson's voice became softer yet deeper. His body language changed. He stared straight ahead, almost as if taking an oath of allegiance. The man meant what he said and intended Allen to understand that.

Years later, reflecting on their conversation, Allen concluded his father's decades of working for the Postal Service must have instilled this sense of unshakable patriotic faith.

Following the familiarity of elementary school, a tall, gangly and slightly underweight Allen found secondary education challenging.

Fairfax High, with a student population approaching 3 000, was complicated and unsettling. The scale of its impressive glass-fronted buildings, spacious atriums and comprehensive facilities for almost every activity combined to distract him. Feeling overwhelmed, he had difficulty focusing on classwork. This soon became evident in declining grades and mediocre assessments.

The summary comment in his school report at the end of second year read:

> 'Allen Ivory's results at the B and C levels have been disappointing. He is capable of As in most or all his subjects. His attitude to education is casual and he often appears disinterested. This has been consistent through the year. He needs to change.'

That didn't worry Allen. He enjoyed playing baseball and his marks weren't *too* bad. He felt he could continue coasting.

Jefferson, however, had other ideas. One Saturday morning he sat at the dining table, with a reluctant and slightly hostile Allen, for what Jefferson called *a little chat* and Allen, in anticipation, *a nagging session*.

Confronted with Jefferson's incisive questions and observations, Allen confessed he had problems with learning and remembering. There was such a volume of material and so many sources. He didn't know where to begin. He'd tended to lose interest. Allen wondered if he was just plain dumb.

Jefferson allowed this to possibly be true and proposed a test to find out.

Handing Allen a thick volume containing the rules of baseball, together with recorded explanations and decisions, he asked him to find the maximum length permitted for the bat and also which materials were permitted as the covering for a baseball. In less than two minutes Allen had the answers and references to support them.

More questions followed, each regarding obscure aspects of the game, all answered promptly and accurately. Jefferson then reached into a yellow-fabric shopping bag, hauled out a thick volume and thumped it onto the table.

'Son', he said 'this is Alexis de Tocqueville's *The Ancien Régime and the French Revolution*. By 5.00pm tomorrow I'd like a summary of the main causes of that revolution. And don't think you'll be missing worship in the morning either, because that won't happen.'

Had one of his teachers made a similar demand, Allen would have worked around the problem, asking colleagues for their opinions, searching the Web for a suitable summary, checking the school and local libraries hoping to find a book to plagiarise, such as *French Revolution for Dummies*. In fact, he'd have done almost anything to avoid tackling de Tocqueville.

Instead, given his experience with the rules of baseball, Allen felt confident, slightly ecstatic. He knew he could do this. It was within his grasp.

At 5.00 pm the next day, Allen presented his father with the list of main causes of the French Revolution *plus* a summary of events leading to the American Revolution and a comparison of the two.

Jefferson confirmed its accuracy and congratulated Allen for his curiosity and initiative in exploring that further step.

But, just as a relieved Allen was leaving the room, Jefferson said 'By the way, I don't think you included mention of the gabelle, the salt tax. Please let me have a note on its relevance. There's no hurry. By next Friday evening will do.'

For the remainder of his time at Fairfax High, Allen never again succumbed to confusion or uncertainty. If a subject seemed to be slipping away, consultation with Jefferson was his first response.

Regardless of whether the challenge involved history, chemistry, physics or mathematics, his father seemed to understand and could offer a technique to tackle it. Allen was both gratified and astonished. His Senior Storeman dad was a truly remarkable and underutilised person.

Allen's spiritual development continued in parallel with his scholastic work, each validating the other. Bible study classes, held at his church each Wednesday evening, introduced moral and ethical issues, all based on the life of Jesus.

One evening, they debated the Lord's action in throwing money changers out of the temple. It was mentioned in the *Gospels* of *Matthew, Mark, Luke* and *John*, so there could be no doubt that it was true.

Had Jesus been heavy handed? Could he perhaps have given these people a few weeks of grace in which to relocate?

The group finally decided there were issues of such importance they had to be addressed immediately, brutally if necessary. Perhaps some injustices might emerge in the short term but eventually the outcome would be positive.

Another week they considered the story, from the *Gospel of Matthew*, where Jesus drove evil spirits from men into a herd of pigs. The pigs ran down a steep bank and into a lake where they'd drowned.

The outcome was rough on the pigs, the pig owner and the pig-herders. However, releasing men permanently from evil spirits was the primary objective. Allen interpreted this as meaning The Holy Bible recognises, we sometimes can justify collateral damage to support a higher cause.

Other insights followed, all pointing to indispensable obligations for us to love both God and country. In *Matthew* and again in *Acts*, St Paul advised us, when people refuse to acknowledge our truth, we should shake their dust from our feet, we must reject them totally.

These indicators pointed toward his obligations to spread God's word about life, liberty and the pursuit of happiness. America was and would remain the New Jerusalem. How fortunate he was to have been raised a Christian, an *American* Christian. The two were inseparable.

His mother put it into memorable context one day when she referred to 'One God, four in one; the Father, the Son, the Holy Ghost and the blessed United States of America.'

Allen graduated from Fairfax High with above average university entrance scores. They weren't high enough for admission into one of the Ivy League establishments, but almost anything else was possible.

As usual, he sought his father's guidance although, so far as Allen knew, Jefferson had never been exposed to tertiary education.

As always, Jefferson's advice reflected his considerable experience in life and was worth listening to.

'Your choice of a university will count for more than you might think.' his father had said. 'Some have a reputation for excelling at management, others at physics; some attract high achievers, others don't.'

'Cross-cutting those criteria is that some campuses are, fairly or unfairly, considered left-wing, others right-wing. You will, to some extent, be associated with the reputation of your university.'

'Finally, when you begin tertiary studies, remember this; your aims are to be well thought of by the hierarchy and then graduate with a quality degree.'

'To achieve those objectives you need to study your professors almost as much as you do the topics they are teaching. Learn what they think and why. Make sure your work is never confrontational except, perhaps, in occasional and marginal ways.'

'As an undergraduate you lack the status to become an intellectual hero, although you could turn into one of the many anonymous martyrs who tried but failed to change anything.'

'That's it; over to you.'

Allen gave his father's advice considerable weight, especially since there was no competition except, perhaps, in prayer. He had no close friends. Without consciously meaning to, he'd strayed far from his youthful peers.

They attended dances, even nightclubs. Allen saw no point to rhythmically bopping up and down, hour after mindless hour. They had cars; he didn't. What was the point? Public transport was adequate and a lot less expensive. His colleagues (for none of them were close enough to be *friends*) wore the latest fashions in denims and sunglasses; Allen was interested only in dressing modestly.

And then there were *girls*, many apparently exuding some strange chemistry. It caused young men to indulge in ludicrous behaviours, to physically fight each other and, in a few cases, become so distracted they'd dropped out of high school. Allen felt relieved the Lord seemed to have let that cup pass from him.

GRADUATION

Allen was accepted by The George Washington University, headquartered in Washington DC. It was a respected institution with a student population drawn from across the US and nations throughout the globe. It had a reputation for sensitivity to social justice issues but was not commonly categorised as an incubator for radicalism.

That was the easy part. The University offered around 2 000 courses. His father had made clear these were to be Allen's own decisions. That left him with only one source of guidance.

Allen's earnest morning and evening prayers resulted in a subtle message from Jesus; not quite a voice in his head but the next best thing. As he prayed, the conviction that he should study the humanities subjects became increasingly strong. This was what The Lord wanted of him.

Armed with the authority of Divine Guidance, he elected to major in international studies with sub-majors in business management and economics.

During the following years, his undergraduate progress was satisfactory although unspectacular. He became a conservative Black student, one who attended church regularly, who wouldn't touch drugs. Socialising pleasantly, he avoided meaningful relationships.

Had Allen Ivory's professors or student peers been asked to describe him, most would have replied, 'Who? No, never heard of him.'

The few who could identify Allen would likely have described him as *'dedicated', 'consistent', 'private', 'conservative,'* or, *'well-balanced and happily self-contained.'* None of them knew the details of Allen's family background, their brief conversations having never got that far.

As the date for graduation approached, Allen toted-up his results and calculated, accurately as it happened, he would receive his bachelor's degree with one of the lesser categories of honours.

It would be a respectable outcome but not strong enough to justify a future as an academic. He'd need identify some sort of career or profession but had minimal idea of what it might be.

Reviewing what he valued most in life, Allen was attracted to serve either God or his nation, possibly both. He yearned, in some loosely defined way, for an opportunity to enrich others by pointing to the wonderous compatibility between God's will and America's destiny.

The biggest challenges facing America, he believed, were social trends obviously contrary to God's will. Prominent among them were homosexuality, especially homosexual marriage, abortion and pornography. These were cancers attacking the backbone of American morality. They had to be struck down and he would enjoy being one among God's army of morality destined to fight the good fight.

Perhaps he could apply to study at the Brownleigh Theological Seminary. An august institution, it had been training ministers with a lineage going back to 1906. As usual, he decided to seek God's guidance.

God hadn't yet responded when, one Saturday morning in a coffee shop facing a narrow Georgetown street, Allen was guiltily enjoying a large mug of cappuccino, sip by creamy, rich, frothy sip.

He was aware his parents paid for his university education and allowed him to continue living at home, rent free. This must have taken a huge percentage of their savings for retirement. He needed a paying job, and soon.

The cafe was crowded and Allen was seated alone at a two-person table. He wasn't surprised when a slim, middle-aged, middle-class-looking White woman approached. With short-cropped greying hair and wearing a beige, long-sleeved blouse, matching calf-length skirt and sensible flat-heeled shoes, she seemed designed to blend anonymously into the background. Nevertheless, with a confidently calm voice she asked if she might use his spare seat.

Allen consented. She sat. Ignoring her, he began reading a Kindle book.

Without further introduction the woman leaned toward him and said 'Hmmm, so *you* are Allen Ivory.' She then reeled-off the marks he'd achieved at George Washington, details of where he worshiped and other aspects of his personal life, all from memory. It was an impressive feat.

Allen was about to protest when she began describing his performance at Fairfax High School. She recalled his record as a pitcher on the school baseball team, the time he'd left his schoolbooks on a bus (something he hadn't mentioned to his parents), names of his teachers, his academic attainments, and the number of the bus he caught when travelling to school.

Next came Mosby Woods Elementary School. She knew some of his classmates' names, details of the time Mr Gladstone spilt lemonade over himself and what happened when Mr Pitt had backed his car into the Ms Addington's motor scooter.

Then she moved onto describing the exterior of the house that Allen vaguely remembered from New Orleans.

Stunned, Allen realised this was way beyond any introductory sales pitch. Besides, the woman wasn't trying to sway him in any direction. But she was a mobile encyclopaedia of his life.

In part forgetting his manners, and responding to the woman having forgotten hers, Allen said, rather peevishly, 'Okay, I admit that was very impressive. What happens next?'

The woman placed a high-quality, mat-surfaced business card in front of him. It had no name, only an address printed in raised copperplate script. She said '9.00 am next Tuesday please. We will then discuss a job offer.'

'You have no conflicting engagements in your electronic diary. I know because I've checked it. If you attend you are to bring this card with you. If you do not attend you are to destroy this card. You may not tell anybody, including your parents, Jefferson and Martha.'

She stood and departed without bidding him farewell, merging with others on the crowded sidewalk. Allen wondered who in hell she thought she was and questioned why he'd bother to do *anything* she wanted.

———————

Returning home to Oakton that evening, Allen consulted a Web-based street map of Washington DC and vicinity.

This address, it's the Washington Navy Yard. Surely it's nothing to do with joining the Navy. They wouldn't compile a dossier such as the one that woman had on me—not even for the United States Naval Academy.

Still, it is an official address in a government-owned facility. These people must have some connection with the Government. Well, perhaps I could work for Uncle Sam instead of the Lord Jesus. It's not as if they're all that different.

Having prayed for guidance several times, only to become frustrated because God obviously wanted him to make his own decision, Allen decided to keep the appointment. But he remained ambivalent.

Foremost in his mind was the impression of his highly intelligent father, a potential-filled man who'd succumbed to the drug of employment security. It was depressing to think he'd ended up in a dead-end job as a senior storeman. Still, Allen supposed, it was only an interview.

On the Tuesday morning, after one bus and a change of train, Allen caught the Metro across to Navy Yard station and walked to the 11th and O Street Gate. Being about 15 minutes early he loitered, admiring the Anacostia River and surrounds.

A warship of the United States Navy was moored nearby, its menacing grey profile and purpose-built design reminding him of the old but true saying that the price of liberty is eternal vigilance.

At five minutes to the hour Allen entered the building marked Visitors Center. He approached a counter where non-military personnel could make inquiries and showed the address card to an official-looking woman.

It seemed to mean something. The woman turned away and pressed several buttons on a communications panel. Following a brief pause she announced 'Good morning, your guest has arrived.'

Almost 10 minutes passed before a hinged door opened in a wall behind the counter. The woman from Georgetown stepped out.

'Good morning Allen. Thank you for attending. Please follow me. You may address me as Carol.'

THE LIONS' DEN

Allen followed Carol through the same door and into a narrow passage. Layers of conduits and other tubes covered most of its high ceiling, reflecting generations of communications technologies installed then superseded. Barely adequate light from incandescent globes, each located behind a heavy metal mesh, was reflected in pale-green walls and a deep-brown linoleum floor.

20 paces later they stopped opposite a grey-metal door. Carol pressed a button at about chest height. The door slid smoothly back, revealing an elevator which they entered. It was one of the old-fashioned metal-cage designs dating from the mid-20th century or possibly earlier.

The elevator had three buttons: *Emergency Support, Ground* and *Not Ground*. The environment wasn't light-hearted, so Allen assumed his destination was a sensitive issue.

Carol selected Not Ground and the elevator seemed to descend for more than 30 seconds, suggesting a deeply excavated destination. When they stopped, the cage door, followed by another steel door, slid open automatically.

Allen and Carol exited onto a platform. In front of them a pair of narrow-gauge railway tracks extended into the gloom in both directions. On the tracks sat an open bare-metal carriage with black upholstered seating for four people.

Carol explained the technology had been installed during the Cold War. It had been designed to distribute mail between Federal agencies regardless of what was happening at ground level. Refurbished and upgraded, it had a new role.

They entered the carriage and sat. Carol slid back a panel between their seats and waved an electronic pass card across it. As the carriage began moving into a pitch-black tunnel Allen felt the unmistakable press of acceleration.

The journey to another illuminated station took about six minutes, leaving Allen to conclude this was one reason Carol needed about 10 minutes to meet him at ground-level.

Leaving the carriage, they entered another almost identical elevator. It ascended for a few seconds before stopping. Its doors opened and they alighted into an apparently normal office building, except it was underground. Its installed lighting had been designed to simulate sunlight, implying the occupants spent many hours, possibly years, in this subterranean environment.

Walking briskly along an unremarkable corridor, Carol leading, they passed several closed rooms with frosted windows, giving no clue as to their content or purpose. There were also open areas filled with workstations, most of which were vacant. Closer inspection would have revealed that all offices and closed meeting rooms had been triple-glazed to form sound-proof capsules.

They stopped and Carol pushed firmly against one of the office doors. It opened slowly, almost elegantly, implying strong hinges supporting a significant weight.

The room they'd entered seemed identical to those found in almost any commercial building. Embedded in the plain white ceiling were rows of downlights. The walls, also white, were covered with unadorned sound-absorbing tiles. An indispensable whiteboard was attached to the front wall. Fixed to the back wall, was a row of small cabinets featuring individual combination locks.

There was no central conference table. Seven of eight office-type swivel chairs were already occupied by middle-class looking people about Allen's age or older. One was a woman. Allen deduced, with some discomfort, he was last to arrive.

Carol pointed wordlessly to the vacant chair. Allen sat. Carol departed, hauling the heavy door closed behind her.

Standing behind a plain, wooden lectern at the front of the room was one of the least impressive men Allen had ever seen.

Middle-aged, skinny and of below-average height, he might have been a retired jockey in poor health. A few tufts of wispy grey hair poked inquisitively from a shining fish-belly-white scalp. His deeply wrinkled forehead flowed onto pock-marked cheeks surrounding sunken eyes of uncertain colour. Beneath a hooked nose was a wide, thin-lipped mouth. Lacking a discernible chin, his face merged into a long, scrawny neck. The man was wearing a dark-blue business suit, white shirt, conservative necktie and highly polished shoes.

The 'jockey', who had a deep and well-modulated voice, said 'Good morning ladies and gentlemen. I am Martin.

You are on a course designed to last nine weeks. It requires you to hold a Top Secret security clearance. The clearance is a sign that the United States of America has placed its faith in you and that you will be loyal to our nation. Six of you already know that you hold a TS clearance and the conditions attached to it. Two of you do not yet have one.'

'Allen and Tom please follow me. You others, while we are out of the room, please introduce yourselves on a first-name basis only. You should not disclose any other personal information. This is not the sort of course following which you might maintain contact with each other. In fact, it is unlikely you will see each other again.'

Allen and Tom followed the jockey into an adjoining room where they were told 'You have been under moderate to intense surveillance for more than two years. In consequence the United States has been able to conduct the checks needed to ensure you are eligible to hold a Top Secret security clearance.'

'If you agree to accept the clearance you will be bound, for a period of ten years, to not disclose anything concerning the training you are about to undertake. Further training will likely extend that period. Any breaches will be viewed extremely seriously, leading to conviction for committing a felony.'

'You need not agree to those conditions. If you do not agree, you will be given a formal warning to not disclose anything about the morning's proceedings for a period of five years. You will then be escorted back to ground level and be free to depart.'

Tom seemed nervous and comprehensively confused. After fidgeting for a few seconds and twice wiping perspiration from his deeply freckled forehead, he opted for the five-year limitation. Martin accepted the young man's decision and, Allen thought, looked quite relieved.

Allen could sense the Lord was, finally, revealing His plan and agreed to sign. Martin spoke to Carol via an old-fashioned looking telephone. She duly arrived to collect Tom and escort him from the premises.

Martin then gave Allen *your own cover story*. So far as the world outside this institution was concerned, Allen had become a trainee executive with the United States Department of Commerce. As a trainee, he'd be rotated regularly and so unable to answer detailed questions about his job with that department.

They returned to the original meeting room.

Pursuing his no-nonsense approach, Martin said 'Some of you come from established agencies in the intelligence community. Following this course you will be returned to your agencies. In other cases, we will decide what to do with you when and if you complete.'

Martin wasn't interested in or inhibited by normal social values. His next revelation, if broadcast to a wider American public, would have been regarded as scandalous or worse.

'In addition to meeting the character and related assessments required for a TS security clearance, you all are considered to meet six prerequisites to be accepted for this training. They are as shown on the whiteboard.'

Pointing his multi-function pen toward an overhead projector Martin projected an image onto the whiteboard:

Prerequisites

- Third generation American. No foreign marriages along the way.
- Devout Christian for at least two generations.
- Family history of service to the United States.
- Either Republican voter or strong Republican leanings.
- Unmarried, no dependants. Likely to stay that way.
- No unconventional sexual engagements.

Martin continued 'As you will appreciate, these conditions fail every known test for political correctness. We don't give a damn. Any one of you might be put in a position to influence the future of the United States of America. Those are the qualities we want for such people.'

'We have other prerequisites not mentioned on the slide. We'll cover them as we progress. As an example, you will not be allowed to have a tattoo, mainly because such markings make you more easily identifiable.'

'So far as we know, none of you has been tattooed, but if you have been then you must tell me at the close of business today. I will arrange for surgical removal.'

'As with all other requirements, if you don't like it then, as the old song says, it'll be a case of "farewell it's been good to know you".'

Following further discussion on the reasoning behind the six prerequisites, they stopped for lunch. It was served in an integrated chrome-and-white themed canteen which provided self-serve, buffet-style meals.

They took trays and selected from an array of soups, pastries, sandwiches, fries, cold meats and cookies. Coffee, chilled water and tea were available, also self-serve. There was no cash register, no menu and no price list.

Each group of workers, students, or whatever the other diners might be, had apparently been encouraged to stay separate. Conversations between individuals were muted and indecipherable. There was no contact between tables except where good manners required some brief acknowledgement.

The Canteen's meals didn't reflect any concessions now common in America. There were no vegetarian options. No religious constraints were acknowledged. No allowance was made for allergies.

Martin later explained that people with such sensitivities were not considered eligible for the range of assignments members of this group, and others in the underground complex, might be expected to perform.

Administration filled the afternoon, most processes requiring completion and signing of paper-forms. Martin gave Allen, on otherwise plain paper, a list of his working conditions.

Although his normal working day was from 8.30 am through 5.30 pm, with 30 minutes break for lunch, he could be required to work non-stop for as long as necessary without regard for weekends. Overtime work would never be financially compensated. The concept of *overtime* didn't exist.

Fully paid absences due to illness or injury would be unlimited. His weekly salary would be approximately three times the highest figure he had been hopefully anticipating and was tax free. He was exempt from submitting annual taxation forms and was not to report or disclose his income to anyone.

Each student was allocated a small locker attached to the rear wall of their classroom. Those unfamiliar with combination locks, which included Allen, were shown how to set new numbers of their choosing. They were warned against using their dates of birth or other easily identifiable numbers. Every evening they would be required to secure all notes and other documents in the lockers. No written or electronic material was to be taken from the room.

Carol reappeared soon after 5.30 pm. One at a time, the remaining seven students entered the elevator with her and vanished. It was after 6.00 pm when Allen's turn arrived. The elevator deposited them at another small railway station resembling their place of arrival that same morning.

She motioned him to climb aboard the waiting carriage, telling him to leave it after it stopped and to follow signs at his destination. He was to note carefully his final point of exit and arrive in reverse order the next morning. A swipe card he'd been given would operate the 'train'.

She pushed a button on the platform's wall. After a few seconds, Allen's carriage began moving into another black tunnel, accelerating as it had previously.

When the carriage stopped, Allen, feeling very insecure, alighted onto a platform and passed through a hinged door which closed behind him with a thud. He climbed two flights of stairs and departed via another door into a foyer. Noting carefully the location of the door, he crossed that foyer and into the open air.

Looking back, he could see the building was signed as *Department of Commerce*.

Being familiar with Washington DC, Allen had no difficulty locating the nearest Metro station and travelling home via two trains and one bus.

Allen made his announcement at the dinner table, after prayers and before Martha had served soup. 'Mom and dad, I've accepted a job offer and can start work immediately. My new job involves a cadetship with Department of Commerce.'

'That's great son. How many applications did you submit before getting the offer?'

'Well, mom, I'd have to check on that...'

'I've been keeping watch on job opportunities for you and haven't seen Department of Commerce 's advertisements.'

'Er, yes mom, I heard about this opportunity and managed to get a head start on other applicants.'

'Will you still live at home, son?'

'Possibly so, if you and Mom are happy with that. I've been told to anticipate frequent job rotations for the immediate future.'

Despite the interrogation, Jefferson and Martha seemed quietly pleased and wished him well.

COAT OF MANY COLOURS

The following day, Wednesday, Allen found his way back to the classroom. Martin and five of the six remaining students also arrived on time.

The missing man didn't appear again. Allen never discovered why but had the feeling it wouldn't be smart to inquire.

From that morning onwards the atmosphere was, in Martin's words, *'Full on! No quarter asked or given.'*

The first topic for discussion was: What are the ultimate goals of the United States of America and how can they be achieved?

The class split into two groups. One argued vigorously for reduction of the burgeoning national debt, increased taxes to fund ageing infrastructure, recognition of the global warming process and stronger support for international security.

How else, they asked, could Americans have a basis for the longer term and the enduring pursuit of happiness?

The other group, which included Allen, took a contrasting stance. Their spokeswoman claimed:

'America's ultimate goal has to be world domination, although it can never be discussed openly. Without that, America's capacity to provide for the life, liberty and pursuit of happiness for its citizens will always be jeopardised. New forces will rise up in opposition to us, as the USSR once attempted and China is trying to do now.'

'This is America's destiny. God endorsed it and He blessed the United States as an exceptionalist nation, the Leader of the Free World. To the extent possible all other considerations have to be subordinated until this great cause is achieved.'

'We might resort to warfare, trade, monetary and fiscal manoeuvring or international law, all endorsed by the absolute guarantee that overwhelming force could be applied if necessary.'

Martin intervened with a further challenge 'Okay, they are both interesting concepts. Now I want each group to spend the next 30 minutes preparing a presentation describing what the United States of America would look like, how it would feel, once your vision of the ultimate goal had been reached.'

They formed into huddles.

As the first group began speaking, Allen felt so angry, so alienated, he couldn't bear to listen. Opening his laptop computer he interrogated a data base of intelligence agency staff. Three *Martins* were listed but only one was in Washington DC. He selected it and located a summary of Martin's record.

'Martin L Mulkamitz

Trained as a penetrating agent with Central Intelligence Agency. Employed on missions associated with drug importation from Columbia. Twice wounded by gunshot. One wound destroyed part of his stomach. Can now eat only minuscule meals. Physique changed from 170 pound amateur-wrestling contestant into jockey-like proportions.

Subsequently deployed for covert operations in Afghanistan. Awarded CIA Distinguished Intelligence Cross. Citation summary follows:

While observing a firefight from an apparently safe distance, a mortar shell struck the mud-brick enclosure sheltering Mulkamitz together with an Afghan woman and her baby. Shrapnel tore away the bottom of his jaw and opened an artery in the woman's leg. Using a combat medical kit, Mulkamitz slowed the rate of blood loss from the woman. With a triangular cloth, intended for use as a sling, he held his own lower face together, binding the cloth around top of his head.

Notwithstanding his wound and his light physique, Mulkamitz partly carried and partly assisted the woman and her child across trackless, steep terrain for almost one hour, reaching a first-aid facility operated by a detachment of US Army forces.

Medical personnel doubted Mulkamitz's version of events, claiming no man with his physique and severe injuries could have assisted or carried the woman and her child for any time or distance.

A patrol was sent to investigate. The patrol located trail of fresh blood and followed it to a mud-brick enclosure matching the description given by Mulkamitz. At the enclosure they found a US Government first-aid kit. It was missing the components Mulkamitz had used on the woman and himself....'

On Thursday morning Martin was already in the classroom when Allen arrived for class, early.

Martin, his eyes narrowed to slits and lips contorted into a snarl, turned to Allen. 'On Tuesday I made the point that you were not to take any interest in other people here, beyond recalling their first names. Yesterday, you interrogated a classified data base spending seven minutes and nine seconds looking through my record of service. *Why?*'

Allen confessed to having been repulsed by what he called the other team's, 'soft and treacherous approach to America's security'. He'd filled-in time by practicing his internet investigatory skills. He'd been fascinated by Martin's obvious confidence and toughness so decided to look for an explanation.

Flattery failed to impress Martin.

'Allen Ivory, you have messed up. This breach is on your record, where it will remain. You are on a formal warning. Any future screw-ups and I'll have you polishing conch shells on an otherwise uninhabited island for the next ten years.'

'And, if you are stupid enough to think I don't mean that to be taken literally, then just try me.'

Shocked and humiliated, Allen had no difficulty believing anything this man said. His remaining problem was, *how* to avoid another screw-up.

What in hell's name comprises a screw-up around here? I still don't understand the objectives of this course. I don't know what they expect of me either here or later. Come to think of it, perhaps exposing me to uncertainty is one of their tests. Who would know what they're thinking.

His first clue came within minutes. Martin announced that the two people who'd been arguing for a softer policy on American security, had been assigned back to their respective agencies. According to Martin it was because the necessary components of their training had been completed.

Noting they were only three days into a nine-week course, Allen doubted Martin's explanation. However, the man's attitude and tone of his voice indicated no further discussion would be tolerated.

Allen was nevertheless relieved that the approach which came naturally to him seemed to fit. However, there'd already been four departures. *He* was on a formal warning. With an attrition rate like this, nobody would finish the course, if it was a course in the first place.

During the following weeks, lectures and exercises considered in detail America's perspective of global history since and including the War of Independence. Singly and in combination every case study was resolved in ways that supported views Allen had tentatively formed while still a teenager.

Martin led discussions but never slanted lessons toward a desired conclusion. The prayer-led and patriotic inclinations of his audience performed that function for him.

A classic example was their conversation on America's War of Independence.

'The War', Martin claimed, 'wasn't caused by British taxation. In fact, the colonists had been getting a very good taxation deal. They were paying lower taxes than Englishmen back in their own country. Following independence, the new American government increased domestic taxes.'

Continuing to demolish widely accepted myths he asserted 'About two-thirds of Americans had opposed or been neutral toward severing ties with Britain. There was no unbroken series of victories by untrained colonial patriots. Washington himself had little patience with militias. The French, especially the French navy, played a major part in defeating the British, although we never gave them the appropriate credit.'

'And so' asked Martin, 'despite all the controversy, notwithstanding all the propaganda spouted by all sides of the conflict, was the long and messy War of Independence a pivotal event in forming our nation? Do any lessons resonate with us, today?'

These weren't easy questions to answer. Eventually, the group identified four key points all supporting the notion that the War had helped define America and was still relevant. Each student presented one.

'The Europeans originally settling in America', it was first argued, 'had been unconventional people. Some, for example, refused to accept limitations on their preferred way of worship. It was inevitable they would oppose oversight by one or more of the old European powers and that this attitude would persist.'

The second speaker addressed the time interval between early settlements and unmistakable battles, such as the Boston Massacre. 'At first,' she claimed, 'the new settlers were focussed on survival. Gradually, they came to understand the incredible gift God had bestowed upon them, to realise they were custodians of a Divine bequest. Responding to Divine Guidance, they waited until they had the critical mass needed to defeat the British.'

Allen was third and, unusually for him, he focussed on people and personalities.

'The leadership mix had been perfect or close to it. Patrick Henry exhibited inflexible determination with his "give me liberty or give me death" speech. George Washington combined military leadership with wisdom and statesmanship. Benjamin Franklin comprehended both science and the value of journalism. Thomas Jefferson and John Adams, an unlikely combination, had nevertheless played a major role in writing the Declaration of Independence.'

'It was beyond reasonable belief these diverse people had come together other than in accordance with a Divine Plan.'

The final speaker represented the War of Independence as more than just another conflict. 'It had been preordained. America has always had to fight for what it had and for what it deserved. It was prepared to spill blood if needed to achieve its objectives. These golden threads of determination and sacrifice have woven the nation together ever since.'

Lessons continued with students encouraged to consider issues from what Martin referred to as a global perspective.

Underlying the War of Independence, they were told, was early opposition to Britain's global empire. But the Brits had not been alone. The Dutch, French, Spanish, Portuguese, and belatedly the Germans competed to capture territory, control trade routes, monopolise markets and generally stamp their imprints upon the globe. By 1898 European powers controlled 67 per cent of the Earth's surface and had expanded that to 84 per cent by 1914.

According to Martin 'The strategic implications of this manoeuvring were not lost on America. To fulfil God's objective we needed to become a global force. Starting late in the race we made some unpleasant decisions in order to establish our credentials as a world power and ensure we had strategic flexibility.'

'But', Martin claimed, 'we did not wait until the 20th century to make a start.'

'In 1823 President James Monroe announced the Monroe Doctrine, effectively warning European powers that the North and South American continents were in our region of strategic interest and we would not tolerate European interference. It was a bold and risky manoeuvre. It was also a classic example of our capacity to make audacious decisions and back them up.'

'Unfortunately, we also created a precedent which China is now using to stamp its dominance on the Western Pacific region. Before long, they'll begin citing Monroe in defending their activities.'

'In 1803 we bought Louisiana from Napoleon. During 1810 we declared West Florida to be a US possession. In 1845 we annexed Texas. During 1867 we began protecting our northern approaches when we bought Alaska from Russia. In 1877 we acquired, through a treaty, rights to use the harbour of Pago Pago, one of our first strategic ventures into the southern hemisphere.'

'In 1893 we effectively toppled the Queen of Hawaii and annexed the islands in 1898. This gave us control over a vital stepping stone between our nation and the Western Pacific.'

'Sometimes we almost fell onto our feet, such as in 1898 when we declared war against Spain, allegedly to protect the Cubans from Spanish tyranny. This, coincidentally, limited the presence of a European power on our doorstep. But it also led to a bonanza with us gaining Puerto Rico, Guam and the Philippines, giving us a potentially strong presence across the Pacific Ocean.'

'One way or another, we never stopped expanding or consolidating or influencing sites and nations globally, in accordance with our ordained destiny.'

'You can see the pattern here. We moved decisively to ensure our security as our highest and most immediate priority.'

'However, you mustn't limit your concept of security to military or territorial issues. The massive economic engine of the United States needs raw materials, fuels and markets. Guaranteed availability is also a component of our national security. This is one reason we intervened militarily in Latin America on 24 occasions between 1900 and 1925.'

'When Japan began doing something similar in East Asia we froze funds to halt trading. This deprived Japan of about 60 per cent of its total supply of steel and oil. Japan found this intolerable and attacked Pearl Harbour on the day "which will live in infamy." As international strategists, we might ask ourselves what America would have done if the roles had been reversed.'

'People with limited strategic vision fail to understand these broader considerations. General Smedley Butler, who commanded several economy-related interventions, wrote a book, *War is a Racket*. But without that racket America would not be the super-power it is today and would not be able to extend its protective wings to cover the free world.'

Allen was ecstatic. Martin's analysis accorded precisely with the spiritual model he'd evolved. This was in your face reality. America had nothing to apologise for, not now, not ever.

The floodtide continued.

On one occasion, Martin said 'There's an old French saying, "You can't make an omelette without breaking eggs." To achieve our objectives, we've sacrificed young American lives. That's something we begrudge and lament. Every drop of American blood has to be paid for many times over.' The First World War was a classic example.'

'For the Europeans who started it, for no obvious reason, the war began in 1914 and lasted until 1918. Between 15 and 19 million people were killed. America joined the fighting in 1917, prior to which we'd gained useful national income from trading with both sides of the conflict. From 1917 to 1918 we lost just over 54 000 American military and civilians killed.'

'But,' according to Martin 'the war was part of our pathway into a bigger power game.'

'President Woodrow Wilson dominated the subsequent Versailles Peace Conference. Having successfully influenced the terms governing formation of the League of Nations, we didn't join it and weren't bound by it.'

'We always expect a return on our investments, in peace or war. Also, the United States does not appreciate competition from any other nation. Those are fundamental principles. Remember them!'

This was pure gold. The news media often presented US foreign policy as incoherent, inconsistent, or at least confused. But Martin understood common threads and objectives. America knew exactly what it was doing and why.

Snatches of Martin's dialogues resonated so strongly that, years later, Allen could recite them *verbatim*.

' ... yeah, Latin America will always be difficult. ... if any fool of a dictator looks likely to overstep the mark we sort him out. If you want a text-book example of a situation well-handled, read up on what happened to João Goulart in Brazil.'

'... Middle East will remain a problem. ... we must stop any player including Israel from getting too powerful, even if our interventions sometimes seem inconsistent for other reasons.'

'Japan is stuck in our strategic corner whether it likes it or not. They've invaded and occupied areas of China, Russia, Korea and most of South-east Asia. Those nations would be happy to dish-out some of what they received. But Japan is under our protection. It's a vital forward base. We intend keeping it that way.'

'India remains a huge frustration. We can't predict its moves. We've offered diplomatic olive branches without much success. If expanded permanent membership of the UN Security Council becomes an issue we might prefer supporting Japan over India, regardless of what one past President told the Indians.'

The dialogue continued more than a week, covering Sub-Saharan Africa, Britain, Near and Far-East, Oceania, Far Northern States, East and West Europe. A few nations merited special concern but, in the main, America's true orientation was regional.

Martin left no doubt about the American concept of leadership. America produced the world's finest leaders, the most hallowed principles. America expected others to fall into line and follow.

'As we've seen, America's most significant strategic moves have been initiated by either one or a very few people. Strong and effective leaders have provided the framework on which we built this great nation. As Allen said in an earlier session, they always emerged when we most needed them. '

'They're still appearing. They've, for example, given us a near global stranglehold on computer-based software and data processing. This has conferred massive financial and strategic authority over other nations.'

'That doesn't sound friendly, but we are talking real-world issues here. Our alliances with other nations are designed to ensure they will support our objectives, or at least won't become strategic competitors. We'll subordinate them if the opportunity arises. Keep in mind that alliances are veneers for insulating America.'

'We're at our most powerful, our most influential, when our power is concentrated and focussed on a small number of American patriots. Our political and economic systems work in tandem to produce that outcome.'

'Our great nation has never tolerated strong labour movements. They aim to spread wealth, which means they dilute power. We crushed the labour movements of the 1870s, 1880s and 1890s, using the US Army when necessary. The Palmer Raids of 1919 and 1929 followed.'

'Even under the Roosevelt reforms during the Great Depression, our largest corporations dominated the National Recovery Administration. And we haven't eased up, although we're more subtle in our techniques today.'

'There's no shortage of critics writing unfavourable comments on America's attitude to organised labour forces in other nations. They forget how tough we were in managing our own.'

'If anybody has doubts about America being on the right track, I ask them why our sea and air ports, our borders, are crowded with people wanting to get into the United States, to share the benefits and opportunities this great nation has to offer. America's never had a viable labour party and one isn't about to emerge.'

COMMITMENT

Without warning or ceremony, one Friday afternoon when they all stood to depart Martin announced they'd performed well. However, two people had absorbed as much as their respective agencies required. They would report to those agencies on the following Monday morning. Complimentary reports on their progress would be sent to their agency heads.

The two nominated students seemed unsurprised. Allen gained the impression they'd started the course, or whatever it was, with a clear idea of what they'd be covering.

Their departures weren't emotional. Both people, known by first names only, handed back their notes, swipecards and laptops, said farewell and walked.

This left only Allen and a woman named Jillian. Her first name was all Allen was supposed to know. However, several days earlier he'd overheard Martin talking with her.

'I've been considering your birth name of Jillian Usherall. It's far too Anglo-Saxon. It needs to be changed, now, before you start training for your assignment in Kiev. Following completion of your time under my wing, you will become Jillian Horrowicz. Changes to all your necessary identity and other documentation are being arranged.'

Classes continued with topics covering more controversial issues than previously.

One was 'How much sensitive information should we share with politicians, including the President, cabinet appointees, their senior staffers and elected members of Congress?'

'Democracy' said Martin 'doesn't mesh well with reality. Following every election, we gain some new congressmen and periodically we have a new President and administration as well.'

'Theoretically, they've been elected to govern us. However, in some cases, we have minimal information on their associates or families, their temperaments or most other criteria we would normally consider in granting a high-level security clearance. Yet, as some of them assert, they hold such clearances automatically and instantaneously, simply because they've been elected.'

'This isn't a problem confined to the United States. Intelligence communities in Britain, Canada and other nations face the same dilemma.'

'Can we or should we trust these untested and unobserved individuals with our nation's most sensitive information?'

'What might happen if we don't?' Will they then make suboptimal judgements or decisions? In one case, during 1973, the Australian Attorney-General authorised a police raid on the headquarters of his own security and intelligence organisation. He suspected they were withholding information from him.'

'There's no comprehensive solution. But, when dealing with politicians, or their staff, you need to keep in mind these people might not hold anything approaching a conventional security clearance. Therefore, don't share information beyond the minimum necessary.'

'For situations which look like getting out of control, it's always possible one of our agencies will have assembled a dirt-file on the most likely troublemakers, just as J Edgar Hoover was alleged to have done. It, speaking hypothetically of course, might be used to modify some enthusiastic behaviours.'

On another occasion the *topic du jour* was use of nuclear weapons. Martin quickly dispensed with small-scale weapons designed for battlefield applications, categorising them as *tactical*.

'Today, I want to consider strategic nuclear weapons, devices capable of decimating an entire town or city.'

'The United States has more strategic nuclear weapons than all other nations combined. We could deliver them, with unerring accuracy, using aircraft, submarines or missiles.'

'The best defences of any other nation might eliminate up to ten percent of our incoming weapons. Nothing and nobody could stop the remaining 90 per cent. We could eliminate any nation on Earth.'

'But there are other factors to consider. If we attacked either one of our most likely opponents, Russia or China, regardless of the circumstances, their early-warning and mobile launch platforms would enable them to retaliate.'

'They couldn't eliminate our launch platforms, especially the submarines, but they wouldn't try to. They'd target our core administrative, financial and manufacturing hubs. Having obliterated New York, Washington and Chicago, they'd turn their attention to major industrial centres.'

'There's debate over just how many US city-targets they'd need to eliminate before the United States became a third or fourth-grade power in the world. Most analysts put the figure between 15 and 30. Russia or China could easily achieve that result with their nuclear inventories.'

'The fact we have ten times more nukes than they do is irrelevant. Our defences couldn't stop them, couldn't eliminate all the incoming weapons. And, if we attacked first, they'd have nothing to lose. A new world order would emerge. We, likely, would become bystanders. Think Hiroshima and Nagasaki multiplied by thousands!'

As the conversation progressed it became shockingly obvious that the American nuclear armoury, was a domestic and political delusion, or possibly a tool for deployment against weak nations without the capacity to retaliate in any significant way.

Even in the latter case, they agreed, using nuclear weapons involved risks. For example, would China tolerate a pre-emptive strike on North Korea? Or would it respond with limited retaliation, such as destroying Guam? And if it did, were the combination of Guam and North Korea justification for escalation leading to the comprehensive destruction of two nations?

And, thought Allen, *for nations so militarily weak they had no capacity to retaliate, what possibly could be the justification for using strategic nuclear weapons against them in the first place?*

The conclusion reached was that their own politicians posed the greatest risk.

Finally, they discussed the touchpoint topic of, would the United States military obey an obviously dangerous political order to launch an attack with nuclear weapons? There was no way to know. This, they agreed, was dangerous territory.

But, deeply within himself, Allen knew the Lord Jesus Christ would never allow God's most magnificent creation in human history to be stalemated, held at bay, by any nation or coalition of nations. Regardless of challenges, the home of the brave would prevail.

Following the nuclear debate, Allen was convinced topics couldn't get more controversial. But Martin had an trump card up his sleeve.

One morning he reminded his audience, now of two people, that, on Day 1 he'd listed Either Republican voter or strong Republican leanings as one of the prerequisites for selection to attend these sessions.

'Is there an unwritten policy of stacking the intelligence community with members of the Republican Party?' The answer was a definite *possibly*.

According to Martin 'The core concept associated with republicans, as contrasted with democrats, was a fundamental focus on protecting, strengthening and projecting the United States. The nation came first. The nation itself was more important than social justice, cultural inclusiveness, health and welfare support, or any other people-related causes.'

Martin added 'The greatest United States Presidents were Republicans: Lincoln, Grant, McKinley, Eisenhower, Reagan, the Bush father and son. However, some democrats also exhibited occasional republican values. Woodrow Wilson was a tough advocate for America on the world stage. Even Barack Obama had his moments when he ramped up the number of targeted killings from drone strikes. There's always hope, even for a president holding the Nobel Peace Prize.'

'The fundamental issue is that you must be totally committed to putting the interests of the United States, as a dominant global power, first at all times and in every situation.'

On the Monday morning of the ninth week Allen arrived, via the Department of Commerce foyer, and sat in what had become his normal chair.

Jillian did not appear. Allen had no way of knowing it, but he'd seen her for the last time. Like an intricate *pas de deux* performed on a moonless night, their paths would cross many times during the years ahead, but Allen and Jillian would never again see or contact each other.

Martin arrived a few minutes later. 'Jillian completed her training with me on Friday. She was reassigned.' he said in a pragmatic tone.

'Does that mean, being the only person still here, still unassigned, that I've failed?'

'No,' said Martin 'the training I estimated would require nine weeks has been completed in eight. You have passed with flying colours. You, Allen Ivory, are a genuine, true-blue, straight arrow.'

'No doubt you are wondering what might happen next. We have several options, but we hope you will accept assignment to the most prestigious, most influential organisation in the entire American intelligence apparatus.'

Martin continued. 'There is a catch, and it is a major one. It you accept induction into this organisation you will be a member for life.'

'Your life might terminate early as a consequence of accident or violence, you might live to a wonderful old age having spent decades of contented years in semi-retirement. But, whatever happens, if you join this organisation your membership will never expire.'

'There are less dramatic options available to you. If necessary, we will discuss them. Meanwhile, I invite you to take a week off work, go somewhere pleasant and peaceful, think about what you want to do.'

Allen had only one question. 'Are you a member of this unnamed but prestigious organisation?'

'Yes. I am.'

Knowing he'd be expected to appear calm and professional, Allen swallowed a rising rush of excitement. This was the target at which his entire life had been aiming. From the patriotism of his home, the many lessons he'd learned from studying the Lord Jesus in his Bible, the content of the past eight weeks, it all meshed perfectly. It was like completing a jigsaw puzzle to reveal a superb landscape.

Consciously steadying his voice, he replied 'Thank you Martin. I cannot imagine that a week or a year of contemplation would change my mind. I am delighted by this offer. It will be my sacred honor to serve our nation, unconditionally.'

'Hmmm,' said Martin 'I was fairly confident you'd say something like that. In anticipation, I've arranged for you to meet the head of our organisation. He is never mentioned by name but always referred to as The Leader. The interview is scheduled in 30 minutes from now. Afterwards, you will sign your Oath of Induction.'

'Thank you. By the way, what's the name of the organisation I'm about to join?'

'It's easy to remember. It's called *The Office*. That's it, *The Office*. Now, I suggest you wait in the canteen and have a coffee. I'll call for you.'

Seated in one of the canteen's white-plastic chairs, Allen decided to dawdle over a small coffee rather than risk the adrenalin rush from a large one.

It was a good move. Within ten minutes Martin reappeared and they set off.

As they approached another unexceptional door at the end of the common corridor Allen heard two pronounced clicks, like heavy metal bolts being withdrawn. He assumed, correctly, a detection system had seen them approach and some invisible approving authority had electronically released a security device.

The heavy door swung open and they entered a spacious office featuring modern, blonde-wood furnishings resting on a thick, beige carpet. Seated behind an impressively large desk was his now-familiar escort, Carol. In front of her desk were several comfortable-looking cream-fabric upholstered arm-chairs. She invited Allen to sit.

Martin, nodded to her and departed, the entry door silently swinging back and clicking into its locked position.

Behind Carol's desk was another door. On its either side, lounging against the wall, was a United States Marine wearing body armour and holding a menacing sub-machine gun.

Carol, with a wry smile Allen couldn't account for, pressed a button on her desk. Picking up a handpiece, she spoke a few indecipherable words then listened intently.

Turning to Allen she said 'The Leader hates keeping people waiting but he is about to take a call from the Vice President. He apologises but invites you to enter and sit while he completes the conversation.'

She nodded to the Marines. One of them opened The Leader's door. Allen thanked him and entered.

The Leader's office met and exceeded Allen's expectations for prestigious accommodation designed to accommodate a very senior executive.

In front of a large, green-leather topped oakwood desk were two modern and comfortable chairs featuring moulded-wood bases and fitted cushions. A few feet back, beside the desk, was a highly polished antique conference table, surrounded by eight chairs. The chairs appeared to be the ultra-thin and elegant pieces once made by Shaker communities.

Papered walls hosted gold-framed oil paintings portraying heroic scenes ranging from the War of Independence to the Vietnam War. Each was illuminated by a brass light fitting.

The Leader was seated on, or in, a high-backed swivel chair turned to face away from his desk. Speaking softly, in a deep voice, he was addressing the handpiece of a red telephone attached to a coiled electric cord.

Allen could just see the top of his head. The hair was grey, turning white. It was also cropped short and tightly curled.

Another African American! So *that* was why Carol had been smiling to herself!

Allen hadn't contemplated racial prejudice in this environment. Nevertheless, it was a good feeling to know his boss was also Black and would understand what that meant.

Less than a minute later The Leader finished talking, replaced the handset and swung his chair around.

Allen felt a sudden, jarring shock ripple through him. His eyes bulged. His mouth fell open. The man facing him, with customary calm demeanour, was his *father*.

Allen gasped 'Good Lord, for all these years you've been saying you were going to the office and what you meant was, *The Office.*'

'Correct', The Leader replied 'and to save you wondering if you can ask me the next two questions now forming at the back of your mind I'll give you the answers.'

'One, until about 30 minutes ago, I knew nothing about you being under our surveillance or your possible induction into The Office. Had you not met the required standards, Agents Carol and Martin would have reallocated you in an appropriate manner and almost certainly never mentioned it to me.'

'Unless something unexpected happens, or you become very senior in our organisation, I will play no part in guiding your future career.'

'Two, your mother knows nothing about The Office, but she undoubtedly has concluded I am engaged in support of the national interest. She and I met when we were both working for the Central Intelligence Agency.'

'I was invited to leave and pursue other opportunities. Fortunately, I did not have to sever my ties with her as well. So far as she is concerned, you are employed by Department of Commerce.'

'Have you any additional questions?'

Allen, already disoriented, was stunned to learn that his *mother,* his dear, kind, domesticated *mother,* had worked for the *CIA.* He could only manage 'N, no sir.'

'Fine', replied The Leader 'I understand you have some paperwork to complete. Thank you for visiting.'

The man opened a paper file marked USEYES ONLY and began reading. Allen, assuming the discussion had ended, stumbled to the door and let himself out, walking past the armed men.

He slumped into one of the chairs in front of Carol's desk.

Evolution

Carol, with an attitude remarkably like The Leader's, said 'Martin left this document for you to read carefully and then sign.'

The single page contained a concise statement that Allen agreed to commit his life to serving the United States of America, without limitation or exemption. There would be no way out, no turning back.

Allen signed. Carol added hers and dated the document. Offering a firm almost masculine handshake, she said 'Congratulations, Agent Allen Ivory. We have every confidence you will be one of our finest.'

'Martin offered you a one-week break for contemplation before you committed to The Office. You felt confident to proceed without further consideration.'

'We accepted that. However, we still believe you should have a week to reflect on the journey you have been taking and to think about the future of our nation in the global context.'

'I am now ordering you to take one week off, to go somewhere peaceful and pleasant. I'll see you here at 0930 hours next Monday.'

Allen, still living with his parents, returned home to Oakton and retrieved an old brown-canvas travelling bag from a loft in the garage.

Along with two pairs of denim jeans, he packed socks, shirts, tees, underpants and spare jogging shoes. A few casual overgarments and a polyester raincoat, together with his toiletries folder and well-thumbed Holy Bible, completed the inventory.

He booked accommodation and arranged to hire a car, finalising both transactions on-line.

Feeling self-conscious as he addressed it, he wrote a note to 'Dear Mom and Dad', saying 'I've taken advantage of a low-pressure period at work and am heading off to enjoy a one-week vacation. I'll be home next Sunday.'

From habit, he almost mentioned a low-pressure period at the office but remembered his father would see the note and caught himself. Life at home had changed.

———

Driving west through green-grassed meadows separated by white-painted fences, he passed several properties stocked with magnificent thoroughbred horses, all quietly speaking to the lifestyle enjoyed by successful Americans. Arriving at the confluence of the Potomac and Shenandoah Rivers, he drove into the historic township of Harpers Ferry.

This village of old and restored buildings was not only picturesque but reeked of American history. George Washington and Thomas Jefferson had visited. The slavery abolitionist, John Brown, had attempted his famous raid there. It had featured in the American Civil War.

Allen was in his element. Feeling close to some of the world's greatest and most historic struggles, he could sense the emergence of this divine nation surrounding him.

A road climbing a steep incline hosted Camp Hill-Wesley United Methodist Church. He wouldn't be here for a Sunday service, unfortunately, but Allen put aside a minimum of an hour every day to visit so he could silently thank the Lord Jesus Christ for blessings beyond words.

Apart from praying, Allen wasn't inclined to do anything in particular. Walking, from his motel, eating at one or other of the locality's traditional restaurants, reading the daily newspapers, happily filled his days. He didn't spend much time contemplating global events either, deciding neither Carol nor Martin had really expected him to.

But during the week, two items in newspapers caught his attention.

The first was highly critical of kangaroo slaughter in Australia. Apparently, the Australians regularly conducted organised raids on kangaroos. Almost unbelievably they used the hides for shoe leather and sold some of the meat *in supermarkets* for *human* consumption. This was, the journalist claimed, worse than eating whales or horses.

The following day, disgust and outrage dominated *Letters to the Editor*. Intervention of some unspecified sort was advocated more than once. One correspondent proposed trade restrictions to bring these barbaric people to their senses.

The Australian Ambassador released a statement arguing that kangaroo populations numbered in the millions, they were breeding at uncontrollable rates and the meat was highly nutritious. It was an unproductive move and generated yet more outrage.

Two days later another indignant item reported an American athlete, competing in Australia, had been disqualified on grounds of drug cheating.

'*How dare they*', thundered one editorial. This was an *American!* Did Australians have the reliable technology needed to conduct such complicated tests? Did they know how to use it, to interpret the data? Was this a politicised attempt to handicap foreign athletes so the Australians could rig the results? These grave insults to America could not be ignored.

Bans on Australian athletes competing in the US were proposed. Details of almost an entire Australian Rules football team caught using a banned substance were highlighted. Another incident, where members of their national cricket team had been implicated in ball tampering, was dissected over and again.

It seemed obvious the Australians couldn't be trusted to compete cleanly or detect drug-cheating *if* it happened. Australian athletes were compared with Russian competitors.

Allen was astonished. The United States and Australia had for many years been viewed as close and compatible allies. Visitors to and from either side of the Pacific were almost invariably regarded as good guys and made welcome. These media articles suggested the tide of friendship might be turning.

During the remaining days of that week, apart from reaffirming his vocation, the only decision Allen made was he'd have to move from his parent's home. Living with The Leader, knowing his mother was a former CIA operative, and camouflaging any knowledge of those startling revelations, would be nearly impossible. Besides, it was time to begin living independently.

Using his laptop, Allen checked the Web and tentatively selected several apartments to view.

———————

On Monday morning a refreshed and eager Agent Allen Ivory reported to Carol on time and as ordered.

Welcoming him back she presented Allen with a photographic identification card, compete with holograph and security markings, showing he was a permanent employee of Department of Commerce. Curious, he asked Carol who she was nominally employed by. For the first time in Allen's experience she burst out laughing, then said 'You'd never guess in a million years.'

Encouraged by her informality, Allen mentioned his intention to find an apartment but Carol stopped him with a dismissive wave.

'Don't worry about that. Your next training and development assignment starts on Thursday and it won't be in this region. Here's a slip of paper with the name of a US Army base, located interstate. Please report to our administration office and collect your travel documents.'

'The transport has already been booked, door-to door-from Oakland. Because of complex connections, travel time will be three days. So, go home and pack your bags. You can expect to be away for about six to nine months.'

Allen was beginning to understand what The Office meant by *total dedication*. This disciplined organisation could respond rapidly to changing situations. Its agents were expected to do likewise.

On the Thursday morning an airport shuttle bus dropped Allen at the guard-gate entrance to a US Army base he had never previously heard of. Located in a remote area of hilly woodland it apparently met requirements for a variety of training.

The rostered guard was not expecting him and was none the wiser after consulting a folder labelled *Guard House Standing Orders*. It took several 'phone calls to officials on the base before he located someone aware of Allen.

Eventually, a captain arrived and identified him from a photograph embedded in a briefing paper giving an almost completely fictitious version of Allen's background. With the rostered guard now satisfied, Allen was issued with a *Temporary Entry Conditional Pass—Civilian*. The captain helped load his two trunks of luggage into the trunk of a dust-covered Kia sedan and together they drove over a slight ridge into the established base.

Allen's first impression was of a regulation banning multi-level buildings. Long, neat rows of almost identical single-storey establishments extended in every direction. Some of these raw-timber-clad structures were domestic houses, others served as offices. A few had been joined together forming larger halls or warehouses. Approaches to the more official buildings were marked by rows of boulders painted in high-gloss white. A flagpole flying the stars-and-stripes stood in front of one edifice labelled 'Headquarters'. *Its* access path was bordered with white-painted warheads from superseded artillery pieces.

There was hardly any sign of human activity, leaving Allen to assume most inhabitants either worked indoors or were engaged on military activities in the surrounding and heavily forested hills,

He'd been nervously anticipating something equivalent to a military boot-camp. However the captain, who'd been assigned as his training mentor, assured him that would not happen. Provided Allen was fit enough to undertake the range of training offered he would not be required to do supplementary exercising or jogging, but....

'For several reasons associated with safety and practicality you'll be required to wear clothing resembling the standard Army issue. Out-of-hours, if that ever happens, you can revert to civilian attire.'

Later that morning, Allen staggered from the military supply store to his allocated bedroom. Draped over and around him was a pile of kit including camouflage uniforms, compatible underwear, various pairs of boots and joggers, hats, sunglasses and a variety of strange items made from webbing.

Navigating by occasionally turning side-on to get his bearings, awkwardly consulting a locality map, he almost dropped the bundle several times before reaching his room. It was in a building marked at each end with a large letter 'M'.

Finding the a key in the door of his unlocked room, Allen opened the door and stumbled into a green-and-cream painted chamber. He dropped his bundle of kit onto the singe-width bed provided.

The room reminded him of an immaculately maintained three-star motel. In addition to his bed and a clothes cupboard, a school-style wooden desk and a chair had been provided. A small bar-fridge (empty except for a tray of ice cubes), a toaster and an electric jug together with rudimentary crockery and cutlery almost completed the contents.

Wall decorations comprised a flat-screen television set, a list of actions to be taken in case of fire or other emergency and an inventory listing all United States Army-owned items in the room. His bedroom led to a small bathroom. Both floors featured grey non-slip tiles.

Within minutes, the captain arrived and taught him how to finish dressing, using the military paraphernalia.

Unexpectedly, at least to Allen, treatment of soiled clothing did not include dropping a bag-full into his local laundromat then collecting it, washed, folded or ironed that same evening. Here, he'd be required to use a washing machine, drying room and ironing board at the communal facility provided in Building J. Soap powder could be purchased from the local Base Store and Supermarket.

Oh well, in some future assignments the normal American facilities might not be available. It's better I learn now. I can always email or text Mom for some guidance if I need it.

His training began later that day. It was to be one-on-one with the captain.

EDUCATION

Although the captain had said Allen was not learning to be a soldier, his training included a range of military skills. This, he was told, would take account of a possibly varied career ahead, 'in your capacity as an employee with Department of Commerce', said the captain with merely a hint of sarcasm. There was no specific timetable for success, which was why his assignment might last for between six and nine months. First up was learning to maintain and shoot a variety of pistols and revolvers.

'But I've never held a gun.' Allen protested.

'Well, that's good. You won't have to forget bad habits.' came the reply.

'Now, contrary to popular opinion, competent shooters begin by understanding how their weapons work and that's where we'll begin.'

A lesson on the basic physics and ballistics of firearms followed. This left Allen shocked at how deceived he'd been by movies featuring gun-toting cowboys. Handguns, he discovered, were essentially short-range weapons and not especially accurate ones either, except in the hands of an expert.

Stripping, cleaning and assembling various handguns followed. The sequence was logical and Allen had no difficulty remembering how it was done, even when the captain hid an occasional component or deliberately mixed it up with the parts of other weapons.

Three days later, buoyed by his success, Allen chatted happily while they walked to a nearby indoor shooting range and donned ear protectors. He then discovered firing a handgun required more skill than he'd anticipated, despite previous and sobering revelations.

No matter how hard he tried with a pistol, Allen found it almost impossible to hit one of the human-shaped targets provided. He continued missing, even when the captain used a series of pulleys to bring targets closer, stopping when they were only 15 yards away. Almost unbelievably, his results with revolvers were worse.

After a week of four long and embarrassing sessions each day, the captain concluded Allen was unlikely to improve beyond his present abysmal standard and decided to move on. The concluding advice, as Allen long remembered, was 'If ever you have to shoot someone, make sure he or she is very damned close before you squeeze that trigger.'

But his training wasn't all about handguns. He also endured a gruesome session of killing people, with a knife. Using well-stabbed mannequins, he learned how to slip the blade in between ribs, sever arteries and mutilate bodies in various other ways.

Lessons on stealing and driving various forms of motor-transport were considerably more fun. Allen also checked-out as a driver of all-terrain vehicles, armoured cars, small trucks and even on commercial buses of Greyhound proportions. 'You might need to make your getaway by stealing one of these someday.'

He mastered offensive driving skills to an exceptionally high level, astonishing both the captain and himself in the process. On one occasion he drove an articulated vehicle along a highway, fishtailing it in a controlled manner to prevent anything from overtaking them while causing mayhem for other traffic. The lesson terminated when he pulled into a truckers' rest-area and they both collapsed with laughter.

Tuition wasn't confined to driving on sealed roads either. Allen had to wrestle off-road vehicles through flowing streams and across rugged terrain, winching them up and down scarily steep hills where necessary.

Following his success as a driver, Allen began convincing himself his progress was now satisfactory, or perhaps better than that. The delusion persisted until the morning, dressed in thickly padded trousers and jacket, he was introduced to motorcycles.

Having never sat on one, he was confronted by a massive black and chrome, multi-cylindered Harley Davidson. The captain, noticing Allen's dismayed expression, laughed and said 'That's your post-graduate steed. Over here is the machine we'll start with.'

Over here was a machine with controls duplicating those of the largest bikes, but with a 100cc engine. After several days learning to ride this sedate version, including on roads and across fields, tumbling off it only three times, the captain considered Allen ready to try the Harley.

'Remember', he was told, 'all the controls are identical. But the engine is much more powerful so be very careful with your acceleration.'

Feeling more confident now, Allen mounted the beast, started the motor, planted his left foot on the gear-pedal to select first gear, and gently twisted his throttle grip.

The chrome-plated monster instantly raised its front wheel skywards and accelerated away leaving Allen sitting, crestfallen, on the ground. It continued, riderless, for a few seconds before slowing and falling onto its side.

'Shit!' said Allen swearing for the first time in years. 'What the hell happened there?'

'Well' the captain replied 'let's agree you're not likely to become a highly competitive motor cyclist. However, we are going to persist until you improve.'

Allen persevered and eventually learned to ride the Harley moderately well. At some stage he also decided to never make motorcycles his first option for the daily commute.

At about this time Allen began wondering what he'd signed-up to. The classroom lectures with Martin, and discussions of grandiose visions where America dominated the entire world, were one thing. Learning how to steal, shoot, stab and even to use drugs or poisons was something else. What was he becoming, a clandestine diplomat or a trained killer? He still had only a vague idea what The Office's mission was or how he might be expected to assist in achieving it.

But, regardless of private doubts, the training continued relentlessly and extended to kayaking, camouflage techniques, escape and evasion, abseiling, rock climbing and living off the land.

On a few occasions the captain was unqualified to manage specialised aspects of the syllabus and passed Allen to other instructors. They taught him the basics of aircraft-piloting, parachuting, shop-lifting, forging, identity theft, lockpicking and detecting listening devices.

One afternoon, with almost eight intense but fascinating months behind him, Allen met with the captain in a small, unadorned office located in a standard-model building. He was handed a sealed envelope addressed to him by name and marked, 'Shred immediately after reading.' The captain pointed to a document shredder in the corner saying 'That's for you.'

The typed, unreferenced and unsigned note directed him to report, four days later, to an address with the US Department of Justice where he would be studying international law. This would be a necessary component of his development as an officer in Department of Commerce.

Allen memorised the new address and shredded his document, all the time feeling bitterly disappointed.

Given his training over recent months, he'd been expecting a more exciting assignment, something with a whiff of danger.

Perhaps not quite so much danger as Martin experienced when getting parts of his body shot away, but surely something likely to get the adrenalin moving. Certainly, a bit more exciting than this.

His only exposure to international law had been reading or watching public announcements by politicians. They'd been either castigating another nation for non-compliance or projecting America as the shining international exemplar of truth, justice and the rule of law. It all seemed formulaic and routine. He wondered what he was supposed to learn.

Turning, he attempted to thank the multi-talented captain for eight amazing months. The woman accepted his compliments and informed a surprised Allen, 'You know, you were my most competent student during a three-year assignment.'

What was more, she said, Allen would retain that title because she'd been promoted to the rank of major and assigned to an installation in Europe where her master's degree in electrical engineering might finally 'get a work-out'.

———

Still convinced that continued living at home in Oakton would be challenging, Allen left the Army installation and flew back to Dulles Airport, carrying a short list of potential apartments. The following day he signed a 12-month lease on a furnished place located close to both the Rosslyn and Courthouse Metro stations.

Having hired a van and collected his remaining possessions from home, Allen spent the first evening at his new address immersed in two Kindle books: *Cooking for Bachelors* and *Cooking for Dummies*. A greater contrast between this and his life during the past eight months could hardly be imagined.

JUSTICE

Editorial Note.

Most details of Allen Ivory's time with Department of Justice remain highly classified and so cannot be disclosed. His assignment to that department continued beyond an originally estimated one year. Following is a synoptic description of selected aspects.

His initial fears of an underwhelming assignment were confirmed when Agent Allen Ivory arrived at a squat, grey, Washington DC-ish address on a miserable, dull, blustery day. Entering a dark-wood panelled, mosaic-floored reception area he met his assigned escort, a tall, thin and acne-complexioned young man wearing jeans, sneakers and a yellow sweatshirt. The escort, Barry, took him to the third floor before pointing to a standard-model workstation in a room full of them.

Allen's ten square-yards of temporarily assigned floor space were defined by chest-high, grey-cloth partitions. Worn fabric around the edges of several panels, supplemented by a few greasy stains on the vertical surfaces, indicated he wasn't this workstation's first occupant, nor a particularly esteemed one either.

Emphasising his foreignness was a sign, thumbtacked to a side panel and marked *Guest, Dept of Commerce*. The implication seemed to be, *Watch what you say. The occupant can't be trusted.*

Seated on the armless swivel-chair provided, Allen opened his briefcase and unpacked a souvenir coffee mug from Harpers Ferry followed by his laptop computer and a foolscap-paper notepad. He supposed he should be grateful for the built-in 110v power point. No other connectivity was provided so Allen assumed he wasn't yet allowed to log into the departmental server or access any of its data bases.

His frustration increased on discovering all three of the workstation's built-in drawers had been either locked or jammed shut.

Nobody had approached him, so he opened his laptop and filled-in time by reading a downloaded version of *The Washington Post*.

It was almost midday when a chubby, pink-faced man arrived and introduced himself as Lionel McKell. He invited Allen into an adjoining office for a chat.

When both were seated in comfortable, if antiquated, wood-framed chairs, Lionel apologised for not making contact sooner. He'd been attending a meeting but returned to find his papers and possessions shoved into a wire shopping basket and deposited in the corridor. Someone else had taken over his well-located workstation as part of the new hot-desk efficiency program. Thinking of his own humble facilities, Allen correctly concluded he was unlikely to suffer a similar fate.

Lionel explained Allen would be given a month in which to tutor himself on the formal basics of international law. Legal theory, he explained, contrasted sharply with reality. However, regardless of whether an issue was theoretical or practical, the same vocabulary would apply. Allen could seek guidance if any questions arose.

Oh well, at least I have a supervisor, or a tutor or something, so I guess that's progress.

Lionel opened his wheeled briefcase, one large enough to support a three-week overseas vacation, and produced two thick volumes, *The law of Nations* and *Introduction to International Law*. He also offered Allen a list of related websites he considered reliable.

Before finishing work for the day, Allen was already immersing himself in exotic terms used by international lawyers, finding them more complicated than he'd suspected. Was an arrangement between nations a treaty, a convention or an agreement, and was there a distinction between them? Had a nation signed, ratified, acceded or succeeded to an arrangement and what were the implications of each? Which states were monist, which were dualist and was the difference worth a damn?

Allen attempted several times to categorise the terminology and its potential applications, using a variety of charts and diagrams. They all failed him. Fortunately, Lionel, approachable and relaxed as his portly physique implied, offered the necessary guidance. He was precise, observant and analytical, leaving Allen no option but to grudgingly respect the man.

Three frustrating weeks later, armed with a modest grasp of legal terminology, Allen began the disenchanting process of learning how international law operated in practice. The first shock came when he discovered there was a fundamental difference between international law and what he had deluded himself into thinking was *global law*, the law to which all nations subscribed. There were no global laws.

Some nations accepted obligations to comply with specific agreements, but it was rare to find any two nations agreeing to be bound by the same menu of agreements. Even when two nations had agreed to be bound by an identical and specific agreement, they were likely to interpret their compliance obligations differently.

Nations apparently in breach of their own commitments were obliged to appear before tribunals only if and when they *consented* to do so, which was seldom the case. Often, they refused to recognise the authority of an international tribunal.

And so it continued, disillusionment following disappointment. '*At the least*' Allen thought '*America will have taken lead in the global compliance, setting an example by fighting for justice.*'

But, on checking a sample of arrangements relating to international security, he discovered the United States had committed to about the same number of agreements as had Russia and fewer than either Japan or Britain.

It got worse. America, he discovered, was one of few nations not to ratify the *United Nations Convention on the Law of the Sea*, a distinction it shared with North Korea, Ethiopia and Liechtenstein.

Lionel, who remained supportive, noticed Allen's growing disenchantment. One afternoon, having balanced his pin-stripe-suited backside on a stool now kept at the entrance to Allen's workstation, he said 'International law is not a shining star Allen, not an ideal or an entity floating aloof from humanity. It is merely one more tool to support America's quest to reach our global objectives. We use it as either a shield or an offensive weapon.'

'Where established laws of nations support our objectives, we use the laws; where not, we ignore them. If circumstances change, well, as the exceptionalist nation we re-evaluate the situation and pretty much do as we please.'

'Nevertheless' he told Allen, 'it is useful to maintain a veneer of compliance. This gives us an excuse for diminishing the reputations of other nations, particularly when we accuse them of breaching an international law, even if it happens to be a law they didn't sign up to in the first place.'

'We can also claim to be *restoring* the rule of law when justifying an invasion or some other form of regime change. Besides, the image of moral and legal superiority is a valuable tool in domestic politics.'

'From time immemorial our politicians have been preaching *international law* to their constituents, as if it were a precise set of rules attached to universally agreed penalties. Such claims aren't much different to a Native American medicine man claiming that a rainbow has all sorts of tribally convenient attributes.'

'The trick' Allen was told 'is to adopt only international agreements which, in the final analysis, don't limit or inhibit America. We achieve this by negotiating until the terms of proposed international agreements are so diluted and vague as to be open to almost any interpretation. Then we recommend that the United States commits.'

'More recently', he continued 'we've been promoting a concept known as 'soft law'.

'Soft laws are not subject to formal commitment at any level. They're plastered with phrases such as *when possible, where circumstances permit* or *as opportunities allow.* This comes close to not having any law at all while feigning a desire to both adopt a law and comply with it.'

Allen, despite some discomfort, got the message. After reading several recently negotiated arrangements he could see the pattern. It was ingenious and well-planned. Better still, it was compatible with his grand strategic vision of an America safe from its enemies because *it* was in control of its own destiny.

Armed with this approach, Allen played a constructive but necessarily minor role in the devious, demanding and intricate manoeuvrings associated with international agreements. In particular, they had to be made compatible with America's defense, trade and foreign policy objectives.

He learned it was easiest to negotiate bilaterally, persuading one nation after another to endorse the American perspective, distracting them from opportunities to form alliances and thus strengthen their own negotiating hands.

Negotiations were not always based on legal issues. Gifts, threats and economic pressures could be applied to gain support for the American point of view. Often there was no public record, no paperwork directly linking meetings and transactions to American policies, yet international law was being invisibly influenced, nudged and evolved in ways ultimately reflecting the harsh realities of global politics.

Allen didn't understand why, but after working on several apparently meaningless projects, he was asked to produce a discussion paper on the Australian concept of international law.

Typically, although unenthusiastic, Allen decided to try for a quality product. He consulted Australian law reports and journals. Controversies were commonplace.

There was an uneasy truce between claims of Australia's Federal government and the governments of individual States, both of which claimed jurisdiction over offshore islands. Australia had legislated for an Australian Whale Sanctuary, including in waters adjacent to the Antarctic continent, but its sovereign capacity to enforce the claim seemed minimal. Japan had consistently ignored it. Other examples of Australian territorial claims might be challenged. Issues of questionable conduct in relation to East Timor had been documented.

This set him wondering about the legality of *American* territorial claims. As he'd anticipated, some were questionable. The legality of America's lease over Guantánamo Bay in Cuba was controversial. Details of land use arrangements in the Republic of the Marshall Islands had not been fully settled. The acquisition of Hawaii might have been unjustified by present-day standards. And the list continued.

Allen began to understand why The Office had sent him on this assignment. They wanted him to see and taste the ugliness of international dealings and, no doubt, emerge better prepared to apply dominance techniques during his future career.

Others in The Office must have survived similar exposures. Perhaps this accounted for the taciturn toughness evident in his father, in Carol and in Martin. But, did he really want to become one of them, a narrowly focussed, nationalistic enforcer?

LAMENTATIONS

Allen's concerns increased following an unplanned meeting with Barry, his original and unimpressive escort. Barry, Allen discovered, was a post-graduate law student attached to the department for a one-year internship. And Barry had become even more disenchanted than Allen.

According to Barry 'The American nation is little more than a grotesque joke. We're the biggest arms exporter in the world. The arms we sell to aggressive nations, some governed by disgusting individuals, are likely to be used as weapons of oppression, not that we give a damn. Then, we keep millions of Americans in poverty, spurn a decent national medical scheme, all because we divert massive funding into a ludicrously huge military. We say we must maintain it to stabilise a world that we contributed to destabilising in the first place.'

'It's no wonder members of the UN General Assembly broke out laughing when one former President of the US addressed them.'

Allen was stunned. Despite a few twinges of conscience, he'd never heard his beloved United States described in such negative terms. In years past, he would have rejected Barry and his attitude. But cumulative exposures over the past two years had revealed the world through a different prism. His future as a component of the grotesque joke was looking increasingly unattractive.

Once again, a chat with Lionel prevented Allen sliding into full-scale disillusionment.

'Allen' Lionel sighed 'please think back to our previous conversation. There's no point to comparing the justice or justification of our international activities with those of other nations. The simple fact is that we're more powerful than they are and so what we do is more right than what they do. This has nothing to do with morality, although we often pretend otherwise.'

'Whenever we confront any actual or possibly emerging threat to our security, which we did to some extent during the years when the Soviet Union temporarily stalemated us, we continued doing the same thing, but more subtly. Even then, we forced the Reds to back down during the Cuban Missile Crisis.'

'Other nations act in the same way, when they get an opportunity. Take India with Goa or Australia with the oil reserves adjacent to Timor Leste for example. Look around you and you'll see China is trying it on as we speak.'

Allen took the message to heart, but nevertheless continued to find the translation of Martin's patriotic classroom discussions into competitive real-world affairs had unsettled him.

But time moved on and new distractions emerged. Soon, for a more mature and enlightened Allen, the most frustrating aspect of this assignment became the requirement for endless bureaucratic consultations covering anything and everything. Almost every American agency seemed to be involved. Some would respond promptly to a request for their concurrence to a proposal; others were invariably tardy.

Occasionally an agency, pursuing its own political agenda, would stop an entire process by not acknowledging invitations to provide input. Heavier administrative artillery would then be required to clear the policy roadblock. Then, if only one agency raised a new and relevant issue, the entire process would begin again.

And that was before Congress bought into the picture with its multitude of overlapping committees, each convinced the entire world revolved around its specific needs. Before congressional dust settled, the White House would often become involved as well, demanding its views be acknowledged, and so the cycle continued.

During his entire period of working in the international-law environment, Allen saw only one agreement escape the bureaucratic threshing machine. It had taken years to get that far. Later, it became bogged down by congressional infighting.

No wonder, he thought, *we never seem to make progress on a domestic issue as emotional as enhanced gun control.*

Nevertheless, as the time to conclude his assignment approached, a wiser but sadder Allen Ivory comprehended the strength and wisdom of thorough, methodical consultation. In its proper place, this was an indispensable tool of democratic governance.

He also appreciated that, sometimes, the United States had to respond rapidly to evolving international events. On these occasions other and parallel mechanisms were needed. Although still ambivalent, he felt relieved to be associated with The Office which, apparently, was one of the rapid reaction components in the American machinery-of-government.

But, regardless of either patriotism or logic, he felt disappointed by the cynicism attached to international law by its practitioners. He could accept it was simply one more tool for manipulating other nations. However, used responsibly, it could also have been a powerful force for global stability.

His discomfort peaked on the day he asked Lionel what had happened to the recently invisible Barry, the post-graduate intern. Lionel's pleasantly plump face converted into an emoji-like image of utter disgust. His response jolted Allen back to the cruel world of global reality.

'That scrawny little turd. I'm not surprised you remember his name. His attitude was deplorable. He seemed to believe that free speech meant he was free to criticise the foundations that support this nation, that which makes us great, makes others fear and respect us.'

"Well, we gave him a lesson in freedom of speech, American-style. We cancelled his assignment and advised his campus he was a dangerous radical. Now, he's free to shout as much treasonable crap as he wishes while serving in the ranks of our unemployed.'

That evening, returning to his apartment, tired and dispirited, Allen skipped the evening meal and immersed himself in prayer. Hour after hour he implored The Lord to restore his focus on progressing his beloved nation's journey toward its sacred destiny, regardless of who or what had to be sacrificed in the process.

Later, sprawled exhausted across his quilted bed, Allen was granted the most powerful spiritual experience he had ever known. Jesus responded unmistakably, reassuring him that his mission should continue, *and* it had the blessing of God the Father.

This sublime enlightenment emerged through the divine words of Katharine Lee Bates's *America the Beautiful*. The blessed verses entered his apartment, gently, peacefully, filling it with pure beauty and embracing him with the comfort he so badly needed.

> 'O beautiful for spacious skies
> For amber waves of grain
> For purple mountain majesties
> Above the fruited plain.......
>
> O beautiful for heroes proved
> In liberating strife
> Who more than self their country loved
> And mercy more than life.......
>
> America, America!
> God shed His Grace on thee
> And crown thy good with brotherhood
> From sea to shining sea.'

Allen slid gently into the deepest slumber he'd enjoyed for months. Meanwhile, in the apartment next to his, a woman switched-off her entertainment system and went to bed. She'd been playing her *Collection of*

American Patriotic Music.

Cynics might claim Allen had experienced a profound case of self-delusion. But those who lack the gift of faith often refuse to acknowledge that The Lord works in many ways. Sometimes He directly employs His spiritual authority. At other times He exploits physical resources made available because He has divinely inspired an inventive humankind.

———

During the following week Allen received a cryptic text on his mobile telephone: *Next Monday, report to Commerce Dept. Proceed to Carol's desk. New assignment.'*

Extricating himself from the US Department of Justice was easy. As usual for Allen, he'd related pleasantly enough to a moving population of co-workers but without making any special friends. For most of the time he'd been regarded as an outsider, even by the ever-tolerant Lionel.

Several senior managers were nevertheless able to tick the *interdepartmental liaison* box on their performance appraisals, having also ensured they'd not created a dangerously well-informed competitor belonging to another organisation.

SACRED HONOUR

The following Monday, following his well-remembered journey down the elevator then along the small railway line, Agent Allen Ivory entered The Office. Walking along the now-familiar corridor, he approached its final door, feeling quietly gratified when two metallic clicks indicated he had been recognised and would be allowed to enter The Leader's outer-office.

From behind the desk a middle-aged man stood and introduced himself as 'Carol Mark II'. The Carol wasn't totally misleading, he explained. He was a fourth generation American but his family had migrated from the Hungarian region. They'd maintained a tradition of baptising their children with Hungarian names. His was Karoly, although everybody called him Karl.

The names Carol and Karoly were phonetically connected, but that was where the similarity ended. Karoly, or Karl, was a mobile monster. Two metres tall, swarthy, with almond-shaped eyes and the build of a heavyweight wrestler, he looked menacing, an attribute he enjoyed and one employed to his advantage whenever it suited him.

Allen asked what had happened to Carol. Karl responded by shrugging his shoulders, leaving Allen to decide that pursuing the issue wouldn't be smart.

'At present, I'm focused on what will happen to you' said Karl. 'In consultation with Martin, and yes, he's still here, I decided you will be assigned to lead a team of one person. You are it, or him if you prefer.'

'You've now been exposed to military activity at the tactical level, to spycraft techniques and to the Machiavellian world of international law. That, together with your previous tertiary studies and your time under Martin's wing has prepared you for the job.'

'Your task, which is of the utmost sensitivity, is to evaluate a proposal for the United States of America to absorb Australia as a component of this nation. You have one year in which to complete your assignment and submit a report. The report is to include three identifiably separate implementation options.'

'You will likely need to bounce some of your evolving ideas off someone else, in which case you can employ me or Martin in that role. You do not have the option of refusing this assignment. You are forbidden to discuss it with any other person.'

'Have you any questions?'

Allen had never vaguely considered what might be involved in absorbing a modern, independent foreign nation, especially an ally of the United States, and tried hard to think of some useful questions. But before he could, Martin appeared, welcomed him back into the fold and escorted him to a small theatrette for what he called the *Australia briefing*.

As the briefing progressed Allen realised, regardless of Karl's constraints, he was not its first and probably not its originally intended audience.

Slides had been produced to a high standard. Points made were crisp, clear and at a uniformly strategic level. Every time he thought of a question the answer would be in the following slide. The presentation reflected detailed planning, rehearsals and, no doubt, refinements.

He began wondering who else had seen and presumably endorsed it but decided any such questions would be ignored and so stayed his tongue.

In any case, he was not an approving authority; obviously the decision had already been reached, at least tentatively. He was expected to put flesh on the bones. Declaring the basic skeleton irrevocably flawed would not be an option. Australia, ready or not, was going to join the land of the free and home of the brave.

According to the briefing, identified justifications for an American take-over were: to counter China's growing influence by ensuring a substantial and enduring American presence in the South Asia region, control Australia's tendency to enable China's economic growth through exporting iron ore and other raw materials to feed the dragon, and acquire control over Australia's rare-earth mineral resources.

Following the briefing, Martin added that a campaign to incline American public opinion against Australia had been quietly progressing for more than two years. As opportunities presented, the print or television media would release an item likely to offend American sentiment by highlighting something the Australians had done or omitted.

But opinion polls still indicated pro-Australian sentiments remained strong and so this initiative seemed likely to fail, although according to Martin the media management folk were reluctant to admit it.

One proposal to be canned was production of a Hollywood film based on Australia's treatment of its aboriginal people. The project was already attracting controversy, mainly because our treatment of native Americans had been as bad or possibly worse. 'Still', Martin reflected, 'how many Australian aboriginal tribes own casinos?'

Allen suspected the Australians would initially resist joining the United States, instead adhering to emotional props regarding their heritage and traditions. But when exposed to the blessings of life, liberty and the pursuit of happiness, they'd soon realise being part of our America was a gift, something beyond value, almost beyond conception.

The briefing over, Martin showed Allen to his newly assigned office.

Located within a larger secured room, it was a glorified work-station designed with walls extending to the ceiling and a lockable door. He'd been equipped with an encrypted telephone, two computers, adequate stationary, a white board, a desk, one chair, and the inevitable paper-shredder. There were no additional seats for guests and not enough floor-space to accommodate them either.

Eight intense months later, during which he explored numerous approaches, Allen felt he had a foundation that might enable The Office to responsibly justify endorsing the Australia Proposal.

The Executive Summary of his report included:

<u>Increase permanent US presence in Australia to counter Chinese influence in South Asia–achievable.</u>

- US personnel and aircraft need permanent bases in northern Australia.
    - ✓ US military personnel now spend time in the Darwin locality, ostensibly for joint-training purposes.
    - ✓ Australia and the US also conduct periodic military exercises in other locations, sometimes with friendly Asian nations.
    - ✓ Australians are accustomed to US military presence. US generally well received.
- Australia could support a massively increased American military presence.
    - ✓ Basic civil services infrastructure adequate.
    - ✓ *But* new capital works probably required.
- Concentrating military personnel and equipment in the one location undesirable. A single target would be too vulnerable in case of military conflict. Three new US bases are proposed, tentatively at:
    - ✓ Darwin.
    - ✓ Katherine (300 kilometres inland from Darwin)
    - ✓ Port Hedland (Western Australia).
- Nuclear weapons and other conventional munitions will be required in all three locations.
- There is no obvious need for permanent Australian basing involving the US Navy although expanded sea-port facilities might be necessary.

<u>Reduce China's access to Australia-sourced raw materials–achievable.</u>

- With Australia under American control, US can categorise Australian mineral resources as critical national assets.
    - ✓ Exports to China will then require approval. US will control

the flow.

- Withdrawal or reductions of exports could tempt China to consider military action.

  ✓ This emphasises the need for enhanced American military presence in Australia.

Manage Rare-Earth minerals—partly achievable, noting these resources are distributed globally.

- Global resources are distributed widely—US, China, Russia, Brazil, India, Australia, Greenland.
- The US strategic preference is to retain domestic rare-earth reserves and import from others.

  ✓ Some specific shortfalls are likely, depending on future demand profiles.

- Australia has 5th largest global reserves of rare-earth minerals, but they are spread across the entire continent.

  ✓ Critical national asset legislation could prevent exports from Australia to China but this would not prevent China importing from elsewhere.

  Bonus One from Takeover

- Australia claims over 40 per cent of Antarctic Continent.
- US has not yet made a claim but reserved a right to do so.
- Takeover of Australia and withdrawal from Antarctic Treaty would give the US this strategic asset.

  Bonus Two from Takeover

- Australia claims as external territories both Christmas Island and Cocos Islands.

  ✓ They could provide useful stepping stones to Indonesia if required.

  ✓ These locations are possibly relevant for close monitoring or combatting of regional Chinese activity.

Allen printed two copies of his report, passing one each to Karl and to Martin. They both accepted the document, neither smiling nor commenting. But having absorbed some feel for The Office's culture, Allen took this as a welcome indication he was probably on the right track.

Later, Karl said to Martin 'That was a damned fine report. I'm glad we picked this young fellow for the job.'

Martin, typically even more cautious than Karl, responded 'Yeah, I agree. So far so good. But let's keep our eyes peeled. This is the biggest thing we've done since the Revolutionary War. It has to succeed.'

Allen's next task, according to Karl, was to review Australia's economic and other environments in which the initiative would unfold.

From preliminary studies it was clear the American plan would be a blessing for this unfortunate nation. Australia was stuck in an economic quagmire and it was getting worse. With a population of around 25 million, its domestic market was too small to support major industries.

Local car manufacturers had already closed-up shop. Its capacity to manufacture other sophisticated goods for export was limited, in part by high labour costs. Successive Australian governments had been spending more than they received from revenue and then borrowing to bridge the gap. Australia's exports, especially minerals to China and agricultural products to a wider customer base, were keeping the nation viable—just.

Trying to kick-start their sluggish economy, past Australian governments had embarked on some absurd campaigns. One had been to repetitiously screech *innovation* at every opportunity, overlooking the reality that Asian, American and European industries were light-years ahead. Another had been an attempt to present Australia as a major exporter of military equipment, despite Australian equipment containing restricted American components.

The Australian Government's capacity to collect taxation revenue was hampered because major multinationals had been avoiding taxes and Australia seemed to lack either the clout or the political will needed to force them into line. This was compounded by a lazy banking sector which focused on financing real estate, leading to ludicrously inflated real-estate prices and distorting the national economy.

One of few things Australian governments had done properly was to create and sustain an economic elite. Wages were still too high but, using a range of monetary and fiscal devices, governments had supported the creation of some very wealthy people. These elites could bring capital and labour together for major projects while providing solid national leadership.

Allen concluded Australian politicians had been successfully bluffing their voters since time immemorial. There were no confirmation hearings to test the mettle of people proposed as prime ministers or as ministers assigned to head the major portfolios. Politicians commonly blamed an abstraction they called *Canberra* for policy or administrative failures, deflecting blame and responsibility away from themselves.

Australia had a governor-general, again appointed without public consultation or participation. He or she had power to dismiss the entire elected national government and had done so in the past. Lurking behind the scenes was the hereditary King of England, who'd been dubbed King of Australia, also possibly with some shadowy capacity to influence political outcomes.

Personal freedoms were a concern. Minimally accountable powers, given to intelligence and police agencies under the guise of fighting terrorism, could be used for political purposes. Ordinary Australians were denied normal liberties to own hand-guns and rifles, especially automatic ones. Thousands of unregistered weapons were held by criminals or had never been surrendered by formerly legitimate owners.

On the positive side, most military equipment in Australia had been sourced from America or was produced under licence from America. Australian military personnel were accustomed to operating with American forces. Reliance on American military support was so extreme that, if Australian defence forces showed any sign of opposition to the takeover, it would be possible to neutralise them using logistics as our weapon of choice.

Surveys showed Americans had almost no awareness of, and therefore no gratitude for, Australian involvement when supporting America in conflicts including Korea, Vietnam, Iraq and others. This was despite Australian governments trumpeting their contributions at every opportunity.

Armed with that preliminary review, Allen believed he should visit Australia to verify, if possible, his tentative assessments and collect more data. Having written a submission explaining his reasoning and including an estimate of costs, he approached Karl to discuss the request.

MANIFEST DESTINY

Standing in front of Karl's desk, Allen was about to speak when asked 'Is that your request for approval to visit Australia?'

Allen said 'Yes, it is.' offering the document.

Without glancing at it, Karl wrote *Approved* across the top and handed the submission back saying 'I knew you'd need to do this. I've determined your budget. It's almost certainly well above your estimate.'

'Don't hesitate to spend if you need to, especially if unanticipated opportunities arise. I'm not prepared to have this mission compromised by penny-pinching. Now go see the folk in Administration to organise your travel and accommodation.'

Six days later, with no fixed agenda, Allen flew from Washington DC to Los Angeles, changed aircraft, then travelled to Sydney, crossing the international date line on the way.

Despite having dined and slept pleasantly enough in his business-class seat, he was unaccustomed to long-haul international travel. Exhausted and jet-lagged, he spent two hours at Australia's Kingsford Smith Airport, queuing and clearing Australian customs, quarantine and immigration. Then he had to rush for a bus which took him to another terminal where he boarded a small propeller-driven aircraft travelling to Canberra.

Allen's mission had no direct association with the United States Embassy in Canberra. But, following a cab trip from Canberra Airport, he visited its entrance gate and left a courtesy note advising he, a representative of Department of Commerce, was in town.

This apparent independence from the Embassy, and from the range of services it offered to visiting officials, caught the ever-alert eye of the Chief Security Officer, an unpleasant individual commonly known as *Scowler*. Downloading an image of Allen from the guard-house security camera he circulated it to his staff with a request to report any sightings or dealings with this individual.

Allen then took the same cab to the Hyatt Hotel in Commonwealth Avenue. Touted as one of Canberra's finest, he'd expected to arrive at a tall, glass-clad edifice. Instead he was confronted by a low, white painted and red-tiled building, its classic-horizontal lines extending extravagantly across an expanse of valuable inner-city real estate.

Following registration, a bellhop wearing a bizarre outfit showed him to his room. The room was larger than normal, especially the attached bathroom. Both were tastefully furnished in a theme he interpreted as updated 1930s *chic*.

Sitting on the edge of a comfortable king-sized bed, Allen began trying to adjust his internal time-clock by staying awake. He lasted almost two hours before falling asleep, still fully dressed.

At 7.00 am next morning a showered, shaved and grey-business-suited Allen entered the hotel's dining room where an elaborate breakfast buffet was appetisingly displayed. The room could comfortably seat 100 people but was already crowded.

Taking a tray and pre-warmed plate, he made two slices of wholemeal toast before adding two packs of butter, two link-sausages, some Boston beans (inexplicably labelled *baked* beans), and two long rashers of a meat which looked, and later tasted, like bacon. He avoided the small, sealed containers of *Vegemite*, having been warned by other Americans that it was atrocious.

Standing next to the buffet, he noticed no small tables were vacant and the longer ones were filling rapidly with people who seemed to know each other.

Slightly disoriented, looking around the room for a second time, he saw a seated woman beckon. She pointed to an unoccupied seat, one of the two at her table. With a relieved smile and a nod he accepted her implied invitation

Seated, and blushing slightly, Allen confessed to ignorance of local protocol.

'Thank you for inviting me to share your tabletop. This is my first visit to Australia. I'm not sure if it's etiquette to start a breakfast conversation with a lady I've never met, or whether I should eat in silence with eyes downcast.'

The woman, quietly delighted at meeting a man who valued good manners, invited him to '*Surprise me!*' Allen, conscious he was on a fact-finding mission, declared he'd prefer the conversation option.

This obviously astute woman claimed to have detected an east-coast American accent, possibly with a hint of the south. It prompted Allen to introduce himself and offer a business card displaying his Department of Commerce credentials.

Responding, the woman said she was Elizabeth Gnagnarra, an Australian aboriginal who lived in Canberra.

Easing gently through their introductory manoeuvres, she chided Allen for being categorised in the US as a *Black. Her* skin, she said, was several shades darker than his and still only brown. Pursuing the now light-hearted theme, they agreed that curly black hair was unmanageable, dreadlocks looked awful and short hairstyles were the only answer.

With breakfast further loosening the conversation, Allen learned Elizabeth was a cardiothoracic surgeon attending a medical conference at the Hyatt Hotel. That was why she wasn't at home in her apartment.

Hoping he wasn't being too intrusive, Allen asked, 'How did you acquire such an accurate ear for American accents?' Elizabeth confessed she'd undertaken post-graduate studies at Yale University's Faculty of Medicine. 'Not Harvard, but close.'

After breakfast, Allen thanked her for the 'gracious invitation to share your table' and they went their separate ways.

But Allen, energised by a rising emotion for which he had no name, nor experience either, made a bee-line for the ornately decorated hotel foyer. There he located a VIP-welcome board indicating the medical conference had two more days to run.

On the second morning Allen arrived earlier for breakfast and took a table for two, placing his suitcoat over the back of one chair while visiting the buffet. A few minutes later he saw Elizabeth enter in company with several distinguished-looking and older men.

They took a table for six and became engaged in an intense conversation, probably, he concluded, concerning some technical aspect of medicine.

On the third and final morning of the medical conference Allen again arrived early and took a table for two. Seated, he began wondering what was drawing him to meet Elizabeth.

Her education and training, especially at Yale, placed her well above his intellectual league. She was probably five years older than him. She was a foreign national and so any significant meeting should be recorded on a contact report. A relationship of any consequence with her would cost him his position at The Office and possibly a lot more, not that anything seemed likely to happen.

Having diluted his enthusiasm, Allen opened his I-Pad, logged on to The Hyatt's guest server and downloaded his complimentary copy of *The Canberra Times* newspaper. Settled back, content, he began reading his way through a leisurely breakfast.

But, as he sipped freshly squeezed orange juice from a tall and elegant glass, another tall, elegant vision appeared before him.

Elizabeth, despite several other tables being unoccupied, approached him with 'Good morning Allen. I wonder if you'd like to return my favour of two days ago and allow *me* to join *you*.'

Hastily choking the urge to say, Well that's a no-brainer, Allen replied 'Good morning Elizabeth, I'd be delighted if you did.'

Hairs on the back of his neck prickled unaccountably when, after sitting, Elizabeth said 'I saw you at breakfast yesterday morning but was engaged in a planning meeting to sort out some issues for the day ahead. By the time I could escape and bid you "good morning", you'd finished breakfast and departed.'

Allen began wondering if seeds of something profound might have been sown within them both. This was new territory for a romantically unattached and still-virgin man. He had no idea how to navigate it. A voiceless murmur, an urge, almost a demand, was pressing him to continue, to explore this sublime possibility.

Today was Thursday but he'd earlier consulted a publication left in his room, *This month in Canberra*. The National Botanical Gardens had looked interesting, so he'd decided to visit on the following Saturday.

Taking a deep and more than slightly nervous breath, he wondered '... if, perhaps, you might show me over the National Botanical Gardens on Saturday and if, as a thank you, you would permit me to host you to a light luncheon at the attached café?'

Wanting to avoid the impression of being intrusive, he added, 'I could meet you at the Gardens, perhaps at 10.30 am.'

Allen was relieved and slightly surprised when she agreed.

———

He filled Thursday and Friday constructively. Confining spiritual nutrition to daily prayer and Bible readings in his room, Allen used Thursday to visit Australia's National Library where he read microfiches, recording previous copies of *The Canberra Times* and other newspapers. He followed-up his findings with further research.

Going back to February 2018, he found alarming accounts of Australian filing cabinets, filled with highly classified and sensitive papers, being sent to an auction room where they were sold to a member of the public. That incident had been followed closely by a folder with sensitive Defence material, and accompanied by security passes, being located and surrendered by another member of the public.

Probing further, he located records of an August 2016 security breach involving the French company with a contract to design Australia's new fleet of submarines. The precise nature of damage done was difficult to determine, but it was a disturbing incident.

There were also reports of intelligence files being found during a drug-related raid in the City of Melbourne.

And these were incidents of which the Australian public had become aware. How many more had occurred then been suppressed, he wondered. How much American classified information had been compromised? Allen took notes.

Thursday evening, he strolled across a bridge linking both sides of Lake Burley Griffin to dine at an advertised restaurant in Childers Street.

Its clientele was mostly undergraduates from a nearby university together with a few youthful government employees. They'd already enjoyed a few drinks and were moving steadily along the alcohol-fuelled scale from chatty though loquacious to rowdy, most having reached *loquacious.*

Accepting this cohort was not representative of Australian society, Allen nevertheless inveigled himself into their conversation.

The youngsters were deeply suspicious of Australia's political establishment, more so than students in some other Western nations, and equally cynical.

One imbiber had suggested there was an inverse correlation between the apparent sincerity of prime-ministerial speeches and the likelihood he was being honest. Others were aware of a survey placing trust in political parties ninth, behind TV news broadcasts and trade unions.

Most agreed their prospects of living the happy and successful lives of their parents were not promising. Unemployment and underemployment were significantly higher than official statistics suggested, they believed.

Finding a job that used their skills would be difficult. Getting a secure job was almost impossible.

Partly because of the way governments had structured taxation deductions, housing costs were through the roof, as were rents. Even a massive decline in housing values would not offer much relief. Something significant and possibly radical had to happen.

Allen noted their dissatisfaction and mentally listed the tertiary student body as a possible future ally.

The following day, he sought opportunities to begin conversations with people in a variety of locations including bus stops, a mosque, coffee shops, two university campuses and the public waiting room at a hospital.

His impression was one of a fracturing society. The traditional Australian image of cohesive families and good blokes was camouflaging economic fissures operating horizontally. Running vertically were gender, racial and religious divides.

For decades, Australian governments had attempted to beat the social unification drum. Their propaganda often reached a crescendo on the national holiday known as *Australia Day*. But it wasn't being heard. In particular, the White/Aboriginal gap was widening.

Traditional social stabilisers, especially religion and the print media, were in retreat. Governments seemed immersed in a contrary illusion. One Government Minister had employed 66 media advisors, none of whom had been able to rein-in the popularity or the independence of social media.

Voters had become cynical when they learned of a senior official in the taxation machinery being investigated for possible implication in an embezzlement scheme, the chief executive of Australia's public broadcaster being dismissed, in part allegedly because she'd refused to bow to political pressures, and the one-time chief of a major police force being fired for allegedly unacceptable behaviour. The national government had cracked down on welfare recipients while strenuously resisting a formal inquiry into Australia's flawed finance sector.

Government had eventually agreed to an inquiry into the banking and finance sectors but it was commonly considered too little and too late.

Australia's unifying forces, Allen concluded, had been diluted. Confidence in governmental processes had eroded. The likelihood of cohesive or widespread opposition to America's plans seemed increasingly remote.

DREAMING

10.25 am on the Saturday found Allen, beneath a cloudless sky, waiting at the head of a path leading from a carpark into the established Australian National Botanical Gardens.

A few minutes later a white BMW-3 zipped confidently into a parking bay. Elizabeth emerged from it, her sophistication and essential aboriginality blending flawlessly. Poised and elegant, she'd tucked a deep-blue silk blouse into the beige-coloured slacks caressing her long, slim legs, terminating at white leather sandals with low-rise heels.

Following almost formal greetings they walked, side by side but without physical contact, along a steep, rocky path and into the garden area.

Allen was shocked. Accustomed to traditional botanical masterpieces of the Philadelphia region, such as Longwood and Winterthur, here in Canberra he was confronted by straggly, unkempt vegetation most of it without flowers or any other redeeming virtue.

Sensing his reaction, Elizabeth explained 'Apart from a separate rainforest gully, this entire collection of Australian naïve flora was planted and then left alone. We neither water nor fertilise or prune except in unusual circumstances.'

'These plants grow much as they would in the wild and, for most of Australia, the wild is an arid place. It's amazing they survive at all. And *that* is the core of the magic, the significance and the beauty of this place.'

Elizabeth continued by showing Allen the variety of techniques Australian plants employed to survive droughts, occasional floods or widespread fires. And that was only the beginning. She also knew the ways traditional aboriginal people used bark, seeds, roots or leaves for tools, medicines and food.

Then gradually, without explanation, she stopped speaking *about* specimens and began communicating *with* them, offering empathy and affection as if they had deeper connections with her. The plants had names, aboriginal names, and individual personalities which resonated for her. Some were old and dear friends.

Their botanical stroll continued along a richly vegetated rainforest gully, through an area of noble trees, followed by the sharp contrast of an almost totally barren region representing a central Australian desert.

Using her combination of modern and ancient knowledge, Elizabeth gave each vista life and meaning, happily sharing her botanical spirituality as if it were natural to feel like that.

Allen had never encountered or imagined anyone like her. After an hour he was emotionally exhausted and suggested they sit for a while on one of the park benches scattered throughout the gardens.

Struggling to frame an appropriate comment he said 'You speak as if plants and rocks are somehow connected to you, are an extension of you or, sometimes, as if *you* are an extension of *them*.'

Elizabeth was surprised and delighted. 'Yes, you've hit the nail on the head. What you have been seeing and hearing is a diluted version of my inheritance, my dreaming.'

Elaborating, she said 'I was born in a small aboriginal municipality located west of Alice Springs in central Australia. Schooling wasn't a high priority, although White authorities tried to insist that aboriginal children attend primary school. So, my exposure to higher education was almost miraculous.'

'When I was six years-old, a primary teacher recognised what she called my "abilities". She spoke to a local politician who was looking for an aboriginal good-news story, probably to attract more aborigines to vote for him. This suited me because it led to a succession of scholarships at some of the best schools in Australia.'

'Can you imagine it? Me, a kid straight out of an aboriginal settlement wearing a uniform tunic, stockings, and gloves; yep, even gloves, and getting *tennis* lessons. Anyway, after that it was all plain sailing.'

But, regardless of formal education, Elizabeth's desert roots, reinforced by periodic visits, had impregnated a timeless aboriginality upon and within her. Her homeland held the core of her dreaming. It included specific rocks, water holes, plants and hills representing the ancient memories of countless generations.

Allen wondered if he could reconcile Elizabeth's experience with his ingrained Christianity. His own inspiration came from the Holy Bible. It introduced him to the Lord Jesus Christ from whom flowed an undeniable connection to America and its manifest destiny. Anything likely to harm his beautiful nation would cause *him* emotional pain, possibly translating to physical discomfort.

For a few minutes he half convinced himself that his abiding love of America, his willingness to dedicate his life to ensuring its security, was at the core of *his* dreaming. But it wasn't, and at a deeper level he knew it. Only another Australian aboriginal could experience what Elizabeth was feeling.

They strolled to the garden's informal café and sat opposite each other for a light lunch of quiche, salad and coffee. Occasionally they attempted to identify and explore new topics of conversation, not so much for the pleasure of exchanging viewpoints but more to prolong their time together. But despite best efforts, the discussion faltered which signalled time to depart.

Coincidentally seated at another table in the same café, was a staff member from the American Embassy's Security Office. He'd recognised Allen Ivory from the image circulated by Scowler. Having observed an apparent level of affection between Allen and the aboriginal woman, he used his mobile phone to text a contact-observation report to his boss.

Allen walked with Elizabeth to her car, confessing he'd like to extend their time together but also admitting he couldn't think of a plausible excuse. She acknowledged being similarly inclined, especially because he'd seemed to grasp the almost unintelligible notion of her aboriginal dreaming. However, she'd been invited to examine a research thesis and needed to make a start on it.

Allen said he was due to travel interstate but wondered if Elizabeth might feel comfortable with seeing him when he returned,' if your schedule allows'.

Elizabeth, her face expressionless, immediately decided her schedule *would* allow time to see him regardless of what had to be moved or cancelled. Instead she said 'Thank you. I'll have to check what's on my calendar.'

From a business card Allen had given her at the Hyatt, Elizabeth already had Allen's mobile 'phone number and so gave him one of her cards. Following an almost dutiful handshake, she fastened her seatbelt, closed her car door and drove away.

———

The next day Allen flew from Canberra to Sydney and then on to Australia's northern city of Darwin. From the air he began to appreciate vastness, the grandeur, the exquisite purple and ochre landscape of central Australia. He'd read statistics on Australian population distribution but travelling above the incredible distances between minuscule townships was unforgettable. Australia's Northern Territory made Alaska seem overpopulated.

After two days in Darwin he flew to Port Hedland where he stayed for three days, then to Perth and afterwards back to Canberra. He'd hoped to visit Alice Springs or Katherine but didn't have time.

Travelling in hire cars around both Darwin and Port Hedland confirmed Allen's impression that both locations would be suitable for American Army, Air Force and Marines bases. They reminded him of some smaller cities in Texas and other mid-Western regions. Traces of the old sleepy, conventional and unexciting attitudes remained. But a new dynamism, motivated mainly by energetic entrepreneurs, had also emerged.

His main surprise was that residents of both localities seemed more cohesive than the Australians in Canberra. The same diversity of race and religion existed in the north, but here was an overriding feeling of mateship, a reluctance to be judgmental and a powerful teamwork ethos. These people were basically Darwinians or Hedlanders, and proud of it.

They also had a strongly independent streak, often expressed as a contempt for laws they considered useless, particularly governing alcohol consumption or speeding restrictions on the highways. Allen decided it would be a significant mistake to alienate *them*.

Flying from Port Hedland and down to the City of Perth, Allen was again impressed by the magnificent strength and rugged beauty of the land below. However, his thoughts were mostly elsewhere. Focussed on the screen of his laptop, he was watching a travelogue of Western Australia's coastline.

He saw thousands of kilometres of exquisite coastline, strings of small islands, reefs, pure-white beaches, magnificent turquoise seas, all seemingly uninhabited or at least unexploited.

What's wrong with these Australians? They've been here for more than 200 years and still are ignoring this potential tourist bonanza. We'll certainly change that, big time!

Having landed in and dismissing Perth as a charming, beautiful city of minimal strategic value, Allen began an emotionally challenging fight back to Canberra.

Crowding his mind came happy memories of his days as an undergraduate. He'd worked one evening each week in a soup kitchen feeding Washington's poor. It was a shock to realise, these days, he'd be more inclined to regard the needy as inevitable casualties along the highway to economic dominance. Or did he? Was that what he *really* believed? In fact, what in hell *did* he really believe?

Then there was the humiliation he'd felt recently when contemplating the treatment of native Americans. He'd been trying to convince himself that these original inhabitants had already been given enough time to adjust and be part of the New Jerusalem. But a lingering empathy for them, for their traditions, kept surfacing, especially after meeting Elizabeth.

Another concern was the near certainty that American tourism and other economic developments in Western Australia would impact on traditional aboriginal dreamings. When in Port Hedland he'd been shown two traditional sites. They'd featured rich and dazzling displays of ancient but elegant rock art carvings, drawings and symbols.

Especially confronting was the way this harsh southern land had expanded his sense of beauty, the attachment he'd felt to Elizabeth's dreaming, to Elizabeth herself. Could he, should he, become part of a plan which might eliminate what remained of this ancient cultural heritage? Added to his discomfort were memories of the harsh realities of international law.

He felt less inclined than usual to pray for guidance and so arrived back in Canberra still emotionally dishevelled.

Returning to the Hyatt Hotel, Allen unpacked, sending his red-dust-stained clothing to the laundry service. For the next three hours he wandered restlessly about in his room, first slumping briefly into a lounge chair, then propping on the end of the king-sized bed before strolling over to balance on a bar stool and from there to his window where he leaned on the railing, looking, without seeing, at the Canberra landscape.

At 8.00 pm he surrendered and telephoned Elizabeth.

It was Saturday evening. Elizabeth was writing her part of a joint-authorship paper.

On hearing Allen's voice, she opened her diary, splitting its screen to view both clinical and personal commitments, meanwhile telling Allen 'I'm pleasantly surprised to hear from you. Given your obviously high-powered lifestyle, I thought you might have had other priorities.'

At that moment Allen couldn't think of any priority higher than seeing Elizabeth. But not wanting to seem overly keen, he invited her to dine with him at The Hyatt. He would be free on either Tuesday or Thursday evening.

Playing a similar game, Elizabeth kept him waiting almost a minute, meanwhile enjoying several sips from the mug of coffee on her desk. Only then did she reply 'Yes, thank you, it looks as if I can arrange to be free on Thursday evening. Should we say 7.00 pm. I have a full program on Friday so can't afford a late night.'

Consolidation

The next few days were so frustrating Allen had no time to think about Elizabeth.

One of his tasks had been to acquire personality profiles on all ministers in the Australian government. He was confident diplomats at the Embassy would already have compiled the same sort of information for their State Department.

But, despite the Ambassador giving directions that Allen was to receive full cooperation, it was obvious subordinate staff intended to resist sharing. Regardless of how many approaches he made at offices throughout the Georgian-style building, their responses were uniformly unhelpful.

Allen recalled one of Martin's observations back at The Office.

'Officials in State Departments and foreign offices worldwide are a special breed' he'd said. 'They act like demigods, causing endless frustration and inefficiency along the way. In the end they're useful only for writing briefs, escorting VIPs and processing visa applications.'

'We should all thank God that any international initiative of consequence originates at the political level and any important operational initiatives are undertaken by attached officers from other agencies.'

Allen's next move was to make an appointment to see His Excellency the Ambassador, a man whose status was apparently defined by the number of table lamps in his expansive office. After Allen had been admitted to the inner sanctum, His Excellency kept him waiting while he finished reading an item on his desk-top screen. Allen occupied some of the time by counting lamps. There were 23. All except one was alight.

Then it was down to business. Showing His Excellency the half-page of notes he'd been given to describe the Prime Minister of Australia, Allen shared his dismay before commenting 'I suspect officials back home will be astonished to discover the minimal content of VIP dossiers at this Embassy.'

The immediately galvanised Ambassador made one internal telephone call.

That afternoon, Allen was deluged with information and data, all provided by surly junior diplomats, but provided nevertheless.

Much of the avalanche had been sourced from public media. Useful for pointing to the characters and mannerisms of people described, it would be of minimal value for applying pressure to individuals if that became necessary. There was also some unpublished information, but it was pathetically tame.

The Australian Prime Minister had enjoyed, or perhaps *experienced,* a protracted sexual affair with his corpulent female Chief of Staff as well as numerous relationships with young women from a variety of backgrounds, some not especially salubrious. He also liked wearing women's underwear, black being his preferred colour.

The Foreign Minister had been observed visiting a gay-men's club in Sydney, but presumably could claim to have been legitimately associating with voters in his electorate.

The Minister for National Security had twice been treated for syphilis, a somewhat spicier tit-bit but not exactly a hanging offence and not unique among elected officials. Several other ministers had been photographed visiting Asian brothels.

Reviewing these slim pickings Allen concluded they would be worth keeping in mind, but not much more.

His research had already revealed that typically, if exposed, Australian politicians would issue a total denial, threaten legal action and claim the allegations were politically motivated. The technique had been employed so often, usually successfully, it had acquired a name—*the good old one, two, three and you're home response.*

Occasionally, the media would persist and be accused of starting a *witch hunt.* An unfortunate politician, or senior official, might then be forced to resign in *'a long overdue decision to spend more time with my family'*, and the media would lose interest.

———————

Thursday evening finally arrived. Disentangling himself from professional skulduggery, Allen returned to his room. He showered then dressed, twice, seeking a casual but refined image.

Aftershave or not? He decided not. *Mouthwash after brushing teeth? Hmm; difficult decision; perhaps not, but I'll avoid garlicky foods. The main challenge will be to imitate the weird Australian technique for handling knives and forks.*

In Allen's mind was a clear image of what happened in American restaurants. Diners employed forks to stab a steak or potato, pinning it firmly to the plate. Knives would then be used to cut off one or two portions. Knives would be set aside. Forks, now retrieved and grasped in the right-hand, would convey severed portions from plate to mouth before repeating the process.

Allen had noticed the Australians holding, and keeping, a knife in one hand and fork in the other. Spurning the benefits of a top-down stabbing motion, they used the two implements cooperatively. It was confusing but achievable.

———————

After walking from his room to the Hyatt's elegant dining facility, Allen followed the *maître d'hôtel* to his reserved table for two. It was covered with a starched, white-linen cloth. Gleaming silver cutlery had been set. Serviettes nestled into matching silver holders. Sparkling crystal wine glasses completed the picture.

He sat and waited.

Elizabeth appeared, a fashionable-five-minutes late, and Allen suppressed a gasp. Approaching *his table* was the most beautiful woman he had ever seen.

Slipping into her chair, unassisted by an almost-mesmerised Allen, she apologised for being late explaining she'd been caught in a lengthy meeting.

That much was true, but Elizabeth had forgotten to add that she'd also been home, showered, spent 10 minutes debating which undies to wear, redone her make-up twice and then dressed in the outfit she'd been planning for the past two days.

The Hyatt's hand-picked chefs provided their usual superb cuisine although, by next morning, neither Elizabeth nor Allen could remember what they had ordered and then left behind, picked over and almost untouched.

Together, thrilled, happy but tongue-tied, their feelings could not have been conveyed in words. Neither knew what they really wanted to say or how to begin saying it. It didn't matter because even the most intimate verbal communications could not have enhanced the warmth and tenderness passing and increasing between them.

Avoiding the central issue of admitting they were falling in love, they filled the gaps between admiring and sometimes secretive glances, discussing some of Allen's impressions from northern Australia and Elizabeth's ambition to join a newly formed medical research team at Australia's Monash University.

Eventually, with dining-related justifications exhausted, they agreed it was time for Elizabeth to depart. Allen walked to her car.

On reaching the BMW, Allen, drawing on his total reserve of emotional courage, said 'I can't imagine never seeing you again. I must travel back to the US on the weekend. However, within a few months I will probably be back here. I'd like to email you in the meantime, perhaps once every two weeks or so, and also catch-up when I return.'

Elizabeth replied 'Good.'

No external observer could have decided if Elizabeth then hugged Allen, or Allen, Elizabeth. Intuitively, they approached, touched and clung to each other, tenderly, inevitably. Breast to chest, abdomen to abdomen, thigh to thigh.

Elizabeth's cheek rested on Allen's shoulder as his one hand softly engaged her hair; the other, with fingers widespread, gently, slowly caressed her shoulder.

Seconds passed before Allen kissed Elizabeth's forehead, the contact with his lips releasing a thrilling vibration that flowed along the full length of her spine.

They separated physically but not emotionally, wordlessly accepting they were drawing together in a new and beautiful way.

———————

Tiring but uneventful flights conveyed Allen over the Pacific Ocean and across the United States, finally depositing him into a cab at Dulles Airport which then returned him to the Commerce Building.

Following the usual elevator and rapid-rail journey, he visited Karl and submitted his report on the Australia visit, failing to mention Elizabeth.

The omission caught Karl's attention, first because Allen should have submitted a formal contact report, second because Karl had already seen a separate summary sent to him by the Embassy in Canberra. It included details of lunch in the café at the National Botanic Gardens, dinner in the Hyatt and that memorable caress in the carpark.

Karl said nothing but made a mental note to analyse Allen's work carefully and ensure he had remained reliable, loyal. He also ordered a special watch be placed on Allen's communications, personal and electronic, to and from all sources. Any contact with the aboriginal woman was to be reported directly to him.

Karl needn't have worried. Immersed in The Office environment, returning to his regime of prayer, boosted by attendance at Sunday worship, Allen reverted to his Agent Allen Ivory persona. Elizabeth, significant though she was, he consigned temporarily to his emotional *too-hard* basket. He would deal with that challenge when time allowed.

Returning to his assigned task, Allen located earlier records of America's plans to invade Australia and New Zealand. Some of the required military intelligence had been collected by America's *Great White Fleet* during its naval good will visit to Australia in 1908. Other invasions or takeovers might also have been planned or proposed.

It seemed possible General Douglas MacArthur, given his personality and his influence over Australia during the 1941–45 War, had contemplated capturing the entire continent. With a massive American troop presence, it would have been almost too easy.

Assembling the now vast amount of information and data available to him, supplemented by briefings from the Australia Desk in Department of State, Allen began searching for patterns, trends and vulnerabilities to support proposals for America to absorb Australia.

Already obvious was the combination of Australia's substantial reliance on America for national security, extensive bilateral trade, American ownership of all categories of property in Australia and American dominance of the software enabling almost every aspect of Australia's government, military, commercial and social activity, had brought Australia to the brink of subordination without *any* additional activity.

This conclusion, denied vigorously by Australian politicians of all colours, had for decades been blindingly obvious throughout America, Asia and further afield.

The main challenge, Allen identified, was to bridge the gap between subordinating Australia and dominating it. This would require a significant strategic move.

Following more months of intense, almost fanatical, work Allen's final 510-page report was ready for submission. It would be the first stage, he suspected, in an almost endless round of bureaucratic and political negotiations.

He'd settled on three primary options absorbing Australia. These were: one, economic strangulation based on aggressive policies limiting trade, investment and finance; two, electronic deprivation focussed on cyber attacks many of which might be blamed on China or Russia; and three, military invasion. Supplementing the military invasion option he recognised the potential to achieve immediate capitulation by deploying one nuclear weapon against a strategic national target. However, he'd added, the loss of life could not be justified.

He also concluded that only Option 3, military invasion, would result in the United States fully absorbing Australia. However, global responses to Option 3 could be highly negative and this might prove costly.

SONG OF SOLOMON

C ontrary to his expectations, Allen's report did not succumb to an
endless cycle of consultations. Karl, having read it over the following
weekend, warmly congratulated Allen on '*a first-class and perceptive analysis*'
before approving it and delivering it by hand to The Leader. The Leader told
Karl to hold all calls and cancel all appointments for the next four days.

Having read and contemplated the document, he sent it, unamended
and via trusted courier, directly to the President, adding a handwritten note
stating, '*President: Sir, I fully endorse this report. Leader, The Office.*'

For three days the report, still in its security-sealed envelope, sat in a
locked safe within a White House outer office. On the fourth day, after a
secretary drew his attention to it, the President, reinvigorated by a golfing
weekend in California, personally opened the envelope. He spent the next
12 minutes reading the Executive Summary component.

Satisfied he was sufficiently familiar with the report, the President told
his Office of Cabinet Affairs 'You are to arrange a meeting of all officials
of Cabinet rank. As background to discussion, I want them to have studied
this report.'

'Send one numbered copy to each of them. Security envelopes are to
carry strict instructions. The document is not to be shown to any deputy or
any other person or discussed with them.'

'I do not consider electronic transmission sufficiently secure. Electronic copies are not permitted.'

Eight days later the President and most of his invitees met in a designated secure meeting room within the White House.

It was a grim venue. The entire room had been lined with special sound and vibration insulation. Dull-brown, unadorned, windowless walls matched an almost identical ceiling. Adding to the sense of high security, a thick drab carpet covered the floor. Transparent chairs were made from hard, moulded plastic. There were no tables or cabinets capable of concealing any listening or recording devices.

All surrounding rooms, including those on the floors above and below, were kept permanently vacant and regularly checked to ensure no intrusive technologies had been installed. No media personnel were permitted within a two-room radius.

The Secretary of Commerce was absent, having been tragically killed when his VIP aircraft crashed into the Andes Mountains. A replacement had not yet been appointed and the President had decided to exclude deputies from the meeting.

Secretary of the Treasury was also a no-show, although nobody seemed to know why. The President responded to news of her absence with 'I usually ignore that stupid woman's advice anyway, so I don't care where she is.'

Nobody wanted to be there. This President viewed the world and almost everybody in it with undisguised loathing. And that was on his better days. More often he was immersed in near pathological hatred expressed through vicious temper tantrums and inconsistent decisions.

Approaching the final year of its first term, his entire presidency had been unremarkable. Having alienated his colleagues, his political party and the media, he'd been elected mainly because the opposition candidate had been so ineffectual. Now moving toward the mid-term contest, he'd made no secret of an ambition to have his name welded onto American history as one of its greatest leaders.

This tall, ultra-slim man, with a pale complexion and sunken eyes lurking beneath an untidy mop of grey hair, normally avoided venues lacking opportunities for media releases. But today's subject was much too sensitive for that. Consequently, as everybody realised, he'd be more vindictive than usual.

What his reluctant audience failed to recognise was that their President's traits were a mirror image of their own aggressive and domineering personalities. They'd all used similar tactics against perceived impediments to their own fast-tracked careers. The President was merely more forceful than they'd been and therefore was committing the cardinal sin of making *them* the victims. No wonder they hated him!

The President opened the meeting saying he assumed everyone was familiar with the circulated report and its recommendations.

He continued by describing the document as 'Heralding one of the greatest foreign policy initiatives in the history of the United States. It is an expression of our manifest destiny and a message to the world that America will not rest until all nations are free under the rules of law and of God, as guided by the United States.'

His audience uniformly interpreted that as implying: a) no meaningful debate would be permitted on the merits or otherwise of the proposal to dominate or absorb Australia; b) the President had already decided on the preferred course of action; and c) it would be smart to agree with him when he revealed it.

As usual, the President would allow a veneer of discussion, mainly because it provided enjoyable opportunities to overrule his underlings, further subordinating them in the process.

One core issue, understood by everyone except the President, was that this meeting would be handicapped because it could access little or no authoritative advice regarding economic, fiscal, monetary, trade or related issues. To proceed without that guidance would be dangerous, they thought.

The Ambassador to the United Nations, allowed to attend the meeting because of his equivalent Cabinet rank, felt more strongly than his colleagues about the lack of economic expertise. At considerable risk, he raised the issue.

'Mr President, in my opinion the plan to simply take Australia over without a clear understanding of the fiscal and economic implications would be irresponsible.'

'Well, who in hell asked you, you useless clown.'

'It's my duty to express my opinions whether you like it or not. And I'd like to remind you of the previous occasion when a President of the United States pressed ahead on a so-called strategic initiative without considering the global economic consequences.'

'What in hell are you raving about?'

'Don't you recall, under a previous Administration, we blockaded Iran to stop exports of its oil and then increased import tariffs on a vast range of products from Europe. Apart from the domestic economic harm caused when the Europeans slapped reciprocal tariffs on *our* products, several European nations considered our actions amounted to unjustifiable and aggressive attacks against their sovereignty.'

'That was a storm in a teacup.'

'Can you seriously call it a "storm in a teacup" when France, Germany, Holland and later Britain all withdrew from NATO, when they reached new free-trade agreements with China and Russia? Just look at the decline in our influence across Europe. We aren't the only nation capable of wielding some political clout!'

'I've heard enough of this crap. You, sir, are fired as from immediately. Your security clearances are withdrawn and if you ever dare breathe a word about the Australia proposal you'll be found guilty of treason. Now get out.'

'Fine, I'll get out, with pleasure. Don't forget to have your spin meisters explain to the global media why you now need your fifth Ambassador to the United Nations.'

Rejecting this and other embryonic mutterings as 'timid hogwash', the President told the meeting, 'Option 1, Economic Strangulation, is off the table. It'll take too long, it's too complex. It allows time and other opportunities for China, possibly Russia or India also, to get involved. Consequently, economic and financial issues are irrelevant.'

With choices narrowed, the meeting began moving toward favouring Electronic Deprivation as the preferred option.

'It seems achievable.'

'It could be casualty free.'

'Yeah, and we would look blameless, or almost so.'

'I like the idea of shifting a lot of blame onto China or Russia. Anyway, they might have done it if they'd thought of it first.'

'It'd meet the critical objective of letting us influence the rate of exports from Australia to China.'

After listening with increasing disbelief, the President exploded, vomiting waves of revulsion, disgust, and sheer fury.

'Call yourselves cabinet officials? Jesus, you couldn't organise a kitchen cabinet between the lot of you.'

The man continued, 'Now listen up and listen good. I have only 12 months remaining in this term as your President. I intend using them to consolidate the United States in its God-given role as the greatest nation the world has ever seen, and to get re-elected on the back of that triumph.'

Raising his voice to screaming pitch, he added 'The greatest! You hear me? The greatest!'

Changing pace, the President began rhythmically pounding his left fist into his right-hand palm, slowing his delivery to emphasise the danger now confronting anyone stupid enough to disagree with him.

'I intend leaving a legacy attached to my name, yes, *my* name. My name will live forever. I need, and will get, a sure-fire strategy capable of being implemented and implemented soon.'

'The payoffs are to be visible, measurable, and attributable during my presidency. No successor will get the credit. This idea is mine, do you hear me, *mine*.'

Noting with satisfaction the shocked faces surrounding him, the President made his move.

'We're agreeing on military invasion using the nuclear option, right?' he said, announcing a decision not even his most ardent supporter would have endorsed.

However, with sick and sinking stomachs they all realised that they'd be sharing collective responsibility for whatever might follow.

Later, the President endorsed his copy of the document, '*Military invasion, with nuclear variation. Agreed unanimously.*'

That decision was passed to The Leader via a written note from the President and delivered by hand.

CONFIRMATION

The Leader's task would be to coordinate the entire exercise. He was to consult with the executive participants and delegate responsibilities. The solution was to be implemented within six months.

Jefferson Ivory understood his orders perfectly. The President would take full responsibility for a positive outcome. Meanwhile, any stumble, any unforeseen negative development or, God forbid, any catastrophic consequences, would be attributed to The Leader.

But, being fair to the President, knowledge that The Office existed was confined to fewer than 10 people outside of its organisation. Jefferson was the ideal man to manage this ultra-sensitive initiative. The 10 additional people included, pivotally, Secretary of State and Chairman of the Joint Chiefs of Staff Committee.

Within a week the three of them met, sitting around the antique table in The Leader's subterranean office. Six months, they agreed, was not enough time to arrange the complicated web of diplomatic and military logistics needed to support this operation. However, knowing the President's temperament and temper, they agreed to make it happen, cutting corners where necessary.

As their meeting ended, The Leader sighed 'Oh well, I've long agreed with von Clausewitz that foreign policy is an extension of domestic ambition. I guess this reinforces the theory.'

The Secretary of State nodded wearily but their long-time acquaintance, Chairman of the Joint Chiefs, replied 'You should watch your what you say Jefferson. Sometimes I'm amazed you were promoted beyond assistant janitor.'

'It's often surprised me too' The Leader mused 'but I guess somewhere in every organisation you need at least one analyst among the dedicated propagandists.'

'In this case, as we all know, the President amassed his incredible wealth by inventing financial products designed to acquire value out of thin air and transfer it into his coffers. His fortune rests on a foundation of illusions. That's his strength. We mustn't expect logic.'

One week later they met again having realised, ironically, that delivering and detonating a nuclear weapon was the least complicated component of their task.

A submarine would be positioned in the Tasman Sea, off the east coast of Australia. When ordered, it would fire a missile. A desk-top exercise had modelled the damage anticipated for a hypothetical city, one similar in most respects to Canberra. A 50 kiloton-yield weapon had been identified as a suitable compromise between making an adequately impressive statement and not eliminating the entire metropolis.

They agreed it would be easy to spoof or otherwise confuse the missile early warning notifications available to America's allies, so no ally would have visibility of the fatal missile's track. Keeping Russia and China in the dark would be almost impossible, so programs of plausible deniability would need to be in place, ready to counter any accusations.

More likely, they thought, Russia and China, especially China, would play a waiting game until they understood what America was aiming to achieve. By then it'd be too late to react in any decisive way.

High-level consultations within Department of State had pointed to central Canberra, known as Civic, as the most appropriate target.

Looking into recent history they realised there had been minimal condemnation when America claimed to have accidentally bombed China's embassy in Belgrade during 1999, or to the 2015 airstrike on the *Médecins Sans Frontières* hospital at Kanduz, among other incidents, although the scale in this case was different.

But further discussion led to a decision that they'd look for ways to protect Canberra-based Chinese and Russian diplomats and their families. If the subsequent diplomacy turned nasty, as it probably would, then this gesture should count for something.

Having considered several options, they decided a conference exploring cooperation for peaceful development in the Pacific region would be a believable pretext for coaxing the most important foreign diplomats away from Canberra. The meeting could be held in Guam or Pago Pago. Hosting would be provided by the families of Canberra-based American diplomats. That should keep most of *them* out of harm's way as well.

A cover-story was invented. America would claim the detonation had occurred accidentally when a USAF aircraft, carrying a nuclear weapon, had suffered a technical malfunction causing the weapon to explode.

To project the all-important image of America as a saviour and friend at a time of need, a massive recovery, support and rebuilding program would be provided to Canberra. It would have to start as soon after the detonation as possible.

The Secretary of State recognised this would be an expensive exercise but commented 'The outlay might run into a few billions of dollars, but we'll have acquired a new nation, and one with extensive mineral resources, as well as giving China a black eye in the process. In both strategic and financial terms, this'll be a bargain.'

The Leader believed another cover-story was required to justify arrangements for stockpiling emergency response materiel and assembling expert personnel for the recovery operation. Nothing seemed particularly convincing. Eventually, they decided to claim the United States was preparing for enhanced responses to natural disasters.

Middle-level planning staff soon wanted more detail to help guide preparations. Was the anticipated disaster linked to climate change, vulcanology, meteorite impact or what? Wiser heads, knowing the President was a climate-change sceptic, insisted on less specific objectives.

The Leader commented 'We'd better all pray like hell that no actual natural disaster occurs prior to the detonation, otherwise it'll be politically impossible to justify corralling all this stuff.'

The US Navy identified an aircraft carrier, the USS *John F Washington*, to carry initial relief aid and then act as a command post for US personnel during the reconstruction phase. At its home-port in Hawaii, the ship was extensively re-fitted.

Briefed on the Military Option, the United States Ambassador to Australia became a valuable resource. During and following Allen Ivory's visit he'd realised something strategically significant was afoot and made a concerted effort to befriend Australia's Prime Minister. This, together with his understanding of Australian politics enabled him to propose a high-risk but potentially high-reward tactic.

If he could convince the Australian Prime Minister of the need to rehearse a nuclear attack and have his senior ministers physically in Parliament House's bomb-proof bunker when the weapon was detonated, the core of a functional government would be preserved. The United States might then be able to create the impression of cooperating with a willing Australian government. The planning group acknowledged the risk but considered his proposal a stroke of genius.

Other elements of the strategy were falling into place when Christmas intervened.

Noel, Noel...

At Christmastime, from the most powerful to the least influential, from the wealthy to the poor, regardless of vocation, despite a range of religious beliefs, most Americans succumbed to expectations that they'd purchase gifts, acquire red poinsettias and decorate their homes or dwellings for the occasion.

Tidal waves of younger family members would criss-cross the nation, compulsively driving or flying home for family reunions. Millions of pre-slaughtered, plucked, gutted and stuffed turkey carcases, hygienically sealed, would become central elements in countless roast dinners to be served on Christmas Day.

For the Ivory family, attendance at Christmas worship was an indispensable prelude to the annual feast. Allen joined his parents as they listened attentively to a sermon on the enduring love of God the Father as expressed through the birth of His Son, the Lord Jesus Christ, who came down from heaven to bring peace and good will to all mankind. Together, they solemnly reaffirmed their Christian values.

Nothing in the Ivory household had changed since the previous year or those before it. Propped in the usual corner of the kitchen was a prematurely harvested spruce tree. As always, it was installed in a bucket covered with aluminium cooking foil. Attached were strings of miniature flashing lights and strips of glittering décor. A golden angel, moulded from plastic, topped the tree. Other traditional decorations included several White House Christmas ornaments, some with military themes.

Martha's cute collection of dancing chipmunks adorned the mantle. Christmas knick-knacks were scattered about.

Jefferson had installed strings of coloured lights around the external window frames. Amidst a thin blanket of snow covering their front lawn was an illuminated ornament featuring four long-haul reindeer pulling a sleigh, satisfyingly one more reindeer than a neighbour's otherwise identical decoration.

Martha had cooked her usual Christmas dinner. But, before indulging, Jefferson intoned their traditional prayer of grace, thanking God for the meal, the family and the privilege of enjoying their time together.

Allen responded silently, offering thanks for the opportunity to play his role in obeying Jesus's command to love your neighbour as yourself by giving Australia the greatest gift possible on this planet, union with the United States of America.

Martha added her customary supplication, seeking Divine protection from the many enemies who surrounded America and wished to do it harm.

Their dining table was covered with a cloth featuring a colourful holly sprig design on a white background, anchored by the family's silver cutlery placed in sets.

Martha then ladled her superb frosted-tomato soup from a huge tureen in the shape of a glistening green and mother-of-pearl fish. Plates and bowls were bright-red fine-china. Gold rims made the crockery unsuitable for either microwave ovens or dishwashing machines, but Martha was prepared to accept these limitations for sake of family tradition. The soup was accompanied by sweetened bread baked to the recipe used by George Washington's mother.

Honey-glazed turkey followed, expertly carved at the table by Jefferson.

It was served with Silver Queen corn and baked vegetables coated lightly in maple syrup, all piled appetisingly into an earthenware baking dish which they passed between themselves. For anyone who wanted yet more flavour, there was a gold-plated jug containing Martha's secret toffee-turkey sauce recipe.

The dessert was Martha's specialty. Spurning common Christmas pudding, she'd baked their favourite, brownies and fudge. Nobody else could fit as much glorious richness into each wonderful mouthful.

Two bottles of brut champagne enriched the meal. This was genuine American champagne, its title having been retained despite pesky French protests. As the label said, additional sugar had been added discretely, raising the Brut palate to a standard required by American connoisseurs. They savoured every sip, enjoying each carbonated bubble.

After dinner, the family sat in reclining chairs around their open fireplace. Central heating kept the house comfortably warm, but they sometimes enjoyed the additional cosiness of a log fire.

In their seldom-used fireplace they were burning logs made commercially from recycled wastepaper. Chemicals in the logs ensured they would burn with a glow coloured to meet the customer's preference. Martha had chosen purple, and they all relaxed within the consistent hue of those glowing logs and dancing violet flames.

'Only in America the beautiful' said Allen, not addressing any aspect of their celebration in particular. Jefferson and Martha agreed.

Allen, although maintaining contact with his mother through emails and occasional telephone calls, had not been home since the previous Christmas. Perhaps, he later thought, it was unsurprising that there'd been a change in his father's attitude.

Previously, he would have described his father as *reserved* or *taciturn*, but on seeing the man today, adjectives such as *melancholy*, *reflective*, possibly even *morose*, came to mind.

Had Allen suspected The Office was coordinating the nuclear option to capture Australia, he would have understood. But he didn't. So far as Allen knew, his report on Australia was progressing through consultations which could continue for years.

Jefferson, noting his son's buoyant mood, was confident nobody had brought Allen into the nuclear picture. *A good decision too,* he thought.

As evening approached, Allen decided to return to his apartment. Despite the atmosphere of deep respect and love shared between them all, it had been emotionally exhausting to camouflage every hint of his vocation and all the knowledge he carried regarding his father's position and mother's former employment. He was driving a hire car and the snowfalls had been light, so travelling back shouldn't present too many challenges.

He arrived home, slightly shaken, following a few scares when the hire car skidded on icy patches. But Allen and the car were unscathed.

Back in his apartment Allen calculated, given the 10-hour time difference between the US east coast and Australia, he'd be able to phone Elizabeth before she was due to leave for her church service.

Selecting her number from his cell-phone memory, Allen pressed the green button to connect. Elizabeth's telephone rang several times before being answered by a male voice, 'Hello?'

Allen, stuttering and suppressing a heavy, sick sensation, asked if he could speak with Elizabeth please.

In the background he heard 'Hey Sis, a bloke here wants you. Got a yank accent. Probably the gorgeous, handsome and refined one you reckon you're not in love with.'

Elizabeth came on the line, happy, anxious to talk.

'Hi Allen, thanks for such a nice surprise with your call. How are you?'

Then, without waiting for his reply 'It seems you've met my brother, Chris. And before I forget, that handknitted cashmere scarf you sent as a Christmas present is exquisite. I'll bet anything *you* didn't knit it.'

Allen, confessing he'd never knitted a stitch in his life, tried but failed to adequately thank Elizabeth for *her* Christmas gift to *him*.

She'd sent two small bottles of essences to remind him of the Australian bush; one of eucalyptus oil and the other with scent from the Brown Boronia plant. Distinctly different, their aromas brought with them a sensation deeper than memory. Somehow it projected the quiet strength, harsh resilience and grandeur of the Australian outback. Both fragrances were hauntingly intoxicating, addictive.

They spoke for almost 40 minutes, particularly discussing Elizabeth's normal place of worship, St Columba's Uniting Church. She said it was within walking distance from her Braddon apartment.

Allen's experience with churches had focused on an all-consuming relationship with God, although charitable offshoots had been organised. In contrast, so far as he could understand, St Columba's pastors and parishioners homogenised prayer and good works.

They welcomed the most vulnerable folk in all of society, opened their Lewis Hall to homeless people during the cold weather, supported others in need, all of which was blended into their humble and dedicated Christian lives. In a strange way this helped explain Elizabeth's compatibility with a Christian church despite the parallel reality of obligations to her extended aboriginal family, to her *mob* and to her dreaming.

They wanted to keep chatting, but Elizabeth had to break-off. The local Christmas service began in less than an hour and she was providing a shuttle service, using her car to collect several elderly people from their homes and take them to the church. She hoped he'd understand that she couldn't let them down.

Transformation

I n Washington DC, following commemorations for the birth of God's envoy for peace and goodwill, it was back to work at The Office.

All planning for the assault on Australia was proceeding, in fact falling into place with unprecedented precision. The Leader, however, was increasingly nervous and kept reminding himself that, *the likelihood of a secret escaping is directly proportional to the number of people who are aware of it.*

Every effort had been made to ensure the many people required to participate in this vast and complicated initiative knew only enough to effectively perform their tasks. However, any efficient analyst could have discerned the essential elements of their enterprise and, if so inclined, connected the dots to cause chaos.

Having no alternative, The Leader and his small group of associates pressed ahead. They kept the President informed as they had been directed to do, hoping and praying *he* of all people would not attempt to resuscitate his declining public popularity by releasing some hint of what was afoot.

The cover story explaining how and why an American nuclear weapon came to be detonated over Canberra was rehearsed and refined then modified by the President himself.

An associated Presidential statement of shock and regret had been drafted but the President wanted some aspects made more emotional '*to enhance the impression of authenticity*'. The version he finally approved included his description of Australians as '*... so close as to almost be members of my personal family,...*' and similar sentiments. The presidentially approved version was then pre-recorded, copied and made ready for widespread distribution across media formats.

The fit-out of USS *John F Washington* was completed ahead of schedule. Emergency relief supplies and equipment were collected in vast quantities, then stockpiled, both aboard the ship and in several other locations, to reduce the risk of attracting attention.

Sealed orders were drafted to the captains of the aircraft carrier and the submarine selected to fire the fatal missile. The President personally signed the orders.

He also signed a letter to His Excellency the Ambassador in Australia, congratulating him on his concept for using the Australian Government as conduit for American policies during the post-attack phase.

The domestic media campaign, designed to reduce public empathy for Australia, was stepped up. Almost any newsworthy item involving Australia could, if desired, be presented in a negative light. There was no shortage of material.

Australian Border Force officials had apprehended huge amounts of illegal drugs. This proved Australians were heavy drug users, and possibly drug exporters as well. The Australians had no sense of responsibility for executives. One former prime minister drowned when swimming alone. Another had died in a brothel. That these incidents occurred decades ago was omitted.

According to widely believed news items, some Australian attempts at enhancing physical security had been a joke, leading to segments on popular comedy programs. Bollards installed to protect the Australian Parliament House from ram-raids had started activating without warning and damaging the luxury automobiles of invited visitors. Australian attempts to install higher speed internet connectivity had, in some cases, slowed the system down. A major bank had been accused of money laundering but the Government had refused to consider a second independent inquiry into the finance sector.

'What sort of jerks are these people?' asked one indignant TV personality during prime time viewing.

Weekly situation reports from the Ambassador were encouraging. He'd consolidated his relationship with the Australian Prime Minister. That man was facing a political crisis. His personal popularity, along with that of his government, was plunging. Every initiative designed to arrest the fall made matters worse.

In the Ambassador's judgement, the Prime Minister's leadership would normally have been successfully challenged by one of his colleagues. But they, sensing a major political train wreck, were isolating their boss and awaiting the chance to rise from his anticipated ashes.

———

Meanwhile, Allen, after submitting his report on Australia, had been given a new assignment.

Still within the inner sanctum of The Office, he was investigating whether clandestine American support for an independent Scotland would open opportunities for the United States to gain more influence over North Sea oil and gas resources.

He'd started by collecting and summarising data available from internal intelligence and economic agencies. But, before he could make substantial progress, his encrypted telephone rang. It was Karl calling. He wanted to see Allen, approximately now!

Karl was unhappy. One of The Office's rising stars appeared to be at risk of becoming a security liability. Each of the now weekly contact reports, describing Allen's evolving relationship with the aboriginal woman, indicated a consolidating relationship. Their affair involved someone who was not an American citizen and unlikely to ever be granted the American security clearance required for spouses of employees engaged on sensitive missions.

'At least' Karl thought, recalling a worse scandal of some years previously, 'it is with a damned *woman*. Perhaps I should be grateful for small blessings.'

In any case, as Karl well knew, Allen was best qualified to undertake the next phase of the Australia project. There was no realistic alternative to sending him back to Canberra and back into the arms of that blasted aboriginal woman. However, he'd make sure Allen was based at the Embassy where the Ambassador and Chief Security Officer could keep an eye on him.

Allen arrived to find Karl less forthcoming than his usual uncommunicative self.

'Agent Ivory, we are sending you back to Australia. You'll be based in Canberra, at the Embassy, but can travel where you wish in Australia without reservation. Our Ambassador is expecting you. You will report directly to him.'

'Your assignment, based on your previous work, is to identify the most influential social and economic issues the United States will need to address while we are assuming control of Australia.'

'We intend using your new report as the basis for planning to keep the Australian population as passive as possible during our takeover process. You are not to consider international implications. They are being managed by other people. You are to start in Australia by 30 January.'

'Leave your work on Scotland with me. Depending on how Australian plans work out, I'll either return that assignment to you or pass it to someone else. It won't be forgotten'

'I am obliged to remind you that you have been entrusted with a key role in the greatest initiative the United States has undertaken since the Revolutionary War.'

Allen had no alternative but to nod in agreement and tell Karl he'd let him know what the travel arrangements were. By the sound of this assignment there was no telling when it would end so he'd book an open return-air ticket.

Karl, his massive hands resting on the desktop, raised then lowered the index finger of his right hand, acknowledging and agreeing. He scowled to indicate that the meeting was over.

Returning to his own office, Allen thought of several questions although, given Karl's mood, it would have been a waste of time to ask them.

It now seemed obvious to Allen that his report on Australia had not bogged-down in bureaucratic debate but instead had moved rapidly toward a decision and possibly even an implementation-planning phase.

Without other guidance, Allen assumed the Electronic Deprivation option had been selected. It seemed the most rational approach and he had no doubt the United States could cyber-attack Australia to the point of capitulation.

He'd become less confident that concentrated electronic warfare could be conducted without America being identified as the aggressor, but his nation had survived worse. Anyway, that wasn't *his* problem.

MORAL IMPERATIVES

At 8.00 am the following morning Karl received a classified email attaching a transcript of Allen's telephone call from his Arlington apartment to Elizabeth during the previous evening.

'I'm coming back to Canberra.' he'd announced excitedly.

Elizabeth had replied 'That's wonderful news. I can hardly wait to see you.'

During the conversation Allen hadn't disclosed or hinted at any classified information, but the relationship between the two was obviously close.

After reading the transcript, Karl directed Allen be *'now placed under intense observation until I authorise otherwise.'*

Allen arrived back in Canberra on January 28th. After an obligatory call on the Ambassador, he settled back into to work, occupying a workstation within a secure room in the chancery.

Later, he visited the Hyatt Hotel to confirm his accommodation booking, get a room pass and unpack.

He telephoned Elizabeth the same evening. They agreed to meet the following day for a late-afternoon picnic on the lawns of Glebe Park. She would cater.

Walking across the park, each saw the other almost simultaneously. This time there was no pretence, no suggestion of a remote attraction. The pace of their steps and heartbeats accelerated. They touched and hugged, the physical proximity cloaking them in a mutual, loving, tender daze.

Sitting on a tartan-design rug that Elizabeth spread across an area of lawn, they chatted happily, while enjoying Elizabeth's crabmeat, crisp lettuce and mayonnaise sandwiches together with a glass each of chilled mineral water.

But the food, the place and time, although pleasant, were wrong. Soon, with arms interlocked, they strolled slowly back toward Elizabeth's apartment in the nearby district of Braddon.

As they passed through the park's gate a man and woman, picnicking nearby, telephoned a waiting car. The car, fitted with a roof-rack concealing a directional microphone and high-resolution camera, followed them. One of its two occupants operated the electronic devices from within its cabin to film the lovers and record their conversation to the extent possible.

Occasionally the driver would park for a few seconds before continuing to drive at walking pace, as if looking for a specific address. Only the most astute observer would have recognised a professional pursuit.

———

It was Allen's first visit to Elizabeth's apartment. He was surprised and disoriented.

His notion of comfort and homeliness had been forged in his parent's home. There, floors were thickly carpeted and walls covered with printed papers. Furniture was made from rosewood or mahogany and it filled the rooms. Ornamentation was abundant.

Allen's rented Arlington apartment had traditional, but imitation, artefacts. The less expensive furniture he'd hired mirrored the real McCoy. Instead of wallpaper, patterns had been stencilled onto his walls. 'Not quite the real thing, but near enough.' Martha had said when visiting her son to '... see if you're looking after yourself properly.'

Elizabeth's apartment had stark, white walls. Its highly polished wooden floors were made from a timber known in Australia as *blackwood*, although the swirls and curves of its complicated grain included every shade from pure blonde to the deepest brown.

Her few art works, if you could categorise paintings on bark as 'art', were dramatically different to anything Allen had expected in a private apartment. One, *The Dark Emu*, was haunting. He didn't realise, and would never know, it represented a series of astronomical observations, all made by the allegedly primitive and traditional aboriginal people.

Her furniture was sparse but elegant. He recognised one swivel chair and its matching footstool from a magazine he'd thumbed through during the flight into Sydney. Its advertised price had been about equal to the cost of a small car. A few contemporary rugs were scattered about.

Allen was still wondering what to say when Elizabeth gently took his elbow, guiding him to her bedroom. They stood, clothed, locked in embrace, overwhelmed by a mutual need they could neither describe nor justify.

Blushing, Allen said 'I have to confess I want to make love to you, to join and blend and commit physically with you. But, I'm almost 30 and I'm a virgin. I could be a humiliating disappointment.'

Elizabeth, standing on her tip-toes, reached up, moistening his lips with her tongue before resting her cheek against his chin and whispering into his ear 'Well, I'm not a virgin. I was raped as a ten-year-old. From that day on I never wanted physical intimacy, until now, until you.'

Their union was neither rushed nor desperate. A soft cloud of tender trust, motivated by a loving desire to bond, descended upon them and obscured all else, or so they thought.

Clinical details became irrelevant in the depths of their togetherness. The only certainty was that they blended, whether nude or partially clothed they didn't know or particularly care.

Later, Elizabeth with eyes moist, said 'Thank you.'

Allen nodded, turning his face away. But she'd seen the tears. Regardless of any legal enactment or religious ceremony, they had committed and married in a sacrament of their own making.

During the previous week, Elizabeth had been experiencing problems with a fluctuating electricity supply. Luckily, her supplier had been on-the-ball. Before she could complain, a phone call told her that an electrical irregularity had been detected and required attention. This was a potential safety hazard and, as such, the issue would be resolved free of charge.

The following day, two technicians had arrived, both wearing photographic ID. They identified and resolved her problem as well as testing every power outlet in the apartment, '...just to be sure, lady.' They'd also installed seven miniature listening and transmission devices covering Elizabeth's living area, both bedrooms, the kitchen and her bathroom.

Outside Elizabeth's apartment, across the road, two women in the electronically equipped car heard and recorded every syllable and every sound made by the lovers. Verbal communications had been sparse but other noises enabled them to deduce, with invasive precision, precisely what was happening.

Within the hour a report, covering the time between the meeting at Glebe Park through to the conclusion of the lovers' intimacy, had been despatched to Karl in Washington DC.

Copies awaited the Ambassador and Scowler when they returned to their offices the following day.

INCORPORATION

Nobody could accuse Allen of laziness. Early next morning he reluctantly climbed from Elizabeth's bed, dressed in the previous night's clothes, tenderly kissed her and returned to the Hyatt. There, he showered, shaved, changed into business attire and, having ignored breakfast, was at his workstation in the Embassy by 7.30 am.

Focussed on achieving his mission, he decided to write a draft report, progressively, as information came to light. He could revise or add to it as necessary.

Three days later, he'd ploughed through a forest of material and identified five of what he referred to as Australia's *common social pacification tools (CSPTs)*. He identified them as: alcohol, other drugs, religion, gambling and spectator sports.

These CSPTs had several features in common: they the absorbed the time, energy and money of many individual Australians, distracted participants away from national or political affairs, promoted similar cohort attitudes, and created target groups with which mass communications were relatively easy.

In summary, according to Allen, each CSPT presented potentially valuable opportunities to win support for US objectives or, at the least, to muzzle opposition to them.

The first section of his draft submission included:

Alcohol.

Australians are 10th highest consumers of alcohol in the world. Nearly 20 per cent consume more than the recommended two drinks per day. Most Australians view consistent drinking as normal.

Heaviest consumption is commonly in Western Australia and Northern Territory.

Governments are ambivalent. Health and injury consequences of alcohol are concerns. Revenue from alcohol-related taxes is welcomed.

Alcohol in many cases is a sedative. Attempts to limit consumption for moral or health reasons could be counter-productive and would likely be opposed strenuously.

Recommendations.

Reduce by half the Commonwealth taxes on alcohol for consumption. Introduce as a trial. This will increase alcohol consumption, along with the associated sedation and attract support from an influential industry.

Negotiate in advance a deal with industry to endorse US objectives through alcohol-related advertising and by other means. No agreement = no tax reduction.

Reduced prices would be popular in the Northern Territory and Western Australia, both being potential sites for new American military bases. If the alcohol industry backpedals, restore higher taxes on the pretext this is a necessary response to evidence of increasing social problems.

Other Drugs

Australian law is intolerant to a wide range of both organic and designer drugs. Opposition to cannabis for medical use is weakening. Illegal drug trade is flourishing. A recent survey indicated high consumption by unemployed people; mainly cannabis and heroin.

Immediate or short-term intervention might not be practicable. We also lack data on the money-laundering cycle leading to investments of drug-related profits in legitimate businesses. The economic consequences of interrupting this source of finance are difficult to estimate.

The capacity of organised crime to cause problems, if this trade is curtailed, is also unknown but might be significant.

Recommendations.

All aspects of illegal drug importation, distribution and sales are too decentralised to enable deals. Take no new actions to either combat or encourage Australian illicit drug trade for the time being.

If opposition to US objectives arises from any emerging illegal-drug cartels, impose crackdowns through increased policing and harsh penalties.

Religion

Australian attendance at Christian churches has been declining for decades. Respect for religion reduced further during and following the global paedophilia scandal.

Despite the decline, religions continue exerting significant influence over public opinion. Specific strategies to win religious support are required. The most senior clergy are aware of church-related wealth and strategic (material) goals. They may be useful points of initial contact.

Religions shoulder significant financial and operational burdens of childhood education and care for the poor as well as for drug and alcohol addicted people.

Recommendations.

As an interim position, guarantee all religions the continuation of their favourable taxation concessions.

Offer to negotiate increased public funding for church schools in exchange for pulpit support for US objectives.

An additional study to identify other avenues to gain the confidence of all major religions is necessary.

Gambling

Gambling is deeply entrenched. Telephone and on-line gambling are popular. Children under 14 years-old are involved. Indulgence is almost universal.

The gambling lobby is powerful and may have strong links to alcohol and organised sport. Past attempts to curtail gambling have been opposed and seldom successful.

Recommendations.

Consult with major gambling executives.

Arrange an agreement to maintain current laws and regulations without further revision in exchange for consistent support from the industry.

If public pressure for reform arises, promise a wide-ranging inquiry but without a fixed timescale.

Avoid head-on clashes with this industry.

Spectator Sports

Australians are more passionate about sport than about religion. About 60 per cent participate. There has been a major rise in women playing traditional male games, and at a high level. Almost 100 per cent of Australians attend events or view them by other means.

Governments at all levels fund sporting events with total assistance running into billions of dollars. The public contributes directly through buying entry tickets to events, acquiring badged clothing and equipment; indirectly via taxes. The first prize for one horse race in Sydney (the Everest) is claimed to be AUD 6 million.

Sport appears closely linked to alcohol sales and gambling, in part through a nation-wide network of social clubs and similar institutions.

Administrators, managers and top-line participants gain significant incomes. Australian loyalty to specific sporting codes and to specific teams is strong.

Recommendations.

Do not rock this boat. Do not dilute existing codes by pressing for greater acceptance of American sports.

Win Australian hearts and minds by sponsoring prizes in various codes. Sponsorship of women's elite sport is likely to be popular.

Major opportunities exist to use (paid) advertising at sporting events.

In Washington DC, at a meeting between the President and his Cabinet, key personnel reported on progress to implement what had become known as *Plan-N*. The Leader attended but sat alone, without speaking, in a second row of seats.

All programs and preparations were either on target or had been completed. Transition proposals by '*our man on the ground in Australia*' had been accepted and advanced to the extent possible at this time.

The attack was planned for the third week in March. The precise day and time had to be identified and an authority to expend the nuclear weapon was required.

The President selected the Tuesday ('*Traditional washing day. We'll clean the joint out.*') and 11.15 am Australian Eastern Daylight Savings Time ('*It'll save wasting a midday meal.*')

He signed an authorisation to use the weapon, commenting 'This, ladies and gentlemen, will carve the record of my presidency in granite. It'll dwarf the Louisiana Purchase. It will be a major contribution to our secure future.'

Security-classified operational orders and directives were issued, in most cases to committed patriots who felt honoured to be participating.

One man didn't participate in the almost celebratory atmosphere. His Excellency the Ambassador to Australia knew how difficult it was going to be to arrange for the Australian Prime Minister and his key personnel to be physically present in Australia's Emergency Security Facility at the moment of detonation *and* without betraying Plan-N. He'd do his best and hope he wouldn't be blasted into hell if there was a miscalculation at any point.

IMPLEMENTATION

Within the Embassy, junior staff were organising a sub-summit conference to be held in Pago Pago. The event involved diplomatic representatives from all Pacific-rim nations. It had been announced as *'intended to examine avenues for reducing international competition and enhancing cooperation in the Pacific region.'*

Spouses of attending diplomats had been invited. A parallel program of *'entertaining and epicurean events'* was being arranged for them. The conference would take place during the third week in March.

Diplomats from perceived smaller nations, and those representing non-Pacific-rim countries, were not invited to what they regarded as the *Pago Pago junket*. Naturally, a few of them were unimpressed. In anticipation, and as compensation, the Embassy had quietly organised a coincidental week of relaxation and refreshments at an Australian seaside resort well-known for its seafoods.

Embassy spouses were press-ganged into providing hosting services at both venues. Given they'd be doing something similar in Canberra, they didn't consider it a burden.

After the alternative event was announced, whispers around diplomatic circles suggested the Batemans Bay affair might be more enjoyable than the

Pago Pago conference. Consequently, there was no shortage of volunteers for Bateman's Bay as well as offers of support from several diplomatic missions.

Five days prior to the closely held deadline, the Ambassador met the few senior diplomats who'd been selected to remain behind in the Embassy, '*to meet a high-priority national requirement*'. Having informed them of Plan-N, he paired them off, each with a buddy. If plans went awry, they'd be responsible for ensuring their buddy could reach a reliable car and drive from Canberra to avoid the detonation.

At Scowler's request, his buddy was to be Allen Ivory, although Allen was not at the meeting.

———

Four days before the planned detonation, six luxury motor-coaches, hired by the Embassy, conveyed party goers to Batemans Bay. That day their diplomatic brethren left by chartered aircraft for Pago Pago.

Allen, still working from his office in the Embassy, knew of these developments but paid scant attention to them. They had no apparent link to either the plan for cyber-attacking Australia or to his transition proposals.

———

Meanwhile, Allen's extracurricular relationship with Elizabeth had continued drifting happily toward a deeper bond.

Shared sandwich-lunches on the Glebe Park Lawns had been supplemented by evening meals at Elizabeth's apartment, not every evening but most of them. Their tender physical intimacy continued, still dominated by loving togetherness, remote from raw sexuality.

But the relationship was altering Allen and he knew it. His entrenched sense of church-induced morals told him that physical intimacy with Elizabeth was fornication, a sin. Yet he was elated rather than troubled.

His capacity to pray evaporated. Kneeling in supplication, emptying his mind, reading normally inspirational texts from his Bible, all failed to produce the spiritual connection that had guided and, he felt, guarded him through his life. Yet he didn't feel deprived. Without consciously realising it, he'd accepted Elizabeth as his beloved, his present and his future.

One evening at Elizabeth's apartment, following a light dinner of cold chicken with avocado salad, he raised the unmentionable topic.

'Dearest, I have to tell you some aspects of my employment with the US Department of Commerce might be a little unconventional.'

He was pausing, wondering how to continue, when she interrupted, 'Yes darling, I'd already figured that out. Australia and the United States don't have any particular trading interests involving places such as Darwin and Port Hedland, which you visited when last you were in Australia.'

'This time you flew to Brisbane and drove a hire car back through various inland townships which are not central to any bilateral trade or commercial negotiations. So, your mission was something quite different.'

'However, knowing you and trusting you, I'm not going to ask unanswerable questions. I accept you are a good man doing what is right.'

Across the street, now occupying a leased apartment, two operatives heard and recorded the conversation. This had been a cosy assignment, but lately they'd picked-up nothing of interest and were concerned their task would be terminated. But Allen's initiative, implying he was engaged on a highly sensitive mission, was dynamite. From experience they knew he'd probably reveal more in the future.

One said 'It looks as if the cat's starting to climb out of the bag. This is damned serious.'

They immediately reported the conversation to Scowler, despite suspecting he'd already be asleep in bed. Normally, Scowler would have informed both the Ambassador and Karl, his Washington DC contact for this case. However, he kept the report to himself.

Allen Ivory, he decided, was on the verge of becoming a major security risk. If young Ivory got even a hint of Plan-N, he'd probably try to save that damned aboriginal woman. The entire plan would be jeopardised. In fact, remembering her apartment was in the zone likely to be destroyed, an Allen Ivory-initiated rescue mission was almost certain.

The quickest and cleanest solution, Scowler decided, was for Allen Ivory to become part of the collateral damage. If, miraculously, he survived the detonation then other means could be employed to manage him.

FORTIFICATION

The Australian Government was suffocating in a politically poisonous atmosphere. Opinion polls consistently indicated the Opposition would comfortably win the next Federal election. Thanks to social media, centralised influence over public sentiment, one of the perks of political office, had become increasingly difficult.

During their previous term in office, a succession of plans to reduce the excessive price of electricity had been underwhelming while various attempts at tax reform had attracted more controversy than endorsement. Claims that electing the Opposition to power would invite unspecified chaos failed to rally public support. Programs presenting Australia as a new epicentre of innovation and a focal point for processing rare-earth minerals had all been ridiculed. Scandals affecting some Cabinet Ministers hadn't helped either.

Now back in office but unwilling, or unable, to learn the lessons of that humiliating defeat, trapped by a philosophical commitment to what was called 'liberal free-enterprise', the Prime Minister and his Cabinet were flopping impotently, like dying fish in a hessian bag. Desperate, they began inventing slogans as substitutes for policies while promising undeliverable outcomes, more in hope than expectation.

Something dramatically new and convincing was required, or they'd suffer yet another catastrophic trouncing at the next election.

During a social round of golf at the picturesque Royal Canberra course, the US Ambassador, overtly in jest, suggested to the Australian Prime Minister that the threat of nuclear warfare might provide a cohesive rallying point.

Normally, the Prime Minister would have dismissed the idea, categorising it as a clumsy attempt at humour. But the number and severity of challenges confronting him had been increasing, day after day, leaving him emotionally exhausted and vulnerable.

During his senior high school years and throughout university this man had never deviated from his quest for political power, for political party leadership. Spurning an opportunity for romance, he'd married a formidable but photogenic ogre, the daughter of an influential politician. Consistently self-promoting, he'd out-manoeuvred, outworked, out-debated and stared down his contemporaries, accepting two major coronary events and a likely shorter lifespan as the price of success.

Now his ambitions were unravelling. His focused fanaticism no longer provided the political traction he so desperately needed. Formerly supportive alliances were evaporating.

Increasingly frequent tantrums followed by contrite apologies were alienating his few remaining political colleagues. They, mainly with an eye to self-preservation, were projecting an image of normality, a process the Prime Minister had noticed and appreciated while privately acknowledging its implications for his political future were ominous.

In this atmosphere, following some well-choreographed encouragement by the Ambassador, the Prime Minister began taking the idea of a nuclear threat seriously. Lying awake at night, he reflected on past political successes associated with skilfully marketed alarmist campaigns.

I should have been paying more attention to scare campaigns. They can be potent weapons. Looking back over my lifetime our side of politics usually gained valuable political capital with 'reds under the bed', '36 faceless men', 'boat people will destroy our way of life', 'the caravan of chaos', 'national debt spiralling out of control', and 'the economic disaster of changing negative gearing'.

Even temporary relief from our increasing unpopularity could offer a springboard for other positive steps. Everything else has failed. This nuclear threat business is a long-odds possibility, but it could be worth a try. What do we have to lose?

That led to more meetings between the two men, all held in the Ambassador's private suite. The details they discussed with such grave and thoughtful focus were never recorded.

A subsequent meeting of Federal Cabinet agreed to endorse the nuclear threat as a possible scare campaign. Cabinet Minutes showed ministers in attendance had accepted the Prime Minister's view that there could be national security implications. After some debate they'd agreed action ought to be taken to address a possible attack on Australia involving nuclear weapons *in a manner not likely to cause undue alarm*.

The reenergised Prime Minister now had the bit between his teeth. He argued it would be consistent with Government policy, as well as electorally beneficial, to set the ball rolling by simulating a nuclear-warfare related emergency. The aim should be, he claimed, to increase alarm incrementally so public insecurity peaked just prior to the next election. This would not cause *undue* alarm.

The Department of Australian Security was directed to resuscitate a 1950s and 60s program of civil response to nuclear warfare. This would require cooperation by the States.

At a consequent meeting, held in a typical glass-fronted Braddon building, State officials were uniformly unimpressed. Following several well-scripted presentations from Department of Australian Security staff they finally decided, when other priorities allowed, they'd form a committee to draft the terms of reference for a standing committee which would consider courses of action.

Departmental representatives pressed for a more robust response but were rebuffed. The States were primarily interested in funding shortfalls, replacement of antiquated fire-fighting equipment and a decline in their numbers of volunteers. The notion of preparing for a nuclear attack on Australia looked ludicrous.

Nothing was released to the media, although the canny Prime Minister was confident that State officials would never respect Chatham House rules, although they'd been asked to.

As he'd anticipated, inquisitive and suspicious journalists soon began sniffing. By prior arrangement, Federal ministers and public officials consistently stonewalled by using the *'can neither confirm nor deny'* line, an approach always guaranteed to inflame speculation.

Less inhibited than the conventional press, social media channels went into overdrive. Something big was going to happen. Government was being excessively secretive.

Countless exotic theories appeared. A new cure for cancer been discovered but pharmaceutical companies were urging Government to suppress it. Government planned to open a new, publicly owned bank and insurance corporation. Australia would be adopting the one, uniform, time zone. Government was trying to distract attention away from credible evidence of a visit by aliens from outer space.

This groundswell of uninformed speculation suited the Prime Minister perfectly. His next move was to take credit for one of the Ambassador's ideas and arrange what he called *'a realistic rehearsal meeting'* of his Cabinet. It would be held in the Emergency Security Facility, a subterranean part of Australia's Parliament House, a venue designed to survive an attack by nuclear weapons.

To replicate reality, and hopefully increase public speculation, he decided it would not be a meeting of the entire Cabinet. Only permanent members of the National Security Committee would be invited. This predictably led to more leaks from the offices of several piqued ministers who were not included.

Adding to apparent authenticity, the Prime Minister had insisted the Chief of the Defence Force attend the meeting as an advisor. Following another timely suggestion from the American Ambassador, he also considered it appropriate to take the unusual step of including representation from Australia's primary national-security ally. Senior officials from the Embassy of the United States of America would be asked to join as observers.

Believing an attack by nuclear weapons might require decisions with constitutional implications, the Prime Minister also offered the Governor-General and Chief Justice of the High Court an opportunity to attend.

But the Governor-General, justifiably suspicious of unorthodox political manoeuvring, politely refused. The Chief Justice felt he would be more gainfully employed by writing his opinion on a complicated case involving the spread of seeds from genetically modified canola crops across State borders.

Always ready for a fight, at least two of the senior ministers would normally have challenged the Prime Minister's melodramatic move. But after further consideration they decided it would do no harm to cooperate.

'Let's face it, the PM is keen. This is his initiative. If it becomes an embarrassment it'll be his problem, not ours.'

'Yeah, I agree. Besides, it can be useful to occasionally delude the poor little fella into believing he actually has some authority.'

Capitulation

At the appointed date and time, all eligible participants assembled among elegant marble pillars embedded into the gleaming floor of Australia's Parliament House foyer. Following an usher along a passage and down several flights of stairs, they passed four airlocks before entering a lower-basement room.

Apart from hosting an impressive array of wine racks, mostly redundant since the introduction of screw-topped wine bottles, the Emergency Security Facility was stark but functional.

Grey concrete walls, still displaying wood grain imprinted by their original formwork, surrounded a honed concrete floor. One offshoot corridor led to a row of bedrooms, each with its own small bathroom. Another corridor opened into a food preparation facility.

The door to a third passage finished at a communications centre. It had been designed to maintain global contact as well as to broadcast national command directives during an emergency.

A steel door separated another large room. It contained living quarters for essential staff such as medical personnel, chefs, stewards, diesel mechanics and communications technicians.

Compressors and filters hissed as they distributed crisp, purified air now blowing gently from industrial-looking ceiling vents located throughout the facility.

Fluorescent-tubed lighting was glaringly bright. It could have supported a collection of orchids, or forest of marihuana, but no botany had been provided.

15 normally extraverted politicians and invited officials failed to dilute the depressing and uniformly barren environment. These unremarkable men, clad in dark-coloured business suits, deprived of the theatrical environments in which they normally thrived, were but marginally more animated than the surrounding walls. Three brightly clad political women failed to make a humanising impression.

The Australian politicians and their guests assembled in the central auditorium for coffee, tea and small-talk. Members of the American delegation remained apart, grouped together in a muttering huddle.

This unusual behaviour from often friendly and gregarious people would normally have attracted speculation. But the Australians, annoyed by this ludicrous waste of time on what one of them called, *'a stupid wild-wombat chase'*, were immersed in their own hostile emotions. It was, they agreed, acceptable to initiate a political scare campaign but this charade was taking things too far.

After 30 minutes, the Prime Minister, following several attempts to make his falsetto voice heard, invited all present to sit on chairs facing a polished wooden table located close to one wall.

Standing alone behind the table, using it as an oversized and hopefully prestigious-looking lectern, now totally convinced *this* was the initiative needed to secure another term in office, his hands and voice trembling slightly from excitement, the Prime Minister began.

'Your Excellency, visiting officials from the Embassy of the United States, other guests, colleagues, I declare this meeting of an expanded National Security Committee of the Government of Australia to be in session.'

'I won't read the agenda. You have had a copy of it for the past three days. No requests for amendments have been received.'

'I have apologies for their inability to attend from the Chief Justice of the High Court and from the Gover...'

The steel door at the rear of the room swung open.

'There's a reading on the nudet' shouted a technician. 'The geolocator's saying its right here, directly over Civic.'

'What's a bloody nudet and what's a geolocator?' asked the National Security Minister.

It was a timely inquiry although her colleagues, equally ignorant, had been prepared to bluff until clarification emerged.

Ignoring the protocol that advisors may speak only if requested, the Chief of the Defence Force answered. 'Nudet is an abbreviation for nuclear detector, an instrument which detects detonations of nuclear weapons. A geolocator tells us where the detonation occurred.'

The Treasurer weighed in. 'Are you trying to tell us someone's nuked Canberra? Your instruments must be crap.'

The technician replied 'That's what the instruments are saying, Minister. What's more, they are regularly calibrated and have triple redundancy circuits. The possibility of a false reading is millions to one against. Canberra has been nuked.'

Mouths hung open, hearts raced, pores emitted cold sweats, some bladders leaked. The enormity of the situation was beyond comprehension. A deluge of unanswerable questions contributed to a rising and turbulent group-babble.

'Will bombing continue and involve other cities? To hell with Canberra but what about Hobart, Perth, Sydney, Brisbane, the places where *our* families live?'

'Is this part of a new global war, part of the nuclear Armageddon?'

'How will the electorate respond?'

'What about radioactivity? How long will it last?'

'Could we blame the Opposition?'

'How and when will we get back home?'

Reactions reached a crescendo before subsiding into incoherent muttering. A sullen and hostile atmosphere descended as some conclusions became self-evident.

This meeting was not a coincidence. The Prime Minister had pressed for it.

'He knew something would happen; perhaps not an attack with a nuclear weapon, but he'd known something significant would occur.'

'That's right. He was nervous as hell.'

'Yeah, he assembled the group capable of maintaining continuity of civil government together with the military chief able to enforce it.'

'And why are the Americans so calm? They must've known something too.'

Sensing potential for the situation to get out of hand, the First Secretary from the American Embassy stood and demanded silence, almost as if his involvement had been rehearsed. A former three-star admiral in the United States Navy he was an ill-tempered, stocky, broad-shouldered individual; someone accustomed to exercising power and influence.

The Prime Minister was shocked, both by this uninvited and undiplomatic intervention and by the man's tone of authority.

Granted, the situation is abnormal, but nobody asked this fellow, an invited guest, to address Cabinet. And just look at the cocky bugger. He acts as if he owns the place. Who the hell does he think he is?

'Prime Minister, ladies and gentlemen, I have been getting a live feed on a classified communication device I am carrying. There *has* been a catastrophic event. All of Civic and most inner suburbs of Canberra have been destroyed.'

'This was caused by the detonation of a nuclear weapon being carried by a United States Air Force aircraft. Its crew will have been among the fatal casualties.'

What 'classified communication device'? This is garbage. He couldn't have got those details unless the Americans themselves planned the detonation from the beginning. Is this a declaration of war?

'In highly sensitive discussions, your Prime Minister has been liaising with senior members of the US Administration to review Australia's strategic posture. It was agreed you required a nuclear deterrent for your protection, politically unpalatable though that was.'

This is total and absolute bullshit! How dare he stand up and sprout lies right in front of me. How does he think he can get away with it?

'The United States, subject to comprehensive guarantees regarding conditions under which they might be used, proposed to provide Australia with five such weapons.'

'The weapons were to be stored in specially designed facilities at the Woomera Prohibited Area in South Australia.'

'At your Prime Minister's request, the first nuclear weapon to be delivered was flown, symbolically, across your national capital, across Canberra. This is where the horrific and regrettable accidental detonation occurred.'

My God, he is persistent, and supremely confident as well. I've seen some brash efforts, but this takes the cake. Maybe I'd best hold back until I can get a better grasp of the situation and figure a way to manage it.

'Garbage!' shouted the less-constrained Attorney-General. 'We know perfectly well the United States' policy when carrying nuclear weapons in flight is to avoid population centres.'

'What's more, this room contains the core of the Australian government as well as its defence chief, and we were all assembled here just before the detonation. That wasn't a coincidence. The detonation was planned, and very thoroughly planned too.'

The American didn't hesitate, although his attitude became frosty.

Speaking slowly and deliberately he said 'Madam, I have informed you of the public-management version of events. Within a few minutes it will be broadcast throughout Australia and globally, using American owned and managed communications satellites.'

'The statements to be released will include expressions of shock and disbelief by the President of the United States together with a promise to deliver medical and other aid. Your remaining media outlets will pick it up and run with it.'

'An investigation, to be conducted by US specialists, will find residual components of the United States aircraft which was destroyed by a nuclear detonation. Those components will be located around the fringe of the region of primary destruction. Sadly, but believably, no trace of its aircrew will be discovered.'

Oh no! The bastards really have planned this one. They've backed us into a corner. I wonder if I can still trust all of my ministers? Have any been compromised?

'You and your colleagues can choose to stand up in opposition to the version released by the United States of America.'

'But hear this. For the short-term future you will no longer have independent access to media channels. We can convincingly present you, madam, or anyone else, as a conspiracy theorist of diminished responsibility because of emotional inability to cope with the nuclear tragedy.'

'And, just in passing, your governor-general has declared a state of national emergency. As a result, your military forces are authorised to act in support of the civil authorities, if necessary, to ensure law and order are maintained.'

Still angry and unconvinced, the Attorney-General replied 'What a load of crap! The GG refused an invitation to attend this meeting. He was likely in Government House when you lot detonated the bomb. He's probably dead and is certainly not issuing declarations without Government's advice.'

The diplomat's frustration increased together with his natural inclination to belligerence. He wasn't inclined to accept opposition from any *antipodean idiot*, one of his favourite names for uncooperative Australians.

'Unblock your ears and listen-up lady. The governor-general just issued the declaration I described and might authorise more of them if convenient'.

'Any corpse found to resemble His Excellency will be forensically tested by US experts and found to be someone else'.

'After a suitable time, His Excellency will die as the result of a stroke. He'll be accorded a solemn State Funeral and then be cremated in a sealed coffin. Any more questions on that score?'

Good Lord, this level of detail is incredible. I'd better watch my step. God knows what else they've got hidden up their blasted star-and-striped sleeves. I wish my ministers would shut their traps. They're not gaining ang ground and are probably worsening an already catastrophic situation.

The Treasurer, by far the most confident but dumbest of them all, still was not getting the message. Persisting, she demanded of the Chief of the Defence Force 'And what are *you* planning to do about this outrage?'

The Chief, aware an incautious statement might further inflame the situation, offered a measured response.

'Minister, my first action will be to use whatever media channels remain available to me and reassure the Australian public that this catastrophe was an isolated incident. Then, I will publicly endorse the official version of what happened.

After that, I will ensure the armed forces are aware that the Government remains in control. I will also arrange for State police forces to be advised of the emergency proclamation and informed of the support they can expect through me.'

From an unidentified voice, 'Jesus! You gutless dog. You've surrendered, you've hoisted the white flag, abandoned Australia.'

'Ladies and gentlemen' the Chief replied 'with respect, I'm going to give you a lesson in Reality 101.'

'The Australian Defence Force cannot function without American approval. Yes, we might have some latitude around the fringes of international policy, but when things get serious the US can stop us dead in our tracks anytime it wants to.'

'America controls the software for operating our naval radars, fire-control systems and primary weapons. Ditto for our submarines as well as our combat aircraft and the weapons they carry.'

'All systems are computer-code reliant and American corporations are responsible for keeping our software virus free, or leaving it vulnerable, or infected, if you understand what I'm saying.'

'We buy our spares and replacement components from them. We purchase ammunition from America. In short, opposing a core United States initiative would be utterly futile.'

'Bear in mind what America did to Turkey back in 2018, and that was merely a mild lesson compared against what the United States could dish out to Australia if it wanted to.'

'Well, how in hell did things reach this state of affairs?'

'You, Australia's most senior politicians, should be able to answer that question better than anyone. For decades, a succession of military leaders has been warning their ministers about this extreme and growing dependency. In response they've been told to keep their mouths shut.'

'Of course, this attitude of blind denial was never associated with maintaining the flow of your electoral funding from America,... or was it?'

That last shot struck home. The Prime Minister, although previously shocked into silence, was not about to let any official become the de facto Australian spokesman.

He now entered the debate telling the man 'Yes, in the past you have been told to keep your mouth shut and now you are being told to do so again. This issue is a problem for Government. *You* will be told what to say and when to say it.'

Observing the discussion, American officials had already decided which Australian should be driving the born-again bus. The Prime Minister and his colleagues would need to be monitored and supervised, especially the Prime Minister because he seemed to have a few brains. But the Chief of the Defence Force was a smarter bear than any of them.

Then it was the Ambassador's turn. A career diplomat, this tanned, handsome, silver-haired man, his calm, grey eyes gazing observantly through rimless spectacles, was an experienced manipulator. Having allowed his First Secretary to absorb the distain following those first, indispensable announcements, *he* was ready to adopt a more conciliatory tone.

'Prime Minister, ladies and gentlemen, the facts are these. Due to the catastrophe that impacted Canberra, your capacity to govern Australia effectively has been diminished. This has endangered your national economic and broader strategic security.'

'The Security Treaty between Australia, New Zealand and the United States, known as *ANZUS*, Article IV, has been interpreted by us as covering the current catastrophe.'

'Being your closest and most committed security ally, the United States of America, as an interim arrangement, will assume responsibility for supporting and guiding your governance in accordance with a request you will be signing shortly.

My First Secretary will provide the document. Your Prime Minister will sign on behalf of your nation. Other ministers are invited to sign as witnessing the event.'

Another pack of hogwash. Jees, they are so confident, so ruthlessly organised. I'd better go along with them for the time being.

'The Secretary General of the United Nations will be informed that Australia has requested a period of consolidation under the oversight and stewardship of the United States of America.'

'The Prime Minister and those other ministers who sign the agreement and assist in its implementation will retain their present Cabinet positions into the longer-term future.'

'Recognising the stress they will endure as a consequence of this unusual arrangement, their parliamentary salaries and all related allowances will be paid by the US Government at a multiple of three times present rates.'

Oh well, at least I'll get some financial benefit out of this unholy mess. Hopefully, the promise of cash will gag some of the others before they make life even more difficult, if that's possible.

'As you know, your Prime Minister has power to choose his own Cabinet and he will replace those ministers not willing to participate. Accordingly, participation will be voluntary.'

The First Secretary, following a whispered consultation with the Ambassador, continued with another unheralded pronouncement.

'At present, nobody is filling the role of Minister for Defence for Australia. Your Prime Minister has agreed to appoint your Chief of the Defence Force to that position. Your new Minister for Defence will also maintain his position as Chief.'

'This arrangement will persist for a period of three months in accordance with Article 64 of your Constitution.'

Well, we'll see about that. He might carry the title of minister but nobody in my Cabinet will trust him for a minute. He's gone across to the enemy.

It was the first time the Prime Minister had heard of this or any other arrangements now being announced. But, accepting the inevitable, he nodded.

The Ambassador sighed with relief. The announcements and the way they'd been delivered, had been among several key tests designed to determine how compliant the Prime Minister was likely to be. So far, so good!

The First Secretary then introduced a 'nuclear-science expert' from his staff.

The Prime Minister and Foreign Minister were almost certain they remembered the man from social functions hosted by the United States Embassy. Tall, pale-complexioned and built like a gridiron player, he'd been hard to miss. He was obviously a conventional member of their diplomatic corps reciting a prepared script. This was further evidence the nuclear catastrophe had been thoroughly planned.

'Prime Minister, ladies and gentlemen, as you were informed, Civic has been comprehensively destroyed as have the inner Canberra suburbs. The human casualty rate in regions of major damage will have been close to 100 per cent either due to the original detonation or the effects of injuries then experienced.'

'As you already know, nuclear detonations cause radioactive fallout. But, the weapon which detonated was a relatively 'clean' bomb. By this time tomorrow, it will be reasonably safe to travel to Canberra Airport, which is likely to have been minimally damaged.'

'In the longer term, some radioactive material will be distributed by winds at various altitudes. It will enter the food chain, conceivably as far away as New Zealand. It is not possible to responsibly estimate the spread of this secondary pollution.'

'The United States had already arranged to lease the Swainotel in Sydney for use by our own new and expanded trade and diplomatic personnel. Given the tragedy that has occurred, we will now make the entire building available for you to occupy and utilise as your temporary parliament house.'

'The hotel comes with its staff and has significant conference or meeting facilities as well as accommodation suitable for your interim government, for support staff from your regional offices and for your senior bureaucrats if required.'

––––––––

The Australians felt they'd heard enough for one day. The situation was beyond surreal. Every foundation supporting personal, corporate, political and national stability, every Australian social and economic value, had either changed drastically or was about to. There was a new hairy mammoth in the room.

'At least', the Treasurer opined, 'the conspiracy theorists who claimed something big was about to happen will be able to say their instincts were valid. Whether they'd be smart to persist in making that claim in public is something else again.'

While gentle but agnostic autumnal breezes continued dispersing the particles that had once comprised Allen Ivory and many thousands of Canberrans, the assembly decided to adjourn for drinks and dinner.

Following a brief opportunity to tidy-up in their now-allocated rooms, the business-attired Australian and American officials assembled back in the mausoleum-like central auditorium. Support staff, despite not knowing if their friends and families were alive or dead, continued working diligently. Trestle tables were erected and set for the evening meal.

The Foreign Minister noticed, although white linen table covers had been laid, only paper serviettes were provided. But, he supposed, the situation was somewhat abnormal. They'd all have to be gracious and accept what was available.

Meanwhile, two male stewards now wearing black-bowties, short-white jackets and immaculately pressed grey trousers, circulated unobtrusively among the guests. The embossed silver trays they so dexterously balanced held offerings of scotch, beer, dry sherry, champagne, orange juice and chilled water. Unsurprisingly, alcoholic aperitifs were almost universally preferred.

The deep hum of liquor-fuelled, male-dominated conversation increased in volume as second and, in some cases, third, drinks were swallowed by seasoned imbibers. Escapist instincts guided the conversations toward sporting events, recently published novels and other uncontroversial topics. One minister, typically insensitive, attempted to recount a humorous event but it fell flat.

The same atmosphere dominated during the meal as diners, their appetites now whetted, consumed entrées of stuffed quail flambeed in cognac with a hint of black truffle in the glaze. Only two main courses were offered so they were forced to choose between lobster thermidor or wagyu beef, each accompanied by lightly steamed seasonal vegetables. Desserts were constrained to crepes suzettes or a cheese platter.

A limited range of white and red wines, including the inevitable *Penfolds Grange*, lubricated the conversation. The *Grange* was considered a pleasant tipple, although a few people thought some bottles hadn't been aired properly after opening.

Much to the relief of a never visible and recently employed catering supervisor, nobody questioned how or why such epicurean dishes had been available in an emergency survival shelter.

———

The subsequent night was uneventful, apart from a brief incident in the Prime Minister's assigned bedroom.

In common with her colleagues, the Attorney-General, anticipating a two or possibly three-hour meeting, had not brought a change of clothing. But, driven by one of her periodic randy urges, she remembered she was wearing a lacey-black G-string. Emboldened, and with the top buttons of her blouse unfastened, she sprayed *eau de cologne* from a handbag-sized capsule into several strategic locations.

With long and shapely legs now extended by green stiletto-heeled shoes, her surgically reconstructed and now bra-less breasts jiggling rhythmically, she sauntered down the corridor to the Prime Minister's room, her high-heels making a sensually feminine clopping sound as each echoing step heralded her approach.

Entering his abode without knocking, having mentally rehearsed a casual greeting to be followed by lounging sexily against his doorframe, she found him sitting on the bed chatting with an attractive young woman.

This woman was, the Attorney-General recalled, a member of their domestic support staff. Following an almost believable assurance that the two had been discussing unspecified aspects of room service, the Attorney-General retired, crestfallen and frustrated, to sleep alone.

Acts

The following morning, a basic breakfast was served from one of the trestle tables used during the previous evening. On offer, to be consumed while standing, were cornflakes (with yoghurt or cold, full-cream milk), toast and Danish pastries. English Breakfast tea and plunger coffee followed.

Having eaten, Australian politicians and American officials began gravitating across the auditorium toward the site of yesterday's memorable announcements.

The more observant were surprised to see *three* chairs behind the polished wooden table. All three were occupied; one by the American Ambassador, one by his First Secretary and, in the third chair, was the newly anointed Australian Minister for Defence. It was a symbolic but potent message.

Dissatisfied, the hierarchy-sensitive Prime Minister began repositioning his chair out to the left of the main assembly, but the Ambassador sent his nuclear science expert to quietly suggest he not persist. He didn't.

With his audience seated the Ambassador stood, ignored the Prime Minister, and began.

'Ladies and gentlemen, I have been advised that, by tonight, it will be acceptably safe for us all to leave this building and travel to interstate locations. The airfield at Fairbairn experienced only minimal damage and is suitable for use. Your VIP aircraft fleet is intact together with associated aircrew. It will provide your transport.'

'A fleet of United States Air Force aircraft is already airborne, flying toward Canberra. It is loaded with tents, bedding, clothing, food and water as part of America's Operation Friendship and Compassion (OFaC).'

On hearing, 'Friendship and Compassion' the Prime Minister felt vomit rising into his throat but choked it back, swallowing hard.

The Ambassador continued, 'As I'm sure you appreciate, we must use all available time constructively and efficiently. This includes making some broad policy decisions today, if possible.'

'To save you being distracted by matters relating to the routine functions of your departments and portfolios more generally, I can tell you we have analysed your machinery of government and related operations in detail.'

'Essentially, your services are contracted out to providers who in turn have sub-contracted to other organisations, many of them on the Indian sub-continent. The remainder are being managed interstate. Your main data bases are either interstate or backed-up by interstate facilities.'

'Almost all Commonwealth functions can continue without much disruption so long as nobody wants to make changes.'

Hearing this, the newly appointed Minister for Defence began appreciating the incredible depth of planning behind America's initiative. Having already been briefed on the Ambassador's remaining announcements, he felt free to disengage and consider some of the more disturbing implications now emerging.

I could and should have predicted this. America and China have been increasingly hostile to each other. Most mutual aggression has been confined to trade, finance and a few minor collisions in disputed waters, but more assertive initiatives have been increasingly likely.

Meanwhile, we've been enabling the Chinese economic machine by selling iron ore and other minerals. We've been indirectly supporting its competition with America.

The Americans planned their move over time and in great detail. Whatever they do next it will probably result in them controlling Australia's exports to China.

'That brings me to the first issue to be addressed today,' continued the Ambassador, already setting the Australian Government's agenda, 'and it requires an Australian decision.'

'As I've said, American aid is pouring into Australia. However, before capital works can be undertaken, we need to know whether Canberra will remain Australia's symbolic focus city. I invite you to address that issue now.'

First out of the blocks was the Prime Minister, who stood and faced his colleagues.

'Colleagues, I'm confident that Brisbane, overlooked in 1912 as a site for the national capital, would today be the perfect location. Think of the climate. Consider Brisbane's proximity to Asia and to the United States. The patriotic dedication of honest Queenslanders stands for something. They're nothing like your tertiary-educated, daylight-savings-endorsing and chardonnay-sipping Canberrans.'

'Whaat', screeched an unidentified voice 'are you delusional, mad, stupid or all the above? Bloody Brisbane with its humidity and history of flooding! What a disaster! Obviously, the new capital city should be in Tasmania, preferably close to or in Hobart or Launceston.'

'Nooooo', yelled another claimant 'it has to be Adelaide with Port Lincoln as an outside possibility.'

'Sydney's the only sensible option.'

'Rubbish! Melbourne is by far the better choice!'

The National Security Minister weighed in with a pitch for Perth as, '...the only bloody option anyone with a bloody brain would even bloody contemplate,' a contribution meritorious for enthusiasm if not content.

The conversation became yet more heated and less constructive, continuing with such intensity that a scheduled pause for morning coffee and croissants was overlooked.

At one point the Foreign Minister, attempting to break an emerging deadlock, opined that perhaps in the electronic era Australia could manage without a physical focus city. Almost immediately he disappeared beneath an avalanche of objections.

'That's just plain stupid. The prestige associated with parliamentary ceremony and protocol is indispensable.'

'Virtual attendance couldn't provide the photographic opportunities available from a physical assembly.'

'Yeah, exactly. And how would we constrain the stupid press corps if there was no centre of political gravity?'

'Where would the significant ceremonies be held? The symbols wouldn't seem truly Australian if they were scattered across the entire continent. Besides, pride and prestige require an aiming point, an anchor which all Australians could acknowledge.'

Having reproduced the arguments with which Australia's Founding Fathers had grappled more than a century earlier, they adjourned for a light luncheon.

The constrained menu offered only garlic prawns on chunky baguette, sliced beef cheek with seasoned basmati rice, and a few other minor offerings, accompanied by a selection of wines from the Margaret River district.

After the meal, a fortified but also chastened Cabinet reassembled. They soon agreed Canberra would need to remain as Australia's capital city. There was no logical alternative.

The American Ambassador noted their decision but suggested references to a *national capital* or *capital city* be muted while the reconstruction process was ongoing.

The Ambassador seemed adamant and, given the Americans were obviously calling the shots as well as responding generously to this crisis, the Australians felt it wasn't too much to ask.

For the remainder of that afternoon the Ambassador asked Cabinet to consider arrangements for the disposal of human remains. An estimated 40 000 people had died, give or take 10 000. No component of Canberra's mortuary, funeral or cemetery facilities could cope with a demand on that scale.

With minimal delay, Cabinet agreed on mass burials in two sites. They would be designated as sacred memorials. There was no time to consult with municipal officials, if any remained. Besides, this was a matter of national significance.

Nobody involved had lived or ever wanted to live in Canberra, so they approached the challenge with a degree of detached objectivity. With the aid of an old, single-sheet street-map found wrapped around a bottle of wine from *Chateau Lafite Rothschild*, they identified land occupied by the Federal Golf Club as the southern mass-burial site and the Mount Ainslie Nature Reserve for the north.

Someone, obviously not thinking clearly, began raising concerns about rare orchids, aboriginal heritage and double-tailed lizards living close to Mount Ainslie, but the Prime Minister's icy glare gagged further debate.

Given almost no capacity to identify the charred and often dismembered bodies of Jews, Christians, Moslems and members of other cultural or religious categories, they decided to make no distinction. A series of symbolic markers, installed later, would substitute for religious rituals.

The conversation then turned to a formal declaration of an official mourning period for the dead. Periods of between one day and a week were proposed. No two participants could agree on the time required. Finally, the consensus reached was 'Almost all the dead were Canberrans, so who would care? A more concrete decision could be taken closer to the first anniversary of the event.'

That evening, a small staff of volunteers remained behind in the Emergency Security Facility. Everyone else, the Australian politicians, American diplomatic personnel and most support staff, tramped, in nervous anticipation, along the sloping exit corridor, up the stairs and out through the airlocks that had sustained them.

Despite hearing summarised reports of damage to Canberra, nothing had prepared them for the revised panorama. Looking north from Parliament House, built on a hill, they could see an alien, almost two-dimensional, landscape covered with lifeless rubble. Apart from a few trickles of curling, black smoke, the fires had extinguished themselves. Nothing else was moving.

A spread of white debris indicated where the Old Parliament House might have been. A gabled wall, still standing, could have been part of St John's church in Reid. The few other still-vertical skeletons were unrecognisable to non-Canberrans.

Their Parliament House had been split into two sections, a large and vacant gap running north-south between them. Its symbolic flagpole, formerly standing 81 metres above the building and weighing 220 tonnes, was warped and leaning toward the south.

The stench of putrefying corpses and decomposing foodstuffs, mingled with other rotting materials, reached into their nostrils and clung to their bodies. Some dry-retched. One man vomited.

Detonation had occurred on the day prior to a parliamentary sitting day. Most other members of the parliament would have been assembled on-site together with their integrated staff. Presumably, they were dead or critically injured.

Within minutes, a camouflage-painted military helicopter, badged as belonging to the United States Marine Corps, appeared. With twin overhead rotor-blades whirling noisily, it descended quickly then, at the last possible moment, raised its nose slightly and landed gently, expertly, on the circular mosaic in front of them.

The first group of passengers climbed on board via a ramp lowered at the rear. Six, including the domestic assistant last seen in the Prime Ministerial bedroom, were flown to the VIP lounge at Fairbairn and the remainder were dropped off at a terminal on the other side of the airfield.

An additional shuttle flight followed, conveying technical, domestic and other staff to Canberra's main airfield terminal. There they were left to fend for themselves.

A waiting V-22 Osprey aircraft then collected the Americans from Canberra Airport, taking-off almost vertically before rotating its wings into the horizontal position and flying to a landing on the USS *John F Washington*, now moored in Sydney Harbour. At the Ambassador's request, the newly sworn-in Australian Defence Minister accompanied the American contingent.

ACCOMMODATION

Flying home to Brisbane, seated comfortably in his VIP-aircraft, the Prime Minister finally found time to reflect. Thinking back on last month's discussions with the Ambassador, he could see he'd not been told lies. But every nuanced statement had been open to interpretation.

Not only that, but an exercise as refined and detailed as this one must have carefully planned over months, if not years. How come we never got wind of it? Perhaps we were too trusting.

The Americans wouldn't have contemplated accepting these major political and strategic risks simply to gain a temporary advantage. They're here for the long haul. Australia as an independent sovereign nation is probably finished, stuffed.

Damn and damn again! Well, at least I'm still Prime Minister of Australia, for the moment, and on a handsome remuneration package too. With any luck, I might enjoy some distracting time with that luscious girl from the Emergency Security Facility. I could've already made a start if it hadn't been for the damned Attorney-General.

Alluringly attractive and a good conversationalist, the short but slim Jill Horrow exuded a tantalising whiff of conservative celibacy overlaying an occasional hint of voluptuous erotica. The Prime Minister was hooked.

This, he later realised, must have motivated him to take a risk and invite Jill to accompany him home.

Seated opposite him, Jill said she'd been born in the US, which explained her accent, but moved with her parents to Australia when she was 12 years old. Sadly, she explained, looking directly up to him through her warm, moist, brown eyes, her father had died from a stroke only a year after their arrival. This, she added, blushing prettily, left her strongly attracted to older men. She really needed a father figure and hoped the Prime Minister wouldn't find her too clingy.

Slowly stroking his Waterford glass-full of gin-and-tonic, the Prime Minister listened analytically, hoping to appear empathic.

Oh yes, m'dear, I'm sure I won't find you too clingy. In fact, with any luck I'll help you elevate that desirable trait to new heights.

Surfacing from this pleasant reverie, he said 'Actually Ms Horrow, I will need a new personal assistant. The job could be demanding and the hours unconventional, so the person selected would need to live in my Brisbane house and travel with me to official engagements. Of course, the salary will be much higher than what you are earning as a domestic assistant. Do you think these arrangements might suit you?'

Fortunately, they did.

Knowing his wife was in England, comforting a slowly dying relative and almost certainly in no hurry to return home, the Prime Minister relaxed into his deeply padded seat, once again allowing his mind to wander.

Ah, yes, Jill! Those velvet-soft lips, the smooth neck and delightfully compact young breasts. Responsive, firm nipples? Almost certainly! Hmmm. Must remember to keep a few Viagra tabs in the bedside drawer.

His Brisbane house was the perfect venue for an amorous venture, although strict oversight by the First Lady meant he'd not yet had an opportunity to try it out.

Their residence appeared to be a traditional beige-coloured *Queenslander*, meaning a two-level wooden house with room for car or boat parking beneath and living quarters above. Surrounded by a wide upper-level balcony and located close to the University of Queensland, it blended tastefully with its pleasant neighbourhood.

That, however, was where the cultural and architectural similarities ended. On the pretext this was the Prime Minister's alternative residence, a venue where he entertained prestigious international guests, he'd convinced the Parliamentary Expenses Branch to authorise '*essential security and related features*' costing millions of dollars. The entire structure had been subtly rebuilt.

Heavily insulated walls and ceilings now embraced state-of-the-art climate control and mood-lighting systems. Smokey-glass doors slid silently in and out from internal wall cavities as did large-screen television sets. Floor to ceiling curtains opened and closed at the touch of a button on a remotely controlled device, permitting or blocking light filtering in from the recently installed triple-glazed windows. Another hand-held controller managed soft music in any or all rooms.

Excavations beneath the house had added an in-door heated swimming pool and a billiards room with a well-stocked bar, all accessible using the discrete electronic elevator.

Ah yes, *silver linings in a dark cloud.*

But he had no idea how dark the cloud could get. A barrage of media releases, usually accompanied by graphic pictures and horrific eye-witness statements, not only stunned the nation but also left it vulnerable to a media campaign of anti-governmental suggestions. They became more specific and damaging as time passed.

One morning, streaming the overnight news on his cellphone, he was shocked to hear:

> 'According to consistent reports from usually reliable and insider sources, our American administration had strongly opposed Australian requests for nuclear weapons. But, ignoring the discouraging political atmosphere, Australia's

Prime Minister campaigned relentlessly.'

'Sources within the White House have revealed that America became increasingly concerned by the persistent Australian demand. It was considered possible the Australians might approach France as a possible provider.'

'Given this, and yet more strategically hazardous possibilities, it seemed preferable to keep some control over this undesirable development.'

'Finally, our President, anxious to preserve the strong bond of friendship built between Australia and the United States, and consolidated over many years, granted the necessary permission.'

'America nevertheless imposed stringent conditions on storage, access to and utilisation of these weapons. Because the precise details were exceptionally sensitive, revealing them would not be appropriate, although the President is believed to have said that the Australian Prime Minister could do so if he wished...'

The following day a recording, apparently of the Prime Minister in an incriminating conversation with the President, appeared briefly on social media. It was quickly taken down. An apology and hints of a denial were released by an official from America's Department of State.

However, it was widely reported. The damage had been done.

———

Regardless of distractions, the Prime Minister and his colleagues retained some responsibilities. The residual Cabinet met in the Swainotel for one day every third week during which they examined routine reports and tried to project the impression they were governing Australia.

Occasionally, a surviving backbencher would arrive and try to appear interested. Their visits were tolerated, mainly because they supported the impression of a democratic and consultative government at work. In any case, the Canberra catastrophe hadn't changed the reality that junior politicians were irrelevant except at election time or when voting on parliamentary motions. These occasional visitors always appreciated shopping excursions in Sydney, their travel having been financed at taxpayers' expense.

On only two occasions did individual ministers ignore guidance from the American Ambassador that new business and innovative policies should be avoided. Both attempts failed, following debates less dignified than would have occurred in the past.

The first came from the Treasurer. Thinking it might be possible to boost the almost undetectably low level of public confidence in Government, she heaved her ample physique into a standing posture, paused momentarily to recover from the exertion, and proposed another investigation into the Australian finance sector by a second Royal Commission.

For years, a previous Government had relentlessly opposed the *first* Royal Commission, but events had forced its hand. With the greatest reluctance they'd then petitioned the Governor-General to authorise the inquiry but constrained its terms-of-reference and imposed a deadline on its completion. Consequently, the Treasurer argued, some issues could have been more comprehensively examined.

Her colleagues, like pack dogs sensing a vulnerable quarry, responded with a chorus of contempt.

'Did the Minister understand what she was saying? We realise you're new to your portfolio, but this is just plain bloody stupid.'

'Compared against us, the big banks are mere amateurs at the game.'

'We're up to our necks in dragging cash out of taxpayers.'

'We impose taxes that drive up component prices, then come our fuel taxes that make delivery more costly.'

'Yeah, and on top of that we apply a 10 per cent consumption tax.'

'And don't forget the punters buy finished items with income from which we extract income tax. Of course, if the item is really expensive, we might impose an additional luxury tax.'

'In only six years we got them paying nearly 50 per cent more in income tax.'

'If anyone complains, the Tax Office can either ignore them or drag-out the complaint until the taxpayer dies, goes bankrupt or surrenders.'

'Hey, hey, and what about the VIP aircraft fleet? We cost it against the Defence budget, so when we travel around in convenient luxury it looks like increased expenditure on Defence. What a deal!'

The group dissolved into laughter, normally signifying the end of a debate, but the Treasurer was so committed she failed to get the message.

'But, but, but, the big banks and some of the loan sharks have been...'

The attacking hounds regrouped.

'We don't care about what big banks or loan sharks do.'

'They are fully aware of *our* financial activities.'

'If we get stuck into them, they'll shoot back with enough ammunition to blow us to smithereens.'

'What do you think would happen if they began publicising our parliamentary allowances? This is a you-scratch-my-back-and-I'll-scratch-yours exercise.'

'Do you get it now, sweetheart?'

The normally ambitious Treasurer withdrew her proposal and sat to nurse a seriously fractured reputation.

Three weeks later a second and more dangerous suggestion was put to Cabinet, this time by the Minister for Education Policy. A tall individual with a greying goatee beard, he'd convinced some of his colleagues that he was their resident intellectual. He'd consciously cultivated this approbation by lowering the tone of his voice, speaking slowly and stating the bleeding obvious.

His reputation entitled him to a respectful hearing although he wasn't a member of the National Security Committee and hadn't been present in the Emergency Security Facility. Then he dropped a shocker.

'Perhaps' he suggested 'the language being used to describe "terrorism" is not appropriate. "Terrorism" and "terrorist" carry some prestige, status, *je ne sais quoi.'*

Continuing, he claimed 'The language we employ is possibly attractive to youths or immature adults. If we changed the emphasis and began describing disruptive actors by using terms such as: deranged, infantile, attention-seeking or cowardly, then the glamour factor would be seriously eroded.'

His audience, at first stunned, spontaneously combusted.

'Reduce the threat? What the hell is he talking about?'

'Terrorism is the greatest political gift in living memory. It's the best thing we've had since the communist takeover scare.'

'Ministers can appear strong, resolute, paternalistic as they speak about national security being the Government's highest priority.'

'Taxes can be increased to pay for essential security. Security constraints prevent details of the expenditure being released.'

'Anti-terrorist initiatives help soak-up unemployment'.

'The Opposition is gagged because anyone questioning anti-terrorism initiatives is clearly a traitor, someone unfit to govern.'

'This is win, win, win, bloody win.'

'Does the Minister seriously want to risk throwing all of that out the window? Does he really want to disrupt this downpour of political manna from heaven?'

The hapless man, seeking to preserve some dignity, responded with 'Yes, but we need to reduce associated outlays. Deaths in Australia due to terrorism are comparable with deaths due to lightning strikes and merely a fraction of the fatalities from drowning and numerous other causes.'

His colleagues, or perhaps former colleagues, were quick to respond:

'The number of deaths and injuries remains low only because our magnificent security apparatus detects and foils the plots. This shows we are doing a great job in protecting the Australian public.'

'Yeah, that's right. What's more we can claim any numbers. Nobody can challenge us because the information is classified. It's "national security."'

The Prime Minister chimed in.

'I've heard more than enough. We, ladies and gentlemen, are in the business of politics. Politics means we strive to *acquire* power and prestige, *exercise* power and prestige, and *retain* power and prestige.'

'We must keep in mind that nations and their economies are robust. They can absorb a lot of mismanagement without much harm being done. In fact, most of the time it's almost impossible to tell what's good management and what isn't.'

'Now let's not be distracted from the fundamental principles of politics by considering any more banking inquiries or other irrelevant brainwaves. A politician's job is to manage emotions, not respond to logic. As Charles de Gaulle correctly said, "It is the task of political leaders to dominate opinion." The analysts, the Noam Chomskys of this world, are not welcome here.'

For the first time since this vertically challenged man accepted his thankless job, all except one minister stood and applauded.

But, regardless of what Cabinet did or refrained from doing, the media-propaganda machine moved into yet higher gear, releasing more details undermining the Australian Government, or what remained of it.

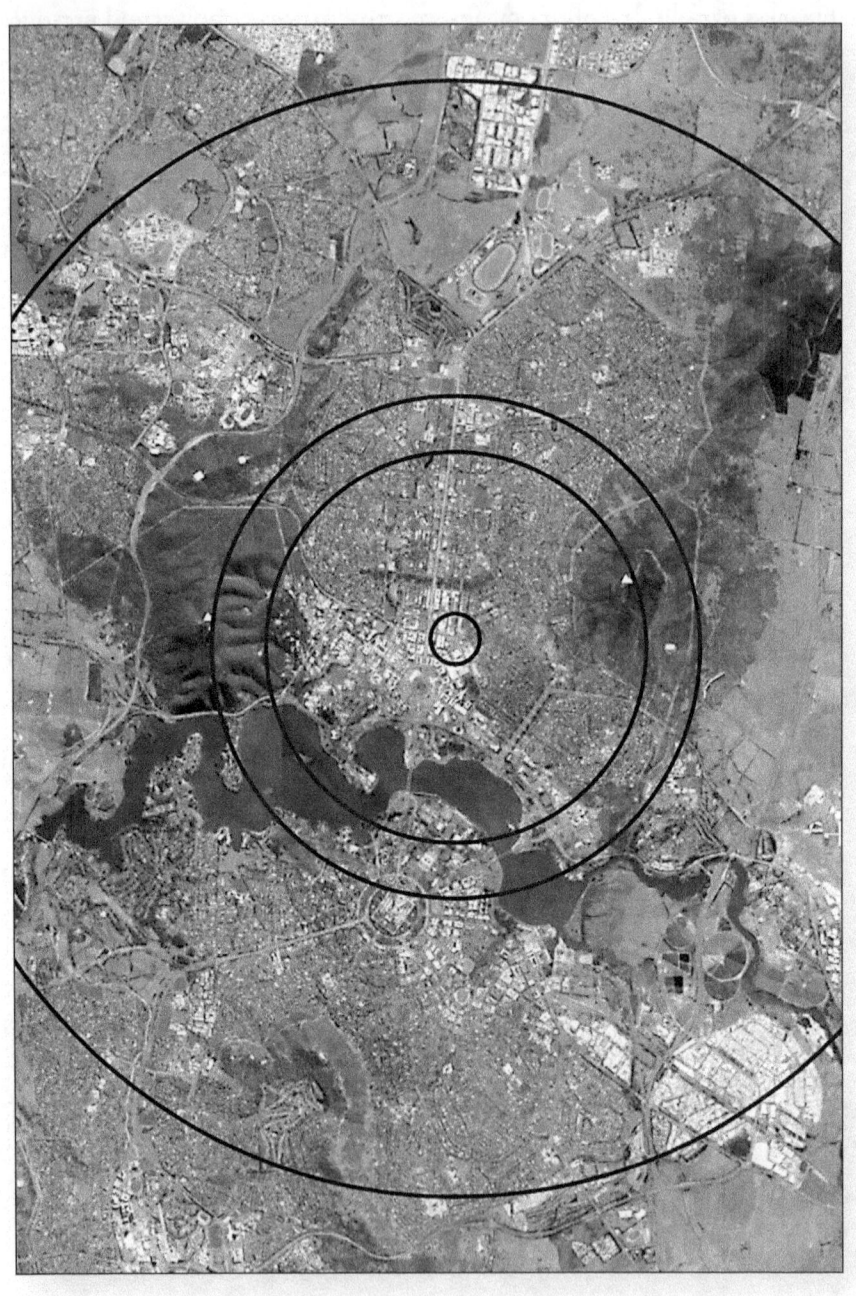

Representative effects of a 50 kiloton, air-burst nuclear weapon detonated over Canberra, Australia, with no allowance made for local topographical and related shielding.

Inner circle. Fireball radius 290 metres.

Next circle. Air blast radius at 5 psi, 2.59 kilometres. (Most residential buildings collapse, injuries to people are universal, fatalities are widespread.)

Third circle. Thermal radiation radius, 3.2 kilometres. (Third-degree burns extend through layers of skin and destroy nerves. Scarring and disabilities can require amputations.)

Outer circle. Air blast radius at 1 psi, 7.28 kilometres. (Glass windows break causing injuries, other minor structural damage.)

Acknowledgements

Data related to the extent of damage sourced from the website NUKEMAP, by Alex Wellerstein, hosted by Stevens Institute of Technology, Hoboken, accessed 17 September 2019, <https://nuclearsecrecy.com/nukemap> Radiation data was also provided but not included. The text of the novel exaggerates the dimensions and locations of some damage.

Data from NUKEMAP was superimposed in a Google Earth map. Publication is in accordance with the Google policy at <https://www.google.com/permissions/geoguidelines> for print material.

The contributions NUKEMAP and Google Earth are gratefully acknowledged.

Canberra's Hyatt Hotel at which Allen Ivory stayed and where he met Elizabeth Gnagarra.

The Pollen café and restaurant in the Botanic Gardens, where Allen and Elizabeth's luncheon was observed and reported.

Apartments in the leafy suburb of Braddon where Elizabeth lived.

St Columba's Uniting Church were Elizabeth worshipped. Lewis Hall in the background.

HUMILIATION

One evening on the 6.00 pm newscast came an announcement by a well-known national television presenter. His backdrop was a screen showing the immediate aftermath of the Canberra catastrophe.

> 'According to leaks from well-informed sources, the idea to fly Australia's first nuclear weapon, symbolically but secretly across Canberra, had come from our own Prime Minister.'

> 'American officials had been unimpressed but, on checking their records, they noted the last airborne malfunction involving a nuclear weapon had occurred near Greenland's Thule Air Force Base in January 1968.'

> 'Since then nuclear and related technologies had advanced to a point where the probability of a mid-air incident was considered less than one in a million.'

> 'But, tragically for Australia, and for the many thousands of Canberrans who lost their lives, nothing is ever absolutely certain.'

Corrosive attacks then began extending to the Prime Minister's personal appearance. He'd always insisted on being photographed from a low angle, making him look taller. Camera shots never included the thickened platform soles on his specially designed shoes. Suddenly, that changed.

Published images looked downwards, emphasising his shortness. New business shirts with slightly overlarge collars, a birthday gift from the American Ambassador, made him look younger, less substantial, almost juvenile.

Then there was the problem of no longer having a professional cosmetician to apply makeup before scheduled television interviews. Jill, now well-established as his indispensable personal assistant, did her best to assist him. But sometimes he'd resembled a clown from a travelling circus.

One newsprint headline read, *Pint-sized Prime Minister Urges Calm*. Another asked, *Will the Little Fella Stand Down?*, before listing the Prime Minister's alleged errors of judgment.

The theme was unmistakable. The Prime Minister and remaining four senior ministers, five if you counted the new American-anointed Minister for Defence, were incapable of providing effective and stable government.

Yet another frustrating challenge confronting the Prime Minister was that his planned romance with the delectable Jill hadn't progressed.

When first they'd arrived at his Brisbane home, her menstrual period had started although she'd been coy about admitting it. Sadly, her libido was always low for a few days after it ended.

'Oh Buffy darling, you are the most wonderful of men. But I've lived a very sheltered life. I've never had an enduring, stable relationship. My hormones are telling me I need one, and soon.'

'Jill, Jill, Jill you know I think the world of you. Sadly, years ago, I made the tragic error of marrying the wrong woman. She's now welded to my public image. Divorce would be impossible.'

'Of course Buffy. You're a sweet, darling honourable man. You do have to respect that commitment. But, you know, I'm so attracted to you that I'd be prepared to play second fiddle. I could be your muse, so long as I was your permanent muse.'

'Jill, you darling, fabulous beautiful girl. Let's work toward some arrangement that suits us both.'

'Yes, yes, my dear cuddly Buffy. Let's work all of that out. We'll make sure the foundations for our truly loving relationship are secure. Then, we'll be able to surrender ourselves to each other, mind and body, when we join as one.'

Still in hope of a carnal outcome, the Prime Minister bided his time, ambivalently accepting an occasional calming shoulder massage or a kiss on the best side of his forehead, Jill consciously avoiding patches of pinkish skin where he'd had basal-cell carcinomas removed.

That aside, political pressures continued to mount until the Prime Minister felt he couldn't, and Australia shouldn't, take any more.

Using an encrypted telephone with access limited to Cabinet Ministers, one of the few purely Australian security assets remaining, he set up a teleconference with the Attorney-General, Treasurer and National Security Minister.

The Foreign Minister was, he believed, inflexibly pro-US and couldn't be trusted. His so-called Minister for Defence had disappeared into the American strategic planning machine.

Opening the conversation, he said 'I believe the Americans have gone much too far. They must be stopped. The ludicrous propaganda they've been pumping into the media has undermined us all. And let's be realistic here; what's bad for us as the nation's leaders, must be bad for Australia. Do we all agree with that?'

The Attorney-General responded 'Yes, Prime Minister, I believe we are all in violent agreement.'

'Yes.'

'Agree entirely.'

'In that case, I suggest we consider options for action. Nothing should be off the table. I propose we consider the issue carefully and again meet by teleconference at 4.00 pm tomorrow.'

But, as the Prime Minster knew, his resources were limited. Discussing the situation with Jill they agreed that the Attorney-General, although a risky choice, would be the most effective representative to send to any foreign power with a plea for help, if that was to be the preferred course.

But still he still hesitated. The Attorney-General was a ruthlessly ambitious woman. Offering her any assignment, especially one that might enhance her reputation, was dicey. Nevertheless, she did understand the legal and constitutional issues involved.

Jesus, now I have to deal with three blasted women. One is sharp as a razor and twice as dangerous, the other two are blustering loudmouths with huge public fan bases. I wouldn't wish this on my worst enemy.

Thinking aloud, the Prime Minster concluded he would need to reach some form of security-related arrangement with either India or, as a last resort, China.

Having taken his first significant step in more than a month, he was inclined to relax a little and consider a strategy for the next day's teleconference.

But even this narrow window of success was soon to close.

Within 30 minutes, his telephone rang. As usual, Jill answered. It was *Scowler,* the Chief Security Officer from the American Embassy. He needed to speak with the Prime Minister.

Yes it was urgent and, yes, the Ambassador was fully aware he was making this possibly unorthodox request. He could fly from Sydney and be at the Prime Minister's residence at 10.30 am tomorrow. The meeting need take no more than 20 minutes.

Jill faithfully relayed the conversation. Knowing he had no option, the Prime Minister agreed.

———————

The following morning an obese, dark-complexioned Scowler arrived at Brisbane Airport. 76 years-old, he was one of the last Cold War warriors. Domineering and inflexible in his opinions, he'd been reluctant to retire because the younger generation had failed to grasp the gravity of Russia's threat to the United States. He'd been assigned to the Embassy in Canberra because nothing of consequence ever happened there.

But every dog has its day, and this assignment was tailor-made for Scowler.

He caught a Yellow Cab to the Prime Minister's residence. On arriving he lost no time coming to the point.

'You, Prime Minister, have been actively engaged in contacting your ministerial colleagues and planning to encourage international opposition to the United States. You have taken this initiative despite everything the US has been doing, and continues doing, for Australia.'

'Do you, Prime Minister, realise you are meddling in a security-classified environment with international and operational implications? American national security is involved.'

That final barb tipped the Prime Minister's balance.

'How dare you talk to me about security classified environments. Of course I accept there's a core of information which must be safeguarded at all costs. But you know perfectly well that about half of this stuff is melodramatic bullshit that we routinely trot out for consumption by the gullible voters. It's stuff that China, Russia and God-only-knows-who is already well aware of. You can't pull that crap on me.'

Unfazed, Scowler lowered his voice half an octave and continued. 'Sir, the United States does not take operational and intelligence issues lightly. There are appropriately severe penalties for breaches and the law does not discriminate on grounds of status, income, race, or anything else.'

The Prime Minister was apoplectic. 'Jesus Christ almighty! That is the exact response I and my Ministers have rehearsed. It's designed to intimidate persistent interviewers. Who the bloody hell do you think you are?'

Scowler could have persisted but, watching the Prime Minister's complexion change from a light-tan to deep purple, decided not to risk it. The fictitious Australian Governor-General was scheduled to die soon. It'd be difficult to manage the almost concurrent death of the Prime Minister.

'Okay', said Scowler 'you win'. 'Prime Minister, we'll forget the crap and finish our business. Although, really I've delivered my message and you'd be well advised to heed it.'

Thoroughly disenchanted at being lectured-to, the Prime Minister nevertheless decided to ignore this gross breach of protocol. However, there was one point he wanted cleared up.

'Well, since we are being candid, I don't understand how you knew about my telephone conversation with the Ministers. The communications link is heavily encrypted, the coding changes often. There's no way your people could've cracked it and listened in.'

Scowler, enjoying every moment of the Prime Ministers discomfort, paused silently for a few seconds, allowing himself the rare luxury of a smile.

'That's easy to explain.' Turning to the smoked-glass door separating the reception room from an adjoining area, he called out, 'Agent Horrowicz, would you join us please.'

In walked Jill, the Prime Minister's trusted personal assistant; lips, neck and nipples still unassailed by Buffy darling.

'Meet Agent Horrowicz.' said Scowler. 'She joined the United States Marine Corps and trained as a helicopter gunship pilot. Her high intelligence and social skills came to the attention of our people during her service in the Middle East. We provided further training.'

'Since then, she's served on challenging assignments in Kiev and Tehran. But you, Prime Minister, are her first one-on-one target. Would you say she did a good job?'

The Prime Minister folded into foetal position. Too depressed, too disillusioned to respond, he stared helplessly at the floor.

Enjoying his victory, Scowler couldn't resist another thrust.

'By the way, I understand that you'd like a long-term relationship with Agent Horrowicz. Well, your wish is granted. Her assignment as your personal assistant won't be ending any time soon.'

Exiting the house, standing halfway down the front steps, Scowler turned and finished the conversation with one final jab, informing the Prime Minister 'Acting on the advice of the Government of Australia, the United

States has agreed that ANZAC Day, Australia's traditional day of military remembrance, will henceforth be rebadged as ANZACUS day.'

'This revision appropriately recognises America's role as Australia's primary security partner.'

A New Covenant

To most of the international community it was obvious. The Australian government had been at fault. Yes, America should have been more cautious about sharing its nuclear weapons, but the Americans had always done things their way and were unlikely to change any time soon.

Ignoring the *Non-Proliferation Treaty*, as it was already doing in its relations with India, Israel and Pakistan, but not North Korea or Iran, the United States had been prepared to forge ahead regardless of treaties or other constraints.

The outcome was regrettable, but the United States deserved high praise for reacting with stunning efficiency and generosity. Essential services were being restored to the City of Canberra, roads had been cleared and temporary schools opened. Damaged foreign embassies were being repaired and compensation paid. Modular housing was pouring into shattered suburbs—all at no cost to the Australians.

Mass graves had already been built to contain the dead and appropriate arrangements were in place to ensure these now sacred sites would be preserved in perpetuity.

Obviously, the United States Government wasn't the only actor on stage. The global community could see the American people were also involved. Wealthy corporations, small communities and private individuals offered assistance. In municipalities, some already labouring under their own economic stresses, residents opened hearts and bank accounts for the Aussies.

One voluntary group raised the funds to purchase an entire fleet of ageing aircraft. They provided a shuttle service taking patients to specialised burns and trauma surgeries along America's west coast. Return flights carried countess thousands of food parcels together with bedding and clothing.

Another charity chartered a commercial cargo vessel, transporting frozen, radioactivity-free vegetables to Sydney and then by rail to Canberra. Volunteer teachers, counsellors, plumbers, electricians, bricklayers, surveyors, doctors, dentists and nurses arrived, often self-funded and ready to start work.

The genuine, warm-hearted, compassionate Americans were, yet again, rising *en masse* to confront a challenge not of their making and beyond their shores.

International organisations, the *Red Cross* and *Médecins sans Frontièrs* especially, made well-organised contributions to medical and sanitation services. Religious movements from various nations collected donations to rebuild Canberra's churches, synagogues, mosques and temples.

Countless foreign families offered to accommodate dispossessed Canberrans, even agreeing to pay return fares for their guests. As a result, several thousand Canberra families removed pressure from overstretched services by temporarily shifting to the United States, Canada, Greece, Japan, Germany, New Zealand and other locations.

But throughout Australia, responses to Canberra's catastrophe were muted. Ignorant of political and statistical realities, many Australians believed the Canberrans and *their* politicians had had it too good for too long.

This, they thought, was just the sort of disaster Canberra *would* bring down on itself. This'd teach them what real-world struggle was all about; give 'em a taste of reality. Maybe they'd learn to act differently in the future.

One political movement, the New Nation Party, identified the nuclear culprits with confident precision. It was *those Moslems* who'd infiltrated naïve, left-wing Canberra and caused the disaster. How *those Moslems* had achieved this feat, one for which America accepted responsibility, was never specified, but they'd done it.

It wasn't clear whether this assertion was compatible or competitive with claims, mostly by the Reborn Christian Union, that the devil had gained a foothold in Canberra because Christian worship was being diluted, impliedly by *those Moslems.*

Throughout the evolving debate, media in all its formats, public and private, remined active. While the personal profiles of the Prime Minister and his colleagues were being diminished, the unquestionably magnificent response by the United States Government was correspondingly elevated, described in detail and accompanied by glowing commentaries.

Graphs and charts were published illustrating progress made toward rebuilding Canberra. Film clips showed grateful Canberrans receiving treatment in American hospitals. A flood of reports covered the magnificent work done by volunteers.

In addition, American-controlled media channels began incorporating statements of humanity's inalienable rights to life, liberty and the pursuit of happiness, words described by the American statesman Alexander Hamilton as having been '*written by the hand of divinity itself.*'

By clear implication, those and other hallowed principles had guided America to become the leader, the sword and the shield of the Free World. Dedication to America's manifest destiny was a sacred honour. Anybody not clamouring to climb on-board *this* freedom train was obviously a fool or a traitor.

A few Australian constitutional law experts and other intellectuals tried pushing back against the propaganda. But their efforts were so feeble it was possible, even useful, for American media to disregard them in the interests of demonstrably encouraging free speech.

The process of indoctrination continued unabated. America's *Declaration of Independence* was held out as an inspirational example to be imitated. It bristled with patriotism, confidence and righteous indignation. There was no Australian equivalent.

The yawn-inducing *Act to Constitute the Commonwealth of Australia*, had been endorsed by the British Parliament, not the Australian. It ploddingly announced:

> 'And whereas it is expedient to provide for the admission into the Commonwealth of other Australasian Colonies and possessions of the Queen:
>
> Be it therefore enacted by the Queen's most Excellent Majesty, by and with the advice and consent of the Lords Spiritual and Temporal, and Commons, in this present Parliament assembled, and by the authority of the same, as follows:
>
> This Act may be cited as the Commonwealth of Australia Constitution Act.' ...

Further eroding capacity for pushback was that successive Australian governments had comprehensively stamped a pro-American imprint, often presented as pro-alliance, across Australian society.

They'd consistently appointed advocates of the American alliance to senior and influential positions in the bureaucracy and the military. Those appointees had provided career-enhancing opportunities to ambitious sycophants. Junior officials knew that any fundamental criticism of Australia's security ally would be a career killer.

Through a variety of channels, the independence of academic and related communities had been diluted. Most of the nation's so-called *thinktanks* and similar organisations were populated by frustrated foreign-policy wannabes dedicated to debating and spreading their own versions of government propaganda.

Even to suggest there was a growing need for rapprochement between

China and the United States, as one brave scholar had done, risked the accusation, *left winger* or worse.

Amid this new and accelerated acceptance of American values, Australia's wise and prudent Governor-General, a man commonly viewed as holding the Australian nation together, dropped his own bomb. Sir Lidian Isaacs issued a media release recording his opinion that, following the Canberra 'event', Australia could not sensibly revert to a business as usual approach.

He proposed a referendum to decide whether Australia should become another State of the United States of America, noting this implied the Australian Government adopting a new *State of Australia Constitution*, one compatible with the United States' Constitution. The decision-making process, he suggested, should be a national referendum of all enrolled voters.

Normally, an immediate, strong and aggressive reaction would have emerged, not because Sir Lidian's proposals seemed to favour the United States but because they were radical and unforeseen. But Australian society had changed.

Constitutional lawyers were effectively gagged. Despite writing volumes analysing how Australia's Constitution could or should be *amended*, there was no recognised process for abandoning it entirely. The law was silent, and the Governor-General's proposal seemed as good as any.

The prevailing academic viewpoint, conceivably influenced by the need to retain research funding, was that the Governor-General's pro-American proposal seemed likely to be acceptable.

It was also adopted enthusiastically by common women and men across Australia, most of whom found appeals to the pursuit of happiness and manifest destiny both inspiring and attractive.

Having for many years been complicit in muzzling anti-American propaganda, the Prime Minister and his remaining ministers could only issue a statement asserting that matters of such gravity should be decided by the Australian people.

Appearing to break ranks, the Minister for Defence provided his own widely acclaimed press release. It analysed the implications of Sir Lidian's proposal and endorsed it as the most appropriate way ahead.

Some observers expected serious opposition from the Australian Broadcasting Commission, known as the 'ABC'. But, as the situation developed, it became clear they'd miscalculated.

For decades, naïve Australian politicians had been claiming the ABC displayed a left-wing or anti-government bias. In fact, it had been the most effective right-wing propaganda tool in the nation. While the ABC occasionally broadcast programs not supporting government policy, it normally reported major strategic and related geopolitical events through a clear pro-American lens.

At times of heightened tension, its broadcasts were peppered with repetitious commentaries from the President of the United States or his senior cabinet officers. Alternative media releases or statements from other nations, Iran, Russia, North Korea and China especially, were often either ignored or broadcast in selectively condensed versions.

If quoted at all, the non-US foreign media releases would sometimes be translated unsympathetically, or literally, leaving the impression that their authors were emotionally or intellectually handicapped.

This delicately managed process had given a broad spectrum of Australian audiences, especially the politically uncommitted middle-class, an impression of impartial reporting from an organisation they could trust.

Some State politicians, keen to preserve their political influence, did attempt to make a fuss. What would happen to the individual States? How would this affect services provided by the States—police, fire-brigades, education? What about State revenues?

Specifically, they asked if South Australia would be forced to accept coal-fired electrical generating facilities, Western Australia a nuclear waste dump or Queensland the horrific scourge of daylight savings. Any emotionally charged objection would do.

Sadly for them, at the national level there was minimal enthusiasm for revisiting the constitutional entitlements of individual States. The idea of rescuing their formerly divisive fiefdoms from a jurisprudential graveyard seemed absurd.

National media, still dominated by American owned and controlled outlets, responded in a benevolent but superior tone. The States had *interesting* concerns which should not be ignored. However, the main issue here was Australia's security, its survival in an increasingly challenging international environment. Other issues could be addressed later.

State premiers had heard it all before. They knew there was no defence against the national security or classified information cards. It was better to quit before someone raised the vexed question of whether they were doing enough to combat terrorism, or more controversially, how they were applying funds provided by the Commonwealth Government for specific projects.

Because Sir Lidian's proposal implied Australia would be resigning from membership in the Commonwealth of Nations, some adverse comment from King Charles III, or the British Parliament, was anticipated. They didn't eventuate.

King Charles was absorbed in repudiating claims that he'd secretly converted to Roman Catholicism. Insinuations of a very long-term addiction to drinking cherry-brandy continued to dog him.

The view prevailing in Westminster was that Australians were more like Americans than like Englishmen. They would have declared themselves a republic sooner or later. Besides, Britain was preoccupied with managing the disaster that followed its attempts to engineer a favourable exit from the European Union. That initiative, at first given the jaunty title *Brexit*, was now more often referred to as *Screwedit*.

CREMATION

According to reports from reliable American sources close to the Governor-General, he'd been monitoring his nation's mood as well as international reactions to his proposal.

Despite several minor strokes, he'd refused to make concessions to his health and was continuing to work 14-hour days and sometimes longer. His health, he claimed, was inconsequential when compared against the well-being of his beloved Australia.

Two weeks to the day after his memorable media announcement, and struggling courageously against the burden of illness, His Excellency Sir Lidian Isaacs, acting on the advice of the Government of Australia, authorised a national referendum to consider the issues he'd originally raised.

The date for voting was set for a Saturday one month away, at which time, in accordance with Australian tradition, it would avoid clashing with any major sporting event.

Included in the announcement was that, because the Australian Electoral Commission had been one of the organisations fundamentally damaged by the Canberra Event, administration of voting on the referendum would be overseen by officials provided generously by the United States.

Two days later, Australians were shocked and dismayed to learn their much admired, indeed loved, Governor-General, Sir Lidian Isaacs, AK, MC,

OBE, LLD, had died following a haemorrhagic stroke. Working through until his last breath, he had passed away while consulting with American officials aboard the USS *John F Washington*.

Because His Excellency had died aboard an American ship, and the Australian government was overwhelmed with pressing political and administrative issues, American representatives kindly offered to coordinate and generally manage all required funeral arrangements. The Australian Minister for Defence would assist.

Print media proclaimed this melancholy event on front pages displaying black and purple borders. Other media acclaimed the merits of this great man, tracing his origins in suburban Melbourne, his subsequent military career, his various academic achievements, his contributions to charities and other successes.

According to syndicated reporters, nothing, including the loss of his beloved wife during the Canberra Event, had distracted him. The strength, courage, dedication and wisdom he'd displayed during his term as Governor-General were analysed in fine detail.

For once, the entire spectrum of public media was in agreement. Australia, indeed the world, could ill afford to lose a man of this calibre.

Sir Lidian's funeral was planned for one week away. The service would be held at St Andrew's Anglican Cathedral in George Street, Sydney.

To give as many Australians as possible an opportunity to pay their last respects, a solemn ceremonial procession would proceed along the full length of Park Street, turn left into George Street and then travel to the Cathedral at the intersection with Bathurst Street.

However, there would be no formal viewing of His Excellency's mortal remains. In accordance with Sir Lidian's specific wishes, he would be sealed within a coffin made from Australian native timbers grown on commercial plantations.

The Anglican Archbishop would preside over the Service, full details of which would be made available shortly.

But investigative reporters, with only minimal assistance from the US press liaison office, managed to locate a draft order of service. They were able to inform a now rivetted Australian public that readings would include the Twenty-third Psalm. Hymns would be *Abide with Me* and *Rock of Ages*.

Subsequent announcements, also from USS *John F Washington*, confirmed that the unofficially obtained information was correct. They also advised that, after the Service, Sir Lidian's mortal remains would be conveyed directly to Rookwood Crematorium. Following cremation, they'd be sealed within an urn of the finest glaze, one embossed with kangaroos and emus, then returned to the cathedral.

Arrangements both spiritual and temporal began. A formation flypast by F-35 Lightning aircraft, and also a 21-gun salute from an Australian naval ship on Sydney Harbour, were planned and rehearsed. An honour-guard of soldiers, on both sides of the road, would extend for the entire length of the ceremonial procession.

A myriad of other essential but less prominent tasks began, including printing the order of service, hiring portable toilets, arranging for barricades, notifying road closures and securing the attendance of first-aid personnel to support members of the predictably distraught public.

———

Sir Lidian's procession assembled on the day appointed. Fifteen motorcycle-riding police in a triangular formation were in the lead. Their gleaming helmets, white ceremonial gloves and chromed machines provided a sense of both ceremony and authority.

A glistening, grey, motorised hearse carried the coffin. It was devoid of flags and flowers so members of the public could see the casket and feel closer to Sir Lidian.

Following the hearse, walking, were the black-clad Prime Minister and his ministers, except for the Minister for Defence who was at the Cathedral ready to give one of the readings.

Behind the political party came an armoured vehicle, included at the suggestion of the American Ambassador, *'just in case a problem arises.'*

Following the armoured car were squadrons of military personnel, immaculately attired and solemnly slow-marching. Gloved officers were holding drawn swords while other ranks carried rifles attached to highly polished bayonets.

As the procession set off, authentic and profound emotions from crowds lining both sides of the road were unmistakable. Many women, men and children were in tears. Men removed their hats. Cries of *'farewell'*, *'thank you', 'you served us magnificently', 'we will always miss you'* and *'mio padre'* swirled around the passing casket.

However, as the procession approached George Street, the mood began to change as the focus shifted from the hearse to the Prime Minister and his colleagues.

First, a few muted but uncomplimentary comments were uttered. Then, the political squadron became a target for shouted threats and abuse. Cardboard coffee mugs, mostly empty, were thrown, insults were screamed and clenched fists shaken.

The situation was getting out of control.

As if on cue, from the crowd emerged a group of burly, grey-suited men, all with either shaved heads or crew-cut hair. Demonstrating practiced efficiency, they formed a cordon around the politicians and escorted them to the now-opened doors of the armoured car.

In that undignified manner, the Prime Minister and the residual Government of Australia, now splattered with food scraps and coffee dregs, arrived at the Cathedral.

The funeral service was conducted without further incident. The Minister for Defence not only gave one of the readings but, being a long-time friend of Sir Lidian, offered a brief homily on behalf of the Prime Minister and Government of Australia.

Formalities finished with the coffin being carried out on the shoulders of six military personnel.

Sir Lidian's police motorcycle escort reformed and led the hearse to the crematorium. There, the coffin and its contents were converted to ash which was cooled before being placed into the vice-regal urn. The urn was sealed.

The same police contingent escorted the hearse and urn back to the cathedral where the urn was deposited beside the altar. Three white-gloved military personnel guarded the urn, standing to attention, heads bowed and rifle barrels pointed downwards. They would be replaced every 40 minutes for the next 10 days.

Meanwhile, along one wall of the cathedral, working discretely, skilled tradesmen prepared a simple but elegant bluestone shrine into which the urn would be placed for permanent exhibition. Some physical protection was considered necessary, so an ornamental stainless-steel grid, backed with thick glass, was also being installed.

Kneeling pads would be provided for those wanting to pray to Sir Lidian for guidance in this uncertain environment.

Over time, many of the faithful did so, although the impact of their earnest prayers might have been diluted by the reality that this urn contained the ashes of a homeless man who had died in New York. Unidentifiable, but of similar height and build to Sir Lidian, he'd become the unknown soldier of the homeless, although only a handful of people knew it.

Editorial Note

Years later, a historian discovered Sir Lidian had purchased a burial plot for his wife and himself at a cemetery in the Melbourne suburb of Brighton. This revelation could have raised doubts regarding the Sydney cremation. However, with some encouragement from cathedral administrators in Sydney, the story was consigned to history's academic trash bin.

The vice-regal burial plot in Brighton was subsequently sold to a man whose racehorse-owning mother, still living, had already purchased her own address for eternity in the same cemetery.

THE COMMANDMENTS

Arrangements for a national referendum, authorised by the now deceased Governor-General, had been proceeding.

The Prime Minister and his colleagues, humiliated, exhausted and no longer capable of mounting any opposition, simply yearned for the nightmare to end. With pragmatism ascendant they were prepared to sidestep or snuff-out almost any argument likely to delay the inevitable outcome.

He grumbled 'As we all know, these are American-inspired initiatives. But there's little we can do to stop them. In fact, attempts to run interference will likely harm *us*, individually, including financially.'

'Yes, we know that, Prime Minister. So let's do what we can to make the processes as quick and painless as possible.'

'Yeah, especially as the Americans have promised us a safe haven on multiples of our anticipated parliamentary pensions.'

The need for austerity, as a mark of respect for the thousands who had died in Canberra, was given as public justification for a low-key political campaign, despite it leading to the most significant referendum in Australia's European-settled history.

Nevertheless, encouragement for a maximum voter turnout was broadcast periodically, offering a veneer of fairness and democracy to the process. Urged by the American press corps, the Government was now referring to the referendum as, *Australia's great leap forward into perpetual prosperity.*

Political opponents, kept distant from related discussions or decisions, had no viable responses other than to trot out their well-worn line that Government couldn't be trusted.

On the chosen Saturday, polling booths opened without fanfare across the nation. The usual lines of enthusiastic advocates, each offering how-to-vote leaflets, failed to materialise.

Voters had already seen a pamphlet purporting to present arguments for and against the proposal. On closer examination, the discussion might have seemed subtly skewed toward a '*yes*' vote. This, however, merely reflected the popular viewpoint that anyone opposing the new opportunity was, to quote one publicised Northern Territorian, '*a drongo and a mug*', vernacular reflecting faithfully the level of intellect apparent throughout the debate.

True to the Ambassador's word, America spared no expense in providing officials to ensure the security of each polling booth, safeguard the ballot boxes and count the results.

The outcome was announced two days later. Except for Western Australia, where the votes for and against were almost equal, the remainder of Australia had clearly supported the propositions.

Stateside, back at The Office, its normally phlegmatic Leader, still not yet aware his only son was dead, shouted 'Thank the Lord for that. We've pulled it off.' before telephoning the President to announce the good news.

Following further consultations between American and Australian officials, the constitutional process was officially titled *The Sir Lidian Isaacs Referendum.*

———————

Across the United States, public reactions were more than positive. Concerns over rising bank interest rates, deteriorating public infrastructure, limited employment opportunities for Hispanics and African Americans together with more mass-shootings of children at primary schools, were all forgotten.

Euphoria reigned as the reality of gaining a resource-rich continent began sinking in. Australia, they suddenly realised, was about the size of Continental United States.

With a 94 per cent approval rating, the President's popularity rating reached an unprecedented level. Media across the political divide touted him as their greatest leader since Washington, a man truly committed to advancing America.

Proposals to commemorate his time in office included erection of an impressive obelisk in Washington DC and rebadging one of the States to reflect his name for evermore. New issues of commemorative postage stamps and coins were a given.

Celebrations in Australia, although not quite so enthusiastic, were widespread. America's assistance and support following the nuclear accident had been appreciated. Its further initiatives in providing economic and other stability during a difficult time in Australia's history were recognised.

People whose lives had been saved by surgery in American hospitals, or who had been accommodated for months in American homes, were vocal supporters of the new arrangements. The Government of the United States was regarded more favourably than any Government of Australia had been in all the years since popularity polling began.

Determined to consolidate this unique situation, the President formed a Transition Team to arrange for the smooth transfer of Australia into the welcoming bosom of the United States.

Core members of the Transition Team included the Secretaries of State, Treasury, Defense, Commerce and the Attorney General. This was to be the Administration's highest priority.

These hardened and experienced executives moved quickly, relying heavily on guidance obtained from insightful and comprehensive reports by an unidentified agent in The Office. However, it became obvious they sometimes needed details and opinions in addition to the written report.

The Secretary of State was strident in saying 'I don't give a dam what the protocols surrounding anonymity of The Office personnel are. This is new territory. We need to speak directly with this man, or woman.'

The Leader, summoned, was informed of the Transition Team's requirement.

He replied 'Yes ladies and gentlemen, I understand what you want and why. I can now share news I received only yesterday. The agent who wrote the reports was a man named Allen Ivory. He is, or was, my son. From available evidence it seems almost certain he was killed in the Canberra Event.'

The Transition Team offered condolences and agreed unanimously that Allen Ivory had been a true American patriot, someone who'd made a magnificent contribution to the nation. Subordinate staff were directed to prepare a submission recommending the President award him a posthumous citation.

Within the Team, the Attorney General accepted two tasks. He'd ensure Australians charged with writing their new Constitution understood the American Constitution and prepared a document fully compatible with it. He'd also arrange for America to rescind the *Antarctic Treaty* of 1959 and assert sovereignty over all Antarctic territory formerly claimed by Australia.

The President, having made clear he wanted to be kept in the picture, didn't hesitate to offer opinions which the Team wisely interpreted as commands.

Discussing arrangements for the new Australian State Constitution he insisted it provide for election of judges and senior police officials by popular vote, their terms being limited to a maximum of five years. He added all senior prosecution officials were to be selected by Stateside processes, '... to stop any possible collusion between government and prosecution. If that sort of thing is going to occur, we'll be the ones to arrange it.'

The Secretary of State wasn't comfortable. 'Of course Mr President, if that's what you want it will happen. However, perhaps we need to recognise that the notion of an apolitical public service and judiciary is integral to

Australian culture, no matter how artificial and misleading it might be.'

The President dismissed that as 'Piffle.'

He added 'I'm told Australians refer to government employees by the ludicrous title of "public servants". I want that to stop, however you do it. Those people work for the government of the day, not for the public. They often work against the public.'

'*If* the term "government employees" is used then the officials' actions will be sheeted home to the government, the new State government in this case. It'll be weakened and occasionally we'll step in, like popular heroes, to resolve issues. This'll keep the Australian government of the day on its toes.'

The Commerce Secretary's highest priority task, but not the most urgent one, was to find a plausible means of negating all Australia-China contracts for the supply of '*ores, minerals and all substances convertible into goods or energy*'.

According to the President 'We'll keep our hands firmly on the supply levers and dial back China's industrial production. When the Chinese try to source supplies from other nations, we'll make negotiations as difficult as possible and, at the least, increase costs to China. China's products will become more expensive and less marketable.'

The President and his Transition Team also agreed that implementation of the minerals and resources constraints were to be postponed until the Defense Secretary had established '*significant US land and air forces*' in at least two of the three areas proposed by The Office.

Nuclear-weapon stockpiles were to be secured in all three locations as soon as possible. This activity was to be completed in '*less than 12 months*'.

Meanwhile, the Commerce Secretary would be kept busy in the short term by guaranteeing the recommencement of live cattle and sheep exports from Australia '*notwithstanding any objections from the pathetic bleeding hearts*'.

This, according to the President '*will assist in calming regional concerns over American expansion and assure them of our intention to be reliable trading partners.*'

She was also to repudiate existing arrangements for water restrictions and resource sharing. Where Australian inland rivers flowed through two or in more of the former States, priority would be *'given to productive agriculture upstream and to hell with the environmental crap.'*

Up-river farming would probably use all the water in the Murray-Darling river systems. This led to seeking tenders from American corporations for nuclear-powered plants to recycle sewage for drinking water. As one of her officials said 'If it's good enough for New York, it'll be good enough for dammed Adelaide.'

The President also emphasised the need to establish a new storage facility for America's increasing volume of radioactive waste. *'You are to find a solution, soon, and not anywhere close to here.'*

A desk-top study identified a location adjacent to the town of Kalgoorlie in Western Australia. It was off the beaten track and had suitable rail transport connections to a seaport. Alternatively, it was worth considering a nuclear-waste site on the Antarctic Continent, which was even more remote. The 'southern location' could become active within nine months, allowing for utilisation during the next Antarctic summer, if this became the preferred option.

To gain a pro-American support in rural Australia, especially in the north-west of the continent, the Team decided to reduce all Australian taxes on alcohol by 75 per cent. The Office had recommended a 50 per cent cut, but the Transition Team decided to make this a flagship policy for promoting warmth and mateship.

It was obvious the United States Constitution and all federal law would apply to Australia. This included the Second Amendment. Gun manufacturers, having sniffed the potential for a significant new market, prepared to ramp-up their production. However, full-blown permissiveness as existed in parts of the United States would, the Team believed, be unsettling in the first instance.

Following consultation with the National Rifle Lobby, they agreed to confine issue of licences for high-powered automatic rifles, automatic shotguns and machine guns to applicants with rural or regional addresses. For the time being, city dwellers would be restricted to automatic handguns up to .45 calibre and other less capable weapons. Changes to firearms and alcohol regulations would be announced and implemented together, within a month.

Recognising the need to gain support from Australia's sporting authorities, the Team agreed America should dedicate US $500 million to supporting Australian sport annually during the foreseeable future. The American Ambassador would distribute these funds in ways most likely to optimise pro-American support.

Of the three remaining items referred to by the President as, '*national sedatives*'—religion, gambling and drugs—two seemed likely to be manageable. Using guidance provided by The Office, the Ambassador would negotiate with leading figures influencing Australian religion and gambling, offering to maintain existing safeguards and exemptions in exchange for overt support for the American takeover. If that policy looked like failing a limited range of additional assistance might be negotiated. For anything further than that, America would abandon carrots and start applying the stick.

Drugs were another matter. The President made clear Australia would not be allowed to drag America down by becoming a source of '...*any heavy drugs including, by the way, all designer drugs*'. Cannabis could be legalised but no other concessions would be made.

The US federal law enforcement machinery would act decisively in its anti-drug role. Any drug-pusher wanting a bare-knuckle fight with the United States would get exactly that. Obvious offenders would be declared aliens who might or might not be granted a trial, eventually, after spending years occupying cages at Guantanamo Bay. The Ambassador was to ensure this message was well publicised.

In the Transition Team's eyes, they'd covered the main items and the President had agreed to all strategies. Implementation programs were achievable. Information would be leaked to the Australian public gradually, beginning with the good news on alcohol and guns. Less palatable news could come later.

And there were, they agreed, categories of less palatable news. Among them were imposition of American labour laws including those covering minimum wages, medical and pharmaceutical entitlements, social security entitlements, and laws governing banking and finance. In every case, a few wealthy and influential Australians would benefit.

The respective Secretaries were put on notice that they had 12 months in which to arrange educational awareness programs with Australian officials and to have computerised data bases ready for registering Australians as citizens of the United States. The Australians were to be given Social Security numbers.

Some officials in the Administration believed this was a dangerous game. The US was counting on its investment in good-will, supplemented by consistent support from the Australian sources of national sedation, to overwhelm an eventual avalanche of bad news. However, it was a once-in-a-lifetime opportunity. *'Failure'* according to the President *'is not an option'* whatever that was supposed to mean.

One of many sensible decisions taken was to minimise potential interference from the invariably fractious Congress. Legislation to consolidate Australia's status as a new American State would be drafted but not presented for debate until Australia had been so decisively incorporated that opposition would have been political suicide.

N-Day Retrospective

4.06 AM.

Shrill ringing from her bedside telephone interrupted Elizabeth's deep and pleasant sleep. Frowning with annoyance, she'd reached from beneath the comfortable warmth of her doona and picked-up.

The caller was a colleague, a specialist surgeon. He was pleading with her to drive a two-hour trip to the town of Bowral and assist with a delicate surgical procedure.

His patient, who had several intrathoracic abnormalities, had been severely injured in a motor vehicle accident during the previous evening. It had taken several hours for the resident medical staff to diagnose the issues and identify associated complications.

The patient was too fragile for transportation to a major Sydney hospital. Doctor Gnagnarra's experience would be invaluable.

Wide awake, Elizabeth moved decisively. During the three paces from bed to her en-suite bathroom she'd hauled off her cotton nightshirt, dropping it on the floor. After splashing briefly beneath a warmish shower, she towelled herself almost dry.

Back in the bedroom, she stepped into the first pair of knickers visible in her dressing-table drawer. Deciding yesterday's bra would be good enough, she snatched it from the bedside chair, stretching it around her chest, fastening two clips at the rear.

Grabbing a plain, white dress from a hanger in the wardrobe, she cursed quietly while fumbling with the row of buttons down its front. Sneakers slipped onto bare feet completed her preparation.

Six minutes after finishing the phone call she was grabbing three muesli bars on her way through the kitchen to her car. She was ready.

Driving along the Federal Highway, Elizabeth remembered agreeing to meet Allen for dinner that evening. It was too early to telephone and let him know what was happening.

She decided it would still be inconveniently early by the time she was due to scrub-up for the surgery at Bowral. Then she'd be effectively entombed in an operating theatre for up to six or seven hours. Afterwards she could phone him to explain and apologise. She'd be too tired to safely drive back to Canberra and so would stay overnight in Bowral.

Then, 16 years of intensive medical training and discipline kicked in. Ignoring Allen or any other personal issues, she began focussing on the medical challenge ahead.

6.30 AM.

In Bowral, she met other members of the medical team. Together they attended a pre-surgery briefing, examined X-rays, reviewed the results of 'bloods' and other test results, before scrubbing-up.

8.01 AM.

Their already unconscious patient was further anaesthetised. The first incision was made.

The surgical team had anticipated some challenges but were unprepared for what confronted them. Procedures, some proceeding in parallel, soon became more complicated than they had imagined. Twice, their patient died on the operating table and had to be revived.

Normally, they'd have postponed further surgery until another day but they'd gone beyond the point of no return. Wishing they'd never started, guided partly by knowledge and experience, and at times by intuition and innovation, they pressed on, hour after meticulous and exhausting hour.

10.00 AM.

At a location almost midway between the southern tip of New Zealand's South Island and its closest point on the Australian mainland, a region in which there was minimal sea-surface activity, a sleek, menacing submarine had been waiting, silent, deeply submerged. Its crew now released a small and unobtrusive antenna which floated to the ocean's surface. The apparatus was capable of receiving signals transmitted from any of three satellites, their orbits having been optimised to provide continuous coverage of the area surrounding the boat's position.

On receiving a prearranged signal, the space-based surveillance platforms began transmitting encrypted reports. They indicated there was no conflicting surface shipping near, or sailing toward, the submarine's position. This was relayed into the hull of the vessel via a wire connected to the floating antenna.

After calmly, professionally, absorbing the surface-shipping situation report, the submarine's captain ordered his weapons officer to confirm completion of final checks on one of his missiles and the single warhead it would be carrying.

A few minutes later the weapons officer confirmed, for the third time over the past 12 hours, that all systems were functioning. He also reported the target coordinates programmed into the missile as 35°17'0.46"S, 149°7'41.05"E. Following a strict and often-rehearsed procedure, the captain checked those coordinates against his orders and agreed that they were correct.

10.30 AM.

The submarine began discharging its seawater ballast, enabling a slow and elegant ascent, stopping when it reached periscope depth.

10.50 AM.

With his boat suspended and motionless, the captain gave the up-periscope order. Then, occupying a seat attached to the column of the periscope, he pressed his forehead firmly against its optical access point. Slowly, he rotated through 360 degrees several times, selecting a different magnification strength with each rotation. His cautious reconnaissance confirmed the report he'd received from the satellites. No surface shipping could be seen.

11.00 AM.

Earlier that morning, the embassy's Chief Security Officer had informed Allen that the Ambassador wanted a short paper on living conditions for indigenous Australians in the country's north-west. Allen, as usual focused and concentrating on the immediate task, was preparing the briefing note when, needing further guidance on one aspect, he went to the First Secretary's office.

11.04 AM.

The receptionist, a locally employed civilian, told him the First Secretary together with the Ambassador and others had gone to a meeting with members of the Australian Cabinet.

She was sorry she couldn't assist him but the combination of that meeting, together with other conference commitments, meant no American diplomatic personnel were present at the Embassy.

It took Allen almost two minutes to deduce what was happening. Most of the diplomatic staff were at an international conference, their spouses were out or town attending some thinly disguised junkets in Batemans Bay or Pago Pago. The few remaining diplomats were at Parliament House.

11.06 AM.

No, no, no! Australia's Parliament House has an Emergency Security Facility, a shelter from nuclear-attacks. That's where they've gone.'

The nuclear option, is imminent. There's been a breakdown in communications. My superiors assumed the Ambassador would pass me details of planned timing for the detonation. The Ambassador probably assumed my own channels had tipped me off.

'The bastards, the incompetent fools, the idiots', he raged, running along a corridor and then down four flights of fire-escape stairs, moving faster than the installed elevator.

God almighty, we had three scenarios and those stupid Stateside bastards chose the nuclear option. Why, why, why?

I should've picked it. No discussion regarding options. Light southerly wind to blow crap away from the embassy region. Perfect conditions.

That lunatic of a President must've had a hand in this. Jesus! How could he have been elected! How could they be so damned crazy?

Racing across a courtyard to the diplomats' garage, grabbing at his cell-phone he ripped his shirt pocket. Speed-dialling Elizabeth's number he was connected to a mechanical voice saying, 'The person you have called is not available.'

Oh God! She was supposed to be at her apartment today, writing a medical paper. Perhaps she's turned her phone off to avoid distractions. I'll try there. If she's not home I'll have no Plan B.

Leaping into his allocated silver sedan, ignoring the beep-beep-beep reminder to buckle his seat belt, Allen accelerated toward the Embassy gate.

His vehicle carried a portable sensor designed to trigger the reinforced steel gate's opening mechanism.

11.07 AM.

Within the comfortable, dimly lighted, almost somnolent atmosphere of the submarine's control centre, facing their respective fire-control panels, the submarine's captain and his weapons officer twisted their independent arming keys one half of a turn to the left. As their indicator lights glowed green, they each pressed their red-coloured *Fire* command buttons.

The confirmed command activated a protective panel on the vessel's deck. It sprang open as a burst of energy converted a tank of water into a high-pressure cloud of scalding steam. The steam forced their missile to the sea surface where its first stage rocket ignited. The now-activated weapon began accelerating into its supersonic trajectory.

'Hurry, hurry, hurry up, move it.' Allen ranted as the inanimate gate slowly slid open. 'Oh God! How did I get involved? I should've been fighting these lunatics, not supporting them.'

As soon as his car could fit through a still-widening gap Allen floored the accelerator. His high-speed, reckless and futile dash toward Elizabeth's apartment had begun.

Allen, focussed on saving his beautiful, beloved Elizabeth, was accelerating along Torrens Street. The weapon arrived overhead. It detonated, precisely as planned.

After almost nine hours in theatre, the team had declared their surgery successful, agreeing to sew-up, clean up and send the patient to an intensive care ward for observation.

Walking from theatre, Elizabeth commented 'That was the most stressful medical event I have ever been involved with. I'm exhausted.' Her remark triggered a chorus of same heres, and me toos.

Elizabeth and her medical colleagues then strolled into an environment they'd never imagined. Everyone, other doctors, nurses, administrative staff, wardsmen, cleaners, all of them, were in shock.

Symptoms varied from compulsive sobbing through to slow and almost mechanistic attempts to perform simple functions. Every face, regardless of race, had paled. Nobody could have been entrusted with any task requiring skill or precision.

'What the hell has happened?' Elizabeth asked a green-dressing-gown-clad patient. Ashen faced, with mouth agape, dribbling, he pointed to a television set in an adjoining waiting room.

Approaching the room, Elizabeth heard the dialogue before she saw the screen.

'*There is now no doubt the City of Canberra, Australia's Capital, has been destroyed by a nuclear weapon.*'

With her eyes fixed compulsively to the screen, fighting against the need to retch, she sat, very slowly, on the upholstered arm of a vacant chair.

According to media reports, central Canberra remained radioactive. But Sydney-based television crews had reached the less damaged outer suburbs before releasing drones to record the worst affected areas.

From televised images it was clear that the Hyatt Hotel where Allen was staying and the American Embassy where he worked had been obliterated. Her Braddon apartment and her church were unrecognisable components of widespread debris.

Elizabeth wondered if, by some miracle, Allen might have been out of town and could have survived. Trembling from head to toe, she ran to her temporarily allocated locker, retrieved her mobile phone and called him. There was no answer, no response.

Returning to the waiting room, swallowing hard, trying not to sob and almost succeeding, she watched and listened intently to a message from the President of the United States.

> '*At this moment of utmost gravity, I speak as President of the United States of America to men and women throughout the world, but especially to my dear brothers and sisters in Australia.*'
>
> '*To say I am shocked by this horrific tragedy would be an understatement. That such an event could have happened to people who are so close as to almost be members of my personal family seems inconceivable.*'
>
> '*I promise you not only America's prayers but much more besides. The United States will provide emergency assistance in the first instance. Some of it is already on its way to you, even as I speak.*'
>
> '*We will not rest until we understand in full detail what has happened, and until Canberra has been reconstructed and is back on its feet again, regardless of cost or effort required.*'

Global media channels heralded the President's address as a masterpiece in diplomacy and empathy, despite having been delivered spontaneously. This, from a man whose public pronouncements had often seemed insensitive or abrasive!

Further newscasts followed. There had been 50 000 to perhaps 100 000 fatal casualties. Nations around the world were sharing their grief, especially Japan where memories of Hiroshima and Nagasaki had burned deeply into the national psyche.

Then the analyses began. From scant information came the incredible story that the Australian Government had pressured the United States to clandestinely provide an arsenal of nuclear weapons.

The first weapon had accidentally detonated while being flown, symbolically, over the City of Canberra on its way to a classified destination. The American aircraft transporting the weapon had been destroyed. Its crew had perished.

Opinionated television interviewers, typically experts in every flavour-of-the-moment topic, began deriding the story. The Australian Government would never do anything so irresponsible, so stupid. China or Russia must have been involved. Why was America taking responsibility and protecting them?

But, as the evening wore on, the United States, releasing fact after detail after fact, confirmed the original version as accurate. *That* was the truth.

Having survived for more than 12 hours on three muesli bars, eaten while driving toward Bowral, and several canisters of liquid sipped while she was operating, Elizabeth felt ill and faint.

Stumbling to a room reserved for relatives of critically ill patients, she dropped onto its narrow bed, too tired to think except to wish she too was dead.

Later that evening, Elizabeth's colleagues assembled a basic survival kit for her, realising she had no additional clothing, and no possessions other than her car, handbag and mobile telephone. She was invited to remain in the hospital's accommodation until something better turned up.

ENLIGHTENMENT

Eighteen months after the Canberra Event, Doctor Elizabeth Gnagnarra emerged from yet another operating theatre, this one in the inner-Sydney suburb of Randwick where she was freelancing as a surgeon.

Discarding her surgical mask and gloves into a trash-bin provided, she dumped her blood-spattered gown into a receptacle marked *Surgical Laundry* before walking across an enclosed garden and onto the canteen reserved for senior medical staff.

Sipping a much-needed mug of coffee brewed from medium-grind *Folgers*, she reflected morosely on the unpredictability of life.

Hell. I trained for so long and with such dedication to become a surgeon.

Never once did I consider that almost one in three of my procedures would involve gun-shot wounds. Now I'm a highly experienced practitioner.

Is this how I'm to spend my days; finding and removing bullets or pellets?

Shotgun wounds seem the worst. I can remove only some of the damned pellets without causing even more damage. The residual lead will take its toll. As for repairing split and fractured human organs, sewing the ruptured veins and arteries, all caused by bullets, that's not what I signed-up for.

Modifications to Australian gun-ownership controls had led to a bloodbath. Australians were unaccustomed to easy firearm access. Gun owners were making their mark, often with fatal consequences. Intentional assassinations, retaliations, family feuds, experimentation, immaturity, exuberance and occasional mass shootings had been occurring at levels above those recorded in America.

Some churches started lobbying for the return of strict gun-control legislation. Elizabeth wondered if she should join them.

But, before they could gain traction, the Born Again Australian Rifle Association (BAARA) retaliated, generously offering a nation-wide program of firearms safety training. A series of firing ranges was to be established so people could practice gun safety while improving their deadly accuracy. This was endorsed by a business which franchised a string of newly established stores selling guns and ammunition.

Further confusing the picture, and conveniently splitting opposition, another program was interwoven and somehow made to appear compatible with weapons training. It highlighted the physical, moral and spiritual dangers of abortion, a disgusting procedure soon to become illegal throughout Australia.

BAARA then began a *teacher protection and enhancement* trial in which schoolteachers were encouraged to carry automatic pistols. But it was abandoned after one teacher, fed-up with the taunts from a particularly obnoxious student, drew her weapon and shot him dead. Other teachers had threatened students with the same outcome. In response, the students together with some of their parents started planning reprisals.

Still in a reflective mood, Elizabeth experienced one of her periodic but unwelcome flashbacks. Over recent months they'd emerged without warning at least once every few days. She wished they'd stop entirely.

In her imagination, she reverted to one week after the Canberra Event. Still living in the hospital at Bowral, she'd used her phone to access a dedicated news website. It included an updated list of Canberra-based American citizens and officials who had survived the event and a second list of those now officially certified as dead.

Looking down the most recent fatality list, her finger had touched the screen where it displayed the name:

Ivory, Allen Jefferson, US Dept of Commerce

The memory shocked Elizabeth back to the present moment, as it always did, away from intense pain and back to a dulled, sickening, melancholy reality.

———

Her emotional health aside, professionally Elizabeth's life had never been better. She was busy. Her income under recently imposed American medical and medical-insurance arrangements was almost four times her previous earnings. But she felt like a loser.

The reduction in alcohol taxes, leading to a massive increase in consumption, had not only anesthetised her mob, her extended aboriginal family, it'd almost obliterated them.

Easy access to high-powered automatic firearms accounted for some others. Chris, her brother, had been a victim. Months after his death she learned he'd been shot in the head while attempting to prevent the rape of a young boy.

Her mob, or what remained of it, had abandoned their traditional tribal grounds. Much of the wisdom and traditions of aunties and uncles had evaporated. She'd lost key parts of her inherited dreaming, the wellspring of her aboriginality. For Elizabeth, living was new form of focused materialistic existence.

In passing, she'd learned there would be no insurance paid out for the destruction of her apartment and its contents in Braddon. Her insurance company, operating on the principle of '*never write a policy if there's a realistic possibility that we'll have to meet a claim*', had argued successfully that Elizabeth's insurance policies excluded damage caused by war. Because a nuclear weapon was a weapon of war, the damage was not compensable.

This, however, was the least of Elizabeth's concerns. Being honest with herself, she didn't give a damn.

Prominent among her growing inventory of woes, was that American medical insurance and pharmaceutical policies had been imposed on a society unprepared to accommodate them. In many cases homeowners were being forced to sell their houses to pay for surgeries, medicines or both.

Peter and Jean Braithwaite, a married couple Elizabeth had first met at a seminar explaining the new medical insurance arrangements, were classic examples.

Peter, a delivery-van driver, now lived with his two children beneath a blue tarpaulin roof stretched across several wooden pallets. Four more wooden pallets, designed for use by fork-lifts, provided a floor, keeping them slightly above a layer of mud and stinking effluent.

The Braithwaites survived, *in situ*, by accepting food every second day from the Salvation Army's brand-new Cart of Hope. Peter dared not seek paid employment because he'd have to leave the children unprotected. The chance of one or both kiddies falling fatally ill was already risky enough.

They were merely one family among the thousands whose tents and other forms of crude accommodation now dotted Centennial, Hyde Park and the foreshore areas of Sydney.

Unoccupied and depressed, Peter often recalled the afternoon he'd arrived home from work to find his wife, Jean, in tears.

'I've been feeling ill lately but didn't want to worry you. I had some tests and they showed I have stage-three pancreatic cancer. The tests are no longer on the pharmaceutical benefits list. They cost $5 400, which is most of our savings.'

That was the start of their financial shocks.

Soon, Jean wasn't strong enough to continue working as a check-out lady at the local supermarket. Under new labour laws she'd become an unwilling contractor with no sickness or vacation entitlements.

Monthly chemotherapy, associated with a mandatory overnight stays in hospital, would cost the family $7 240 on top of regular specialist fees.

Being prudent, they'd maintained private health insurance, despite high and regularly increasing premiums. But their application for reimbursement was rejected.

The letter, in part, read:

> We are obliged to draw your attention to Article XXIV, Section 27, Clause 5 of the policy you signed and committed to. As you should be aware, it states:
>
> No reimbursement will be made with respect to cancers or related malignancies which the claimant has allowed to progress to stage-three. There is a clear obligation on claimants to undertake regular and comprehensive examinations by one of our approved clinical providers and thus ensure such conditions are detected early in their development.

But the Braithwaite's were resilient people. They borrowed funds from Peter's parents then organised a second, and soon a third, mortgage on their house. Peter began two additional jobs. In total, he was working an average of 17 hours each day for six days each week, statistics which flowed into an improving Australian economic outlook.

Four months later, with Peter at work as usual, Jean attended the Cancer Clinic for her routine tests. They showed the progress of her cancer had slowed. Her forecast life expectancy was increased from 'about three months' to '18 months and possibly longer.'

Travelling home on a bus, Jean opened the envelope addressed to her local doctor and read revised prognosis. Conscious of the financial implications for her family, she sadly but calmly decided to kill herself.

Arriving home she wrote a note to Peter, retrieved a container of weedkiller from their small garden shed, poured herself a glassful, sat on the marital bed and drank it.

Later, Peter arrived home to cook the evening meal before heading to his evening job. From the mailbox he retrieved a formal-looking envelope, stuffed it into his pocket, then walked along the garden path to his wood-panelled front door.

Two wailing children greeted him, each grabbing one of his legs. *'Mummy's dead, mummy's dead, she's dead.'*

Moving carefully to avoid injuring the clinging children, Peter walked to the bedroom. His darling beautiful Jean, fully clothed, was lying on the bed. Her blanched face, contorted into a chilling snarl, reflected the agony she'd endured during her final conscious moments.

On the bedside table, was an empty glass and a bottle labelled *'Caution. Weedkiller. Poison. Concentrate. Avoid all contact with skin'.* Her white pillow, splattered with blood and vomit, testified to her body's instinctive attempt at survival. Jean had won, or lost, as she'd resolutely forced herself to persist and swallow a fatal dose.

Her handwritten note signed with *'every bit of my deep love for you and the children'* explained why she had to die.

Peter could never account for his next move. He sat on the bed beside Jean's still-warm corpse and calmly opened his mail. The enclosed correspondence was headed, *Bankruptcy at Creditor's Petition.*

An assessment had been made of his property value, his debts and his capacity to service his financial obligations. The conclusion drawn was that Peter had become insolvent and had no capacity to trade his way out of his mounting debt.

He was invited to sign papers attached and relinquish all claims to ownership of the house. He would then be required to vacate within 21 days, although a gratuity of $2 000 would be provided if the house was in a *'clean and rentable condition.'* Alternatively, the matter would be decided by due legal process.

———

The combination of new and restrictive medical and pharmaceutical regulations applied nationally. In Hobart, Perth, Adelaide, Melbourne and Brisbane also, thousands of formerly employed homeowners became destitute and began living under the ubiquitous blue-plastic tarpaulins. In every such locality there was minimal access to toilets or to water for bathing or for washing clothes. They couldn't hygienically store or cook food, if they could obtain some.

On hot and humid days they'd sweat without relief. As the weather turned colder, they'd huddle together in odoriferous proximity. Suitable clothing was scarce, sufferers from dysentery and pneumonia abundant.

Babies and the elderly became the default victims of a demographic cleansing process. People with physical or intellectual disabilities were trapped in situations too horrific to describe. The strong and able-bodied survived, just.

Despite '*a few regrettable situations*', categorised as '*teething problems*', this aspect of the takeover strategy was succeeding. The economic framework was creating a population of workers, commonly employed on two or more jobs to make ends meet, desperately trying to support their families, prepared to move anywhere and do almost anything.

The ghettoes provided an ideal breeding ground for a new underclass of uneducated children and youths. Soon they'd be required as domestic servants, window cleaners and shoe-shine boys.

Every move to suppress workers increased the wealth of employers and investors, most of whom were *winners*, to use the in-fashion word. National accounts improved; almost full employment was achieved for those able to seek work.

Opportunities abounded for the major Stateside retailers and other businesses, most of them able to supplant Australian competitors by taking advantage of economies available from massive commercial scales. This led to a minor and politically popular bonanza on Wall Street.

As the President said '*What better demonstration of the benefits of capitalism could possibly be found?*'

But for every Australian winner there were at least 50 losers. Under different circumstances the social and economic disruption could have boiled into civil warfare, especially as the Australian population was becoming increasingly well-armed.

However, Allen Ivory's prescient identification of Australia's national sedatives had led to the emergence of skilled public-opinion manipulators from the stables of professional sport, gambling, religion and alcohol.

GRATIFICATION

Enthusiastic supporters of the new leap into Australian prosperity were bombarding a vulnerable majority from every angle. Poverty was good. Jesus himself had been materially poor but rich in spirit. For those still unconvinced, the phrase '*work will make you free*' was resuscitated although, for reasons understood by few, the Jewish community seemed unsettled by it.

Gambling through lotteries offered potential for an even easier path to wealth for 0.0001 per cent of the population. If none of that was happening for you, well, why not relax with a few Aussie beers! And then there was always the exciting distraction of football or cricket.

Confused, dispossessed, bankrupted and homeless Australians were getting the message. It was drummed into them, day and night. *Failures* could become *winners*. *Everyone* could seek life, liberty and the pursuit of happiness.

Employment opportunities, combined with cheap alcohol and readily available firearms, were warmly welcomed in the Australian north, demonstrating once again that Allen Ivory's reading of the national psyche had been perceptive.

Participating in a 24/7 work schedule, thousands of Australians contributed to building combined US Army and Air Force bases near to

Darwin and Port Hedland. The capital works were completed in record time and within budget. A third base at Katherine was almost half finished.

Echoing many of his predecessors, one politician from Darwin said 'This is bloody marvellous. We'll leave the southern nanny-States for dead!'

And so a new mongrel nation began limping along, a veneer of Americanism camouflaging a rapidly decaying and dysfunctional Australian society.

More bad news awaited.

Satisfied that Australia had been sufficiently Americanised for the time being, and with two of the required military bases in Australia having full operational status, Washington's Department of Commerce began adjusting Australia's mineral export quotas. Iron ore, bauxite and coal exports to China were cut drastically, then increased, then cut again.

This didn't interfere with Chinese manufacturing because China already had massive mineral reserves and stockpiles. However, sales of these minerals to India, one of China's main commercial competitors, alarmed China as did America's signalled determination to curtail all or most of China's trade and manufacturing.

For Western Australians the effects of Washington's on-again/off-again export strategy were catastrophic. Before long, the mining and raw materials processing industries collapsed, unable to survive rapid fluctuations in demand. Investments in mining, transport and processing became meaningless and almost valueless. The State Government's capacity to collect revenue from taxation evaporated.

Workforces, comprising fly-in-fly-out workers from Perth, disbanded. Consequences flowed to and curtailed almost every form of economic activity, from airlines to tertiary services, construction and retailing.

Entire departments of civil servants, formerly employed by the State of Western Australia, were dismissed. Education and police services were reduced by half. Remnants of the Commonwealth Government were powerless to assist.

For different reasons the outcome was similar in South Australia. The American policy of giving high priority to water for upstream cash-crops had resulted in the River Murray being reduced to a trickle before it reached the State border.

With water resources already strained in '*the driest State in the driest inhabited continent on Earth*', the loss of more than a third of its water supply was catastrophic. The planned nuclear-powered purification plant had not eventuated. Domestic water reticulation was no longer viable, sewage systems ceased to function or became unreliable, businesses closed.

Many South Australians abandoned their houses and moved, homeless, to the tent ghettoes of the eastern States, hoping to find work. This was *Grapes of Wrath* on steroids.

Across Australia's east coast, coal production fluctuations caused numerous mine closures, although the harm was muted by opportunities for labouring jobs in agriculture and fisheries. But an influx of desperate interstate immigrants led to employment bargaining. Newcomers began accepting weekly cash incomes at amounts below the new and barely survivable minimum wage.

Australian trade-unions attempted occasional strike action and other protests, but the growing hordes of economic refugees guaranteed a plentiful supply of low-cost labour. Nobody seemed to care what the unions did or tried to do.

One potentially major protest march was organised in Sydney. It disbanded when soldiers of the Australian National Guard (a new name for the former Australian Army) fired into the crowd, wounding 17 people.

As usual, the police and military organisations had become enforcers. They followed a long, if not always proud, tradition of supporting whoever or whatever was pulling the strings of political power.

America's plans were working. What could possibly go wrong?

In Washington, the Commerce Secretary, was delighted. Unused Australian resources would remain in the ground, providing a wonderful strategic reserve for the future.

At a micro-level, one of many pleasing outcomes was that South Australia's most famous export, its fine wines, had collapsed due to water restrictions. This opened opportunities for Californian vintners.

Overall, the Australian labour force had been comprehensively castrated and was looking increasing similar to its American equivalent. Some Australian individuals and organisations had benefited magnificently from the new arrangements and they were keen to consolidate their wealth by maintaining the new normal.

REPUDIATION

Despite this avalanche of good news, the President, having surfaced from his orgy of self-congratulations, was becoming paranoid again.

American analysts were certain China would not stand for blatant American interference with its economy. But the intelligence agencies had been unable to detect so much as a hint of Chinese intentions.

Perhaps, as one operative suggested '...they've recognised America's superiority and are going to swallow their medicine without a fuss.'

Others, more attuned to the inevitable aggression and competition of international relations, disagreed. China *had to* be planning *something*.

At yet another meeting of intelligence chiefs the Director of the National Security Agency put it succinctly. 'We are fairly confident we managed to spoof or otherwise negate the missile monitoring systems of most countries. They seem to be accepting our cover story about a nuclear accident in Australia. We are also highly confident our activities were visible to Chinese and Russian space-based observation systems. They know exactly what we did.'

'The Russians don't give a damn. They realise we have China in the crosshairs. That suits them just fine. They've never trusted the Chinese.'

'In any case, the damage we caused to NATO, when prominent

European nations resigned from it, has given the Russians opportunities to resume westward expansion. They should be happy as pigs in mud.'

The FBI Director, a West Point graduate, agreed and felt it was safe to assume there would be a military response from China, an assessment the military chiefs endorsed.

'What we've lost sight of is the extent to which totalitarian regimes will go to when protecting or even consolidating their own grip on national power.'

'In the Second World War the USSR threw men into battle like handfuls of chaff. They lost 22 million. A decade earlier they starved about seven million Ukrainians to death simply as part of an economic restructuring. China's been the same. Mao starved millions of his own people to death.'

'If we open the totalitarian can of worms we'll be in for a fight without precedent. If it includes nukes then it'd pay to remember that America is the most concentrated, most industrialised nation on the planet. While we have massive capabilities we are also a target-rich environment.'

These and similar disturbing analyses persuaded the Administration to focus on preparation for a possible Chinese military response, hopefully one that would not escalate into nuclear conflict.

The forward bases at Darwin and Port Hedland had full operational status. Completion of the third base at Katherine was accelerated. Plans were made to call up all US Reserve forces.

An attack on Continental United States was considered an outside possibility, but nevertheless a possibility.

With the United States' machinery of government now focused on preparations for a shooting war, the first hint of Chinese retaliation slid beneath the official radar.

A previous Administration had forced several automobile manufactures to abandon plans for assembling vehicles outside the United States. Those arrangements had resulted in more American jobs and a higher output of *Made in the USA* products. But the policy had also increased America's economic and technological dependence on China.

Suddenly and unexpectedly, components essential for maintaining the robotic equipment used in motor vehicle manufacture became either unavailable or in short supply. Automobile production slowed and was unable to meet demand.

Simultaneously, and still without so much as a diplomatic note of protest, China stopped exporting a range of electronic safety and convenience components. They'd become accepted as standard automobile features.

A limited number of cars still rolled off American assembly lines, but they lacked backing cameras, speed-sign recognition, proximity warning, electronic braking, entry-key recognition, and other accessories. Within weeks, the myth of a good old mom-and-apple-pie, made in the USA, automobile began crumbling.

Surrendering to public pressure, as he put it, although public outrage would have been closer to the mark, the President issued directions allowing increased imports of European, Korean and Japanese cars. But China had already blocked that move.

While America was focused on preparing for a shooting war, China had been busy offering international automobile manufacturers its own version of *a carrot or a stick* or, as one commentator put it, *a rice bowl or a turd-noodle soup*.

China was ready and able to increase its imports of European, Japanese and Korean automobiles to levels allowing continuity of current production. But, as it also warned, any increased exports to the United States would attract component restrictions tailored to inflict maximum harm on production capability.

When replying to American overtures seeking increased imports, the major international manufacturers had no option but to say *'Sorry, we'd love to help, but... And, by the way, when will the blockade on Iran's oil be lifted?'*

Shaking their collective heads in disbelief, American automobile manufactures met for a strategic conference.

They agreed they could continue building automobile bodies with completed interiors, wheels, tyres, windows and engines of various sizes. It would be possible to ramp-up American production of previously imported components. In fact, they could restore productivity, complete with all common accessories, in about four to six years although there would be price penalties for consumers.

Meanwhile, American cars, technologically similar to the old clunkers still being driven in Havana, could be built and would sell for about twice the price of fully optioned luxury vehicles.

On the up-side, executives recognised that these new *national-environmental cars* would have fewer components and so high reliability could be a sales feature. American drivers would also have the pleasure of *really driving* once again. American cars would be *made in America and by Americans.*

Ford and General Motors planned their new strategies accordingly but Chrysler, never a company to follow the herd, decided to produce several variants of a Soviet-era automobile known as the *Lada Niva.*

China's next move was to expand restrictions on its exports to include the integrated circuits used in America for a vast range of devices, despite many of the finished products being labelled, *Made in the USA.*

Some of these components were central to aircraft manufacture and servicing. Production of new commercial aircraft, most intended for export, ceased except for the simplest single-engine recreational aircraft. Clients fled to factories in Europe, China and Russia, each of which offered such well-tailored services they seemed likely to retain their new customer base into the future.

The shockwaves didn't stop there.

Executives in America's armaments industries, the world's largest, were aghast to discover they'd unwittingly been using Chinese circuit boards, producing items on lathes enabled by embedded Chinese components and using Chinese precision measuring equipment for quality control.

Production of some weapons and equipment stopped. The performance of other armaments, especially those with precision guidance capacities, was reduced. America's reputation as a reliable supplier of high-end military equipment declined.

Collateral problems soon surfaced. Spare parts needed to support farm tractors, harvesters and road building machinery were suddenly unavailable. No longer could a skilled man fix almost anything using his spanners, a welder and good old American know-how. The modern machinery was too complicated, too intricate.

Each blow to the American economy, and American pride, led to unrest. Thousands of skilled and semi-skilled workers lost their jobs. Increases in the automotive industry's labour force merely modified the problems for Detroit and a few other cities. As had happened in Australia, negative multiplier effects rippled across the entire economy.

A shortage of popular consumer items such as cellphones, headphones and microphones attracted both attention and animosity from university students and, later, their professors. This led to hard questions being asked.

The Administration reacted with a high-intensity campaign designed to blame China for America's woes.

But economists in the universities began asking what had motivated China to change its trading policy, especially as this must also be damaging the Chinese economy. The academics also speculated on the Administration's obviously reduced capacity to collect revenue. They started wondering how much additional borrowing was happening to keep the US of A afloat. How would it be serviced or repaid?

Predictably, the Administration punched back with a barrage of abstract insults, accusing its interrogators of being *left wing*, *anti-capitalist*, *anti-American* and *usual suspects*.

But the academics struck again, demonstrating though social media that their unrest was aimed at shoring-up America, not damaging it as the Administration seemed to have been doing.

China, still low-key, responded to the blame game by sending a cordial letter to the United States Embassy in Chaoyang, inviting the Ambassador to an informal meeting with its Foreign and Commerce Ministers.

The meeting, held in a room lavishly decorated with red and shining gold on every surface, involved only the head officials and their interpreters from the China side.

It began in the customary manner. The Ambassador was recognised by name and formal title, then honoured with typically stiff Chinese bows from the shoulders only.

Invited to sit, he was asked 'How is your wife coping with the humid weather? Is your daughter still happy at Princeton?'

Also, and intended to convey a clear message, 'We noted you bought some powdered porcupine quill from the traditional pharmacist in Quang Chi Road on Tuesday. Did it help with your tinnitus?'

Hearing the Ambassador's positive response, the Chinese officials decided enough *guanxi,* or empathy, had been established and moved directly to business.

Their Foreign Minster opened with 'We know when the United States fired the nuclear armed missile that destroyed Canberra in Australia. We can give you the precise coordinates in the Tasman Sea where the weapon was launched. We know with better than 90 per cent confidence which of your submarines was involved.'

The Ambassador, having never been briefed on the Australian initiative, contained his sense of shock and dismay saying nothing.

The Minister continued 'Candidly, we do not care what happened to Canberra. Australia has for decades been your puppet State, not ours. For us it is a source of raw materials and a venue for real estate and agricultural investment.'

'Had you bombed Sydney or Melbourne, cities in which important Chinese people own many investment properties, the situation would have been different; but you didn't. Why not? We do not know or care. Our rural investments in Australia have profited nicely from your economic reforms.'

'However, Your Excellency, and this is intended to be a significant "however", we note your Administration has been interfering with the flow of raw materials from Australia to China.'

'You have also been dumping raw materials in India at prices below production cost.'

'We regard those actions as examples of blatant economic aggression. If normal arrangements are not resumed within 30 Days from today, China will reduce its exports to your nation of clothing, footwear and glassware, causing yet another spike in your already uncomfortably high inflation index. We might also initiate other economic measures or additional responses.'

The Ambassador swallowed several times. He'd been raised from birth believing America was the most powerful nation on Earth. When America said *jump,* smart nations asked: *how high?* Yet, here were these communist skunks trying to lay down the law. Too shocked to respond, he proposed the meeting conclude while he sought directions from Washington DC.

A tall, broad-shouldered rancher from Texas, he'd been nominated for the diplomatic post in recognition of his two-million-dollar donation to the previous Republican election campaign. He'd accepted the appointment, imagining it would involve endless and pleasant social events some of which would be useful for establishing contacts to support the beef-export arm of his own business. Besides, wandering through Beijing wearing his trademark white, ten-gallon hat offered opportunities to introduce the poor Chinks to some genuine American culture.

Ill equipped to engage in a complicated diplomatic tussle, he remembered the Secretary of State's pre-departure instruction to, 'contact me through the direct and encrypted email installed at the Embassy for anything significant and out of the ordinary.' This meeting seemed to qualify.

The reply from Washington DC arrived within an hour.

'All noted. Never refer to or argue about the Australian nuclear accident. Report directly to me with full details any other time it is raised, as you did on this occasion. Thank you. Maintain normal reporting to your established channels in my department without any, repeat any, discussion of the nuclear accident...'

Slumped into his red-leather chair, the Ambassador almost vomited. Six hours earlier he'd felt like a senior, trusted representative of the United States of America. Now he realised he was merely a pawn, moving one square at a time, in the dark, unable to glimpse the huge strategic game in which potent moves were being played out.

'Damn.' he muttered 'Well at least I know we intentionally nuked Canberra. What the hell were we thinking? Is the President crazy?'

REORIENTATION

Regardless of economic turmoil, in the United States the banking and stockbroking businesses continued making money. Adroit, accommodating and manipulative they'd moved funds from the manufacturing sector into bankruptcy administration, foreclosure specialists, used-car-parts and automotive repair shops, all of which were onto a bonanza.

Simultaneously, American capital began flowing abroad. Stock exchanges as diverse as Singapore, Sarajevo, London, Paris and Moscow rose toward record trading levels. The S&P Global, FTSE, MSCI and IPSA indexes boiled over.

The United States Treasury was horrified by the enthusiasm for investments through China's Shanghai and Shenzhen bourses. Financial markets were clearly betting on China to win the commodities brouhaha. But having loudly trumpeted the manifest benefits of capitalism and the uninhibited flow of capital, this Administration could only monitor the accelerating trend, depressed but impotent.

China's next step was to subtly use media channels to spread speculation about the possibility of floating its currency, without restraint. It then intensified the economic typhoon by releasing statements incapable of clear interpretation. Beijing claimed that popular speculation regarding China's currency '*might be*' premature, and later consolidated circulating rumours by asserting that '*no final decision had been taken*'.

As one senior Chinese economist said 'We need do nothing more. The international media is achieving our objectives. We will let the Americans harvest fish from their own peach tree.'

As the US dollar nosedived, the cost of imports into America of almost anything from anywhere skyrocketed. American domestic inflation climbed into the double figures and kept rising. Social unrest made the United States a dangerous destination. Widespread riots broke out.

Believing it had no option, the Administration responded with violence. Police, National Guards and the regular military forces were ordered to suppress '*this uprising of the communist minority*'. Live ammunition, mobile light-artillery, tanks and armoured vehicles together with riot suppression vehicles, were thrown into the fray.

But the tacticians' main problems were: which fray and where was it? Decentralised opposition from a uniformly hostile but uncoordinated citizenry meant the rebels could and did attack pubic facilities at will. Military and para-military forces were often taken by surprise when confronted by cooperating Whites, Blacks, Hispanics and Asians, many rioters being as well or better armed than their uniformed opponents.

Unfortunately for the Administration, increasing social and economic grievances applied equally to members of the police and military forces. Some uniformed personnel deserted, suspecting they'd been directed to fight against the Constitution, not for it.

Despite this, most members of the uniformed forces *were* willing to support the Administration and many uprisings were suppressed, eventually. But one undeniably serious incident occurred in New Orleans.

Standing on a platform in Louis Armstrong Park, an orator had urged his followers into defiant action.

'We have unemployment at 26 per cent in this State. Inflation is at 22 per cent. Interest rates on loans are skyrocketing. Decent and hardworking folk are losing their homes to the foreclosure bandits.'

'The President and his fellow travellers have declared an intifada on honest, decent Americans. We need a regime change and...'

A call on his cell phone interrupted the dialogue. It came from an outposted sentry who, leaning casually on her ornamental-iron front fence, looked like a conventional housewife. Several blocks away an assembled Police and National Guard force was on the move, she said.

The attackers, with live ammunition and flexible rules of engagement, started marching toward the Park. Trooping along Orleans Avenue as well as parallel streets across to Ursulines Avenue, they intended forcing the rebels down to the Mississippi River. There, the defeated rabble could choose to surrender, swim or die.

But, after a few orderly paces, a mob mentality emerged. Uniformed forces began charging ahead, leaping, whooping and yelling as they ran, eventually bursting enthusiastically onto an almost deserted Louis Armstrong Park.

The 'defeated rabble' was ready and waiting, having dispersed into two streams, one each side of the Park. With the attackers trapped in a killing field, the crowd unleashed a deadly barrage. Uniformed survivors found cover wherever possible and returned fire. Blue-grey smoke filled the air carrying the ammonia-like stench of cordite and other propellants.

One elderly rebel claimed he'd seen *'nothin' like this since Nam.'*

Not yet beaten, the uniformed contingent radioed a nearby USAF base asking for air support. But its commander, absent orders from a superior formation, refused to authorise bombing or strafing of American civilians.

However, two US Marine Corps gunship helicopters were transiting near to the battlefield. Overhearing the radioed conversation but lacking authorisation to join the fight, they offered to hover overhead in an attempt to intimidate the rebels.

The leading pilot, anticipating minimal opposition, descended for a terrain-following approach. But as he appeared above a line of trees bordering the park, the aircraft dissolved into a fireball. A surface-to-air missile had done the damage.

The remaining helicopter executed a tactical withdrawal.

Under no circumstances could such a weapon have found its way, legally, into civilian hands. But legality was never a priority for the local biker gang. Two years ago, it had acquired several SAM missiles through an arms dealer in Mexico. This, they'd thought, was a good opportunity to test one out.

After a firefight lasting 11 minutes, the uniformed forces surrendered.

They received a stern lecture on their moral responsibilities toward American citizens, were disarmed and directed to help in arranging medical support for the wounded. They then assisted with the body count.

Still in Sydney, Elizabeth, from her secure and comfortable apartment, watched the Australian social and economic disaster evolve and consolidate. Day after day the sight, sound and stench of a slowly disintegrating society gnawed into her and began fracturing the shell she'd built around her most sensitive emotions. Her humanity, never far from the surface, began re-emerging together with a slow, strong and unquenchable rage.

One blustery Monday morning she telephoned her medical associates and resigned from all positions, all commitments.

Ignoring their pleas to reconsider, Elizabeth drove her BMW to a used car lot and traded it for a truck-like Toyota Land Cruiser.

By week's end she'd arranged for her electricity meter to be read, paid the account, reimbursed her landlady with one month's rent in lieu of notice, packed her clothes along with other personal possessions and was ready to depart.

CONVERSION

Realising she had no capacity to influence the morass of misery dominating Sydney, Elizabeth had decided to find a community where she might make a positive difference.

So far as she could figure the most neglected, the least visible, the lowest of the low, were her aboriginal brothers and sisters. Having heard that the few remaining members of her mob had drifted into a settlement located in the Northern Territory, about an hour's drive east of Tennant Creek township, she headed there.

After five days of driving alone, struggling to stay awake at the wheel, Elizabeth found the remnants of her old mob. They and other strays had settled on Mordiloc tribal lands where their presence had been tolerated, even to some extent welcomed, by the traditional tribal owners.

'Why not?' had asked one Mordiloc elder when questioned by his wife. 'Haven't we got lot of land? We can share a bit. Plenty to go around.'

Elizabeth's new home, a location unbaptised by a postal address, would have daunted the most determined immigrant. Its fluctuating population averaged about 80 adults, more than 100 school-deprived children and at least two dogs for every human.

Four fibro-clad huts provided the epicentre of their settlement. The huts, long abandoned by their first occupants, had been constructed for seismic testing teams employed by a now-bankrupt oil exploration company.

Rougher, rusting dwellings, made from corrugated iron sheeting, were scattered across the equivalent of five city blocks. Typically, two or three ramshackle buildings would be clustered together, followed by a gap of a hundred metres or so to the next group.

Punctuating the landscape were skeletal remnants of abandoned structures, now too dilapidated to accommodate anybody. Their few usable components had been scavenged and added to more recent makeshift housing.

Most occupied buildings lacked doors. Window frames typically supported panes of broken glass, the gaps having been filled with cardboard from beer cartons. There were no streets, sidewalks or gutters. Four long-drop pits, when used, served as toilets for the community.

Two wells, each attached to its rusty-iron hand-pump, provided communal water. The water had a brownish tinge and a slightly acrid aroma. Some among the older generation claimed it could cure arthritis, although their limping gaits and contorted fingers suggested otherwise.

Impressively large piles of empty beer and wine bottles leaned against, possibly supported, the side walls of every building, occupied or abandoned.

Most shacks hosted rusting car or truck bodies. Engine blocks and differentials were also scattered about together with the remains of discarded children's toys and an occasional metal bed frame.

A huge bulldozer blade provided a windbreak for one of the *ad hoc* buildings. Nobody knew or cared who owned it or where it had come from.

A small petrol engine powered their one electrical generator. It was in high demand for recharging mobile phones with satellite linkages. Provided by the Federal Government in the pre-Canberra-bombing era, cell phones were popular with both adults and children.

This concentration of deprivation was, nevertheless, a happier place than any of the new tent communities in major cities. The aboriginal occupants were accustomed to poverty. With low expectations, they'd adjusted to it.

Whiteman's food, with its fat, sugar and other carbohydrates featured prominently in their typically unhealthy diets. But supplementation from Blackfella's tucker, including kangaroo, emu, snake, goanna and native fruits, provided some relief. Sharing was both a tradition and an obligation. Nobody starved.

Alcohol-induced oblivion dampened the occasional outburst of discontent, along with any subtle stirrings of enthusiasm or ambition. Many inhabitants, born to alcoholic mothers, experienced Foetal Alcohol Spectrum Disorder, resulting in intellectual limitations. This offered a frictionless glide into next-generation alcoholism as teenage-years coincided with juvenile pregnancies.

The setting for these unfortunates was an undulating landscape of grey-brown soil, weighed down by occasional clumps of large, rounded boulders, secured by salt bush, spinifex and the root systems of grotesquely distorted gum trees.

Elizabeth occupied one of the original fibro huts, now abandoned by the aboriginal community. Renovating it, she nailed five blue-plastic tarpaulins across its roof and around the worst two walls. Using a broom she'd made by binding dead grass to a stick, she swept her earthen floor before furnishing her new home with a stretcher, sleeping bag, a collapsible table and two folding chairs.

Scavenged wooden boxes supported her washbasin and spirit stove. From a rusting nail on one wall she hung a date-calendar. Advertising a Sydney pharmacy, it now comprised her total art collection. Elizabeth's indispensable medical kit, donated by professional well-wishers in Sydney, she kept locked in the Land Cruiser.

Most of the community ignored her, believing no woman, especially one of their own downtrodden race, could have understood Whitefella medicine. Their contempt became tangible when, one morning, Elizabeth noticed the two front wheels of her Land Cruiser were missing, having been replaced by tiers of house-bricks.

Fortunately, she was accepted and enthusiastically endorsed by the remaining members of her original mob. Swollen with pride, and happy to gain some prestige by association, they became her envoys and advocates, claiming to anyone who would listen 'We know Doctor Elizabeth. She's one of our mob. She's the real deal. Good doctor.'

Also, fortunately and against all odds, some traditional tribal structures had survived. They included a medicine man, or healer. Elders, referred to as aunties and uncles, were still recognised by the younger generations as having wisdom.

But buried within these layers of poverty, tradition, alcoholism and the slowly evaporating spirit of aboriginal dreaming, was another potentially potent, ambitious and intelligent spirit, impatiently searching for and waiting its chance to emerge.

Three weeks of treating minor wounds and ailments had passed when, without warning, Elizabeth's medical skills were needed under circumstances she'd never contemplated.

A gaunt, bare-footed, dust-covered aboriginal man arrived, wearing what remained of a once-white business shirt and threadbare jeans. He was carrying an obviously ill and semi-conscious child. God only knew how far he'd travelled and for how long he'd been carrying the little girl. He was at the point of total exhaustion.

His darling girl, he explained, was experiencing 'bad pain in gut.' She'd also been vomiting, sweating and couldn't eat. Elizabeth's external examination pointed strongly to appendicitis.

The child would die unless she could access almost immediate surgery. But it would take more than two hours for an ambulance to complete the return trip to Tennant Creek, some of it across challenging terrain, *if* an ambulance was available, *if* it could cross the two watercourses that would be flooding following a rainstorm last night and *if* they could raise thousands of dollars up-front for medical treatment.

Facing grim reality, Elizabeth began accepting *she* would have to either let the child to die in agony or perform the surgery, although she'd never even *observed* an appendectomy.

There was no operating theatre and her medical equipment was totally inadequate. There was no back-up blood supply and, naturally, no anaesthetist.

Feeling almost as sick as her patient, Elizabeth approached the tribal medicine man and made a deal.

'Johnny Sugarman, I have to make Whitefella surgery on sick girl or she will die. She might die anyway.'

'Why you tellin' me this?' came the suspicious response.

'I want you help with your biggest spell. You do this and the girl lives I give you all the credit. I tell everyone, say it was your magic.'

Then, conscious of his potential vulnerability should the surgery fail, 'What if she die?'

'We share blame fifty-fifty.'

'Hmmm, well, okay it's a deal.'

'Thank you' said Elizabeth, adding ' Johnny, if your spells make smoke you must stay downwind. No smoke is to drift over little girl. '

Elizabeth had no idea who or what she was dealing with. The diminutive Sugarman had long ago concluded that medicine-man ceremonies and secrets were little more than superstitious garbage. He'd clung to them as status symbols, to give himself some prestige, some influence over other members of the mob, but intended maintaining the façade only until he could find the way to realise *the dream*.

His days and nights were filled with his own fantasy, his conviction, his illusion, that he would become the leader of a revitalised aboriginal people, wherever they were located throughout the entire nation.

Semi-literate but exceptionally intelligent, sandwiched between two cultures but moving rapidly toward European concepts and attitudes, he'd been educating himself using his Government-provided iPad to access books for the print-handicapped. He'd memorised significant moments in the inspirational history of the United States of America, and also noted similarities in the rise of post-revolutionary Russia, the development of China under Mao Tse Tung and the consolidation of Vietnam under Ho Chi Minh.

America's growth, from a few small colonies until it consolidated and was able to fight a revolutionary war against the British, offered the most useful model for his new nation.

With minimal comprehension of the challenges ahead, Sugarman had been studying the techniques employed by America's founding rebels. In particular, their appeals to the supernatural and their insistence that they were morally superior, provided indispensable weapons, weapons available to be imitated and used again.

His review of America's consolidation and territorial expansion had also contributed to Sugarman's swelling core of ruthless, rebellious energy. Sometimes the urge to dominate almost overpowered him, forcing him to consciously put his research aside and focus on some mundane artefact until he could regain control. He was a driven man and he knew it.

Doctor Elizabeth was merely an unanticipated but welcome tool, one to be integrated and employed in his quest for power, when he identified an opportunity. Meanwhile, he'd adopt a subordinated, respectful and compliant veneer.

Using her satellite-compatible phone Elizabeth called a colleague, a cardiothoracic surgeon, in Sydney and explained her predicament. She needed on-line guidance from a general surgeon, if such a person was bold enough to become involved.

She then set about preparing. The only places with enough light to perform surgery were outdoors. One almost level area, beside a gum tree, seemed the best option.

Community members provided two, small, wooden tables. Elizabeth laid a sheet of flattened roofing iron between them and then doused the iron with antiseptic liquid mixed in a bucket-full of bore-water. A clean, white-linen bed sheet, folded double, completed her bush operating theatre.

With an almost comatose child resting on the table, Elizabeth appointed two women to wave bunches of gum leaves nearby to discourage flies.

After applying more of the antiseptic solution to her own hands and the child's abdomen, she tied an old nylon stocking so it covered her now unruly hair and prepared her few surgical instruments.

Morphine was only potent pain killer in her medical kit. She filled a syringe with an adult-level dose and waited, hopeful, tense, impotent, for an unknown surgeon who might or might not call from Sydney.

Awareness of an emerging drama reached across the aboriginal community drawing them into its emotional theatre. Early arrivers sat in scanty shade beneath trees. Most others stood, hatless, in the full sun. Children were hushed. For once, the dogs were constrained using assorted straps and ropes. Those daring to bark were rapped sharply on the nose.

The call arrived after 14 almost silent and increasingly agonising minutes. From Sydney came the reassuring voice of an unseen man who was risking his career.

And so began one of the most bizarre surgical procedures since Hua Tuo's experiments with anaesthesia almost two thousand years ago.

Elizabeth, tall, skinny, shoeless, looking more like a caricature than a modern surgeon, leaned over the patient, cell phone jammed between her right cheek and her shoulder.

Two barefooted aboriginal women, clad in shapeless frocks of uncertain origin, energetically waved their bunches of gum leaves while chanting a prayer invoking the support of their totem, the Snake God.

Standing sightly aside from the women was Johnny Sugarman, a grotesque mask covering his face. Tufts of vertical red feathers featured among his natural hair. His body, apart from a bright-red loin cloth, was covered, head to foot, with yellow, powdery clay onto which his rib-cage had been highlighted using red ochre mixed with saliva. He was carrying an instrument which made a low, rhythmic-growling sound when twirled around his head.

Sugarman had done everything within *his* capacity to give himself a prominent role in the emerging drama. Willpower and habit sustained Elizabeth as she injected her total supply of morphine into the child.

The telephone-directed procedure began.

'Right, now I want you locate McBurney's point, in the location I described earlier.'

'Yes, I think I'm there.'

'Make the incision, running north-south. Keep it shallow.'

'Done!'

'Begin opening corresponding layers of the abdominal wall and enter the peritoneum.'

After a two-minute delay, 'Right, I'm there.'

'Now, you should be able to see the swollen appendix. It looks a bit like a small, overblown sausage.'

'Oh, hell! I can't! Have I gone into the wrong location?'

Holding the iron sheet to stop herself swaying, Elizabeth began panicking. Drops of perspiration from her forehead fell into the open wound. Adding to her growing list of concerns, a murmuring breeze started blowing wisps of fine, grey dust along the ground.

Then, horror of horrors, the child's left foot twitched, the toes curling and uncurling, as if stretching as a precursor to awakening.

Immersed in shock, Elizabeth failed to notice the movement. But several members of the observing community saw it and word of a potentially horrific outcome spread among them.

But only two sounds penetrated Elizabeth's wall of fear. The rapid thumping of her heart, which seemed to fill her head, and the rhythmic moan of Johnny's spell-caster which began surrounding her like a protective cloak.

After a few seconds, Elizabeth shook her head forcing herself back to reality. But the surgery had changed. Now, with her reemergent spirituality considerably stronger than Sugarman's, she was engaging two cultures simultaneously.

The Sydney surgeon was telling her how to remove an inflamed appendix. Her resuscitated dreaming was directing her to find and remove the malevolent spirit inhabiting this innocent young girl's body.

'Concentrate, concentrate.' she told herself and, as if on command, the Sydney surgeon's voice gained ascendency.

'Can you hear me? Can you hear me? Is all okay?'

'Yes, I'm still good to go. What's next?'

'Don't worry too much. Those damn things turn up in various locations.'

'I feel I want to look further to the right and a little lower.'

'That's as good an approach as any other. Go for it!'

After a few moments of nervous prodding 'I'm there, yes, I can see it, I've got it.'

'Okay. Ligate the appendix. Be careful how you handle it. The damn thing's toxic as hell.'

Later still, 'Done!'

'Now, close each layer of the abdominal wall in the same way you've done plenty of times during surgeries within your speciality. Clip or sew the epidermis and you're home free.'

A few minutes later 'Yes, all done, finished.'

'Congratulations! I know how difficult that procedure was, especially under the conditions you were working with. By the way, is your patient still alive?'

'Yes, of course she is, you silly, beautiful, wonderful bastard' said Elizabeth, surrendering to tears as she attempted to thank her anonymous lifeline. The Sydney surgeon, breathing his own sigh of relief, ended the call.

Sugarman was next. 'Johnny, please take that mask off.'

'Why?'

'So I can hug you, that's why.' And she did, gaining an imprint of clay and ochre in the process.

While hugging Johnny she whispered 'At one stage I lost it. Courage gone. No hope. You saved me and you saved little girl.'

Johnny, despite his more recent atheism, had been temporarily recaptured by the spiritual legacy he'd gained as a young man. He replied 'I know. It happen when you sway and put your cutting thing down. I work very hard then.'

Acting on a spur of the moment impulse, Elizabeth asked if he would be responsible for the child's post-operative care, under supervision. He accepted.

Sugarman took this to be another opportunity. He had no idea where it would fit with his grand strategic vision, but some good would likely follow. Consequently, for the next two weeks no patient in a hospital could have received more fanatical, tender, and comprehensive care, within the limitations of facilities.

Later, Elizabeth remarked it was a good thing the child had recovered quite quickly. She wasn't sure how much longer the dedicated man could have survived on his hastily gulped meals and less than an hour's sleep each night.

Nevertheless, Sugarman's reputation as a conduit to the metaphysical world, a healer and now a bridge into Whiteman's medicine, was assured.

Also, at some stage during that anxious post-operative period, the bricks propping up Elizabeth's Land Cruiser disappeared and were replace by gleaming new wheels fitted with expensive off-road tyres. Her original wheels had been coloured black, these were dark green, but she decided it would be best to acknowledge the gesture by appearing delighted while ignoring minor discrepancies.

Incarceration

The New Orleans Incident was one of many across the United States. The combination of deteriorating economic conditions and widespread protests had remained politically potent. Despite many tactical victories, fatal casualties within Government forces were increasing while enthusiasm for crushing the rebels had decreased.

The presidential election campaign should have been at full throttle but there was no doubt about the outcome. It would be a clean sweep for the Democrats. They'd take the White House and gain a majority in both Houses of Congress. The political process was stumbling along, as if by habit.

The more immediate problem was, what to do with the incumbent President.

Day by hair-raising day he was becoming less likely to responsibly exercise presidential power, while still able to do so legally. Among many irrational actions, he was firing, replacing, and sometimes rehiring senior staff and advisors on an almost daily basis.

Occasionally, Members of Congress would be bussed, *en masse,* to the White House and showered with a barrage of expletive-enriched accusations followed by entreaties, a few of them inconsistent with directives issued a few days previously.

The man had to be stopped, somehow.

Most Members of Congress were convinced America's economic woes originated with attempts to constrain minerals exports from Australia to China. The first step in treating this infection was, they believed, to implicate and neutralise the primary cause, their President.

The Justice Department, unopposed except by the hysterically enraged President, appointed a Special Counsel with unprecedented power to investigate the background to China's palpable discontent. Reflecting the intensity of the crisis, he was given a mere 10 days in which to submit his final report.

The Special Counsel, feeling unreasonably pressured, protested loudly. But a tight timeframe was vindicated when, on the second day, an organised crowd approaching two million people descended on Washington DC, forming an impenetrable human barrier around the White House.

With world-wide media recording every moment of this *People v. Administration* contest, nobody was about to risk an American version of China's Tiananmen Square incident. National guardsmen, police and other security forces were kept away from the action.

The dense, almost endless, crowd chanted in unison 'Death, restraint and the pursuit of misery; death, restraint and the pursuit of misery; death, restraint and the pursuit of misery' over and over while pointing their collective fingers into the air with each repetition.

When one tranche became hoarse or exhausted, another would take over. Hour after hour they persisted, all through the day, the following night and the next day.

News channels in Russia and China, enjoying a propaganda bonanza, pointed to capitalism's catastrophic consequences. American media headlines supported the protestors. '*Redcoats*', '*Traitors*' and '*enemies of the Republic*' were among insults directed toward the President and his Administration.

One blog went further, headlining increasing civil unrest as, '*Our Second War of Independence*'.

Congress understood the implications. Civil war was possible, if not imminent. Waiting for an election to replace the President was no longer a viable option.

Fortunately, the Special Counsel's task proved remarkably easy. All members of the President's original Cabinet had been dismissed, some several times over. They either weren't available to run interference campaigns or had decided to cooperate under hastily drafted plea-bargaining arrangements.

Members of the President's personal staff were not motivated to conceal anything. Exhausted, they only wanted the President, as one senior aide said, 'somewhere else, anywhere else, anywhere but in the White House.'

The Special Counsel was obligingly directed toward classified records of meetings involving the President and a few carefully selected members of Cabinet. A shadowy figure from a previously unknown organisation, referred to only as *The Office*, had also been present.

Almost unbelievable documentation surfaced, some of it recording a conscious decision to employ a nuclear weapon against Australia. The main logistics and strategies for assisting with recovery and reconstruction of Canberra had been recorded, attached to agreed timeframes and tracked through to implementation.

The President's compassionate statement of shock and horror, transmitted globally on the day of the nuclear attack, had been drafted months earlier. The President had fine-tuned the text in his own handwriting, having personally authorised the use of the nuclear weapon.

Other plans to undermine and eventually replace the Government of Australia were on the record. Evidence of the President's participation, even domination, was unmistakable.

This was lethal. Implications extended beyond any American precedent in either law or politics. The reputation, standing and influence of the United States throughout the world were at stake.

The Special Counsel informed the Attorney General. He in turn arranged a crisis meeting with the Vice President, the Speaker of the House and the minority leaders of both houses.

10 days after the Special Counsel's appointment, the hunched physique of a shocked and ashamed man, propped-up by a rumpled business suit, walked hesitantly into an oak-panelled meeting room at a building on Pennsylvania Avenue. Two aides followed, each hauling a wheeled container resembling a supermarket shopping trolley. Both trolleys were filled with laptops, spring-back folders, other files and cardboard boxes of papers. The aides deposited their cargo then left the room.

The Special Counsel, standing behind an elaborately carved lectern, occasionally clutching at it for support, began his briefing. Every point made, he said, could be validated by irrefutable records. They could be viewed by anyone present wishing to do so.

'The United States used a nuclear weapon against Canberra. It was carried on a missile launched from one of our submarines. The entire plan was designed and finally executed during a six-month period. The President was personally involved. His objective was to make Australia a State of the US. This would allow us to control Australian exports and rein-in China's economy, which we have been doing. Russia probably knows that we fired the missile; China knows for sure.'

His introductory briefing over the Special Counsel, still standing, awaited questions. None came. The revelations were so shocking it took the audience several silent minutes to grasp them.

Then, as often happens in times of crisis, everyone talked and nobody listened.

'So that's why China has been so stroppy. They're screwing *our* economy, not the other way around.'

'If this story ever leaks out the US of A will be a global pariah.'

'What sort of secretive organisation is The Office? It's obviously dangerous. It'll have to be stopped'.

'This is gonna get messy.'

'Never thought I'd say this, but we're gonna have to get rid of this President, popularly elected or not.'

Attempting to focus on identifying a plan of action, the Attorney-General asked some pointed questions.

'Do we agree that the public process of impeaching the President would highlight what the US did to Australia and this revelation would cause grave and irreputable harm to the US?'

'Do we agree it is not tenable to let this President remain in office?'

'Do we agree the people in this room will be unable to achieve that outcome? We will need additional support.'

Endorsement was muted and reluctant. Nobody present could think of an alternative approach.

The normally energised Vice President, looking weary and dispirited, stood.

'We need to act and soon. I propose to summon the Director of the United States Secret Service to this meeting and acquaint him both with the evidence and the meeting's unanimous opinions regarding the future of the President.'

Within five minutes of receiving a call to his mobile phone, the uniformed Director arrived. Panting and annoyed, he demanded an explanation for the extreme urgency. But having been briefed on the Special Counsel's findings he sat, ashen faced, rocking onto two overstressed rear legs of his chair.

Finding voice, he addressed the ceiling. 'God almighty this is unprecedented. If we act within the law we'll bring disgrace to our nation. If we act outside the law we'll be committing a heinous crime. Jesus, and I'm sworn to *protect* the President.'

After more than a minute of quiet reflection, possibly prayer, he added 'It seems there are times when we must be guided by morals instead of laws, when we must put the nation before our careers, before our liberties, our lives. This, I believe, is one of them.'

'I propose you leave it to me to restrain the President on grounds of his insanity, his likely incurable insanity. The VP can then take over.'

All present agreed. The Secret Service Director asked only that he be authorised to meet with the Director of the FBI to arrange necessary logistics.

———

At a hastily arranged meeting, the Secret Service head was relieved to find the FBI's Director and his senior staff had also become deeply concerned by the President's obvious instability.

The FBI had already resisted several informal proposals to act decisively. But an approach from Director of the United States Secret Service, speaking on behalf of the Vice President, the Speaker of the House, the minority leaders of both houses as well as the Attorney General, carried significant force.

'Given' the FBI Director said 'some action must be taken before we have a civil or possibly a global war, I welcome the support of both the Secret Service and the most senior members of Congress. I also agree that restraint on grounds of insanity is the most practical and achievable plan. Please inform the Vice President that action is underway.'

The most senior FBI executives then began the extreme step of plotting to remove the President although, as one participant muttered 'This is damned ironic. A former President constantly accused us of doing something like this when we were completely innocent.'

Innocent or not, the FBI had the necessary weapons. Following an example allegedly set by J Edgar Hoover, the agency had amassed a data base of unpalatable information on individuals from all walks of life.

Potential accomplices weren't regarded by the FBI as serious criminals. Typically, they'd been recorded indulging in experimental homosexuality, enjoying the favours of an attractive prostitute or sampling a forbidden drug. No formal complaints had been lodged against them. But the FBI had its sources and people involved would have done almost anything to protect both their professional reputations and their families from a manufactured blaze of humiliating publicity.

The list of candidates was whittled down. People with the relevant skills would also have to be among the most deeply compromised of all 'innocent offenders' on the FBI's books. They had to be competent in professions relevant to the task at hand and mentally tough enough to survive protracted examinations from Congressional committees, if it ever came to that.

Finally, two psychiatrists and three psychiatric nurses were selected. Inconspicuously arrested, they were brought to an interrogation centre.

Deals were stuck, one at a time. They could be convicted and imprisoned for various humiliating felonies, as well as exposed to wide publicity. Their professional careers would almost certainly be terminated by deregistration. *Alternatively,* they could meet with the FBI Director who would personally request they undertake an unorthodox mission on behalf of the nation. Known sins of the past would then be forgiven and records deleted.

Unsurprisingly, each chose the latter option. In due course they appeared together before the tall, unsmiling, white-haired FBI Director, each of them shocked at recognising some of his best-known colleagues and realising they were fellow offenders.

Their initial shock was minor compared with the horror of learning what they would be required to undertake. One false move, one mistake, any uncontrollable development, could see them facing the death penalty. But, as the Director made clear, they had no choice.

Guided by experts trained to retrieve American criminals who were being protected by uncooperative nations, plans for a presidential kidnapping were formulated.

Every step in the process was rehearsed under realistic conditions, exposed to possible contingencies, modified and rehearsed again. An unanticipated advantage was that all five accomplices had already been accredited to medical establishments with links into the White House.

The FBI Director was close to accepting that their mission had a reasonable prospect of success when one agent raised the possibility that the President's wife, a formidable First Lady, might '*smell a rat and scream blue murder*'. The woman obviously relished the privileges of her elevated status and would be reluctant to lose them.

A trusted agent, posing as the envoy for a charity aiming to conserve native flora, was despatched to Los Angeles. There, the bubble-gum-chewing First Lady occupied the entire eighteenth floor of a luxury hotel, enjoying a vibrant social life, blissfully distant from her ill-tempered husband.

During discussions with this skinny, jewel-encrusted woman, the agent asked if the President might also be interested in lending his support to the charity.

Responding, the First Lady made no secret of her opinion that 'The man's a damn fool and a menace. I wouldn't trust him to manage a carousel. America'd be better off without him. The sooner he leaves office the better it will be for our nation.'

With fears of a First Lady pushback abated, the following Thursday morning one of the psychiatric nurses, now clad in a green surgical uniform, climbed behind the wheel of an ambulance. It resembled a shortened version of the familiar American school bus. His four colleagues were already onboard.

The protesting crowds having dispersed, he navigated to a White House entrance normally used by staff and delivery vehicles. A list of anticipated arrivals on the gate-guard's iPad had been expertly cyber-attacked. It now featured the ambulance and a description of its authorised passengers.

But, being more cautious than usual, possibly because of recent civil strife, the experienced guard conscientiously inspected the security passes of the driver and his four now-nervous passengers before waving them through.

Driving slowly past immaculate lawns with a backdrop of exquisitely placed shrubs, magnificent flower beds and small trees, the driver followed detailed directions he'd learned by rote.

He parked the ambulance outside a nondescript doorway marked *Deliveries* and they all walked to the downstairs kitchen entrance.

A member of the President's personal staff met the plotters. Their medical bags were x- rayed and passed by a stern-looking security guard. This woman had only the vaguest notion of what she was seeing on her screen but was reassured by the prestige and presence of a presidential staffer.

By prearrangement they were taken directly to the President. Now, as the plotters told themselves, the challenge was to keep their nerves as they confronted the hallowed symbol, the untouchable one.

Seated in a comfortable executive chair, thickly padded with mid-tan coloured leather, the President, enraged as usual, leaned onto the edge of his desk and shouted to his personal secretary 'Where the hell are those media jerks. Weren't they supposed to be here two minutes ago? They're on my diary. Who the hell do they think they are? I'm the President of the United States.'

'Nobody keeps *me* waiting.'

'Hey! What's going on? You lot don't have an appointment. Who the hell are you? No! Hey! Stop iiiit!'

With two experienced psychiatric nurses holding him to his chair and a third tipping his head to one side, a psychiatrist quickly swabbed the presidential neck and inserted a hypodermic needle.

A brief massage assisted the sedative chemistry to spread. Within fewer than 10 seconds the most powerful man on the planet was unconscious.

As planned, the President's pre-briefed personal secretary called the White House first-aid center, ordering staff to bring a stretcher. The President, staff members were told, had suffered a nervous event during a routine examination. Fortunately, appropriate medical specialists had been present. The situation was nationally and internationally significant, so absolute confidentiality was essential.

Impressed by a request from the President's personal staff, the first-aiders complied immediately. Two of the plotters, waiting at the door to the

President's office, accepted the stretcher. The first-aid staff departed, aware of the trust placed in them and determined to never discuss the event with anyone.

The President was then strapped to the stretcher. An oxygen mask was fitted to cover his face and attached to a small cylinder of plain air. Together, they carried him to the ambulance where his stretcher was clipped into place.

Departure was easy. Several years previously, time taken to conduct a comprehensive ambulance inspection at the White House gate had been assessed as contributing to the death of a patient. Nobody wanted a repeat performance. Consequently, only one guard performed the obligatory examination. Seeing a prostrate body strapped to a stretcher, its face covered by an oxygen mask, he quickly cleared them to depart.

Driving through light to moderately dense traffic, with unmarked vehicles carrying armed FBI agents to the front and rear, transportation to Bethesda Naval Medical Center went without incident.

Authorised media releases now began informing America and the world that the President had been taken ill and was undergoing treatment. To ensure privacy at this sensitive time the President's physical location would not be revealed. Details of the illness and the treatment were not disclosed. Prayers for his quick recovery were requested.

It took less than an hour for Washington-based reporters to survey every possible medical venue, note that physical and personnel security around the Bethesda facility had been increased, and to draw the obvious conclusion. However, fearing reprisals, no editor dared publish the information.

Typically less constrained, social media soon placed the President at locations across the United States and in several European countries, Switzerland being the most favoured option.

With the President in a secure facility, remote from normal medical supervision, parallel sets of treatment records were raised. One set, accessible to routinely assigned staff, recorded the care and treatment applicable to a patient who had suffered a serious psychotic episode. The other contained details of potent psychotropic drugs administered periodically and in large doses by the collaborating psychiatrists, both of whom still enjoyed accredited access to the patient.

Nine days later, both psychiatrists agreed that, regardless of whether the President had or had not been insane before his incarceration, he certainly would be now.

Sedative medication was withheld and a new man, one physically resembling the President, awoke. This charming person, sadly unable to recall almost anything for more than a few minutes, soon endeared himself to all members of the staff.

Allowed freedom of movement he wandered about the wards, clad comfortably in striped pyjamas and fluffy slippers, chatting happily to other patients and offering to assist staff where possible. His infectious laughter and hilarious habit of telling parts of jokes then forgetting the punchline rapidly made him one of their most popular inmates.

Every subsequent observation, from a cursory examination to the most detailed diagnosis, reached the same conclusion. This patient was *insane-safe* and highly unlikely to recover. He would need to be retained in a compassionate and empathic environment for the remainder of his life.

The White House media apparatus moved immediately. Within hours of receiving the detailed diagnosis, carefully avoiding any reference to mental illness, America and nations around the globe were informed that the President was now out of danger, thanks to the best of medical treatments as well as the prayers of the millions. However, extensive medical examinations had led to the unanimous opinion he would never again be able to perform presidential duties.

Special condolences were extended to the First Lady. She was gracious, or smart, enough to appear shocked but courageous and determined to carry on with her life. Messages of thanks for the President's deliverance flooded in. Some were sent by well-wishers but most had been composed by the White House press corps using phrase-generating software to provide believable content.

The Chief Justice, convinced from medical evidence that the President would never again be mentally capable of holding high office, administered the inauguration oath to the Vice President, in accordance with the United States Constitution.

The Vice President had already consulted with senior members of Congress across both Houses and all parties. Confident of broad political support, he appeared on national television and social media.

'My fellow Americans, I come before you as an appointed but not elected President. However, I am totally dedicated to restoring the United States to its former status as a great nation, in fact the greatest nation. With the help of God and your prayers we will together achieve that objective.'

'Our nation has been engaged in a campaign designed with the best possible motives, a campaign supportive of our global interests, but executed in ways that have damaged our economy and our international standing. That campaign must cease and not be resurrected.'

'Working with leading lawmakers from all parties, we have unanimously agreed that restraints on exports of raw materials from Australia to China will be abandoned.'

'All pre-existing Australia-China contracts for supply of raw materials will be restored to the extent feasible. Trade relations between the United States and China will be normalised.'

'With one exception, all action to welcome Australia as a State of the United States will be abandoned.'

'American arrangements to govern Australia under the Stewardship Agreement will be unilaterally cancelled. Australia will again become a self-governing nation. We will negotiate with Australia on the future of three new US military bases built there.'

'The exception is, having rescinded the Antarctic Treaty, America will maintain its absolute right under God and under international law to exert sovereign ownership and control over the former Australian Antarctic Territory, thus finally activating the undeniable right we have patiently held in reserve for decades.'

Reactions were instantaneous. Electrified lobbyists from every industry, religion and political faction began pressing for beneficial outcomes. The New York Stock Exchange had a nervous breakdown with both the Dow Industrial and NASDAQ rising to unprecedented heights before falling to depressed lows not seen in 20 years. They then recovered to the previous day's average trading levels.

An evangelist in Oklahoma self-immolated while standing on a packing case in Tulsa's Owen Park and declaring the devil had captured the United States. He died before explaining why.

Meanwhile, *Sanity Returns* street-parties were held across America, while corporate wakes were simultaneously organised by small-arms and pharmaceutical manufacturers as well as representatives from the health insurance industry.

Exodus

In Australia, the first tangible evidence of a new American policy was when the Harbour Master of Sydney Harbour took a telephone call from the bridge of USS *John F Washington* advising the ship was about to depart. And no, the vessel would not require a pilot.

The Harbour Master issued a *Temporary Notice to Mariners* warning ferries and other regular transport shipping to keep a sharp lookout for a 95 000-ton aircraft carrier. The massive vessel, now displaying a skirt of seaweed along its waterline, weighed anchor and moved majestically across Sydney Harbour. After passing through The Heads its huge, grey profile blended into a light mist covering the solemn leaden sea and it disappeared.

The entire United States diplomatic delegation went with her as did Jillian Horrowicz.

After the ship departed, a deflated Ambassador telephoned the Prime Minster of Australia to explain.

For the time being the United States Ambassador in Jakarta would assume diplomatic responsibility for Australian issues. Later, a new American Embassy and diplomatic mission could be established in Canberra.

'Meanwhile' the Ambassador continued 'all work on the new American bases has ceased. US personnel together with aircraft and equipment are being withdrawn. Australia is welcome to what will remain of the facilities. In accordance with its policy, the United States will not remediate any sites on foreign soil.'

The situation seemed bizarre but, as the Prime Minister mused,

I suppose I can understand America's position. If the real story of Canberra leaked out American diplomats would be in grave danger. The moderating effect of American influence in the Pacific Region and elsewhere would be yet further reduced.

And so, as is sometimes the case in global affairs, a major crime was swept away by the broom of strategic convenienc

---

Meeting at their now-normal Swainotel facilities in Sydney, the remnant Australian Government, an organisation of questionable legitimacy, had to move quickly.

The Minister for National Security provided the most radical suggestion.

'We're facing a power vacuum. There is no Australian Constitution. It was voted into oblivion. We can simply declare *we* are Australia's new government and then remain in power indefinitely. So long as we can persuade the military and police chiefs to back us, we'll have it made.'

Remaining Cabinet members agreed this approach had some merit. It would be quick, simple and could lead to a more efficient national reconstruction program, one unhindered by political posturing.

But wiser heads could see the potential for civil war if the now well-armed Australian public objected. Australian society had changed, perhaps not for the better, but changed nevertheless.

With sanity ascendant the residual Cabinet decided its first priority should be to acquire political legitimacy. A new Australian Constitution would be necessary. Elections would be held to create a legally empowered government.

Only then would it be possible to tackle the chaotic mess gripping most towns, cities and industries across the nation, except for the sporting, gambling, alcohol and religious organisations, all of which were thriving.

Australia's Attorney-General, despite being distrusted by almost everybody present, was directed to coordinate drafting of the new constitution but given no authority to act unilaterally. Not the most charming of people, she was acknowledged as the smartest member of Cabinet.

The energetic woman set to work. After digging into the backgrounds of available judges and academic lawyers, most of them residing outside of Canberra region, she assembled a short list of 83 people to advise on Australia's new constitution.

Hamstrung by the limitation she had no authority to act unilaterally, she spent a gruelling six days interviewing each of her potential constitutional counsellors, some by telephone. That done, she selected 15 of them on the basis that their opinions most closely reflected her own.

She then sold her selections to the Prime Minister and Cabinet on grounds of *diversity*.

'Prime Minister, colleagues, I am able to report I have assembled a team of eminent Australians to assist in writing a new Australian Constitution. Recognising there is a range of opinions and perspectives at play here, all of which must be respected, I have selected a diverse team of highly qualified jurists and related academics.'

'You will see from the biographical notes I provided on each of them that the team includes women and men, a native aboriginal person, people whose parents migrated from Europe, and people from each of our former States.'

The Prime Minister failed to see why anybody would consider including an aboriginal on the writing team, regardless of whether he or she was eminently qualified or not.

'That, in my opinion is simply asking for trouble. Before we know it there'll be a demand for some form of beefed-up indigenous constitutional recognition, a blasted peace treaty, and who knows what else.'

The Attorney-General, having anticipated that objection, welcomed it as a distraction from the main game. Well prepared, she put forward her reserve candidate, another man whose opinions coincided with her own, Professor Thoc Quo, Australian born but of Vietnamese parentage.

Following a brief discussion, the Prime Minister and his colleagues agreed the Attorney-General had done an excellent job and endorsed her amended list. Unspoken, was the general impression that perhaps this prickly bitch had finally learned how to be a team player.

On departing the Swainotel, the Attorney-General thought to herself, *Well, that was easy. I've got those idiots where I want them.* She then released media announcements to guard against any political backpedalling.

———

At the first meeting of the Eminent People's Constitution Drafting Advisory Group, held in a former Swainotel dining room, the Attorney General made clear to delegates that they had not been invited to produce a rehash of the Constitution proclaimed by the Parliament of Great Britain.

'One of the few desirable outcomes of American stewardship' she said 'was the development of a draft State Constitution in anticipation of Australia becoming an American State. It will serve as the basis for a new national document. It will enable Australia to clean out its inherited mess'.

'This means there will be no constitutional link to Britain. Australia will become a republic and each new head-of-state will be appointed by the Prime Minister, as effectively happens with governors-general already.'

'Australia will no longer have individual States, therefore we will no longer need a States' house, or Senate.'

'Election of judges, police chiefs and senior prosecutors will be mandatory. This will help break any impression of a cosy interdependence between politicians, judges, prosecutors and the police.'

'Future amendments to the Constitution will be made difficult and likely to fail.'

The Drafting Advisory Group was aghast when told they had three weeks in which to complete their task. However, as the Attorney General said 'This is a national emergency. We do not have a legitimate national government.'

'The governance of Australia will be effectively paralysed until a new Constitution becomes law. Besides, the original document, combined with the American-inspired draft and my guidelines have already filled most of the blank squares.'

The Group, placated by a written promise they would all be recognised and thanked, by name, in the prologue to their document, set to work.

With the Drafting Advisory Group labouring feverishly, and politicians across the nation beginning the traditional process of distorting public perceptions in anticipation of an election, the People's Republic of China made a dramatic and unforeseen move.

LEGITIMATISATION

On an otherwise unremarkable Tuesday morning, Beijing's suave, tall, Ambassador to Australia requested an urgent meeting with the Prime Minister and Foreign Minister. Wondering if some aspects of international law might be involved, the Prime Minister agreed, but stipulated the Attorney General must also be present.

At 2.15 pm on Friday, 14th April, in a small, drab meeting room at the Swainotel, the Chinese Ambassador detonated his own strategic weapon.

'It is obvious to my country, no less to each of you' he claimed 'that Australia's extensive societal and economic woes were either caused or exacerbated by the United States.'

Ignoring diplomatic modalities, he continued for more than an hour, describing the incremental way Australia had become militarily subordinated by America, hinting also that China was aware of the background to the allegedly accidental detonation which destroyed central Canberra.

Little had escaped him. He was aware of America's announced intention, several years previously, to impose punishing tariffs on Australian steel and aluminium, a move Australia had narrowly avoided and only then by making undisclosed concessions.

Continuing, he said 'The United States has demonstrated through many small and incremental initiatives, more recently with a major assault, that it views Australia as a subordinate pawn rather than a friend. In the past, the US has often treated Australia with contempt.'

'You will remember the rust-bucket landing craft the US sold to the Australian Navy, the high prices you had to pay for American military equipment, the insult implicit in America not bothering to appoint ambassadors to Australia for varying periods.'

With the audience now malleable, His Excellency took a deep breath and made his pitch.

'China is willing to offer Australia a genuine treaty-based security guarantee. It will align Australia's economic and security relationships with the same nation.'

'The proposed treaty will not resemble *The Australia, New Zealand, United States Security Treaty*. That document is a classic example of negotiated evasion instead of a commitment to cooperative action.'

'The agreement China proposes would be a joint undertaking that an armed attack against either one would be considered an attack against them both, following which they would exercise the right of individual or collective self-defence as recognised by Article 51 of the Charter of the United Nations.'

'This would be a serious and binding defence commitment.'

His Excellency added China understood, following Australia's commitment to a new security treaty, the United States would withdraw all its military technology from Australia. It would render the remainder useless via a combination of cyber attacks and denial of spare parts. It would refuse to provide munitions.

'In anticipation I am authorised to offer a separate and binding security assets agreement to be signed simultaneously with the security guarantee.'

He continued 'China will, within 30 days of joint signature, provide Australia with 100 Ghost Bird J-35 fighter aircraft, together with a full suite of transport, maritime, tanker, helicopter and training aircraft to numbers at least equal to the levels held by Australia before the Canberra Incident.'

'The aircraft provided will be supplemented by ships' fire control systems, missiles and their launchers, submarine electronics, land force armaments and the latest terahertz radiation devices. You will have full access to intelligence collected by our satellites.'

It seemed an amazing offer although the Australians, still smarting from memories of excessive dependence on the United States, were concerned to avoid getting into the same situation.

But the Ambassador had answers.

'China has recognised the strategic vulnerability of producing all munitions on our mainland. We would seek your permission to establish outposted munitions production facilities in Australia where there is normally a skilled and stable workforce. The facilities established would produce the most common munitions used by Australia.'

'It would be impractical to duplicate production of our most complicated combat systems, such as fighter aircraft, but my country is prepared to increase your logistics security by storing in Australia a more extensive inventory of spare engines and other components than has ever previously been contemplated.'

The discussion continued with additional issues being raised and despatched.

'Yes, China will enter into an agreement to not interfere in Australian governance.'

'Yes, all military equipment in Australia will be under the command and control of Australian personnel.'

'Yes, China will provide all necessary skill and technical training.'

'Yes, Australia will continue to exercise its own sovereign rights and trade internationally as it pleases.'

No, China does not want Australia to become part of the People's Republic and will sign a declarative statement if asked.

'China's only ambition', he said, 'is to replace the United States as Australia's primary security ally.' 'And' he added 'do a better job of it too.'

'Let me be candid. America, as result of its own follies, alienated Western Europe. This left a vacuum that Russia is racing to fill. It will make Russia uncomfortably more powerful. China needs to counterbalance Russian expansion and a security alliance with Australia is the ideal way to achieve that objective.'

To describe the Australian political and social environment as *chaotic* would have been an understatement.

The Eminent People's Constitution Drafting Advisory Group had been subjected to a barrage of passionate and special pleadings. Firearms representatives wanted a simple 'right to bear arms' inclusion. Christian religious advocates hoped to consolidate Christianity as the State religion but were openly brawling among themselves regarding an appropriate form of words. Interests representing sport, alcohol and gambling had also been unable to agree on clauses to provide for protection of their fiefdoms but were determined to ensure their privileged status was maintained.

Adding to the turmoil was the possibility of a new security arrangement, with *China* of all nations, news of the sensitive and classified discussion with the Australian Government having been leaked to the media by China itself.

It was also obvious a general election was imminent, although nobody, including the Prime Minister, could have named the date.

Long-established and genuinely warm relations between many Australians and their American business or personal contacts seemed to be at risk, a notion many Australians deplored. The kindness and generosity of Americans after the Canberra Incident had consolidated favourable impressions.

This, combined with widespread confusion and uncertainty, especially regarding constitutional issues, allowed the Prime Minister to use one of the oldest tricks in the political book. In a well-publicised speech, he acknowledged the value of contributions being made by lobbyists to the Drafting Advisory Group.

'Being committed to open and democratic government and wanting to ensure all Australians have a voice in deciding our future, I guarantee any government I lead will be more consultative than formerly and will hold a national referendum designed to offer the new parliament clear guidance on how to proceed in the national interest.'

'That' he later said triumphantly 'is so vague it will be bogged down for months in debates, even if our side has to cause them. The heat will dissipate and ultimately we'll do whatever we think is in our own political interests.'

Slightly placated, Australian voters failed to focus strongly on the rumoured Chinese offer, although it would, if accepted, have led to the most radical strategic realignment in the nation's history.

Also escaping scrutiny was that the so-called *Australian government* no longer had any obvious legal or constitutional status, yet it seemed to be calling all the shots

---

The Drafting Advisory Group submitted its draft to the Attorney General three days before the deadline. In accordance with her original promise, she ensured all members were identified by name in the prologue to the draft, although she had no intention of including any such nonsense in the finally endorsed version.

By both intent and design, the document was unnecessarily wordy, densely legalistic and heavily seasoned with obscure Latin phrases. The insecure and quasi-legitimate Cabinet, mesmerised by the prestige of its advisory group and distracted by the alleged diversity of the group's membership, endorsed the draft following a cursory examination.

When acknowledging the need for a new constitution, some members of Cabinet, following the Prime Minister's lead, had assumed the document would be made available for a period of public comment, then made the subject of a national referendum. However, the Treasurer began wondering aloud if a period of public consultation would produce any constructive outcome.

'Perhaps' she suggested 'it would create obstacles, especially when those damned constitutional lawyers got their collective teeth into it.'

The threat of interminable delays was acknowledged by Cabinet as unacceptable. Plans for public consultation were abandoned. The Attorney General then offered *her* opinion that no legal mechanism existed for adopting a new Australian Constitution.

Following the *Statute of Westminster* and the *Australia Act,* she claimed, Australia could not request Britain's Parliament to pass legislation applying to Australia. Consequently, the government was in a similar position to the American rebels who broke away from Britain and *adopted* the American Constitution, relying on their own collective authority.

The concept of an illegitimate, or barely legitimate, government simply proclaiming a new Australian Constitution was tantalizing but unacceptable. However, given the possibility of delays following widespread public and professional debate, *tantalizing* won the day.

On a Saturday afternoon when most media reporters were focused on sporting events, the Prime Minister made his announcement. He claimed Australia's new constitution had been drafted fully in accordance with the fundamental principles underlying international law and reflecting the essential requirement to assert Australia's nationhood.

'Only those who wish us harm' he intoned 'could argue against this solemn duty to proclaim our proud country as a member of the fellowship of nations. We will, all of us, be able to tell our heirs and successors that *we* were present when our new Australia came into existence. This momentous event will occur at the stroke of midnight on 1 July.'

Later, sweeping aside questions as to which time zone would be referencing the stroke of midnight, he told media representatives to 'give this moment the dignity it deserves by focusing on the strategic picture.'

Two days later the Prime Minister also announced a general election. It would take place on the fourth Saturday in July.

His announcement included the traditional lies that had accompanied every Australian election for decades, regardless of which political party made the call.

'This will be one of the most important elections in our nation's history. The contrast between Government and Opposition policies will be stark. The outcome will be fundamental to our future and to the future of our children and our grandchildren'.

'We must therefore join and make the right decisions for Australia. Our government will represent all hard-working Australians regardless of who and where you are. We will protect and preserve our families and our way of life...'

As was already happening in the United States, the Australian election campaign then dissolved into a desultory and lacklustre affair, although for very different reasons.

In the United States, the majority party had so alienated voters there was no likelihood it would retain power. In Australia, the opposition parties had been kept so remote from political and related economic concerns that they faced extreme difficulty identifying issues to oppose, advocate or endorse.

Despite being damaged by revelations it had supported the clandestine importation of nuclear weapons, the formerly governing party seemed the only organisation capable of restoring effective control and tackling Australia's economic woes, a point it pressed home at every opportunity.

One of few noteworthy incidents during the election campaign occurred when the Prime Minister dismissed the former Minister for Defence, the man imposed on him by the American Ambassador.

The new, acting, replacement Minister immediately asked for a briefing from the military top-brass regarding their current activities.

Army and Air Force provided details of plans to work closely with China, in view of the prospective bilateral alliance. The Navy reported it was reviewing badges of rank, uniform-buttons, banners and ensigns in anticipation of Australia becoming a republic. The acting Minister immediately directed Navy to make the China relationship its first priority, an insult the Navy never forgave or forgot.

———

The election was held, as scheduled, on the last Saturday in July.

Management of polling booths, safeguarding of ballot boxes and counting of votes all went smoothly, the Australian Electoral Commission having not been quite so badly damaged by the Canberra holocaust as American officials had claimed.

The former Government was re-elected in a landslide victory, mainly because nobody, including opposing politicians, seemed able to identify sensible alternative policies. It was a classic example of casting swine before pearls.

Proverbs

The Prime Minister's party voted him back into his old job, he having claimed that continuity would be essential in these turbulent times. His colleagues, unimpressed by the continuity argument, considered him so weak and indecisive it would be easier to manipulate him to their own advantage than to manage some of their more strong-willed associates.

Jointly, they decided that ministerial portfolios would be allocated without the need to placate State-based interests as formerly. Selection criteria were now to be focused on gender balance, ability to debate in the parliament and capacity to attract electoral funding.

The ministerial selection process was just beginning, the old Praetorian Guard confidently reasserting itself, when one naïve backbencher proposed that ministers should have some qualification or experience relevant to their responsibilities.

Leading contenders for positions in the new ministry recoiled, sensing a prospective competitor, and worse, a possibly talented entrant into the race for status. Political fangs were bared, the bloodlust boiled and a snarling attack began:

'Where in hell did you get that ludicrous notion from?'

'What are you, a starry-eyed bloody idealist?'

'Two major fields of governmental activity are defence and social security; now you tell us when was the last time Australia had a Minister for Defence with any military experience or a Minster for Social Services who'd ever experienced economic hardship.'

'Gees, we've had successful Finance Ministers who thought take-aways referred to fish-and-chips.'

'Yeah, and what about the one who got a kick from sucking on six-inch long, dark-brown phallic symbols!'

Contemptuous versions of what had been said '*by that radical young fool*' were shared with subordinate staff. They, as usual, imitated their Ministers, claiming the opinion to be their own and spreading the story.

The original interlocutor, formerly a professor of engineering, became a long-term backbencher doomed to standing behind Ministers and nodding compliantly while they made announcements to the media.

After the dust settled this new government, still without a Head of State, swore itself into office. It declared the Swainotel to be Australia's national House of Parliament for the foreseeable future.

One of the new Government's first initiatives was to use its overwhelming majority in Parliament and pass a bill forbidding any amendments to the new Constitution for a period of 10 years, '*to let things settle down*' according to the Prime Minister.

The legality of this move was questionable, but so was the legal basis for the entire Constitution. Fortunately, thinking almost as a bloc, experienced jurists and academics decided it would be best to leave those stones unturned.

But powerful lobby groups were incensed. Responding to their furious protests, the Prime Minister agreed he had acknowledged the importance of heeding voices seeking special representation. He had also promised national consultation to collect community views on how parliament might proceed in this new environment.

However, the Prime Minister replied, he hadn't said *when* these processes would occur. Now, he'd provided stability and certainty for planning purposes. They would begin 10 years from now.

At an early meeting of his new Cabinet and subsequent sitting of Parliament, the Prime Minister, feeling more confident than he had for many years, turned up the heat with a series of initiatives he described as 'interim measures'. Chief among them was the restoration of taxation on alcohol to the level formerly applied by the highest taxing Commonwealth and State levies combined. The former regulations governing weapons and ammunition were also restored. A guns buy-back scheme was announced. It would be funded by revenue from alcohol sales.

Still pushing his luck, the Prime Minister announced to startled colleagues that the gambling industry should take a significant hit. He proposed restrictions on the number of poker machines permitted in any single venue together with regulations constraining the machines to a maximum of eight bets per minute.

The gambling industry threatened to withdraw financial sponsorship from community organisations and began a nation-wide television campaign of protest. Tearful members of the Greenburgh Girls Softball Team informed viewers that the girls themselves would now need to raise funds to buy their own uniforms. Other advertisements showed dour-faced punters complaining that new restrictions on bets per minute had taken the thrill out of gambling. *Nanny State* became the phrase *de jour*.

The Prime Minister tried hard to seem empathic. 'Yes I do understand that every major reform brings to light both winners and losers. Of course, we will do our best to understand and address those problems in constructive ways.'

But the most potent reaction, gleefully transmitted by the media, came from comments made by the National Security Minister when standing too close to a live microphone.

'He doesn't give a damn. He knows perfectly well Greenburgh has the highest per capita income in Australia. He reckons the spoilt little brats can afford to buy their own bloody uniforms. As for the geriatric gamblers, the

Prime Minister thinks if they've got enough cash to waste on poker machines then there's scope to reduce their old-age pensions.'

Nevertheless, individual ministers met with senior personnel from peak bodies representing religions and professional sports organisations. Taking a leaf from the book employed so effectively by the United States, they used a carrot and stick approach.

Offers to maintain favourable taxation provisions encouraged religions to cooperate through pro-Government advocacy from the pulpits. The threat of withdrawing all public funding from sport, including from all professional training institutes, converted sporting bodies across the nation into enthusiastic advocates of Government policies, this despite their reduction in revenue from alcohol and gambling.

The Murray-Darling Basin Authority was resurrected with enough staff and sufficient powers to rigidly enforce water restrictions on the up-river users. Down-river agriculture was revived.

Ore exports to China were restored and in some respects increased by the addition of larger rare-earth minerals contracts. Plans to build a huge radioactive-waste depository near Kalgoorlie were shelved.

Ministers and their overworked departments adroitly managed a multitude of challenging problems as they brought former State police forces, fire brigades, education authorities and other institutions under a national umbrella. They also had coins and postage stamps redesigned while arranging for England's symbolic crown to be removed from various national symbols and the Union Jack deleted from flags. No longer was it prestigious to have the prefix *Royal* associated with entities as diverse as horse-racing tracks, public gardens and automobile servicing organisations.

Some of the worst affected cases were people who'd lost their homes either during the Canberra Incident or because they'd been declared bankrupt in the following economic hiatus. The Government offered assistance in the form of emergency financial relief and low-interest loans, but the Braithwaites and many other families never recovered from their economic devastation.

However, tent-camps of the dispossessed in Brisbane, Sydney and Melbourne began shrinking as families trickled back into better accommodation and returned to the cities of Adelaide and Perth along with regional centres.

America's decision to activate its claim to the Australian Antarctic Territory, when publicised by the Australian Government, diluted traditional pro-US public affection. This, in turn, provided an atmosphere significantly more supportive of pursuing the new security relationship with China.

With the tide of pubic opinion turning, and given the now accepted legitimacy of an Australian Constitution and its Government, Australia was finally able to sign the *Treaty of Mutual Security between the People's Republic of China and the Republic of Australia.*

It included the key provision that an armed attack against either one would be considered an attack against them both.

Simultaneously, an *Agreement to Provide Arms and Munitions to Ensure a Republic of Australia Defence Capability* was also signed.

The restored Australian Defence Force stepped up language training in Standard Chinese, known as *Putonghua,* and began conducting intensive cultural awareness seminars.

Military facilities designed by People's Liberation Army were being constructed, as rapidly as possible, to provide for the servicing and maintenance of Chinese military equipment. Australian personnel, as soon as they became moderately competent linguistically, were shipped in their hundreds to China for technical conversion training.

Navy's top brass was finally given permission to allocate resources for the redesign of its symbols, badges and pennants. This concession did not lead to improved relations with the now-confirmed Minister for Defence because they'd been clandestinely doing so anyway.

Despite Australia's strengthened commitment to Asia, a new and chastened Administration in the United States was highly motivated to cooperate. This was partly because of guilt but mainly from gratitude because Australia had never disclosed to the world what it knew about the Canberra Incident, although it could have done so at any time.

Australian exports to the United States increased. Any Australian product was welcomed, tariff-free. Related Australian industries began to boom.

The full suite of US military equipment, some purchased at exorbitant cost, was sold back to America as scrap metal, this being one of China's suggestions.

Slowly, like a sleeping giant awakening, stretching and then standing, shakily at first, the entire Australian nation began its long climb toward a different normality.

After ten months at the helm of his new government, the Prime Minister made the first of what he promised would be a *Periodic Account to the People*. Unaware of the unfortunate acronym, he made several memorable points:

'Friends, fellow Australians, I have some important things to share.

Resulting from what we now refer to as the Canberra Incident and its aftermath, our country has changed dramatically.'

'We are now one nation, not a collection of former colonies attempting, often unsuccessfully, to cooperate through attempts at coordination. We are a republic, a democratic republic. Our economy is mending and will continue to improve.'

'We can look forward to a secure future under the nuclear umbrella provided by the People's Republic of China, with which we have a security alliance stronger than we ever previously enjoyed.'

'We also maintain a robust and friendly relationship with the United States of America. It has become our major trading partner.'

'Some of you may feel concerned that the balance of power in the Asian-Pacific region has changed. But I say to you, unless any nation decides to act belligerently toward another nation, or more belligerently than is normal, the concept of balancing powers is not particularly meaningful.'

'Yes, there are unresolved territorial disputes in our region and elsewhere, as there have been since the dawn of humanity. They need not escalate and should not do so, provided parties involved act responsibly, with respect and maturity.'

'Other matters you should be ...'

———————

The Prime Minister had every reason to feel satisfied with his role, and that of his government. They'd made impressive progress with getting Australia back onto its economic feet. The first of his PAPs had been well received.

Bilateral relations with China and America were progressing. His ministers, almost overwhelmed by the avalanche of challenges confronting them, had temporarily abandoned their aggressive and competitive behaviours, or so he thought.

Consequently, the Prime Minister was shocked and dismayed when, out of the blue, came a media campaign disclosing details of improvements made, at public expense, to his Brisbane house.

According to widespread reporting, the improvements had cost at least five-times the amount he'd paid for the property.

The obvious fall-back position—that he'd needed to make the house suitable for entertaining or accommodating VIP visitors—fell through. Various media outlets had already obtained comprehensive records of such activities and had been waiting patiently for him to fall into that trap.

In total, they claimed, the VIP entertainment had amounted to three events totalling slightly more than 11 hours, spread over four years. One reporter had also started asking questions about a mysterious person with a name something like *Jill Horrow*. She'd lived at the Brisbane address for months while drawing a senior executive salary.

The Prime Minister telephoned the Attorney-General and asked her to meet with him in his now notorious house. She was happy to oblige.

The following day, they were seated comfortably in artisan-carved chairs. The attached wooden legs were reflecting in highly polished ebony floorboards while they sipped long-glasses of iced tea. Ignoring these aesthetic distractions, the Prime Minister came quickly to the point.

'This nonsense about the cost of renovations to my home is politically damaging. I'd like you to get it shut down and keep it that way.'

'That won't be possible.' she replied. 'We're in new territory now. Perhaps in the old days some hints to a police chief could lead to a politically convenient raid on a media office, or a word in the right quarter might encourage a prosecutor to pursue or ignore a case, in the public interest of course, but things have changed.'

'Under the new Constitution police chiefs, crown prosecutors and judges are to be elected officials. They are sensitive to public opinion, not your personal or political preferences.'

'Yes, but we haven't held the elections for police and judicial officials yet.'

'True', she said 'but we soon will hold them and, guess what, almost all incumbents will be candidates. You've already lost that influence.'

'Well, damn it' said the Prime Minister, becoming increasingly irritated at not getting his own way 'then we'll just have to amend the Constitution.'

'I don't think so. We made constitutional change almost impossible, first by the conditions embedded in the document, second by that bill of yours which attempts to prohibit amendments for 10 years. Do you recall your strong support for it?'

'But, Jees, this means I could be successfully prosecuted. It'll mean the end of this government.'

'Oh no,' she responded with a sardonic smile 'it'll mean the end of *your* time in government. But other ministers, including me, will emerge purer than Caesar's wife. We'll retain our portfolios. One of us will subsequently become the new PM. Now, why don't you and I have a chat about identifying ways to ensure that the new PM will be *me!*'

'You bitch. I'll see you in hell first.'

'No, you'll see me as PM first. With prime ministers, hell comes later. For now, I'll bid you farewell, "Buffy darling".'

The Attorney-General departed with a spring in her high-heeled steps. She held all the aces and knew it, having leaked details of the prime ministerial home renovations (available from parliamentary records) as well as copies of his social calendar and diary.

She'd obtained the calendar and diary from Jill Horrow who'd become irritated by the PM's periodic sexual advances; in fact so annoyed that, a few days prior to the American withdrawal, Jill had enjoyed a brief *tête à tête* with the Attorney-General.

Given a new and stable Administration, working cooperatively with Congress, the United States, also began recovering from its economic meltdown.

Through diplomatic contact, China had passed the message that American economic revitalisation would be allowed to continue so long as there were no attempts to interfere with either the Chinese economy or the China-Australia security arrangements.

This was a bitter dram for the most powerful nation on Earth to swallow, but America was finally beginning to accept that, in the 21st century, all nations are to some extent interdependent. The bigger their economies are, the more interdependent they become, like it or not.

HELL

Within the United States scores remained to be settled and villains brought to justice. A closely held investigation into the bombing of Canberra revealed the tactical architect of America's overall strategy to capture Australia was a man named Allen Ivory.

Further inquiries indicated Allen Ivory, whose status remained frustratingly vague, had likely been killed when the bomb was detonated. However, the new Administration was not content to let matters rest.

Evidence pointed to the existence of a shadowy but highly influential entity known only as *The Office*. It took months of concentrated detective work to uncover the extent and purpose of that organisation and arrest its principals.

Jefferson Ivory, its leader, was captured in his underground office together with his chief lieutenants known only as Carol, Martin and Karoly (aka Karl).

Other personnel located when The Office was raided were questioned comprehensively before being reassigned, following reorientation, to various intelligence agencies. They were forbidden to communicate with each other and directed to report any inadvertent contact. Not one of them would be promoted again; their careers had plateaued.

Jefferson, Carol, Martin and Karoly were charged with treason and tried by a closed tribunal. The evidence against them was damming and undeniable. In accordance with a legal precedent established by the United States in war-crimes trials following the Second World War, *superior orders* was not an acceptable defence. They were found guilty.

Jefferson Ivory received a sentence of life imprisonment without prospect of release. The other three were given 20-year terms.

Jefferson Ivory's life sentence lasted 23 days. He allegedly committed suicide by hanging himself using a strip of bedsheet tied to a conveniently accessible bar on the ceiling of his concrete-walled prison cell.

Investigations also uncovered the involvement of some former Cabinet-rank officials who were not protected by plea bargaining deals. Warrants for their arrest were issued, but not one of them was brought to trial.

The Chairman of the Joint Chiefs of Staff Committee had been killed in an automobile accident, the brakes on his car having failed while he was driving along a scenic cliff-top motorway. Unfortunately, because of an administrative error, the wrecked vehicle had been sent to a car-crushing facility where it was converted to a cube of scrap metal before a comprehensive analysis of its braking system could be conducted.

The Secretary of State had migrated to Azerbaijan from which neither promises nor threats to the resident government had extricated him. However, following an anonymous tip-off, a stealth drone had been despatched and imaged him sunbaking on the deck of a yacht sailing placidly across the Caspian Sea. Also on deck was a bikini-clad young woman, her presence implying that the former official would likely remain abroad. Further surveillance was called off.

Two others had moved to Vietnam with a similar outcome, Vietnamese officials feeling they did not owe the United States any favours. A more cautious Administration had abandoned the earlier program of kidnapping alleged American criminals in foreign countries, so the miscreants were safe for the moment.

Others had disappeared without trace although suspicions lingered that they remained in the United States after acquiring new identities.

During consultations between the heads of intelligence agencies and the new President, it was decided to not pursue American diplomatic officials from the former mission to Australia. The precedent of punishing them could have made other diplomats reluctant to implement occasionally less-than-palatable directions from Washington. The captain of the submarine which fired the fatal missile was not censured.

Following her husband's arrest, Jefferson Ivory's wife, Martha, was quietly informed of the changed circumstances and told it would not be possible to visit him while he awaited trial. She never saw her husband again.

Martha relocated to New Orleans where she had relatives still living. She died 18 years later, having become a much-admired interpreter for the profoundly deaf. Martha worked until the final hour of her final day.

Born Again

While global politics and economics were adjusting to a new strategic landscape, and the Australian Government was re-establishing itself, Elizabeth continued residing, subsisting really, in the same outback settlement.

Still treating the many ailments and injuries afflicting her aboriginal brothers and sisters, she relied on friends in the conventional medical establishment to supply dressings, drugs, and surgical instruments. They were sent via the Tennant Creek post office which she visited monthly in her Land Cruiser.

Medically difficult cases sometimes arose when senior members of the community conducted initiation rites or meted out penalties for breaches of traditional customs. Initiation ceremonies involved slashing arms or chests and inserting unsterilised stones into the wounds, or conducting circumcisions using shards of glass from broken beer bottles. Punishments for perceived crimes might include stabbing an arm or leg with a spear or striking an offender's head with a heavy wooden club.

Elizabeth worried that someone would be killed. Under Blackfella's law, a revenge killing might then be required, leading to further violence.

One Saturday morning she sat down with her Senior Medical Assistant, Johnny Sugarman, and his two Supporting Medical Assistants, the women whose first contribution to Western medicine had been to wave away flies while Elizabeth conducted her now legendary appendectomy.

They agreed some improvements to facilities, and even more to attitudes, were needed. But Johnny wisely proposed that changes should be done in the Blackfella's way. Elizabeth agreed and decided to take a back seat.

She had considerable faith in the Blackfella's way. As she knew, *that* appendectomy had been the catalyst for a local reformation. Encouraged by Johnny Sugarman, the entire community had rallied to build her the *Doctor Elizabeth Surgery*.

They'd started by scrounging the best building materials available from across their ramshackle village. These were supplemented by new or almost new components from a mysterious location referred to, invariably with broad grins and shrugging shoulders, as '*good place north or west of here,... hmmm, maybe south*'.

Even more impressive than the inventory of building materials were the tradesmen who emerged to create this new and substantial white-walled, four-roomed building.

Elizabeth's mob of alleged rejects, failures, no-hopers, alcoholics and derelicts included two qualified carpenters, one plumber and two electricians.

A combination of inability to cope with the pressures of city life, loneliness, racial prejudice, alcohol, occasionally drugs and brushes with the Whiteman's legal system had combined to usher these skilled artisans, unprotesting, into impoverished obscurity.

By any measure, the quality of her new building was exceptional. Foundations had been sunk deeply into exactly vertical post-holes then packed solidly with concrete. Every component of the framework was fixed into place with absolute precision. Mortice and tenon joinery dominated where nails and metal brackets would normally have been used. Cross bracing was dovetailed. Gable-roof trusses were without bulge or dip.

Roofing, drainage, cladding and windows were installed with dedicated attention to detail. The perfectly smooth, level, hardwood, tongue-and-groove flooring was immaculate.

Watching this astonishing edifice emerging, Elizabeth sometimes turned from the others lest they see her lips trembling with pride and gratitude.

An attached water tank, with filters, provided potable water and flushed any sewage into a deeply buried septic tank system.

The building processes had been impressive, but the septic sewage was in another league entirely.

Inspired by Sugarman's urging, every woman and man, every child old enough to stand and push a hastily made toy wheelbarrow, had participated in excavating the pit for Doctor Elizabeth's septic tank.

Labouring through day after day of remorseless heat, glistening with sweat, eyes reddened and watering from fine dust, hands covered with raw and breaking blisters, ignoring profound physical and emotional limitations, they'd carved, hacked and dug this massive pit, entirely by hand, down, down through layer after layer of iron-hard geology.

Less orthodox means were used to acquire a reverse-cycle air-conditioning unit, and the diesel generator to power it, as well as a lighting system.

The local mob learned, in Alice Springs an air-conditioning technician and his diesel-mechanic mate had joined forces to seduce a runaway 13 year-old aboriginal girl. They'd abandoned her when she became pregnant.

As is common, a local aboriginal community had taken the child to its collective heart, caring for her and, eventually, her baby. Complaining to the local authorities would, they thought, have been a waste of time. The deed had been done and nothing could reverse it.

Similar events occurred regularly and seldom caused a ripple on the social surface. But, in this case, the fact that one miscreant knew about air conditioners and the other about diesels attracted some attention.

After consulting Johnny Sugarman, four elders set off for Alice Springs. Borrowing Elizabeth's Land Cruiser, the community's emergency ambulance, was out of the question and they knew better than to ask. So, they walked the first 35 kilometres before an old farm truck, driven by an acquaintance from another mob, offered them a ride into Tennant Creek. From there they hitchhiked to Alice Springs.

Alice Springs had only a small industrial region, so it was easy to locate the air-conditioning installation business where their two targets worked.

Armed with information gained during satellite phone discussions with the Alice Springs mob, these uncles entered the air-conditioning premises through a side gate. It led to a yard littered with wooden pallets and assorted lengths of discarded conduit.

They immediately recognised the two men. There they were, together, lounging against a shaded wall having slipped outside for a smoke.

One had bright-orange hair with a matching beard and the other sported a form of mohawk hairstyle revealing tattoos on each side of his scalp. Approaching them with a malevolent glare, one uncle said 'I want to talk with you two.'

The redhead responded 'Well, we're busy so you can get stuffed.'

But the atmosphere changed when three distinctly unfriendly looking uncles appeared from behind a pile of packing crates.

'Well, yeah, okay, okay, maybe we can talk then. What do you all want?'

Following a rehearsed script the uncles described the shock and dismay felt by the 13 year-old and her family.

'That sort of thing is known as statutory rape, brother' said one uncle, recalling his conviction years earlier for the same offence.

Embellishing their story, the uncles revealed they'd been selected to impose Blackfella's justice and described some horrific measures considered to fit the situation in accordance with tribal custom.

The now intimidated duo accepted the uncles' assurances that there would be no escaping retribution. If they tried to leave town the bush telegraph would track them down.

Expressions of contrition began emerging from trembling lips and bone-dry throats. Noting this welcome development, the uncles drew aside, pretending to consult.

Again, they approached the duo, acquainting them with '...an ancient tribal law, brothers...' (actually one they'd invented while hitchhiking between Tennant Creek and Alice Springs.) Forgiveness could be offered to genuinely sorrowful offenders who offered compensation for sins.

In this case, provision and installation of a state-of-the-art reverse-cycle air-conditioning unit and a new diesel-powered generator, both with manufacturer's valid warranties thank you, would likely do the trick.

The two much-relieved villains, having saved enough funds to finance a planned year of backpacking through Europe, decided they could afford to buy the equipment and include a full lighting set, for good measure. The following weekend they travelled to Elizabeth's community and installed the lighting set, air-conditioner and its diesel generator, all under the watchful supervision of Elizabeth's two electricians.

Constructing the Doctor Elizabeth Surgery changed the small community profoundly but not, as it later emerged, irreversibly.

There was no miraculous epiphany in which people damaged by alcohol, drugs, malnutrition or domestic abuse were suddenly transformed into fully functioning and exemplary adults. But in small ways the change was yet more remarkable, and unexpected, than any standard clinical model might have predicted.

The surgery and its septic pit demonstrated their capacity to achieve. They'd excelled on a come-as-you-are basis, without external encouragement, threats or supervision. Encouraged by Sugarman to consider bigger possibilities, they'd recognised success, enjoyed its flavour and wanted more from this hopeful step toward a new, beautiful addiction.

Over the following weeks, with Sugarman and the community children setting an example, piles of domestic trash were collected from outside every dwelling. The detritus was deposited in a natural depression out-of-sight and, as Sugarman insisted, *'out of smell too'*. Rats and other vermin migrated with the trash. All bottles found were collected and set aside.

Unexpectedly, one of the children proposed to Sugarman a plan for *'our small village'*. Merely 12 years-old, this gifted girl understood that the current community arrangements merely consolidated their insularity. Every family group lived separately, immersed in misery and isolation.

The child also realised that cramming people together could be equally destructive. Her village plan allocated almost four standard building blocks for each dwelling. She'd also proposed wide and defined, but necessarily unpaved, avenues.

As Sugarman commented 'This will be luxury living. If we had water for growin' grass instead of spinifex and saltbush, everyone'd need a Whiteman's ride-on bloody mower.'

News of this self-motivated community spread. Within weeks, a team of government men arrived to offer support.

Their leader, impressed with the town plan, proposed to bring a heavy drilling rig and make long-drop toilets for each of the new housing sites. Sugarman accepted, on the condition that Whitefellas not take over the entire project.

Other aboriginal groups in the region also got the message that something unusual was happening. Elders of the Mordiloc Mob took a special interest.

Sugarman's so-called community included people who'd drifted-in from all over the country. They weren't a tribe, had no totem and no tribal language '...yet look what them fellas plan to do on *our* land.'

Building the doctor-surgery had been acceptable, especially as Elizabeth offered her professional services to all. However, this business of starting to build a town, a substantial settlement, without permission or even consultation, went against long-established custom.

A delegation from the Mordiloc Mob, wearing their most formal sandals and trousers together with a traditional talking display of ochre skin-decoration, visited Johnny Sugarman's community.

Complying with tradition, they sat at the approximate boundary of this loosely defined area and awaited an invitation to enter.

Sugarman saw them approaching but, knowing what they likely wanted to say, and having no responses which might be acceptable under traditional law, he ignored them.

The visitors had anticipated Johnny's response and were prepared for a big, big wait.

By prior arrangement, each day, a relay of supporters from the Mordiloc Mob made the 14-hour return journey, on foot, from their camp to the delegation. They brought food, water and, it must be admitted, a bottle or two of overproof rum because '*it give water better taste.*'

Sugarman surrendered on the third day, sending a five-year-old child to invite the men in for the talking. Lounging on ground beneath the shade of a special gum tree, now known as the *Doctor Elizabeth Surgery Tree*, the three Mordiloc men and Johnny Sugarman, together with two of his community uncles, got down to business.

The Mordiloc position was clear and uncompromising. This was Mordiloc land. If Johnny Sugarman and his mob wanted to build on it then they'd have to provide regular compensation. The detail could be negotiated. After two days of thinking and consulting, Sugarman gave his answer. It was '*No bloody way.*'

According to Sugarman, his mob had the support of aboriginal gods. The Great Emu, the Moon Man and the Rainbow Serpent had agreed that *his* mob was different from all the others. Johnny once heard an American talk about *manifest destiny*. He wasn't too sure what it meant, but it sounded important so he used it.

'Yeah, my mob have manifest destiny. The ancient gods who made this land, who made all the dreamings, made all the totems, they guided us here to show you other Blackfellas the new way. We make better life for all.'

The Mordiloc Mob could come across and join if they wanted to but there was no way Sugarman's mob would be paying anything remotely like a Whitefella tax to anybody.

The delegation reported back to their tribe, urging retribution. But some of the more energetic younger people, sensing a new and welcome renaissance, agreed with Sugarman's viewpoint. Abandoning traditional affiliations, they walked across the intervening 37 kilometres to offer their services and join him. The residual Mordiloc Mob wasn't happy.

The Whitefella's dunny drilling went ahead, notwithstanding, or possibly ignorant of, any disagreement between the Mordiloc Mob and the Sugarman community.

PSALMS

Two huge, orange-coloured trucks arrived carrying a drill rig and a massive diesel engine in matching livery. They were followed by the biggest mobile crane any of them had seen. Next, a tanker filled with diesel fuel arrived. Portable vans to house the workers were installed and supported by another diesel engine providing lighting and air conditioning. A specialised portable building contained toilets and showers. These were linked to yet another tanker filled with water.

Early in the morning of the planned day, an awed Sugarman community watching every move, the impressive rig was raised into vertical position, its drill-bit poised above the ground. At the press of a button the diesel engine started with a cough and a whine before settling into its deep, consistent, rhythmic *foof, foof, foofing; foof foof foofing*.

A deeply tanned, workman wearing a high-viz singlet and red hard-hat pulled a lever. The massive bit began spiralling its way into the harsh terrain

These drill-crewmen were another race. Almost uniformly clad, hard as steel, disciplined, precise and organised, their vocabulary was beyond normal comprehension.

Foreign phrases filled the air. *Link the drill string. Pull-back, pull-down capacity. Apply top-hammer. Try the down-hole hammer. Prep the oversize bit.*

Watch the engine temp.' All commands heavily punctuated with more familiar profanities.

'At least' Sugarman thought, *'they* seem to understand it all.'

Before midday three holes had been drilled, leaving a central core which, in turn, was demolished by a fourth and final drilling. The first long-drop toilet was done, finished. The pace of operations then quickened and two more of the total were done by nightfall.

Ten days later the project was completed to everyone's satisfaction, except perhaps for the contracted drill-operator. He'd seldom stopped complaining about how hard the local rock was, what damage it was doing to his equipment, the cost of new drill-bits, the isolation and the overhead expenses.

Watching this progress, some of the younger men began asking why they hadn't asked for a Whiteman's drill to help with digging the septic tank. But senior women, the aunties, stopped that conversation dead in its tracks.

One tough-looking old lady, her chin covered with curly grey whiskers, a partly-smoked, home-rolled cigarette dangling from her distended lower lip, told the disgruntled youths 'If we not work together on that diggin', we not be gettin' together to do other things' adding 'The diggin' bring us all together, all one people. So you lot can shut up or piss off.'

And some of the community did leave. While most of the mob could sense something new and good was happening, a few others, immersed in depression and alcohol, found the thought of change intolerable. They drifted away to join more compatible pockets of hopelessness.

Their departure was offset by the arrival of new escapees from pervasive misery, including yet more youngsters from the Mordiloc Mob. They wanted to improve their lot, not as directed by Whitemen but as motivated by fellow aboriginals. The beginnings of the Sugarman dream were unfolding.

———————

New and old residents alike soon had plenty to keep them busy. Sugarman, in consultation with the uncles and aunties had identified a natural gully which could be dammed to provide supplementary water when it rained.

All available buckets, plastic clothes baskets, children's wheelbarrows and other containers were pressed into service as the community began the collecting rocks left in piles beside each long-drop toilet excavation.

During thousands of repetitive trips, they transported this material across hundreds of metres to the gully. Guided only by intuition, they built a stable dam wall thick enough to withstand the pressure from a gully-full of water when next it rained.

A local cattleman supported their introduction to civil engineering. Having heard rumours of what was happening at this inconsequential location, he flew a cattle-mustering helicopter to visit the community and look for himself.

There was a lot to see. The area had been tidied up. A fully functioning surgery, built by the local mob, was in operation and staffed with a qualified doctor. They had a town plan. Long-drop dunnies had been dug to support the proposed dwellings. The rock-walled dam was almost completed.

Realising, without a waterproof membrane, the dam would leak like a sieve, the cattleman asked Johnny Sugarman how he proposed to complete the project.

Sugarman had to admit, 'I know we need to seal him dam tight but we need concrete. I plan pass word all around and see if any brothers can help us. Don't worry, we won't stop until we get it all working.'

From beneath brim of his sweat-stiffened Akubra hat, the tough, rangy cattleman fought hard to block tears threatening to roll down his leathery complexion. This outpost of hopeless welfare cases was achieving miracles.

Without another word, he turned and walked back to his helicopter, retrieving a satellite phone from a compartment under the seat. Following a quietly spoken conversation lasting about two minutes, he returned.

'Johnny Sugarman, if you'll accept it, my pastoral company would like to provide and install the concrete and other waterproofing materials needed to complete your community dam.'

'The wet season's still about three months away but, to be safe, I'd prefer to complete this within around six weeks.'

Sugarman accepted. The cattleman was as good as his word, and that is how the community dam was completed.

With the dam built, Sugarman and the other elders started two more projects.

Youngsters, who should have been at school, were sent into the bush to collect manure for a planned community vegetable garden.

'You kids, take bags, go find all shit in the bush. Cattle, camel, kangaroos, all of it. Bring it back here.'

The beamingly beautiful children, still enthusiastic and trusting as children worldwide tend to be, worked hard at their assigned task. Bag after bag was filled with manure and dragged laboriously back to the camp. Aunties, with an encyclopaedic knowledge of bush chemistry, mixed the manure with the leaves of designated plants and began converting it into a potent compost.

This almost magical ingredient, combined with water from the dam, would eventually fertilise a community garden-full of fresh vegetables for up to nine months of every year.

Sugarman then proposed to his now-energised community that they use their huge piles of empty bottles for building one or more walls of new houses. 'We now a new and better mob. We don't have to live like slobs. We set the example for others'.

Nobody had attempted such a project and it led to vigorous debates.

'We should have bottle necks face inwards, make nice looking walls on outside.'

'Bullshit. That good for spiders and stuff to breed inside the house. We have bottle necks face outside. Nice smooth walls inside.'

'Best walls will be high. Better air flow. Cooler. Easy to stand up.'

'You not a fair dinkum aboriginal. We *always* have low roof. Tradition. Besides, uses less bottles, faster to build.'

Sugarman was delighted when the most intense discussion focussed on glass colours and designs to be incorporated. Whatever was decided, these dwellings would be lasting expressions of their accomplishments, artefacts to be admired by others.

Once again, their friendly cattleman came to the party.

Johnny Sugarman was cautions, expecting the Whitefella to begin imposing conditions, giving directions on how things should be done, or imposing deadlines as Whites typically did. That would have been unacceptable.

This was a Blackfella's project. It had to be done in accordance with lunar and other rhythms which motivated his people to work steadily, even frenetically, at times. On other occasions they'd sit, apparently idle. Sugarman wasn't happy with these superstitions but was smart enough to let them prevail for the time being.

Fortunately, the cattleman was a fourth-generation outback man. Long ago, he'd abandoned any attempt to understand aboriginal spirituality. But he knew these were powerful forces and understood that interference on his part would be counterproductive.

Everyone in the community was grateful, but not surprised, when he offered materials to mix concrete for foundations of the first two houses, and also provide a new, hand-operated concrete mixer for them to keep.

He was also prepared to give them cement to glue their bottles together and fill the inevitable gaps. But the aunties politely declined *that* offer.

By combining the sap from several native plants they could mix a glue almost as strong as any Whitefella product and could use it to stick the bottles firmly into position. Gaps would be filled with a mixture of mud and the hair scraped from kangaroo hides, a formula they knew would endure.

———

Sugarman and his fellow elders, the uncles and aunties, began planning to raise funds for building the remaining houses.

After occasionally heated debates they decided to operate outback, dry-country food tours for cashed-up Whitefellas from the cities.

At first, the notion of getting Whitefellas to pay money for eating native food seemed ridiculous. 'Let's face it' said one of the uncles 'most of that tucker tastes crook. You all know we prefer Whitefella tucker when we can get it.'

But the aunties weren't so dismissive. 'Course it tastes bad' said one of them 'because we treat it bad. We throw kangaroo or goanna onto coals of a fire. Then we drag it off, part burned, part cooked, part bloody raw. What'd you expect?'

'Yeah', said another 'we cook it proper in Whitefella's Dutch-oven, plenty herbs, native limes, all beautiful.'

The man persisted. 'But why would Whitefellas pay money to eat stuff anyone can pick up for free?'

An auntie struck back. 'That's all you know, you lazy bastard. It hard to find. Take lot of work. Some stuff, if not cooked proper, can make you sick. Whitefella not know where to look or how to cook it.'

The aunties won the debate although they did concede that week of eating native foods could become dreary.

However, someone remembered that several naturally growing plants had hallucinogenic properties. Normally used only during corrobborees and traditional dances, they could be included with occasional meals to leave the Whitefellas believing they'd found the foods of the gods. 'Yeah and find plenty sex too, so watch out!' said one aunty.

Elizabeth, a willing participant in the scheme, prepared a submission for the Whitefellas' departmental consideration. It sought financial aid to establish an indigenous enterprise. Included in her business case was an Environmental Impact Statement describing the geographic boundaries of the food gathering initiative. It included evidence illustrating the activity would be sustainable.

Guided by Sugarman, and without her knowledge, the region she described included the entire Mordiloc tribal lands as well as the regions recognised by aboriginal people as belonging to three other tribes.

Officials from the Aboriginal and Torres Strait Islander Development Department, keen to encourage any hopefully viable aboriginal enterprise, fast-tracked the approval. Further motivated by a significant underspend in their new budget allocation, they completed all formalities within three weeks.

A letter was hand-delivered to *Mr J Sugarman, Chief Executive Officer, Indigenous Nutrition Project,* advising him of the outcome.

The community would receive a fully equipped overland bus, able to carry 20 passengers, together with a full set of camping equipment as well as a mobile kitchen to be towed behind the bus.

The Department noted four members of the community held current driving licences and they would be designated bus drivers. A generous allowance had been made for enterprise advertising. The Environmental Impact Statement had been approved.

Sugarman, highly intelligent and equally cunning, decided to further implicate Elizabeth in supporting his scheme. He called a community meeting, highlighted her contribution to a successful outcome, and asked her to read the letter.

She did so. As expected, everyone was ecstatic. For the first time they could anticipate a viable future.

Privately, the bit that most pleased Sugarman was Whitefella's approval of the region over which they could sustainably collect native foods. Remembering his argument with the Mordiloc elders, he'd become convinced that his own disparate community really did have some special but indefinable attributes.

The facts were obvious. No other mob could have built Elizabeth's surgery. Other gifts had followed in the form of the community plan, the dunny drilling, the new dam, and on it went. Every success, all their achievements, clearly demonstrated they would be the core of a new aboriginal nation.

And now he had that precious piece of paper giving his community a formal right to gather foods over the entire Mordiloc tribal lands, and other lands as well. His dream, his plan, was underway now.

On a roll, he decided to create aboriginal history by doing something that probably hadn't happened for hundreds of years, possibly longer. He'd create a new tribe and adopt a new totem for his mob. The totem would be impressive, awesome, not something small like a gecko or a lizard. Perhaps it would be a fire-breathing eagle or a giant kangaroo. It'd have to look menacing to suit a community about to become the greatest, the most powerful, mob ever.

Looking back over recent months, Elizabeth felt she'd made the correct decision. A core of aboriginality, a deep and abiding dreaming throbbed deeply within her, but years of exposure to Western education and science had blunted her perception of the tribal mentality. This, she felt, limited her capacity to provide leadership. Sugarman had become the community's go-to person, its headman.

Just the same, she believed other corrosive influences were affecting the entire community and they were either not recognised or, more likely, well known but considered too difficult to tackle.

REVELATIONS

One humid, hot afternoon, with powerful, bubbling clouds signalling the approaching wet season, Elizabeth stood near to the wall of the still-empty dam. Sugarman was approaching, walking slowly, lost in thought. As he drew near, she made her move.

'Y'know, Johnny, the community's been making wonderful progress and achieving many things. I'm very proud to be here and see it happening. But most people continue to suffer from two really bad things.'

Sugarman knew what was coming. 'You mean grog and drugs.'

'Precisely. They're so much a part of life here. I don't know if anything can be done, or even if trying to do something might be harmful. We don't want to damage the wonderful new community spirit you have been building.'

'I've been thinkin' same thing' said Johnny. 'It very big problem. Almost all of us is addicts to grog, drugs or both. Not easy to stop but it is holding us back'.

'Maybe we can do this the Blackfella way. We do one thing at a time. We accept many times we fail, but we keep pushin' on. We use tribal law.'

Now united as joint-schemers, they sat together on the smooth, weather-whitened trunk of a fallen tree, using their toes to casually trace lines in grey dust covering the rocky ground.

Johnny spoke first. 'There no way to stop drugs. If nobody can get Whitefella drugs the aunties know how to make brews from native bush. We say it not as bad as Whitefella drugs but I not so sure. You have an overdose of Blackfella drug it will kill you just the same. I've seen it happen.'

Agreeing to ignore the drug problem at present, they took a pragmatic look at the alcohol challenge. Improved morale, a sense of purpose and a potential string of community objectives had offered incentives to drink less. In fact, alcohol consumption, although still too high, was already falling.

But, they wondered, could there be a trigger, a catalyst, to start something radical, to begin a reform not yet recognised by other members of the mob?

They decided to throw this problem across to the community, with perhaps a little guidance. Specifically, a meeting could be held to seek advice from the powerful Moon Man. The next full moon would shine upon them three nights from now.

Normally, only initiated men would have been allowed to witness communications with Moon Man. But this time, Johnny Sugarman, happy to employ superstition when it suited him, received a message from the heavens telling him to invite all women and little children as well.

When the predetermined evening arrived, the entire community sat on dusty ground in an open area. Women and children remained together. Men congregated in their own group.

The sun slowly set, taking with it the remaining glow of daylight. They continued sitting, waiting, not particularly patiently, for the moon to rise above a flat, distant horizon.

None of the women or children really understood why they were assembled, but the sense of honour at attending such a significant event was palpable. The women were also curious to see what men had been doing at these ceremonies.

With everyone seated and Moon's appearance imminent, according to an astronomical App on Sugarman's satellite phone, he appeared from the darkness. Dressed in his Moon-costume of pure white clay supplemented by white feathers from the local cockatoo-parrots, highlighted by strips of reflective aluminium cooking foil he'd been keeping for a special occasion, Johnny projected a supernatural presence.

Stomping quietly, almost gracefully at first, he increased the pace of his movements before whirling and stomping, stomping and whirling, now silent, now chanting in a strange language.

After almost an hour he fell to the ground, facing upwards. Extending his arms and legs to form a human crucifix, he gave himself up to the now clearly visible Moon Man.

Before the startled eyes and ears of his audience, particularly the women and children, Moon began speaking through Johnny Sugarman. The voice was similar to Sugarman's, but somehow strangely altered. Moon had a message for them, first in English, then in a lunar version of the Kaytetye aboriginal language.

'All people listen to me. I want to talk about grog. Grog bad for you. Cause bad health, cost money, make for wife bashing. Grog mean children not cared for good enough. All caused by grog. You have many good things happen but grog can ruin them all.'

The supernatural communication faded into indecipherable mutterings, leaving Johnny twitching and trembling. Another hour passed before he was able to lever himself into a sitting posture and from there to stand on both feet, feigning almost total exhaustion.

Observers would later recall that their leader had indeed contacted the Moon Man in a way that affected everyone who witnessed the event.

As Sugarman regained his feet, the entire community stood with him shouting, dancing, jumping, singing, celebrating. 'Yes, yes, yes, grog the enemy. Let all us fight grog. We will win.'

Seated again, after many requests from the rapidly recovering Sugarman, they began to consider the practical implications of fighting against grog. They knew it wouldn't be possible to stop alcohol consumption immediately. They accepted some people could never stop drinking yet they were brothers and sisters, integrated members of this rapidly consolidating community.

The mob agreed on two things; they should stop drinking alcohol within the newly defined boundaries of their village settlement, and breaches would be punishable by traditional law.

In days following, several men and women departed to live with neighbouring mobs, leaving their children with other families, 'to give 'em a chance for future'. They'd agreed with the anti-grog policy but knew they could never comply and were horrified at the thought of traditional retribution.

Of those who remained, nobody was prepared, or possibly able, to stop drinking alcohol immediately. Sugarman, cagey old man that he was, passed the word around that Moon Man had returned to him, late in the night, and told him to postpone the retribution aspect while new arrangements bedded down.

Drinking binges continued outside the community's borders but in plain view of everyone else. Participants felt a sense of weakness, shame and vulnerability. Worse, they weren't allowed back until they seemed sober, or close to it. The attraction of 'hangin' on a good one' waned.

Within what passed for privacy in their ramshackle dwellings, people continued tippling in secret, gulping an occasional drink when temptations prevailed. But the overall rate of alcohol consumption plummeted. To be seen staggering and drunk was taboo.

All might have been well if Sugarman had been satisfied. But he wasn't. The heady thrill of power and influence were clutching him in their vice-like grip. It was exhilarating. Increasingly confident, he started giving orders, contrary to almost universal aboriginal traditions.

Assembling his elders, the uncles, he told them, 'We now top dog. We need make other mobs see the best way is our way. Best thing they can do is be part of us, part of the new aboriginal world.'

The uncles also felt a sense of destiny, although they might not have put it that way, and were willing supporters.

'Yeah' said one 'we tell them other mobs they join us, make everyone strong. First step, they must cut back on grog.'

Motivated by Sugarman's enthusiasm, inspired by a sense of reflected superiority, the uncles agreed to become envoys. They'd meet all four tribal groups within the Whitefella-endorsed area of influence, acquainting them with the new reality, the better way to live.

Them other mobs would be offered the privilege of joining this new and expanding nation within a nation.

During the next week, other mobs cordially welcomed Sugarman's ambassadors, even organising smoking ceremonies for the occasion. They listened attentively to the message delivered.

But over many years they'd heard too many unfulfilled promises: guarantees that children would no longer live in poverty, that there'd be a treaty between Whites and Blacks, that land-rights would be a priority for the Australian Government. None had happened and so they were inclined to be sceptical.

Latent suspicions consolidated when mobs began comparing notes and found neighbouring communities had received an identical approach. Common to every case was that Sugarman's mob would be top dog, would be calling the shots.

Networking via their satellite-linked mobile phones, the tribes arranged to meet at a recognised location for conducting secret men's business. Sugarman's mob was not invited.

As recently as two decades ago, such an arrangement would have been difficult or impossible. Sugarman's mob would have intercepted and read messages sent between tribes by smoke signals. To use runners would have been impracticable. Every question or suggestion would have required a new and laborious round of running.

Technologically enabled but motivated by tradition, seated on tussocks of grass in the lengthening afternoon shade of three enormous reddish-brown rocks, the uncles were barely aware they had one foot in an aboriginal past and another in the Whiteman's present.

Following a hurried smoking ceremony, they got down to business and began discussing yet another external challenge, something the Aboriginal people had done countless times since European settlement of Australia began.

'This Johnny Sugarman plan no different to other things Whitefellas do to us', one uncle said. They want to rob aboriginal people of their dreaming.'

'That's right' exclaimed another 'and that bloody bush tucker business is no good. Johnny's mob want to make money from teachin' bloody Whitefellas how to steal from *our* food.'

More thoughtful heads among them conceded that cheap alcohol and the recent period of gun-enabled violence had been disastrous. But solutions would have to be their own, not something imposed by Johnny Sugarman regardless of what paperwork the Whitefella's had given him, typically without consultation.

They all agreed, regardless of how it was done, Sugarman had to be stopped. 'He can do what he likes with his own mob but he can't make us hop to the tune of *his* bloody didgeridoo.'

First, they considered a campaign to disrupt Johnny's native-food tours, but soon realised any such action would attract Whitefella retribution, which could be swift and devastating.

After further consultation they decided to attack Johnny's mob by using the Whitefella himself as a weapon.

'Yeah, we need what Whitefellas call a "great and powerful ally" and nobody better at doing that than the Whitefella himself.' Opinions then became divided as to whether Whitefellas were especially *great*, but they were certainly powerful.'

Within a week of that clandestine meeting, a tribal delegation dressed themselves in going-to-town gear. Led by uncles from the Mordiloc mob, they mainly walked and partly hitchhiked into Tennant Creek. On arriving, they made a beeline for a familiar alcohol-sales outlet.

It was a single-level building with a rusting corrugated-iron roof. Old tractor tyres, painted white, surrounded the most vulnerable posts and walls, protecting them from drunken drivers. Yellowish, possibly once white, paint was peeling from external sheet-metal walls. They also featured faded and almost illegible advertising. A thoughtfully provided annex served as a drive-through facility so thirsty customers could more easily fill the trays of their pick-up trucks with cases of beer.

'Hey boss' their spokesman said, addressing the head barman 'have you heard what that Johnny Sugarman mob is trying to do? Cut right down on grog for their mob and now try to force *our* mobs to do same thing. We agree maybe too much grog sometimes, but we not goin' to do what that mob tell us. No bloody way!'

The barman extended the courtesy of listening. An alcoholic escapee from Sugarman's community had already told him about the Johnny Sugarman anti-grog campaign for his own mob. It was, the barman had decided, nothing to worry about. Sooner or later it would fail spectacularly.

But a regional expansion of an anti-grog concept would be a worrying development. First, the new Australian Government had restored the former taxes on alcohol, reducing sales and profitability. Now that aboriginal medicine-man seemed hell-bent on making matters worse. Johnny Sugarman might damage one of the most efficient and market-driven business cycles ever invented.

For decades, the aboriginal population had been receiving financial support, mainly in the form of unemployment payments, commonly known as *Whitefella's sit-down money*, much of which they spent on alcohol. This cycle, according to the barman's reasoning, brought funds back into the White population from which it had come, as taxes, in the first place. It was a win-win situation.

Urgent consultation was clearly a priority. It happened the following day.

Representatives from local pubs met. From the outset it was obvious the maxim, *always back the horse named self-interest*, was alive and galloping toward the finishing post. It took them less than an hour to settle on a plan. The concept was as simple as it was brutal.

TEMPTATIONS

Three days later a small truck fitted with an insulated van left for the drive to Johnny's community. The van was filled with ice-cold beer together with cases of scotch, gin and rum. Scrawled along each side van was, '*FREE GROG*'.

On approaching the Sugarman community, the truck driver and two companions parked under a tree. In the gaps between tussocks of dried grass they set-up a circle of the folding chairs that they'd transported on the roof of their van.

'At least some of our valued clients will be able to enjoy a drink in comfort' sneered one.

With the set-up completed, first one and then all of them began shouting 'free grog, free grog, free grog.'

Their invitation punctuated the quiet environment and drew people toward the van. At first, they were motivated by curiosity, then thirst and finally by a resurgence of naked craving.

From various tasks, from beneath small trees where a few had been relaxing and from inside the dilapidated dwellings, they came and continued coming.

The enticing summons offered more than free grog. It implied relief from recently acquired and challenging commitments to working, thinking, worrying, planning and achieving.

Vivid memories of day-long alcoholic orgies provided an irresistible magnet. The familiar warmth of booze, of immersion in a soft, compliant daze, could replace everything. No worries mate!

The uninvited visitors were delighted. One session like this was all it would take. That mob would be back to their old ways and the good old profitable life could continue.

———————

From the surgery where they had been listing medical requirements for the next two weeks, Johnny Sugarman and Elizabeth heard the call. Sugarman, by far the most politically astute, immediately understood this was a confrontational attack on the new aboriginal nation.

Rushing to his donga, Sugarman retrieved an eight-cartridge, pump-action shotgun acquired during the period of relaxed firearms controls. He'd bought the weapon from a friend who knew a friend, meaning it was probably stolen. He'd hidden it in case of need. This was a need!

Sugarman, although armed, did not look threatening. Wearing a white surgical gown, holding the weapon with both hands on its stock, the barrel pointed skywards, he gave the impression of never having wielded either a shotgun or a rifle.

Unaware of his comical image, Sugarman marched toward the van calling to his community members, 'Stop here, stop here, stop here,' his cries mingling with the calls of 'free grog, free grog, free grog.'

The mass migration toward free grog faltered as people began milling in confusion. The temptation of alcohol was potent but Sugarman also had considerable authority.

He'd reached the front ranks of his community when Elizabeth, seeing Johnny with a weapon she didn't know he owned, ran towards him.

Grasping the shotgun's barrel, she tried to keep it pointed skywards, adding to the cacophony by shouting 'No, Johnny, no, no, no, no.'

Sugarman reacted intuitively. Barely aware Elizabeth was involved, fanatically intent on pursuing his vaguely defined objective, he wrenched the weapon into a horizontal position, dragging a still-attached Elizabeth to the ground with it.

Between them, both struggling for physical supremacy, they released the safety catch and pulled the trigger. A shot was fired. The weapon kicked backwards. Both Sugarman and Elizabeth almost lost their grips on it.

Despite now painful wrists, the two continued arm-wrestling. The weapon discharged again, also ineffectually except that it recoiled into Elizabeth's abdomen.

Dropping to her knees, she folded, doubled-up in shock and pain.

When the first shot whined past their heads the men were convinced this was an attempted deadly attack. Retreating to the rear of their van, one man opened the near-side cabin door. Resting on two brackets was a high-powered rifle, kept loaded in case of attack by a wild bull or buffalo.

He retrieved the weapon.

Now armed, one man scrambled forward beneath the van. He took up his firing position using a front wheel for cover. Johnny Sugarman continued standing in the open, clearly silhouetted, holding his weapon, intent on using it as a threat.

The experienced shooter, rifle nestled firmly into his shoulder, steadied, aimed carefully and fired. His bullet penetrated Sugarman's abdomen and travelled through his body before continuing its trajectory.

Sugarman stiffened and fell forward.

Elizabeth, sufficiently recovered to see what had happened, ignored her painful attempts at breathing. Dashing forward, she snatched the now blood-covered weapon. Unlike Sugarman, *she* was determined to kill.

Inbred and ancient survival instincts guided her as she rolled her body across the dusty ground to present a smaller and more challenging target.

Pausing briefly, without consciously aiming, she twice fired toward the shooter, her second shot blasting his face into a mush of gore. Some of the pellets entered both eye sockets and penetrated his brain.

Suspecting the men had only one weapon between them she sprang to her feet, running forward, intent on shooting the remaining two interlopers. But she could see only one of them.

He was running toward a clump of small trees, his bulging thighs and pathetically fat bum jiggling repulsively with every step.

By now, she'd figured how this weapon worked. Pressing it into her shoulder, leaning forward to better absorb the recoil, she took careful aim.

Baang!

The noise filling her ears, her entire head, arrived simultaneously with the bullet that entered the upper-right-side of her rib-gage before boring its way through her chest.

The missing man, lying under the van with his now-deceased shooting companion, had grabbed their rifle. Realising Elizabeth was now the primary aggressor, and a seriously dangerous one, he'd aimed, fired and killed her—almost.

Critically wounded, with shock suppressing her agony, Elizabeth, her nurturing instincts now dominating, dragged herself toward Johnny Sugarman.

The second shooter didn't interfere.

Her progress toward Sugarman was slow, methodical, determined and consistent. It took almost 30 seconds to reach him.

He wasn't moving. His immobile chest indicated he wasn't breathing. Stretching forward she felt the side of his neck. It had no pulse. Sugarman was dead.

Rolling onto her back, Elizabeth surrendered to a wave of physical, emotional, intellectual and spiritual exhaustion. It washed over and through her. She was about to die, she was ready to die. The ancestors were calling, reaching out to her. She welcomed then, yearned for them with an aboriginal spirituality stronger and more compelling than Johnny Sugarman's had ever been.

Elizabeth's last thought was of Allen Ivory. She hoped, in some undefined but supernatural way, they would meet again. Her final breath, unheard by anybody, gently exhaled his name, '*Allen, ...Allen*'.

And that is how cardiothoracic surgeon, Doctor Elizabeth Hope Gnagnarra, died. Longing for the man who had been pivotal in planning for the invasion of her nation, leading to its unintended but horrific consequences, including the events that had killed her. In her final moment of life she'd illustrated, yet again, the impossibility of understanding the thoughts and motivations of another human being.

Shocked by what they'd seen, the entire community was for a few seconds frozen, uncomprehending, unable to react.

Their leader and Doctor Elizabeth were dead, together with their motivation, their hopes, the potential for their children to have futures of any value. All was lost. Tears and wails of inexpressible grief began.

The remaining two interlopers were first to recover. Sensing this mob would now be more susceptible than previously, they changed tack and joined the community in expressive mourning for Johnny and Elizabeth.

It had been a horrible misunderstanding. As everyone could see, the Whitefellas hadn't started the shooting. One of their own dearly loved mates had also died. Everyone needed to sit down together for a comforting drink.

And they did drink! Within two hours, the entire vanload of alcohol had been consumed.

Men, women and children were hopelessly drunk. Some staggered about making pests of themselves. Others sat quietly, sucking on bottles of scotch or rum. A few flopped, comatose, in the dappled shade.

Meanwhile, the Whitefellas, convinced they were fireproof in accordance with the law, had used a satellite phone to notify the Tennant Creek police and ambulance service, reporting what had happened.

They also telephoned the coordinator of the 'back to booze' campaign, ordering another van with free grog. 'Just send beer and rum this time. It's what they seem to like best. With Sugarman dead, it'll be the final nail in their no-grog campaign.'

And it was.

At nightfall, the second van-full of free grog arrived to service community members still able to imbibe, with extra supplies for those who would awaken, hungover, desperate for a refreshing *hair of the dog*.

The *status quo* had been restored. Power and authority had been satisfactorily redistributed, as it usually is, eventually.

Police investigated the shooting incident, recommending no action be taken following this regrettable event. The matter was closed.

Elizabeth and Johnny Sugarman were buried in separate but adjacent graves. They were laid to rest in a section of the Tennant Creek cemetery set aside for aboriginal people who wanted to be among their own people. Traditional smoking ceremonies and chants evoking deep and sincere sorrow were held as the ancestors took two more spirits unto themselves.

The only surprising incident in the entire grieving process was the arrival, as a mourner, of Johnny Sugarman's handsome, athletic-looking son. Nobody in the mob had a clue this man existed. But here he was, wearing an immaculate white uniform, displaying a row of impressive medals, the clear-sighed, ambitious Lieutenant Commander John Namatjira Sugarman PhD, electronics engineer, Republic of Australia Navy.

As the softly spoken but confident man said later 'I'm not so different to my dad. We often see peculiar electronic effects in our radars. Diagnosing and eliminating them requires something like a witch-doctor mentality.'

Three weeks later, an enterprising Tennant Creek resident established a small but profitable general store in the disused Doctor Elizabeth building. It sold fizzy drinks, tinned and processed foods, some toiletry items and, of course, alcohol.

COMPULSION

The Government of the People's Republic of China was well satisfied. Its supplies of minerals and raw materials were now more secure than formerly. Export and import arrangements had been restored. Russia's opportunism had been counterbalanced and the United States was diminished.

From his ultra-modern office on an upper-floor of a glass-clad building, Premier Wen Jintao was in a reflective mood.

Bringing Australia within our strategic umbrella created a magnificent pincer effect. We've ensured Chinese dominance of South Asia. The South China Sea and Western Pacific have become our ponds. We balanced Russia's expansion.

How pleasant it is that the United States was stupid enough to injure itself in ways that will take at least a decade to heal. Even then, its role as a dominant world power will likely remain diminished.

Nevertheless, the Americans are a very determined and dangerous race. They'll need to be watched carefully.

Hmmm, I wonder what the Chinese Dragon might do to ensure the United States remains permanently weakened.

Perhaps we could increase our trade with Canada and Mexico, gradually consolidating our ties with them. Both are feeling they've been treated badly by America. Bringing them into our sphere of influence would press against the

American land borders both north and south. The Americans deserve nothing less.

We would need to move gently, sensitively at first. But, yes, I think this is achievable.

In Washington DC, an elected President of the United States was focused on rebuilding his nation.

He had no intention of resuscitating the slogan used successfully by one former White House occupant, to '*make America great again*'. His new and well-publicised objective was to make America *function* again, both domestically and as a cohesive, responsible international citizen.

Hanging remorselessly over his head was a Damoclean sword, suspended by the thread of Australian, Russian and Chinese knowledge about what had happened to Canberra. They could, he knew, sever the cord at any time.

But regardless of constraints, the President knew America wouldn't remain passively and inwardly focussed. From early childhood he and countless millions of Americans had been taught that this, the land of the free, the home of the brave, had a global duty, a destiny. It was part of the national psyche.

Somehow, someway, the United States will have to reassert itself. It's a duty we owe to God and to the free world. This is not the time to act, but we can begin planning for a future, one in which our enemies will be vanquished.

Looking at his schedule for the morning, reflecting briefly that presidential power rested significantly with his senior personal secretary, he noted an unusual entry. *10.00 am. Prof R Harley-Laver, South-West Biology Lab (TOP SECRET/EXTREME)*

He knew *South-West Biology Laboratory* was a synonym for one of the most sensitive organisations in the United States. It was dedicated to developing new biological weapons. Soon after assuming office he'd been briefed on their latest initiative.

They'd been developing an apparently undetectable microbiological strain. It was claimed to function on humans by subtly reducing intelligence and reasoning capacity by up to 20 per cent. Widespread, it could render a nation uncompetitive.

At the time of his briefing they'd been running experiments to determine if the new biology could be linked, as he recalled, to DNA in ways that allowed for racially profiled attacks. Tests had been underway to confirm the potential for targeting *Chinese* DNA.

Normally pragmatic, he allowed himself a moment of optimism.

I sure hope that damned scientist can report good news on the Chinese DNA tests. With a weapon like this we could eliminate them as a global force and they'd never know what hit them. It'd take more than a decade to pull it off but that'd give us time to recover, consolidate and be ready to act. We'll do better this time around, much better.

It was 9.00 am. One hour to go.

Editorial Note.

After the Canberra Catastrophe, and following the creation of Australia as an independent republic, dedicated scholars attempted to recreate some individual accounts of people's reactions in the days following the nuclear detonation, filling inevitable gaps with hopefully believable invention and dialogue. Following are three such stories.

Xavier

Father Xavier Westmeath had been appointed Assistant Priest in a parish covering several recently built Canberra suburbs. Signalling his religious vocation only by a chrome-plated cross attached to the collar of his shirt, the slightly built, sincere young man was dedicated to his perceived role as a loving spiritual shepherd.

Often seen visiting Catholic families in streets lined with single-level, brick-veneered houses, he'd been welcomed and accepted by most. Typically seated on a recently assembled Ikea chair, avoiding toys scattered across the floor, he'd listen attentively to parishioners' repetitive worries, as if hearing them for the first time.

Ignoring the cacophony of attention-seeking children, he'd often and empathically nod his head-full of curly black hair. Parishioners felt he treated them as equals.

However, Fath'r Xavier wasn't a push-over either, as some of his flock discovered.

'No Jason and Patricia, the purpose of marriage is to procreate and you both made it clear to me you are not going to have children. I feel I can't perform your marriage ceremony.'

'Sorry Helen, I accept you are only 16 years old and your friends were complicit in feeding you alcohol, but the Church reveres human life. If you have an abortion instead of carrying your child to the full term then you'll be committing a serious sin.'

A few parishioners stopped attending Mass, alienated by Xavier's orthodoxy. However, when a complaint reached the Archbishop's ear, he made clear he thoroughly approved of Xavier's ministry.

Not only that, but the Archbishop's media advisor noticed this young priest had a *photogenic face*. Xavier's mop of hair sat atop a broad forehead which supervised his straight nose, thin lips and strong jaw. High cheek bones completed the picture, ensuring he presented visually as a believable, scholarly and almost physically attractive person.

In addition to his demanding parish duties, Xavier was directed to attend several courses in media studies. They led to occasional appearances on television breakfast sessions and talkback programs.

One morning, Xavier pulled his ageing white Toyota Corolla to the curb, stopping in response to the insistent ringing of his cellphone, thinking yet again he really must find time to install a Bluetooth connection.

'Father Westmeath.'

'Good morning Father, this is Monsignor McGantry from the Sydney Archdiocese. Our respective Archbishops have been in discussion and I've been asked to inform you of their plans.'

'A plan involving me? Are you sure? I'm only recently ordained. What could they want with me?'

'The situation is this. As you know, the long-simmering movement seeking to legalise assisted dying for the terminally ill has been gaining ground. Two States have already passed enabling legislation. A vigorous and effective campaign is needed to stop this nonsense in its tracks before it begins to erode the Church's power and influence at a national level.'

'You will be required to use your media-related skills and become part of the push-back. You'll be seconded to the Sydney Archdiocese for an indefinite period.'

'Please hand over your current responsibilities to Father O'Grady and report to my Archbishop's city office for a consultative meeting at 2.30 pm tomorrow.'

'Well, if you put it that way Father, yes, I'll be there.'

———

The following day, Xavier and seven other men he'd never met were seated on matching office chairs at a round, glass-topped table in an ultra-modern meeting room. One wall of floor-to-ceiling glass offered a view onto the busy street located two levels below them. A framed oil-painting was the only adornment on the three remaining beige walls. It was a modernist interpretation of the Resurrection.

Feeling mystified and slightly intimidated, Father Xavier Westmeath sat quietly, comprehensively insulated from the reality of cars, exhaust fumes, city sounds and pedestrians outside. His companions, also taciturn, were undaunted for they were by nature competitive, ruthless, remorseless and aggressively successful businessmen.

Already known to each other, they realised they'd been invited here to lead a fight and likely a tough one too. Moderately superstitious, they each anticipated their participation would be rewarded by requirements for minimal acts of contrition when next they confessed to some of their more vicious commercial activities.

On the stroke of 2.30 pm the tall, plump and energetic Archbishop of Sydney strode in. Accompanying his business-suited eminence was a whiff of incense and an obviously stressed, vertically challenged priest-secretary. The secretary was burdened with a heavy bag, presumably containing a laptop and numerous documents.

Although one chair was vacant, the Archbishop remained standing, a posture emphasising the distance between him and his audience. 'Thank you, gentlemen, for attending. As you already have been informed, I called this meeting to begin planning for an anti assisted-dying campaign. You have been hand-picked because of your capacity to get things done and your faithfulness to the Magisterium of the Catholic Church.'

'As you know, there has been, nationwide, increasing pressure to legalise what has been described as "dying with dignity". But the Church considers any such activity a sin. We require our view to apply across Australian society to the extent possible, including to Catholics, other believers and even atheists. If we fail then our influence across the political spectrum will be diminished. We do not intend to confront that outcome.'

'As a minimum, I want any enabling legislation stopped in its tracks. Preferably, existing criminal law, where relevant, will also be reinforced, although I suspect that might be too ambitious.'

'To deflect attention from the reality that this is a religion-inspired crusade, all except one of you is a lay-person. Laity will dominate planning and execution. I have already consulted with leaders of other Christian faiths and we all agreed with this approach.'

'At the same time, our Church cannot afford to appear disinterested. Consequently, the man on my left, Father Xavier Westmeath, who has a track record of effective media presentations, will be our primary public personality.'

Everyone looked at the slightly blushing Xavier. Those with visual-media experience could see he was a good choice. If his voice wasn't up to scratch, well, they could always dub the dialogue.

The Archbishop added that every reasonable initiative would be fully funded. There would be no additional guidance. They should, 'formulate plans between yourselves then get on with this crusade for the Church.'

The one-sided conversation ended as abruptly as it began. Without pausing to answer questions or ascertain reactions, the man turned and haughtily strode away.

In one brief but almost luxurious moment the priest-secretary calculated he had only 147 days to serve in this wretched assignment before handing it over to some other poor bastard. He then turned and jogged behind his master as they rushed toward their next tightly scheduled commitment.

Remaining in the same room, the team held its first meeting. They arranged for augmentation by an experienced Christian journalist as well as a senior solicitor. Seminaries were asked to provide their brightest students to act as research assistants. They also agreed a media campaign was needed to emphasise potential dangers of assisted dying.

With Xavier temporarily out of the room answering a 'call of nature', they decided that compassion and social justice could be either ignored or used as a convenient veneer. Public or political opinion, if not supportive, would simply be made to change. They'd fill in the details later.

Within days, television advertisements and media releases began. The visual media included gruesome details of euthanasia disasters, almost amounting to mass murder, all invented or adopted from distorted versions of reality. They were vaguely attributed, so it was almost impossible for objectors to repudiate them. Successful assisted dying arrangements operating for decades in other nations were never mentioned.

One often-replayed 'community announcement' showed a family, delighted by new laws, celebrating with champagne the financial windfall they'd gained following their grandmother's premature death. Father Xavier was phased-in with a voiceover containing an admonitory warning which faithfully conveyed his dedicated and compassionate sincerity. He was the perfect man for the job.

When published studies supported assisted dying, statisticians were employed to attack the data by injecting confusing terminology or raising doubts as to methodologies. Less orthodox strategies, including physical and legal threats together with cyber-attacks, were also used. Reputations of leading opponents were smeared.

Threats to withdraw lucrative advertising from the hard-pressed print and television media led to editorial policies opposed to assisted dying. Letters in support of assisted dying were ignored by the print media except for an occasional irrationally argued and grammatically deficient submission. Major publishing houses uniformly rejected manuscripts arguing for legislative change.

This was war. Week by week, threatened politician after politician, one vulnerable sporting hero at a time, it became obvious the assisted dying camp was being routed.

For Father Xavier, the public face of this campaign, it was a major and profile-raising triumph. Eventually, the devilish enemy would no doubt regroup and try again but, for the present, assisted dying was a beaten cause.

———

With the potent campaign almost completed, Father Xavier received a phone call advising his father had suffered a serious coronary event and his elderly mother was not coping.

Both parents had requested Father not be informed because his work for the Church was so important. But the local social worker, knowing Father Xavier to be an only child, had decided otherwise.

Xavier requested compassionate leave from his duties before driving his faithful old Corolla, overnight, directly from Sydney to the township of Jindabyne, a small village perched among Australia's Snowy Mountains. Fortunately, the roads were neither icy nor snow-covered and he made the trip without incident.

Arriving in the pale and chilly light of dawn, he located the recently built bright-orange building housing the local medical centre. It had been designed as little more than a transit point at which injured skiers and other adventurers could be stabilised before an ambulance transported them to Canberra. But a limited capacity to treat more significant trauma cases had been included.

After walking the length of a glossy tile-floored corridor, following signs indicating *Intensive Care Facility*, Xavier located his father's room. The man, pale and semi-conscious, was lying beneath a grey blanket covered with a mesh of tubes and wires connected to various drips and electronic monitors. His breathing was consistent but shallow.

Finding his exhausted mother at the bedside, Xavier first escorted the thin, white-haired woman to the medical centre's cafeteria where he encouraged her to sip a mug of hot tea and eat a microwave-warmed pastry. Leaving her there, he returned to the Intensive Care Facility and administered to his father the Sacrament of the Anointing of the Sick.

He spent the next two days at the stricken man's bedside, occasionally stroking a white and often unresponsive hand while watching the attached cardiac monitor indicating a steady but weak heartbeat. Despite deep compassion he could do no more. Medical opinion was that his father might live for hours, months or even longer.

Minimally rested, Xavier decided to return to Sydney, visiting his Canberra parish on the way.

After giving his mother a hopefully reassuring farewell hug, Xavier, a paper roadmap on his lap, navigated to intersect the Monaro Highway then began driving along a road crossing windswept, silvery-grassed plains.

At the instant the nuclear weapon detonated he was six kilometres south of the tiny Michelago settlement. Wide-eyed with surprise, he stared directly into a flash of light as bright as the Sun, immediately joining the legions of the blind, in his case the temporarily blind.

Travelling at almost 100 kilometres per hour he began braking gently to avoid skidding or rolling over. But with minimal vision he failed to detect a slight bend in the road. Continuing straight ahead he crossed a gravel surface through which occasional clumps of fibrous grass struggled to survive.

When noise from his tyres indicated he was no longer on a sealed surface, Xavier began braking harder, hoping no trees or large rocks were in his path. Eventually, and at much slower speed, his car entered a gully and crashed through several shrubs before stopping.

The vehicle was leaning at an unstable angle when, uninjured and already regaining some vision, Xavier heaving and grunting, hauled himself through the driver's side window before sliding down over the car's slanting roof. But the car, destabilised by his movement, rolled another few degrees trapping his feet and ankles beneath it.

Ouch. Ouch. Oh boy. I'm in serious trouble now. The ground is iron-hard and compacted. I'll have no hope of digging myself out. Nobody is likely to hear me yelling. The car will be invisible to passing traffic.

Several throbbingly painful minutes later, his spiritual courage reasserting itself, Xavier prayed 'Lord Jesus, my faith in you tells me there are signs, even here, of your boundless love. Yes, within reach I can feel the cold water of a small spring. Are you sending me a message?'

'Yes, yes you are. Water is the fountain of life. Thank you, dear Lord. You intend me to live and to continue my ministry in your name.'

––––––––––

At Cooma, another mountain township, one larger than Jindabyne, people had learned of the catastrophic event in Canberra. Unbelievable though it seemed, they heard that the city had been blasted apart by an atomic bomb.

Mobile telephone calls to and from people on Canberra's southern limits, combined with information from several amateur radio operators, portrayed a situation almost beyond help. Vast areas in the city and surrounding suburbs had been flattened. Fatal casualties were in the tens of thousands. At this early stage nothing seemed to be working; not the water or electrical supplies, not the sewage or the gas. Nobody in Canberra seemed to be taking responsibility for relief coordination, for prioritising support requirements, or anything else.

Shocked but undaunted, the local hospital administrators, the mayor and the Chamber of Commerce's chairman met and decided it would be unacceptable to remain passive in the face of so much suffering. The agreed, as a first response, to send three of the town's five paramedics to Canberra.

Each paramedic would be provided with a hired van containing analgesics, bandages, splints to stabilise fractures, antiseptics and salves. The paramedics would have independent authority to decide which first aid to administer and to whom.

Coordinated by their young and energetic mayor, the local hospital, doctors' surgeries, supermarkets, pharmacies and private homes were urged to contribute as much of their sealed medical stockholdings as possible. Donations would be assembled in the hospital's small foyer.

Compassionate and generous rural people, they emptied their shelves and cupboards. Senior citizens, keen to participate, also offered morale enhancers. Knitted face-washers and exotic hand-soaps, most reeking of the mothballs with which they'd been stored for years, came in brown-paper bags.

Too many volunteers arrived to assist with sorting and packing, adding to the confusion.

Despite the avalanche of generosity each van was loaded, eventually, fuelled then farewelled. Wilson Chubb, a paramedic for almost a decade, had been selected to drive one of them.

Of average height and build, with short-cut hair and a freckled, almost boyish face, Wilson was a deeply compassionate man. Intelligent, self-disciplined, able to work efficiently for long hours, he'd been considered an ideal choice for the Canberra mission.

However, the Cooma medical community had never grasped the implications of Wilson having once served six years as a member of the Australian Army's elite Special Forces. Now trained to sustain life, he could also terminate it, quickly, efficiently and with minimal remorse if the circumstances justified it.

Wilson had recently become the single parent of two boys, aged seven and ten, now being cared for by a friendly neighbour. His beloved wife, Jane, had died from cancer of the oesophagus.

During the previous five months he'd watched Jane's health decline. Her body had wasted from an eye-catchingly athletic profile to a skin-covered skeleton. Chemotherapy had destroyed her shining auburn hair.

Toward the end, she could barely move her limbs. Her speech became slow and confused. Her shocked children, not knowing how to respond withdrew into themselves, quietly panicking.

When she lost control of her bowels and began feeling pain at levels no longer managed by prescribed drugs, Jane was transferred to a local palliative care facility.

Lying in a small room overlooking pleasant gardens, Jane was fed through an intravenous drip leading into her, skeletal arm. A second intravenous tube attached to her abdomen allegedly contained enough drugs to anaesthetise her. A third tube running from her kidney drained urine into an attached bag.

The stress on her face and tension through her arms and torso indicated she needed something different or stronger. Regardless of how often she asked, increased medication was denied because it could have killed her.

From time to time, while still semi-conscious, she'd hold her breath hoping the stress of oxygen deprivation would cause a fatal trauma. But it never did. She'd fall into blackness for a while, then surface and try again.

The nurses, having noticed Jane's suicidal intentions, asked the visiting chaplain to intervene.

This sincere priest, in gentle and confident tone, told Wilson, 'We can see your dearest Jane is experiencing a physical trauma. She might be attempting to surrender God's gift of life. What we can't see is that she's undergoing a truly beautiful spiritual transformation.'

'At a level we can barely comprehend, except through prayer and faith, Jane is relating to the Passion of Christ, coming closer to Him and assuring herself of new life in His Heavenly Kingdom. So, Wilson, we look on you to convey this message of comfort to her so she can fully endorse her remaining time on Earth.'

Wilson was convinced these people were insane or, in his own words, *'fucking crazy'*. Although she could no longer talk, he could see, almost feel, Jane's increasing agony.

For more than a week, hour by hour, Jane became increasingly desperate. Dark rings consolidated under her eyes, her cheeks were sunken, blue veins covered her face. She dribbled uncontrollably.

Her eyes, looking directly at him, silently begged for help. Nothing would have been more welcome than the compassionate release available from an overdose of some gentle, sleep-inducing chemical.

Finally, Jane began vomiting her own effluent. At first it flowed from her mouth as yellowish-brown liquid. Then a large stool emerged to seal her airway. Jane, heaving weakly, her eyes panicking, suffocated.

On his way toward Canberra, Wilson, having tolerated the pressure of a full bladder for the past few minutes, decided he had to stop for a comfort break. A modest man, he drove several metres away from the highway to a location invisible to passing traffic. It faced a small, wooded valley.

Looking from the cabin of his van, a gleam either of metal or glass, he wasn't sure which, distracted him. Not expecting to find anything reflecting here, he walked forward to investigate and discovered a man pinned beneath the side of a crashed car.

Xavier had spent almost 24 hours alternatively praying and cursing, hoping to live and wishing death would arrive. Now this still unseen vehicle had left the road almost opposite where he was trapped. Its engine had stopped. A door had slammed shut.

'Thank you, thank you Lord Jesus your servant will be saved', he prayed in gratitude.

At first, both men were delighted; Xavier because salvation had arrived and Wilson because here was an unanticipated opportunity to help a suffering fellow human.

Wilson crouched to better understand how he could release the injured man, then instinctively recoiled. Despite the camouflage of dirt, dried tears and the distortion of countless insect bites, there was something familiar about that face.

Incredulous, he asked, 'Are you, by any chance, Father Xavier Westmeath?'

Xavier, accustomed to praise and reinforcement from admiring colleagues and fellow Catholics, made the worst mistake of his life. 'Yes,' he said, smiling despite his pain, 'I've been leading the successful anti-assisted dying campaign. Perhaps you've seen me on TV or social media.'

During recent weeks Xavier had experienced some anger from an opposition which had consistently comprised about 80 per cent of the Australian adult population. A smattering of poorly composed but angry letters to the editors of various newspapers had been published. One radio shock-jock had criticised him before a call to the station's owner led to a change of heart. But nothing had prepared him for Wilson's response.

'You bastard, you little prick,' he said, 'my wife and thousands like her have died in mental or physical agony because of you and your bloody fellow-travellers. How dare you use the law to force your stupid, depraved, grotesque superstitions on people. How could you possibly spout that bullshit about experiencing the Passion of Christ.'

Xavier, already exhausted, attempted a feeble defence but triggered another deluge of abuse.

'Don't you dare talk to me about protecting the weak. Throughout history your stinking church has exploited the weak, subordinated women, isolated gays, opposed effective contraception and then prohibited abortion. You lot have sexually exploited countless innocent children. You're experts in abusing the weakest members of our society; yes always the bloody weakest and most vulnerable.'

Belatedly, Xavier comprehended one of life's most sobering realities; many venerated principles were designed to control *other* people.

Enlightened, he began goading Wilson. He pressed the merits of adherence to doctrine, obedience to the Word of God as interpreted by His Church on Earth. Palliative care, he claimed, could manage the ills of pain and fear while preventing recourse to the cowardly sin of suicide.

Wilson, furious though he was, had been trained to evaluate tactical situations, to analyse enemy courses of action. And he was several steps ahead of Father Xavier.

'This prick's trying to rile me,' he thought. 'He hopes I'll smash his skull with a rock and end his misery. Well, I'll give the little bastard an opportunity to experience his own purifying acquaintance with the Passion of Christ, just as my darling Jane had to.'

Calmly, he told Xavier it was time to put their differences aside. Father should now relax and give thanks for this miracle of deliverance. Wilson would retrieve a tow-cable from his van and return in a minute to free him.

After walking back to the van and urinating against a front wheel, Wilson climbed into the cabin, clicked on his seatbelt and started the engine. Without a backward thought or glance he re-entered the highway and continued driving toward Canberra.

Xavier, accessing an occasional palm-full of water from the spring, lived for another two horrible days and miserable nights. Mosquitoes, after attacking all his accessible skin, stopped biting. Instead, small black beetles began devouring the wet, oozing flesh from his ankles and calves. Immobilised, he was forced to defecate and urinate into his trousers.

A feral cat arrived to make occasional grabs at the still-living corpse. But until the very end Xavier was able to beat it away at the cost of a few bites and scratches to his hands.

On the final day, too weak to move his limbs, Xavier began dozing and awoke to find a bush rat gnawing into the side of his neck. The rat punctured a carotid artery. Father Xavier Westmeath bled to an anonymous death.

HEATHER

Sixteen year-old Heather Newseas, pressing against her restraining harness, leaned forward and grasped a handful of the mini-bus driver's grey hair. Gently drawing the head back toward her, she felt a floppiness in its neck.

Sucking in a deep and hopefully calming breath, she moved her right hand across the warm but unresponsive face, pressing against the woman's temples. She couldn't feel a pulse. Heather concluded the woman was dead.

She'd obviously been dazzled by the sudden flash of intense light before driving into a concrete barrier positioned near the corner of Swinden Street. The speed limit in that locality was 60 kilometres per hour but most drivers ignored the signage. The bus and all surrounding traffic had been travelling at almost 80.

Thanks to regulations requiring comprehensive seatbelts and other safety mechanisms, wheelchair-bound Heather and all five of her intellectually handicapped colleagues had survived the crash. They were uninjured apart from a bad fright and few bruises,

Pushing aside her own wavy light-brown hair, she pointed to the burliest and most energetic youth saying, 'Paul, here's a job for you. I can see the side door has been twisted. I want you to release your harness and kick it open so we can all leave the bus.'

Paul, gurgling with flush-faced pleasure, was delighted to help.

Responding to her encouragement, the remaining passengers unbuckled and filed out amid a cacophony of complaints, hysterical tears and shrieking laughter. Except for Heather.

Her next challenge was to coax her colleagues to release a wheelchair from a rack at the rear of the vehicle, unfold it, carry her from the bus and help her to sit. Although she was slimly built, and the wheelchair mechanism uncomplicated, compliance was difficult. They succeeded after several awkward and uncoordinated attempts during which they banged Heather's head on the doorframe before almost dropping her.

Now mobile, or as close to it as she could be, Heather saw other crashed and some upturned vehicles in the vicinity, most with apparently dead or severely injured occupants. Looking toward Canberra's flattened and smoking inner suburbs she saw, in the distance, still on its tracks, what remained of a streamlined tram. It had melted into an oblong blob, presumably together with its passengers.

The few ambulant people in their vicinity were self-absorbed, clearly distressed and in no condition to assist anybody. Most of the nearby houses had lost parts of their roofing and suffered other damage. Obviously, the situation was worse toward Civic, probably much worse.

Heather, the intellectually astute victim of a previous motor-vehicle accident, understood that an unprecedented disaster had occurred and might still be unfolding. Some form of strategy would be needed to give her and her colleagues some hope of survival. But it would be easier said than done.

Their normally supportive families all lived within the inner suburbs. From what Heather could see, they were probably dead or immobilised. A platoon of six disabled youths venturing in that direction would receive minimal priority or, more likely, no help whatsoever.

Heather decided, despite daunting challenges, they would have to leave Canberra. It seemed almost insane but there was no realistic alternative.

After a brief but confused discussion, her five companions agreed to turn north in search of what Heather described, with an enthusiasm she didn't feel, as, '...*our most exciting adventure ever.*'

One of the most pathetic detachments in human history then turned its collective back on Canberra. Lacking suitable clothing, food, water, tentage, bedding, anti-psychotic or sedative medications, they were going to walk, wheel, sing, moan, laugh, weep and stagger to the regional township of Yass, about 60 kilometres away.

Heather reckoned they could cover about 20 kilometres each day. There would be traffic along the road as others, similarly motivated, took to the highways. However, Heather doubted anyone would stop to collect her uninviting flock.

The afternoon of their first day was almost tolerable. Travelling on the gravelled strip running parallel with Barton Highway, they scavenged food scraps from discarded roadside trash and slurped drinking water from puddles. But some problems emerged.

Two hadn't developed reliable toileting habits. Before long, a mixture of faeces and urine clung to their ample legs, increasing the discomfort for themselves and others. Some footwear was lost, leading to blistered and bleeding feet. Other items of clothing, discarded petulantly during the day, would be needed for warmth at night.

Several minor fights broke out, leading to bruising and facial lacerations along with temporarily fractured friendships.

Heather, hoping to minimise the likelihood of food poisoning, had insisted they ignore remnants of meat, fish or chicken in the partly eaten snacks they found. She told them to eat only the bread rolls, fried chips and salad ingredients, all of which were surprisingly plentiful.

When the first night approached, they passed through an unlocked farm gate and entered a paddock of brown, grassy stubble. Dragging bales of newly mown hay, still uncollected by the farmer, they formed a square windbreak which would become their home for the night.

At first, Heather was reluctant to take water from a nearby dam surrounded by waist-high grass. The risk of snakebite would be high and it was unlikely her companions would be suitably cautious. But she needn't have worried. They were so boisterous that no snake would have dared emerge.

At one end on the dam the two soiled youths washed themselves down, complaining bitterly about how cold they felt. At the other, several old beer bottles found by the roadside were filled with water for communal drinking. It wasn't ideal, but the best they could manage before lying down and trying to stay as warm as possible.

At dawn on the second day one youth had an uncontrollable anger fit. Shrieking abuse and rejection, arms flailing, he left them and staggered back along the highway toward Canberra.

Lacking any capacity to restrain him, they continued their journey northwards still devouring road-side scraps while tramping past hobby farms and brick-veneer houses in dry, brown paddocks. Later that day they encountered areas of irrigated grape vines, offering verdant relief from the dry countryside. But the harvest had already been gathered.

By the second night they were within a kilometre of the traditional Murrumbateman Village but lacked the energy to make one final push and reach it. Heather, having noted the clear sky, anticipated a freezing and possibly frosty night.

Finding a small patch of grass surrounded by shrubs, she directed her charges to huddle together for warmth, thankful that the two normally incontinent youths had managed to control further urges to relieve themselves without warning.

Within this slight depression, offering some protection from night-time breezes, they again huddled together for warmth, except for Heather and one ashen, almost cadaverous girl with memorably long, straw-coloured hair. The girl, faced with the prospect of again sleeping while huddled against her colleagues, had become hysterical and insisted on sleeping alone atop a mound of roadside gravel.

Sitting alone and confined to her wheelchair, Heather could only don her lightweight woollen cardigan, together with a baseball cap she'd been carrying, and hope for the best.

During that miserable night, the temperature fell to below zero and a frost formed, as Heather had predicted. At dawn they found the solo girl dead, frozen stiff.

The child had been born with minor developmental challenges and physical deformities. For her, reality had emerged within the confines of what passed for a cradle—a grubby cardboard box padded with a few rags provided by parents who were chronic drug addicts.

The dominant influences in her infancy had been danger, hunger, neglect and, before she was four years-old, sexual assaults causing injuries. With conveniently limited capacity to resist or communicate she'd been vulnerable to almost anything. One year and eight months ago, aged nine, the child welfare authorities had placed her with a foster family.

In her final moments of life, the now comprehensively damaged child had dreamed of a beautiful, gentle, loving woman approaching then lifting her into a tender embrace, softly stroking her hair and telling her she was a very good little girl.

It was the most wonderful moment she had ever known. A final, unmistakable smile on her face shared the joy of that sublime vision.

With nothing available for breakfast, the little group moved on, reluctantly leaving the child's corpse behind, unacknowledged, uncovered.

It was fortunate they hadn't sought succour in Murrumbateman because its normally hospitable inhabitants, had been unexpectedly inundated with strident demands for food, shelter, clothing, petrol and other goods. In response, they'd uniformly adopted a garrison attitude. Signs stating, 'No Visitors' and 'No, we have nothing for you' were commonplace together with more aggressive instructions to 'Piss Off'.

Having walked through Murrumbateman without pausing, on the third and hopefully final day of their trek, Heather's now diminished band continued breaking their enforced fast with scraps of food from the roadside.

Six worm-filled apples on a tree, originally planted by the occupants of a now ruined cottage, provided welcome supplementation. Fortified, they tramped, stumbled and wheeled along the undulating road leading to Yass.

As the kilometres passed feet Heather began to understand that the Fortress Murrumbateman attitude would be duplicated in the township of Yass. Another plan and a different objective were now required.

Her resolve solidified when two young men rode past on motorcycles bearing pannier bags and racks almost overflowing with carrots and other vegetables. One had a rifle slung over his shoulder. There had to be abundant food somewhere in this district.

Recalling the history of that region, Heather was aware that changes to agricultural policy and practice had led to numerous small holdings being abandoned. Some of the old dwellings should still be habitable. Perhaps, she thought, they could repair one and make it their home until something else became available.

They began exploring every overgrown track leading into the bush. But their efforts were futile. Hunger and exhaustion began to slow progress. The few, hopefully edible, roots and berries they found barely kept them going.

Toward nightfall, they followed a two-grooved track until stopped by a farm gate. Mindful of the hostile reception they might receive, Heather and her remaining three charges prepared to settle down beside the path and bivouac for the night.

They were pooling their meagre resources for what would become an evening meal when a woman approached from behind the gate. Simply but modestly dressed, of olive complexion and with prominent dark eyes, she was wearing a khimār.

'*Moslem*', thought Heather. Living within confined environments of her home and the disabled community, Heather had no first-hand experience of Moslems. TV newscasts with a multicultural theme had portrayed them as different to most Australians, but not necessarily hostile or dangerous.

The Moslem woman, which she was, remaining on her side of the gate, leaned over and in accented voice asked what was happening.

Heather decided to abandon all caution and explained their predicament. She was describing the little girl's death when the Moslem woman began weeping, not subtly but with strong and chest-expanding gasps.

'But this must stop', she sobbed, 'it must stop now.' 'Follow me! You will follow me please. Follow me!' 'You need to be bathed.' 'You must be dressed.' 'This is terrible.' 'Clean clothing.' 'This is very bad.' 'Food! Yes, yes, you need proper food.' 'Warm beds.' 'A safe place to sleep.' 'Cuts and blisters bandaged.' 'Shelter, yes shelter.' 'Another very cold night tonight.'

The inventory of loving support flowed compulsively, unabated, as together the waifs tramped and trundled through the now widely opened gateway and followed the woman toward a structure resembling a house.

Its architecture defied formal categorisation. Self-assembled sheds were attached to a larger motor-vehicle garage of identical provenance. Walls of the bespoke interior décor featured polystyrene containers of every description providing insulation. In a corner of the main living room-kitchen a cast-iron stove had been lit and was radiating soft, welcoming warmth.

On arriving in Yass 15 years ago, Yasmin and Ahmed had encountered some racism and religious bigotry. Those attitudes had since moderated but at that time there were indications that the situation could worsen.

It seemed prudent to minimise contact with the established community and focus on self-sufficiency to the extent achievable. In response, the former physicist and occupational therapist had invested in 20 hectares of land located several kilometres from town. Trees and scrubby bushes concealed their land from traffic passing along the sealed road.

There, at first living in an aluminium-walled garden shed, they'd expanded incrementally, one self-assembly kit at a time. Fences, followed. Two natural springs provided their initial water supply.

Eventually, beehives, a herb garden, livestock, photovoltaic panels and other acquisitions became possible as the couple cooperatively saved and invested incomes earned from casual employment as a truck driver and a laundry maid.

But, throughout their otherwise successful marriage, despite a frugal lifestyle, strict religious observance and countless thousands of earnest prayers, they had not been given the happiness of children. Now, suddenly, typical of the mysterious ways in which Heaven can move, a ready-made family had arrived.

Filled with gratitude, they recalled Islam's teaching from Quran 42:49; *Allah creates what he wills and gives to whom what he wills.* It followed that they had been especially blessed. Allah, in his mercy, had granted them four disabled children to be loved and nurtured so *they* in turn could contribute to this world and later to the Hereafter.

GRAEME

ooking anxiously across the neatly ploughed fields of a market-garden
property, an increasingly concerned little boy greeted a second day of
waiting, alone, for his father.

Graeme had seen the distant aftermath of the Canberra catastrophe.
Knowing his father had been visiting business acquaintances in the inner
suburbs, he dreaded the worst. Television news, relayed from Sydney, had
shown a horrific situation in repulsive detail.

Graeme was motherless. Almost six months ago, affected partly by
alcohol but more by undiagnosed and chronic postnatal depression, the
woman had departed, her heart filled with inexpressible grief. She had not
left a forwarding address.

The suntanned, slightly gangly boy often missed her and, just now, felt
especially lonely.

But he wasn't in immediate danger. There was food in the pantry and,
of course, in the surrounding fields of vegetables. He could lock the house
doors at night. Electricity, generated from a grid external to Canberra,
remained available. And, lonely or not, since his mother's departure young
Graeme had developed into a self-reliant young fellow.

On the morning of the second day he'd arisen and showered, perhaps
too briefly and without using soap. He'd dragged on a pair of denim trousers

followed by a plain-brown tee-shirt then matching socks and his favourite elastic-sided boots.

After feeding the cat and two dogs, breakfast was next on his agenda. Perhaps he would allow himself a small treat such as some extra jam on his toast. After all, today was his birthday. He would be eleven years old.

Following breakfast, he emerged from the kitchen and onto the back porch of the green-metal roofed house, ready to resume his melancholy surveillance. Almost immediately, Graeme thought he heard the faint noise of an approaching car.

Carefully placing his mug of tea onto the floorboards, he stood and squinted into the distance. Moving toward him, partly hidden by a row of gum trees, was the reddish profile of a car, or something similar. He could hear its engine revving, spluttering, revving some more, occasionally seeming to stop for a moment before kicking into life once again.

The source was an old MG-A sports car, or what remained of one. As it got closer, Graeme could see a cloud of blue-grey smoke squirting out behind the vehicle. Its windshield, doors and engine-hood were missing. Numerous dents in the remaining bodywork had been filled with a grey substance.

Graeme, knowing nothing about classic cars or vehicle restoration, saw only a mobile wreck approaching. Then he recognised the familiar figure of his father in the driving seat.

It was his best birthday present ever, which was fortunate. He would not live to see another.

On the day the weapon detonated, Peter Poutross (or *Pedro* as he was commonly known) had finished his business in the Canberra suburb of Dickson. Hauling his tall, fit and olive-skinned physique up into the cream-coloured Ford Territory, he drove to a carpark at the rear of that solid, defiant, stone edifice known as the Australian War Memorial.

His son Graeme would turn eleven years-old the next day and the boy was mad-keen on military aircraft. Happy to encourage the lad, Pedro located the Memorial's gift shop. After some hesitation, he decided to buy an F/A-18 fighter-jet in kit form. They'd have fun building it together.

'Yes, I will have it gift-wrapped please, and thank you for asking.'

He was walking back to his vehicle when a flash of intense light followed by an overwhelming wave of pure energy, something he'd never vaguely contemplated, demolished the front of the massive memorial building, leaving areas of its side walls still standing.

Blocks of stone tumbled and bounced around him, miraculously missing him. But he didn't survive unscathed.

The building had sheltered Pedro from the main pressure wave but it was followed by an intense blast of heat. Eddying around the-still disintegrating remains of the AWM building, it caught him from behind. Second-degree burns reached from the top of his head, across his shoulders, over the full length of his back.

Still standing but in severe shock, Pedro was pleased to see his boots were undamaged as was Graeme's birthday gift which he'd pushed down into the front of his formerly brown leather jacket.

Acting intuitively, Pedro knew only one thing. He had to get home. After that, he'd worry about everything else. But on reaching his vehicle he realised driving would not be an option.

Oh shit. The heat's melted my back tyres as well as the spare. I'll never get that rubber goo off the rims by myself. There's been some sort of massive disaster. I'm not likely to get my hands on replacement parts any time soon.

He turned toward Limestone Avenue, hoping he'd have enough energy to walk home. Despite constant pain, and unscheduled roadside breaks to manage an occasional and humiliating squirt of diarrhoea, he covered the first kilometre.

Still clutching Graeme's gift, doggedly determined, feeling progressively weaker, he was passing one of many roofless and smouldering red-brick family homes when he noticed a large shed in its backyard. Roller doors had been torn off and were lying on the burned embers of what had once been a lawn. Inside the shed he glimpsed several vintage cars at various stages of restoration. An elderly hobbyist, standing nearby, was ruefully surveying his metallic passions.

'G'day mate', said Pedro, 'not exactly the best day we've ever had, eh!'

'True mate. I don't know what's caused this, but sure as hell the insurance industry won't be able to cover it. I'll be screwed.'

'And', indicating his collection of cars, 'just look at my passion for the past 35 years. They've cost me a small fortune, plus two divorces. Not much use now. By the way, you don't look too good. Can I help you?'

Pedro, encouraged by that last remark, hoped this man could become his lifeline. Explaining his situation, he asked if he might be trusted with one of these valuable icons of classic motoring, just for a few days, just until he could return it.

He was in luck. The former vintage-car fanatic, faced with having to prioritise his life in favour of food, water, clothing and shelter, was beginning to view the mechanical acquisitions as nothing more than encumbrances.

'Yes mate. I'd be happy to help. It'll be a useful distraction from whatever in hell's name has happened to Canberra. None of my chariots is driveable but I'm pretty sure we could get one going good enough to get you home.'

Using chains and pulleys, supplemented by a lot grunting and heaving, they linked an engine from one vehicle onto the gearbox and manual clutch of another. Components for steering, and what passed for brakes and a suspension system, had already been partly assembled so the task was manageable.

Toward nightfall their car was road-ready although far from roadworthy. Without lights it would have been impossible to drive on debris-littered roads at night. They'd have to wait for dawn to try her out. Pedro hoped he'd still be alive.

Damage to the man's house had been extensive. The few remaining roof trusses were balanced precariously across partly demolished and unstable brick walls. They decided to spend the night in the shed.

Now hungry and thirsty, they'd had nothing to eat or drink all afternoon, the vintage-car man mainly because he was focussed on the reassembly task and Pedro because of fear that food would trigger another bout of diarrhoea. Luckily, stored in the shed were several cases of red wine and some packets of party-foods including potato crisps and something described as *roasted seaweed*.

They consumed a modest night-time snack, in Pedro's case a very modest one, before wrapping themselves in greasy tarpaulins and bedding down on the unforgiving concrete floor. Sleep was impossible so they passed the time trying to understand what had caused the catastrophe as well as exchanging stories, memories and opinions on politics and religion.

On day two, soon after first-light, Pedro, blood spraying from his mouth when he coughed, climbed into the red MG. There was no seatbelt and the plastic crate serving as his seat was unsecured. Using a fully charged battery offered by a supportive neighbour, he cranked the reluctant engine into life.

Despite poorly coordinated ignition timing, an occasional heart-stopping backfire and clouds of blue-grey smoke, the car moved off, its gearbox and clutch performing flawlessly. Pedro's burns prevented him twisting around to wave a grateful farewell to the most gracious man he had ever met. But he held one arm above his head for as long as possible, hoping his saviour would understand.

Watching him depart, the Good Samaritan thought, 'Bet I'll never see *that* car again. But, what the hell. If the poor guy makes it home to his son then my entire restoration venture will have been justified.'

———

Graeme, although delighted and relieved to see his father, saw immediately the man had been seriously injured. Dragging himself from the car, Pedro mumbled a greeting to the boy and began stumbling toward the house.

After a few steps he stopped, turned, and told Graeme how proud he was to have such a wonderful son. Wishing the lad happy birthday, Pedro produced the gift. It was slightly crushed at one end but still wrapped.

Reaching the house, Pedro slumped across an ancient chaise lounge kept on their porch. Calling the boy over he made sure Graeme understood the operation of the deep-well pumping system and knew the routine for watering their crops of organic vegetables

Prominent signs at the side of the Federal Highway, and again at their farm gate, still advertised fresh-from-the-soil guaranteed-organic produce. The signs had been a good investment, having in happier times attracted numerous food tourists prepared to pay premium prices for superior quality vegetables.

About an hour after Pedro returned home, three such visitors arrived. Uniformly clad in black-leather jackets topped by dull-black helmets, each was mounted on a deeply throbbing, chrome-encrusted motorcycle. Two were brothers and the third their best mate.

Confronting young Graeme, they made clear their intention of taking as much of the crop as they could carry. That would include potatoes, onions, carrots and melons. No, they would not be paying.

Graeme, his young frame shaking with rage at this injustice, ran to the house. 'They're stealing the crop, daddy', he yelled.

Rushing then to a nearby shed he snatched a pitchfork from its rack. Pedro kept all implements in tip-top condition so the tines on this tool were filed to deadly sharp points.

Holding the fork in front of him, intending to use it if necessary, the little fellow ran toward this unwelcome trio, already pulling vegetables from the soil. 'You can stop right now', he shouted in his young voice.

Normally, the men might have ignored the kid. 'But', as one of the brothers said on the following day, 'you can't take risks when someone is rushing at you with a deadly weapon.'

The man pulled a heavy-calibre pistol from his jacket pocket, aimed it, calmly waited until the lad was less than three metres away, then squeezed the trigger. A .45-calibre bullet smacked into the boy's chest.

Graeme stopped as if he'd run into an invisible brick wall. Dropping the pitchfork, he folded into a compact, quivering heap. The gunman pocketed the weapon and resumed his agricultural pursuits.

Pedro, having been alerted by young Graeme's warning cry, had stumbled into the house where they kept an ancient Lee Enfield ex-military rifle. After loading the magazine with several bullets, he clipped it into place.

Painfully, slowly, he drew back the bolt before pressing it forward again, loading one round into the chamber. He returned to his chaise lounge in time to witness Graeme being shot.

Leaning forward, propping the wood-sheathed barrel onto his porch rail, Pedro sucked several deep breaths into pain wracked lungs, cleared his head and regained control over the tremors in his hands and arms.

Taking long and deliberate aim, he applied first then second pressures to the trigger and retaliated. The Lee Enfield's notorious recoil broke his collar bone.

Pedro's bullet struck the assassin in the centre of his spine. From past hunting trips, Pedro knew there would be a small entry hole, about the size of the bullet, followed by a massive exit wound, bigger than a man's fist. This would be fatal.

The two remaining intruders paused. Seeing Pedro with his rifle pointing skywards, trying to lever a second round into the chamber, they ran toward him, drawing their own pistols and firing a volley of poorly aimed shots.

But two bullets struck home. One entered Pedro's left shoulder. The other lodged in his right-side groin. Standing over the now writhing but prostrate man, they could see he was incapacitated.

Removing the rifle, they propped it against a tree stump beside their motorcycles. Exactly how and when Pedro would die wasn't their problem.

Lying conveniently close was a concrete fence post with remnant wire still attached. Tying their friend's body to the post, they dragged it to the farm dam and rolled it in. The now surplus motorcycle followed.

Then, after pulling and picking as many vegetables as they could fit onto the remaining two bikes, the brothers shoved, pushed and tied their booty into an arrangement secure enough to last until they could reach home.

The younger of them slung the Lee Enfield over his shoulder and they rode away to their mother's humble, white-painted cottage on the outskirts of Yass.

———

Following the catastrophe in Canberra their mother, still harbouring childhood memories of the Second World War, had been desperate to fill her larder as insurance against whichever pestilences might yet arrive.

Fearing massive price increases she'd given her boys all the money she had in the house, asking them to find and buy some produce. Being wonderful sons, they'd delivered more that she could have hoped for.

After hugging each in turn, she hauled out her reliable Fowlers Vacola Kit; boiler, jars, clips, seals, the lot. Happily engaged in preserving this wonderfully fresh and nutritious food, she reflected on how fortunate life had been.

Yes, her husband had died but she had two tall, strong and loyal sons to care for her in her old age. While working, she hummed a traditional tune learned as a child at her family's home in Italy.

Later, in her small bedroom, she knelt before a glazed-china statue of The Blessed Virgin. There, she prayed the rosary and asked for Mother of God's protection over her two wonderful boys.

Finally, with pain from her arthritic knees increasing, she gave thanks for the many blessings she, although not worthy, had received, then undressed and went to bed.

———

Back on the farm Pedro, having regained consciousness, used his final moments of life to drag himself across to where Graeme had fallen. The boy, weeping and not quite dead, sensed his father's approach and said, 'Sorry, sorry daddy. I did try my best.'

Pedro, unable to talk, reached forward and patted his son's ankle.

Their lives ended within minutes. Pedro died first.

www.ingramcontent.com/pod-product-compliance
Lightning Source LLC
Chambersburg PA
CBHW061513020726
47502CB00006B/2058